MYST: THE BOOK OF TI'ANA

MYST

THE BOOK OF TI'ANA

RAND MILLER

with david wingrove

HYPERION

NEW YORK

Text and Fill © 1996, Cyan Inc.

Illustrations by Tom Bowman

Cover Design © 1996, The Leonheardt Group

Designed and typeset in Centaur by BTD/Robin Bentz and Ann
Obringer

Library of Congress Cataloging-in-Publication Data

ISBN 0-7868-8920-9

First Mass Market Edition

10 9 8 7 6 5 4 3 2 1

TO DEB AND THE GIRLS

ACKNOWLEDGMENTS

IT'S AMAZING HOW LITTLE WE KNOW, after all these years, about the history of D'ni and the story surrounding Myst Island. Over the years the story is revealed piece by piece, like a large puzzle waiting to be put together. It's only with the continuing effort of a core group of people that the pieces are uncovered and assembled to make a book like this possible.

It has been my pleasure to uncover the past events in D'ni history even as Robyn continues to bring the events surrounding Myst Island to its final chapter. Not having Robyn's help for this translation, the burden of discovery was taken up by Chris Brandkamp, Richard Watson, and Ryan Miller working closely with David Wingrove. Our task was large and yet the results are stunning, as for the first time the public gains a glimpse into the richness and complexity of the D'ni civilization.

So it is to these four close friends (particularly David and Chris for their long hours of work) that I extend my sincerest thanks and admiration. This story reaches you because of their dedication and brilliance.

RAND MILLER

MYST: THE BOOK OF TI'ANA

THE SOUNDING CAPSULE WAS EMBEDDED in the rock face like a giant crystal, its occupants sealed within the translucent, soundproofed cone.

The Guild Master sat facing the outstretched tip of the cone, his right hand resting delicately on the long metal shaft of the sounder, his blind eyes staring at the solid rock, listening.

Behind him, his two young assistants leaned forward in their narrow, metal and mesh seats, concentrating, their eyes shut tight as they attempted to discern the tiny variations in the returning signal.

"Na'grenis," the old man said, the D'ni word almost growled as his left hand moved across the top sheet of the many-layered map that rested on the map table between his knees. *Brittle.*

It was the tenth time they had sent the signal out on this line, each time a little stronger, the echoes in the rock changing subtly as it penetrated deeper into the mass.

"Kenen voohee shuhteejoo," the younger of his two assistants said tentatively. *It could be rocksalt.*

"Or chalk," the other added uncertainly.

"Not this deep," the old man said authoritatively,

flicking back the transparent sheets until he came to one deep in the pile. Holding it open, he reached beside him and took a bright red marker from the metal rack.

"Ah," the two assistants said as one, the carmine mark as clear an explanation as if he'd spoken.

"We'll sound either side," the old man said after a moment. "It might only be a pocket. . . ."

He slipped the marker back into the rack, then reached out and took the ornately decorated shaft of the sounder, delicately moving it a fraction to the right, long experience shaping his every movement.

"Same strength," he said. "One pulse, fifty beats, and then a second pulse."

At once his First Assistant leaned forward, adjusting the setting on the dial in front of him.

There was a moment's silence and then a vibration rippled along the shaft toward the tapered tip of the cone.

A single, pure, clear note sounded in the tiny chamber, like an invisible spike reaching out into the rock.

"WHAT IS HE DOING?"

Guild Master Telanis turned from the observation

window to look at his guest. Master Kedri was a big, ungainly man. A member of the Guild of Legislators, he was here to observe the progress of the excavation.

"Guild Master Geran is surveying the rock. Before we drill we need to know what lies ahead of us."

"I understand that," Kedri said impatiently. "But what is the problem?"

Telanis stifled the irritation he felt at the man's bad manners. After all, Kedri was technically his superior, even if, within his own craft, Telanis's word was as law.

"I'm not sure exactly, but from the mark he made I'd say he's located a patch of igneous material. Magma-based basaltic rocks from a fault line, perhaps, or a minor intrusion."

"And that's a problem?"

Telanis smiled politely. "It could be. If it's minor we could drill straight through it, of course, and support the tunnel, but we're still quite deep and there's a lot of weight above us. The pressures here are immense, and while they might not crush us, they could inconvenience us and set us back weeks, if not months. We'd prefer, therefore, to be certain of what lies ahead."

Kedri huffed. "It all seems rather a waste of time to me. The lining rock's strong, isn't it?"

"Oh, very strong, but that's not the point. If the aim were merely to break through to the surface we could do that in a matter of weeks. But that's not our brief. These tunnels are meant to be permanent—or, at least, as permanent as we can make them, rock movement willing!"

Still, Kedri seemed unsatisfied. "All this stopping and starting! A man could go mad with waiting!"

One could; and some, unsuited to the task, did. But of all the guilds of D'ni, this, Telanis knew, was the one best suited to their nature.

"We are a patient race, Master Kedri," he said, risking the anger of the other man. "Patient and thorough. Would you have us abandon the habits of a thousand generations?"

Kedri made to answer curtly, then saw the look of challenge in Telanis's eyes and nodded. "No. You are right, Guild Master. Forgive me. Perhaps they chose the wrong man to represent our guild."

Perhaps, Telanis thought, but aloud he said. "Not at all, Master Kedri. You will get used to it, I promise. And we shall do our best to keep you busy while you are here. I shall have my assistant, Aitrus, assigned to you."

And now Kedri smiled, as if this was what he had been angling for all along. "That is most kind, Master Telanis. Most kind, indeed."

THE EXCAVATOR WAS QUIET, THE LIGHTING subdued. normally, the idle chatter of young crewmen would have filled the narrow corridor, but since the observers had come there was a strange silence to the craft that made it seem abandoned.

As the young guildsman walked along its length, he glanced about warily. Normally he took such sights for granted, but today he seemed to see it all anew. Here in the front section, just behind the great drill, was the Guild Master's cabin and, next to it, through a bulkhead that would seal automatically in times of emergency, the chart room. Beyond that, opening out to both right and left of the corridor, was the equipment room.

The excavator was as self-contained as any ship at sea, everything stored, each cupboard and drawer secured against sudden jolts, but here the purpose of the craft was nakedly displayed, the massive rock drills lain neatly in their racks, blast-marble cylinders, protective helmets, and analysis tubes racked like weaponry.

The young guildsman stopped, looking back along the length of the craft. He was a tall, athletic-looking young man with an air of earnestness about him. His dark red jumpsuit fit him comfortably rather than tightly; the broad, black leather tool belt at his waist and his long black leather boots part of the common uniform worn by all the members of the expedition.

His fine black hair was cut short and neat, accentuating his fineboned features, while his eyes were pale but keen. Intelligent, observant eyes.

He passed on, through the crew quarters—the empty bunks stacked three to a side into the curve of the ship's walls, eighteen bunks in all—and, passing through yet another bulkhead, into the refectory.

Master Jerahl, the ship's cook, looked up from where he was preparing the evening meal and smiled.

"Ah, Aitrus. Working late again?"

"Yes, Guild Master."

Jerahl grinned paternally. "Knowing you, you'll be so engrossed in some experiment, you'll miss your supper. You want me to bring you something through?"

"Thank you, Guild Master. That would be most welcome."

"Not at all, Aitrus. It's good to see such keenness in a young guildsman. I won't say it to their faces, but some of your fellows think it's enough to carry out the letter of their instructions and no more. But people notice such things."

Aitrus smiled.

"Oh, some find me foolish, Aitrus, I know. It's hard not to overhear things on a tiny ship like this. But I was not always a cook. Or, should I say, *only* a cook. I trained much as you train now, to be a Surveyor—to know the ways of the rock. And much of what I learned remains embedded here in my head. But I wasn't suited. Or, should I say, I found myself better suited to *this* occupation."

"You *trained*, Master Jerahl?"

"Of course, Aitrus. You think they would allow me on an expedition like this if I were not a skilled geologist?" Jerahl grinned. "Why, I spent close on twenty years specializing in stress mechanics."

Aitrus stared at Jerahl a moment, then shook his head. "I did not know."

"Nor were you expected to. As long as you enjoy the meals I cook, I am content."

"Of that I've no complaints."

"Then good. Go on through. I shall bring you something in a while."

Aitrus walked on, past the bathing quarters and the sample store, and on into the tail of the craft. Here the corridor ended with a solid metal door that was always kept closed. Aitrus reached up and pulled down the release handle. At once the door hissed open. He stepped through, then heard it hiss shut behind him.

A single light burned on the wall facing him. In its half-light he could see the work surface that ran flush with the curved walls at waist height, forming an arrowhead. Above and below it, countless tiny cupboards held the equipment and chemicals they used for analysis.

Aitrus went across and, putting his notebook down on the worktop, quickly selected what he would need from various cupboards.

This was his favorite place in the ship. Here he could forget all else and immerse himself in the pure, unalloyed joy of discovery.

Aitrus reached up, flicking his fingernail against the firemarble in the bowl of the lamp, then, in the burgeoning glow, opened his notebook to the page he had been working on.

"AITRUS?"

Aitrus took his eye from the lens and turned, surprised he had not heard the hiss of the door. Jerahl was standing there, holding out a plate to him. The smell of freshly baked *chor bahkh* and *ikhah nijuhets* wafted across, making his mouth water.

Jerahl smiled. "Something interesting?"

Aitrus took the plate and nodded. "You want to see?"

"May I?" Jerahl stepped across and, putting his eye to the lens, studied the sample a moment. When he looked up again there was a query in his eyes.

"Tachyltye, eh? Now why would a young fellow like you be interested in basaltic glass?"

"I'm interested in anything to do with lava flows," Aitrus answered, his eyes aglow. "It's what I want to specialize in, ultimately. Volcanism."

Jerahl smiled as if he understood. "All that heat and pressure, eh? I didn't realize you were so romantic, Aitrus!"

Aitrus, who had begun to eat the meat-filled roll, paused and looked at Jerahl in surprise. He had heard his fascination called many things by his colleagues, but never "romantic."

"Oh, yes," Jerahl went on, "once you have seen how this is formed, nothing will ever again impress half so much! The meeting of superheated rock and ice-chill water—it is a powerful combination. And *this*—this strange translucent matter—is the result."

Again Jerahl smiled. "Learning to control such power, that is where we D'ni began as a species. That is where our spirit of inquiry was first awoken. So take heart, Aitrus. In this you are a true son of D'ni."

Aitrus smiled back at the older man. "I am sorry we have not spoken before now, Guild Master. I did not know you knew so much."

"Oh, I claim to know very little, Aitrus. At least, by comparison with Master Telanis. And while we are talking of the good Guild Master, he was asking for you not long back. I promised him I would feed you, then send you to his cabin."

Aitrus, who had just lifted the roll to his mouth again, paused. "Master Telanis wants me?"

Jerahl gestured toward the roll. "Once you've been fed. Now finish that or I shall feel insulted."

"Whatever you say, Master!" And, grinning, Aitrus bit deep into the roll.

AITRUS STOPPED BEFORE THE GUILD MASTER'S cabin and, taking a moment to prepare himself, reached out and rapped upon the door.

The voice from inside was calm and assured. "Come in!"

He slid back the heavy bolt and stepped inside, closing the door behind him. That much was habit. Every door in the craft was a barrier against fire or unwelcome gases. Turning, he saw that Master Telanis was at his desk looking at the latest survey chart. Facing him across the table was Master Geran. Also there were the four Observers who had joined them three days back. Aitrus took a step toward them and bowed.

"You sent for me, Guild Master?"

"I did. But if you would wait a moment, Aitrus, I must first deal with the news Master Geran has brought us."

Aitrus lowered his head, conscious that the Legislator—the big man, Kedri—was watching him closely.

"So, Geran," Telanis went on, indicating the bright red line that ran across the chart in front of him, "you recommend that we circumvent this area?"

The blind man nodded. "The fault itself is narrow, admittedly, but the surrounding rock is of low density and likely to collapse. We could cut through it, of course, and shore up on either side, but I'd say there is more to come the other side of that."

"You know that?" Kedri asked, interrupting the two.

Geran turned his blank, unseeing eyes upon the Legislator and smiled. "I do not *know* it, Master Kedri, but my instinct is that this is the mere root of a much larger igneous intrusion. Part of a volcanic system. Imagine the roots of a tree. So such things are. As excavators, we try hard to avoid such instabilities. We look for hard, intact rock. Rock we have no need to support."

Kedri looked puzzled at that. "But I thought it was your practice to support everything?"

Telanis answered him. "We do, Guild Master. As I said, we are very thorough. But if it is as Master Geran says—and long experience would tend to bear him out—we would do well to drill sideways a way before continuing our ascent. After all, why go courting trouble?"

"So how long will this . . . *detour* take?"

Telanis smiled pleasantly. "A week. Maybe two."

Kedri looked far from pleased, yet he said nothing. Relieved, Telanis looked to Geran once more.

"In the circumstances I approve your recommendation, Master Geran. We shall move back and across. Arrange the survey at once."

Geran smiled. "I shall do it myself, Guild Master."

When Geran was gone, Telanis looked across at Aitrus.

"Aitrus, step forward."

Aitrus crossed the narrow cabin, taking the place Geran had just vacated. "Yes, Guild Master?"

"I want you to place yourself at Guild Master Kedri's disposal for the next eleven days. I want you to show him how things work and explain to him just what we are doing. And if there's anything you yourself are uncertain of, you will ask someone who *does* know. Understand me?"

Surprised, Aitrus nodded. "Yes, Guild Master." Then, hesitantly. "And my experiments, Guild Master?"

Telanis looked to Kedri. "That depends upon Master Kedri. If he permits, I see no reason why you should not continue with them."

Kedri turned to Aitrus. "Experiments, Guildsman?"

Aitrus looked down, knowing suddenly that he ought not to have mentioned them. "It does not matter, Master."

"No, Aitrus. I am interested. What experiments are these?"

Aitrus looked up shyly. "I am studying volcanic rocks, Master. I wish to understand all I can about their nature and formation."

Kedri seemed impressed. "A most worthy task, young Aitrus. Perhaps you would be kind enough to show me these experiments?"

Aitrus looked to Telanis, hoping his Master would somehow get him off the hook, but Telanis was staring at the multilayered chart Geran had given him, flipping from page to page and frowning.

Aitrus met Kedri's eyes again, noting how keenly the other watched him. "As you wish, Guild Master."

THE CAVERN IN WHICH THEY RESTED WAS A perfect sphere, or would have been but for the platform on which the two excavators lay. The craft were long and sinuous, like huge, segmented worms, their tough exteriors kept buffed and polished when they were not burrowing in the rock.

Metal ladders went down beneath the gridwork platform to a second, smaller platform to which the junior members of the expedition had had their quar-

ters temporarily removed to make way for their guests.
It was to here, after a long, exhausting day of explana-
tions, that Aitrus returned, long after most of his colleagues had retired.

There were thirty-six of them in all, none older
than thirty—all of them graduates of the Academy;
young guildsmen who had volunteered for this expedition. Some had given up and been replaced along the
way, but more than two-thirds of the original crews
remained.

Two years, four months, Aitrus thought as he sat on the
edge of his bedroll and began to pull off his boots. It
was a long time to be away from home. He could have
gone home, of course—Master Telanis would have given
him leave if he had asked—but that would have seemed
like cheating, somehow. No, an expedition was not
really an expedition if one could go home whenever one
wished.

Even as he kicked his other boot off, he felt the sudden telltale vibration in the platform, followed an
instant or two later by a low, almost inaudible rumble.
A Messenger was coming!

The expedition had cut its way through several miles
of rock, up from one of the smaller, outermost caverns
of D'ni. They could, of course, have gone up vertically,
like a mine shaft, but so direct a route into D'ni was
thought not merely inadvisable but dangerous. The

preferred scheme—the scheme the Council had eventually agreed upon—was a far more indirect route, cut at a maximum of 3825 *torans*—22.032 degrees—from the horizontal. One that could be walked.

One that could also be sealed off with gates and defended.

The rumbling grew, slowly but steadily. You could hear the sound of the turbine engines now.

Slowly but surely they had burrowed through the rock, surveying each one-hundred-span section carefully before they drilled, coating the surfaces with a half-span thickness of special D'ni rock, more durable than marble. Last, but not least, they fitted heavy stone brackets into the ceiling of each section—brackets that carried air from the pumping stations back in D'ni.

Between each straight-line section was one of these spherical "nodes"—these resting places where they could carry on experiments while Master Geran and his assistants charted the next stage of their journey through the earth—each node fitted with an airtight gate that could be sealed in an instant.

The rumbling grew to a roar. For a moment the sound of it filled the node, then the engines cut out and there was the downward whine of the turbines as the Messenger slowed.

Aitrus turned and stood, watching as the metal snout of the machine emerged from the entry tunnel, passing through the thick collar of the node-gate, its pilot clearly visible through the transparent front debris shield.

It was a large, tracked vehicle, its three long segments making it seem clumsy in comparison to the sleek excavators, but as ever Aitrus was glad to see it, for besides bringing them much-needed supplies—it being impossible to "link" supplies direct from D'ni into the tunnels—it also brought letters from home.

"Aitrus? What time is it?"

Aitrus turned. His friend Jenir had woken and was sitting up.

"Ninth bell," he answered, bending down to retrieve his boots and pull them on again.

Others had also been woken by the Messenger's arrival, and were sitting up or climbing from their beds, knowing there was unloading to be done.

He himself had been temporarily excused from such duties; even so, as the others drifted across to the ladders and began to ascend, he followed, curious to see if anything had come for him.

When the last Messenger had come, three days back, it had brought nothing but the Observers—those unexpected "guests" billeted upon them by the Council. Before that it had been almost three weeks since they had had contact with D'ni. Three solid weeks without news.

The Messenger had come to rest between the two excavators. Already its four-man crew were busy, running pipelines between the middle segment of their craft and the two much larger vehicles, ready to transfer its load of mechanical parts, equipment, drill bits, fuel, and cooling fluid to the excavators.

Aitrus yawned, then walked across. The young men of the Messengers Guild were of nature outward, friendly types, and seeing him, one of them hailed him.

"Ho! Aitrus! There's a parcel for you!"

"A parcel?"

The Messenger gestured toward where one of his colleagues was carrying a large mesh basket into the forward cabin of the left-hand excavator.

Aitrus turned and looked, then hurried after, almost running into Master Telanis coming out.

"Aitrus! Why such a hurry?"

"Forgive me, Guild Master. I was told there was a parcel for me."

"Ah," Telanis made to walk on, then stopped, lowering his voice. "By the way, how was our guest?"

Tiring, he wanted to answer. "Curious," he said after a moment, keeping his own voice low. "Oh, and imaginative."

Telanis frowned. "How so?"

"It would seem we are too cautious for him, Guild Master. Our methods are, well . . . *inefficient.*"

Telanis considered that, then nodded. "We must talk, Aitrus. Tomorrow. Early, perhaps, before Master Kedri has need of you. There are things you need to know."

Aitrus bowed. "I shall call on you at third bell, Master."

"Good. Now go and see what the Messengers have brought."

Master Tejara of the Messengers had commandeered the table in the chart room to sort out the post. Surrounded by shelves of bound surveys, he looked up from his work as Aitrus entered.

"Ah, Aitrus. And how are you today?"

"I am well, Guild Master."

Tejara flashed a smile at him. "You've heard, then?"

"Master?" But Aitrus's eyes had already gone to the large, square parcel—bound in cloth and stitched— that rested to one side of the table.

"Here," Master Tejara said, handing it to him.

Aitrus took it, surprised by how heavy it seemed. Unable to help himself, he held it to his ear and shook it gently.

There was a gentle chime.

"Well?" Tejara said, grinning at him now. "Are you going to open it or not?"

Aitrus hesitated a moment, then set the parcel down on the table and, taking a slender chisel from his tool belt, slit open the stitching. The cloth fell back.

Inside was a tiny wooden case, the top surface of which was a sliding panel. He slid it back and looked inside.

"By the Maker!"

Aitrus reached in and drew out the delicate, golden pair of portable scales. They were perfect, the spring mechanism of the finest make, the soft metal inlaid with tiny silver D'ni numerals. Nor were they the only thing. Setting the scales down carefully, he reached in once more and took out a flat, square rosewood box the size of his palm. Opening it, Aitrus stared openmouthed at the exposed pair of D'ni geological compasses, his fingertips gently brushing the tiny crystal magnifier that enabled one to read the tiny calibrations. For a moment he simply looked, studying the minute transparent dials and delicate adjustable attachments that overlay the simple circle of its working face, then shook his head in wonder.

"Is it your Naming Day, Aitrus?" Tejara asked.

"No," Aitrus said distractedly as he reached in a third time to lift out an envelope marked simply "Guildsman Aitrus" in an unfamiliar hand.

He frowned, then looked to Tejara, who simply shrugged. Slitting the envelope open, he took out the single sheet and unfolded it.

"Aitrus," it began,

You might remember me from school days. I realize we were not the best of friends, but we were both young then and such misunderstandings happen. Recently, however, I chanced upon a report you wrote among my father's papers and was reminded of those unfortunate days, and it occurred to me that I might do something to attempt to reverse your poor opinion of me. If the enclosed gifts are unwelcome, please forgive me. But I hope you will accept them in the same spirit with which they are given. Good luck with your explorations! Yours in friendship, Veovis.

Aitrus looked up, astonished to see *that* signature at the foot of the note.

"It is from Veovis," he said quietly. "Lord Rakeri's son."

Tejara looked surprised. "Veovis is your friend, Aitrus?"

Aitrus shook his head. "No. At least, he was no friend to me at school."

"Then these gifts are a surprise?"

"More a shock, to be honest, Guild Master. Yet people change, I suppose."

Tejara nodded emphatically. "You can be certain of it, Aitrus. Time teaches many things. It is the rock in which we bore."

Aitrus smiled at the old saying.

"Oh, and before I forget," Tejara added, handing him his mail, "there are three letters for you this time."

AITRUS LAY THERE A LONG TIME, UNABLE TO sleep, staring at the pattern of shadows on the smooth, curved wall of the node, wondering what the gifts meant.

His letters had contained the usual, cheerful news from home—chatter about old friends from his mother, word of Council matters from his father. But his mind kept going back to the note.

That Veovis had written at all was amazing, that he had sent gifts was . . . well, astonishing!

And not just any gifts, but just those things that he most needed in his work.

Oh, there were plenty of scales and compasses he could use—property of the guild—but not his own. Nor were the guild's instruments anything as fine as those Veovis had given him. Why, they were as good as those that hung from Master Telanis's own tool belt!

When finally he did manage to sleep, it was to find himself dreaming of his school days, his mind, for some strange yet obvious reason, going back to a day in his thirteenth year when, tired of turning his back on Veovis's constant taunts, he had turned and fought him.

He woke to find Master Telanis shaking him.

"Come, Aitrus. Third bell has sounded. We need to talk."

THE CABIN DOOR WAS LOCKED. MASTER TELANIS sat behind his desk, looking up at Aitrus.

"Well, Aitrus, how did you fare with Master Kedri?"

Aitrus hesitated, not sure how much to say. The truth was he did not like the task he had been given. It made him feel *uncomfortable*.

Telanis coaxed him gently. "You said he felt our methods were inefficient."

"Oh, indeed, Guild Master. He constantly commented upon how slow our methods are. How overcautious."

"And do you agree with him, Aitrus? Do you think, perhaps, that we *are* too pedantic in our ways?"

"Not at all, Guild Master. There is, after all, no hurry. Whether we reach the surface this year or next does not matter. Safety must be our first concern."

Telanis stared at him a moment, then nodded. "Good. Now let me tell you a few things, Aitrus. First, I am aware that this task is not really to your liking."

Aitrus made to object, but Telanis raised a hand. "Make no mistake, Aitrus. I realize you are not at ease looking after Master Kedri, but I chose you for a reason. The good Master seeks to sound us out on certain topics—to *survey* our attitudes, if you like."

Aitrus looked horrified at the thought. "Should I watch what I say, Master?"

"Not at all, Aitrus. I have no fear that you will say anything that might upset Master Kedri. That is why I chose you. You are like basalt, Aitrus, solid through and through. But it would help me if, at the end of each day, you would note down those areas in which Master Kedri seemed most interested."

Aitrus hesitated. "Might I ask why, Master?"

"You may. But you must keep my answer strictly to yourself." Telanis paused, steepling his fingers before his chin. "There is to be a meeting of the Council, a month from now. It seems that some of the older members have had a change of heart. They have thought long and hard about whether we should make contact with the surface dwellers or not, and a few of them now feel it might not be quite so good an idea as it first seemed. Indeed, they might even ask us to abandon the expedition."

Unable to help himself, Aitrus slammed his fist down on the desk. "But they *can't!*"

Master Telanis smiled tolerantly. "If that is their final word, then so be it. We must do what they say. We cannot argue with the Council."

Aitrus lowered his head, acknowledging what Master Telanis said. The Council was the ruling body of D'ni and their word was law. His own opinion was irrelevant—it was what the five Great Lords and the eighteen Guild Masters decided that was important.

"That is why," Telanis went on, "it is so important that we impress our guests, Aitrus, for they represent the Eighteen and the Five. What they report back might yet prove crucial in swaying the decision . . . either for us or against us."

"I see." And suddenly he *did* see. Master Kedri was not just any busybody, butting his nose into their affairs; Kedri was a potential enemy—or ally—of the expedition. All of their hard work, their patient progress through the rock, might prove to no avail if Kedri spoke against them.

"I am not sure I can do this, Master."

Telanis nodded. "I understand. Do you want to be relieved of this duty, Aitrus?"

He stared at Master Telanis. It was as simple as that, was it? And then he understood. It was like going home. He *could* go home, at any time, but it was his choice *not* to go home that gave this voyage its meaning. So with this. He could quit, but . . .

Aitrus lowered his head respectfully. "I shall do as you wish, Guild Master."

Telanis smiled broadly. "Good. Now go and eat. You have a long day ahead of you."

FOUR LONG, EXACTING DAYS FOLLOWED, ONE upon another. Aitrus was ready to go back to Master Telanis and beg to be taken from his task when news came to him that they were ready to start drilling the next section.

Master Kedri was in the refectory when the news came, and, delighted that he could at last show the Legislator something real and tangible, Aitrus interrupted him at table.

"Yes, Guildsman?" Kedri said, staring at Aitrus. The conversation at table had died the moment Aitrus has stepped into the cabin. All four of the Observers seated about the narrow table had turned to stare at him.

"Forgive me, Masters," Aitrus said, bowing to them all, "but I felt you should know at once that we are about to commence the next stage of the excavation."

There was at once a babble of sound from all sides. Some stood immediately and began to make their way out. Others began to hurriedly finish their meals. Only Kedri seemed unmoved by the news.

"Thank you, Aitrus," he said after a moment. "I shall finish my meal then join you. Wait for me at the site."

Ten minutes later, Master Kedri stepped out of the excavator and walked across to where they had set up the sample drills. The other Observers had already gathered, waiting for operations to commence.

"Let us see if I understand this correctly," Kedri began, before Aitrus could say a word. "Master Geran's "sounding" is a rough yet fairly accurate guide to whether the rock ahead of us is sound or otherwise, correct? The next stage—*this* stage—is to drill a series of long boreholes to provide us with a precise breakdown of the different kinds of rock we are about to cut through."

Aitrus nodded, for the first time smiling at the Legislator.

"Oh, I can retain some minimal information, Guildsman," Kedri said, a faint amusement on his own lips. "It isn't only contracts I can read. But there is one thing you can tell me, Aitrus, and that's where all the rock goes to."

"The rock?" Aitrus laughed. "But I thought you knew, Master. I thought *everyone* knew! It is reconstituted."

"Reconstituted?"

"In the fusion-compounder. The machine reconstitutes the very matter of the rock, reforging its atomic links and thereby reducing its volume by a factor of two hundred. The result is *nara*."

"So that's what nara is!" Kedri nodded thoughtfully. "Can I *see* this fusion-compounder?"

Aitrus smiled, suddenly liking the man. "See it, Master? Why, you can operate it if you want!"

AITRUS TOOK A SHEET OF PAPER AND, FOR Master Kedri's benefit, sketched out a cross-section diagram of the tunnel.

"This," he said, indicating the small shaded circle at the very center of it, "is the hole made by the excavator. As you can see, it's a comparatively small hole, less than a third the total circumference of the tunnel. This," and he pointed to the two closely parallel circles on the outer wall of the tunnel, "is the area that the Cycler removes."

"The *Cycler?*" Kedri looked puzzled.

"That's what we call it. It's because it cuts a giant ring from the rock surrounding the central borehole."

"Ah, then that would be the big spiderlike machine, right?"

Aitrus nodded. Only two days before they had exhaustively inspected all of the different excavating tools.

"What happens is that the Cycler removes a circular track around the outer edge to a depth of one and a quarter spans. We then fill that space with a special seal of D'ni stone, let that set, then chip out the "collar"— that is, the rock between the inner tunnel and the seal."

"Why one and a quarter?"

Aitrus sketched something on the pad, then handed it across. "As you can see, we insert a special metal brace a quarter of a span wide, deep in the cut, then pour in the sealant stone. Then, when the collar has been chipped away, we remove the brace and set up the Cycler ready to start all over."

Kedri frowned. "Forgive me, Guildsman, but once again it seems a most laborious way of going about things."

"Maybe so, Master Kedri, but safe. When we make a tunnel, we make it to last."

"Yes . . ." Kedri nodded thoughtfully. "Still, it seems a lot of effort merely to talk to a few surface-dwellers, don't you think?"

It was the first direct question of that type Kedri had asked him, and for a moment Aitrus wondered if he might not simply ignore it, or treat it as rhetorical, but Kedri, it seemed, was waiting for an answer

"Well, Guildsman? Have you *no* opinion on the matter?"

Master Telanis came to his rescue.

"Forgive me, Master Kedri. Guildsman Aitrus might well have an opinion, but I am sure he would be the first to admit that at twenty-five he is far too young and inexperienced to express it openly. However, if you would welcome the opinion of someone of greater years?"

Kedri laughed. "Oh, I know *your* opinion, Master Telanis. I simply thought it would be refreshing to seek a different, *younger* view on things."

"Oh, come now, Kedri, do you really think our Masters on Council would be in the least interested in what a young guildsman—even one as brilliant as Aitrus here—has to say? Why, Lord Tulla is near on eleven times young Aitrus's age! Do you think *he* would be interested."

Kedri bowed his head, conceding the point.

"Then let us proceed with more important matters," Telanis continued quickly, before Kedri might steer the conversation back onto more tricky ground. "Normally we would take bore samples at this stage, but as you are so keen to see us in action, Master Kedri, I have decided to waive those for once and go direct to drilling."

The news seemed to cheer Kedri immensely. "Excellent!" he said, rubbing his hands together. "Will we need protective clothing of any kind?"

Master Telanis shook his head. "No. But you will need to be inside the second craft. When we drill, we drill!"

THE NODE-GATE WAS CLOSED BEHIND THEM, its airtight seal ensuring that not a single particle of rock would escape back down the tunnel. The temporary camp had been packed up and stored; the sounding capsule attached to the back of the second excavator, which now rested against the back wall of the node, slightly to the left of the bore-site. Two large observation lenses had been mounted on the ceiling to either side of the site, high up so that they'd not be hit by flying rock.

All was now ready. Master Telanis had only to give the order.

Aitrus was in the second vehicle, standing at the back of the chart room behind the Observers, who looked up at the big screen, watching as the excavator was maneuvered into place.

In operation it seemed more like something living than a machine, its sinuous, quiet movements like those of a giant snake.

Aitrus looked on with quiet satisfaction. He had first seen an excavator in action when he was four—when his father, a guildsman before him—had taken him to see the cutting of a new tunnel between the outer caverns.

Kedri, in particular, seemed impressed. He was leaning forward, staring at the screen in fascination.

"In place!" Master Telanis called out, his voice transmitted into the chart room where they sat. A moment later a siren sounded, its whine rising and then falling again.

The snout of the excavator came around and seemed almost to kiss the bore-mark on the rock face, so gentle was its touch, but the great drill bit had a brutal look to it, and as they watched, they saw the cooling fluid begin to dribble down the thick grooves of the drill.

Slowly the drill began to turn, nudging blindly into the rock, the mechanical whirr of its slow spiral accompanied by a deeper, grinding sound that seemed to climb in pitch as the bit whirrled faster and faster until it was a squeal, great clouds of dust billowing out from all around it.

The noise was now deafening, the vibrations making the second excavator ring like a struck bell. Slowly the great sphere of the node filled with dust, partly obscuring their view. Yet every now and then they would glimpse the excavator again, each time buried deeper and deeper into the rock, like some ferocious, feral animal boring into the soft flesh of its victim.

From time to time there would be a clang or thud as a large fragment of rock struck their craft, but there was no danger—the excavators were built to withstand massive pressures. Even a major collapse would merely trap the machine, not crush it.

After a while, Kedri turned and looked to Aitrus. "It's a fearsome sight," he said, raising his voice above the din.

Aitrus nodded. The first time he had seen it he had felt a fear deep in the pit of his stomach, yet afterward, talking to his father, he had remembered it with wonder and a sense of pride that this was what his guildspeople did.

Perhaps it was even that day when he had decided to follow his father into the Guild of Surveyors.

"Watch the tail," he shouted, indicating the screen as, briefly, the excavator came into view again. It was almost wholly in the rock now, yet even as they watched, the tail end of the craft began to lash from side to side—again like a living thing—scoring the smooth-bored wall of the tunnel with tooth-shaped gashes.

"Why does it do that?" Kedri shouted back.

"To give our men a purchase on the wall. Those gashes are where we begin to dig out the collar. It makes it much easier for us!"

Kedri nodded. "Clever. You think of everything!"

Yes, Aitrus thought, *but then we have had a thousand generations to think of everything.*

IN THE SUDDEN SILENCE, THE EXCAVATOR backed out of the hole, its segmented sides coated in dust, its drill head glowing red despite the constant stream of coolant. Inside the node the dust was slowly settling.

"Can we go outside and see for ourselves now?" One of the other Observers, Ja'ir, a Master in the Guild of Writers asked.

"I am afraid not," Aitrus answered him. "It is much too hot. Besides, you would choke on the dust. Even our men will have to wear breathing suits for a while. No, first they will have to spray the node with water to settle the dust. Then, once the drill bit has cooled a little, we shall start pumping air back into the node from out-side. Only then will they start the clearing up process."

"And the next stage of drilling?" Kedri asked, turn-ing fully in his seat and leaning over the back of the chair to stare at Aitrus.

"That begins almost at once, Master," Aitrus answered. "Look."

Even as he spoke, a door opened in the side of the excavator and two young guildsmen stepped out, suit-ed-up, air canisters feeding the sealed helmets they were wearing. They were both carrying what looked like spears, only these spears were curved and had sharp, diamond tips at the end.

"They'll set the Cycler up straight away. We should be able to start the second stage of drilling as soon as that's done. Meanwhile, the rest of the men will begin the clearing up operation."

As the two suited guildsmen began to put together the great cutting hoop of the Cycler, two more stepped out, trailing flaccid lengths of hose behind them. Getting into position in the center of the platform, one of them turned and gave a hand signal. Almost at once the hoses swelled and a jet of water gushed from each, arching up into the ceiling of the great sphere. As the two men adjusted the nozzles of their hoses, the foun-tain of water was transformed into a fine mist that briefly seemed to fill the node.

It lasted only a minute or two, but when the water supply was cut, the node was clear of dust, though a dark paste now covered every surface.

Aitrus smiled. "If you ever wondered what we surveyors do most of the time, it's this. Cleaning up!"

There was laughter.

"You talk as if you dislike the job, Aitrus," Kedri said with a smile.

"Not at all. It gives me time to think."

Kedri stared at him a moment, a thoughtful expression in his eyes, then he turned back, leaving Aitrus to wonder just what was going on inside the Legislator's head.

THE FOUR OBSERVERS STEPPED OUT FROM the excavator, their movements slightly awkward in the unfamiliar protective suits Master Telanis had insisted they wear. Kedri, as ever, led the way, Aitrus at his side as they stepped over to the tunnel's mouth.

The Cycler had done its job several times already and the cadets had already chipped out a section twenty spans in length and sprayed it with a coating of D'ni stone. Further down the tunnel, they could see the dark O of the central borehole running straight into the rock and, surrounding it like some strange, skeletal insect, the Cycler, encased in its translucent sheath.

Two brightly glowing fire-marbles the size of clenched fists were suspended from the ceiling. In their blazing blue-white light a number of cadets loaded rock onto a mobile trailer.

"This is more like it," Kedri said, with an air of satisfaction. "This is just how I imagined it."

They walked slowly toward the lamps. Surrounding them, the finished section of the tunnel had the look of permanence. Moving past the young guildsmen, they approached the rock face, stopping beneath the anchored feet of the Cycler.

They looked up, past the sleek engine of the Cycler to where its great revolving hoop was at rest against the face. The transparent sheath surrounding the Cycler was there to catch the excavated rock and channel it down into a chute that fed straight into the central borehole. From there the cadets would collect it up, using great suction hoses, and feed it into the pulverizer.

Kedri looked to Aitrus. "You remember your promise, Aitrus?"

"I have not forgotten."

"Then what are we waiting for?"

Aitrus turned and signaled to his friend, Efanis, who was working nearby. At once, Efanis came across and, positioning himself at the controls of the Cycler, gave two long blasts on the machine's siren.

Kedri made a face. "Yours must be the noisiest of guilds, young Aitrus. It seems you do nothing without a great blast of air beforehand!"

Aitrus smiled. It was true. If anyone was up there, they would surely hear them long before they broke through to the surface.

"If you would make sure your masks are kept down, Masters," he said, looking from one to another. "It should be perfectly safe, but if the sheath was to be punctured your headgear should protect you."

"Cautious," Kedri muttered. "Ever cautious!"

Slowly the great cutting-hoop of the Cycler began to spin, slowly at first, then faster, at first only skimming the surface of the rock, whistling all the while. Then, abruptly, the whole top of the Cycler seemed to lean into the rock face, a great grinding buzz going up as if a thousand swarms of bees had all been released at once.

Chips of rock flew like hailstones against the clear, thick surface of the sheath. Slowly the arm of the Cycler raised on its hydraulics, moving toward the horizontal as the spinning cutting hoop bit deeper and deeper into the rock, carving its great O, like the outer rim of an archery target.

In less than three minutes it was done. Slowly the machine eased back, the hoop slipping from the rock, its surface steaming hot. As the Observers turned, four of the young Surveyors wheeled the great metal hoop of the brace down the tunnel toward them. They had seen already how it was mounted on the cutting hoop, then pushed into place.

So easy it seemed, yet every stage was fraught with dangers and difficulties.

As the guildsmen took over, removing the covering sheath and fitting the brace, Kedri and his fellows stood back out of their way. Only when they were finished and the brace was in place did Aitrus take them through, past the base of the Cycler and into the central borehole. It was darker here, but the piles of rock stood out against the light from outside.

Aitrus pointed to two machines that stood to one side. The first was recognizably the machine they used to gather up all the fragments of rock, a great suction hose coiling out from the squat, metallic sphere at its center. The second was small and squat, with what looked like a deep, wedge-shaped metal tray on top.

Ignoring the rock-gatherer, Aitrus stooped and, picking up one of the larger chunks of rock, handed it to Kedri. "Well, Guild Master? Do you want to feed the compounder?"

Kedri grinned and, taking the rock over to the machine, dropped it into the tray.

"What now?" he asked, looking to Aitrus.

In answer, Aitrus stepped up and pressed a button on the face of the fusion-compounder. At once a metal lid slid across over the tray. There was a low, grinding sound, and then the lid slid back. The tray was now empty.

"And the nara?"

Aitrus crouched and indicated a bulky red cylinder that rested in a mesh cage on the underside of the machine.

"The nara is kept in there," Aitrus said, "in its basic, highly compacted form, until we need to use it."

"But surely it would just . . . solidify!"

Aitrus nodded. "It does. The cylinder is just temporary; a kind of jacket used to mold the nara into a storable form. When we have enough of the nara, we load up another machine with the cylinders. In effect, that machine is little more than a large pressure-oven, operating at immensely high pressures, within which the cylinders are burned away and the nara brought back to a more volatile, and thus usable, state."

"The sprayer, you mean?" Kedri said, staring at Aitrus in open astonishment.

Aitrus nodded.

Kedri crouched, staring at the bright red cylinder in awe, conscious of the immense power of these simple-seeming machines, then, like a schoolboy who has been briefly let off the leash, he straightened up and, looking about him, began to gather up rocks to feed into the machine

THAT NIGHT MASTER TELANIS TOOK AITRUS aside once more.

"I hear our friends enjoyed themselves today. That was a good idea of yours to let them operate a few of the less dangerous machines. They're bookish types, and such types are impressed by gadgetry. And who knows, even something this small may serve to sway them for the good."

"Then you think it *is* good?"

"Making contact with the surface-dwellers?" Telanis smiled. "Yes. Just so long as it is done discreetly."

Aitrus frowned. "How do you mean?"

"I mean, I do not think we should mix our race with theirs. Nor should we think of any extended relationship with them. They are likely, after all, to be a primitive race, and primitive races—as we have learned to our cost—tend to be warlike in nature. It would not do to have them pouring down our tunnels into D'ni."

"But what kind of relationship does that leave us?"

Telanis shrugged, then. "We could go among them as Observers. That is, providing we are not too dissimilar from them as a species."

"But why? What would we learn from doing that?"

"They might have certain cultural traits—artifacts and the like—that we might use. Or they might even have developed certain instruments or machines, though, personally, I find that most unlikely."

"It seems, then, that Master Kedri is right after all, and that ours is something of a fool's errand."

Master Telanis sat forward, suddenly alert. "Are those his words?"

"Something like. It was something he was saying to one of the other observers—Ja'ir, I think—as they were coming away from the rock face. Ja'ir was wondering aloud whether there was anyone up there on the surface anyway."

"And?"

Aitrus paused, trying to recall the conversation. "Master Kedri was of the opinion that there would be. His view was that the climatic conditions are ideal for the development of an indigenous species."

"And on what did he base this claim?"

"It seems that all four of them have seen copies of the Book."

"The Book of Earth," Telanis said, nodding thoughtfully. "It was written by Grand Master Ri'Neref himself,

Aitrus, perhaps the greatest of the ancient Writers. Yet it is said that it was one he wrote as an apprentice."

"So Master Kedri also claimed. Yet most troubling, perhaps, was what Master Ja'ir said next."

Telanis's eyes seemed to pierce Aitrus. "Go on."

"Ja'ir said that whether there was a humanoid race up there on the surface or not, he nevertheless wondered whether so much time and effort ought to have been spent on such a speculative venture."

"Speculative . . . he said speculative, did he?"

Aitrus nodded.

Master Telanis sat back and stared thoughtfully. For a while he did not speak, then, looking at Aitrus, he asked. "And what do you think, Aitrus? Is it worth it?"

"Yes, Guild Master. To know for certain that we are sharing a world with another intelligent species—that surely is worth twice the time and effort that we have given it!"

WHILE THE EXCAVATION WAS IN PROCESS, THE young guildsmen had been permitted to return to their quarters on the ships, while the Observers had been moved into the Guild Master's cabin in the second excavator.

Aitrus returned to his bunk. Briefly he smiled, thinking of Kedri's comment, but the smile quickly faded. The endless secondary process of clearing up normally gave him time to think of his experiments, something he had little time to do these past few days. Indeed, it made him wonder how others could stand to live as Kedri so clearly lived, constantly in someone else's pocket.

Personally, he needed space, and quiet. Yes, and an adequate supply of chemicals and notebooks! he thought, recollecting how his mother used to tease him about his obsession with rocks and geological processes.

Unnatural, she had said, but the old cook, Master Jerahl was right, there was nothing more natural for a D'ni. Stone was their element.

As he sat on the edge of his bunk, he could hear the whine of drills and the sudden crunch as rock fell to the floor. Let others think birdsong and the sound of a river flowing were natural; for him, this was the most natural of sounds.

"Young worm," his father had called him as a child, as if anticipating his future calling, and so he had become. A burrower. A seeker of passages. An explorer of the dark.

Aitrus stood, meaning to undress for sleep, when there came the sound of a commotion outside. He hurried along the corridor and poked his head out, looking about him. It was coming from inside the tunnel. The sound of a human in pain.

He heard a scuffling behind him. A moment later, Master Telanis joined him in the doorway.

"What is it, Aitrus?"

"Someone's hurt."

The two men ran across. At the tunnel's mouth, one of the young engineers met them, his face distraught.

"Who is it, Ta'nerin?" Telanis asked, holding his arms.

"It's Efanis. The cutting tip shattered. He's badly hurt. We've tried to staunch the blood but we can't stop it!"

"Fetch Master Avonis at once. I'll see what I can do!"

Letting Ta'nerin go, Master Telanis ran, Aitrus close behind. The tunnel was almost finished now. Only the last 5 spans remained uncut. There, at the far end, beneath the burning arc lamps, they could see a small group of cadets gathered—some kneeling, some standing—around one of their colleagues.

The moaning grew—an awful, piteous sound.

As the two men came up, they saw just how badly Efanis was injured. The wound was awful. The shattered tip must have flown back and hit Efanis full in the chest and upper arm. He had not stood a chance. Even as they stood there he gave a great groan. Blood was on his lips.

Pushing between the guildsmen, Master Telanis tore off his shirt and poked it into the wound. Then, looking about him, he spoke urgently, trying to rouse them from their shock. "Help me, then, lads! Quick now!" And, reaching down, he gently cradled Efanis's head even as the others crowded around, putting their hands under Efanis's shoulders and back and thighs.

"That's good," Telanis said softly, encouraging them as they gently lifted the groaning Efanis. "Now let's get him back to the excavator. The sooner Master Avonis gets to look at him, the better."

THERE HAD BEEN ACCIDENTS BEFORE, BUT never anything more severe than broken bones, or bruising, or rock splinters. Master Telanis prided himself on his safety record. Efanis's accident had thus come as a great shock.

When Aitrus reported to Kedri the next morning, it was to find the Legislator crouched over a desk in the chart room, writing. He looked up as Aitrus entered and put down his pen.

"I'm sorry, Aitrus. I understand that Efanis was your friend. A bad business, eh?"

Aitrus nodded, but he felt unable to speak. Efanis was not yet out of trouble.

"I'll not be needing you today, Aitrus, so take the day off. Do your experiments, if you wish. We'll carry on tomorrow."

"Yes, Master."

Leaving Kedri to his work, Aitrus went straight to Master Telanis. He found him in the tunnel, crouching beside the temporarily abandoned excavation, staring at a dark patch in the rock. At the center of that small, irregular ovoid was a tiny, slightly flattened circle of what looked like glass.

It had the look of a bruised eye staring from the rock.

"What is that?" Aitrus asked.

Telanis looked up at him. "It appears to be a pyroclastic deposit—a 'volcanic bomb' deposited in this strata hundreds of millions of years ago." The Guild Master pointed to the outer, darker area. "The outside of it is simple obsidian—a glassy basalt—but this pellucid nugget here was already embedded within it when the volcano spat it out. It looks and feels like diamond."

Aitrus nodded.

"My guess," Telanis continued, "is that the cutting tip slipped on the glassy surface, then snagged on this much harder patch here and shattered."

He sighed heavily. "I should have taken core samples, Aitrus. I was in too much of a hurry to impress our guests. And now *this* has come of it."

"You cannot blame yourself, Guild Master," Aitrus said. "The bit must have been flawed, anyway. One cannot foresee everything."

"*No?*" Telanis stood. He looked about him at the abandoned tools, his eyes, for the first time that Aitrus could recall, troubled by what he saw. "If not me, then who, Aitrus? It is *my* job to ensure the safety of my crews, *my* responsibility, no one else's. That Efanis is hurt is my fault. If I had done my job properly . . . "

Aitrus put out his hand to touch his Master's arm, then withdrew it. In a sense Telanis was right. All of their patient checks and procedures were designed to avoid an event like this.

He cleared his throat. "Master Kedri says he does not need me today, Guild Master. I came to be reassigned."

Telanis glanced at him, then made a vague gesture with his hand. "Not now, Aitrus. We'll do no work today."

"But, Master . . . "

"Not now."

AITRUS PACKED A KNAPSACK FOR THE JOURNEY and set off, walking back down the nodes to where—almost two months before—they had drilled through a small cave system.

Though they had labored long and hard in the rock, it took but an hour or so to reach his destination. For the first part the way was fairly straightforward, zigzagging back and forth in the normal D'ni way, but then it branched to the left, where they had been forced to detour around an area of folds and faults.

His way was dimly lit. Chemicals in the green-black coating of D'ni rock gave off a faint luminescence bright enough to see in. But Aitrus had packed two lamps and a small canister of luminescent algae for when he left the D'ni path.

Coming to his destination, he rested briefly, seated on the rock ledge outside the circular door that led through into the cave system, and ate a brief meal.

The sphere of this node had been peppered with openings—some tiny apertures barely large enough to poke one's hand into, others big enough to walk inside. One—the one he now sat outside—had been large enough to drive the excavator inside. Indeed, with Master Telanis's permission, they had shored up the entrance and bored almost fifty spans into the rock, widening the passageway to give access to a large cavern that lay just beyond. But time had been pressing and they had not had

more than a day or two to explore the system before they had had to press on with their excavations. They had sealed the tunnel with a small gate—similar to those that linked the nodes to the lengths of D'ni tunnel—leaving the caverns for future investigation, then they had sprayed the rest of the node with a smooth coating of nara.

Aitrus had made extensive notes of the cave system at the time. Now he had the chance to go back and resume his explorations. The thought of it cheered him as, finishing his meal, he stood and, taking the protective helmet from his pack, he strapped it on and, slipping the sack onto his shoulder, walked over to the lock.

It was a simple pressure lock. Turning the wheel, he could hear the air hiss out from the vent overhead. A moment later a crack appeared down the very center of the door and the two halves of it slid back into the surrounding collar.

Inside was darkness.

In a small cloth bag he carried in his pocket he had a collection of fire-marbles. Taking one from the bag, he opened the back of the lamp mounted on his helmet and popped it into the tiny space. Clicking it shut, he waited for a moment until the fire-marble began to glow. After less than a minute a clear, strong white radiance shone out from the lamp into the darkness, revealing the smooth, uncoated walls of rock within.

Aitrus smiled, then stepped inside.

AITRUS PAUSED TO SPRAY A TINY ARROW ON the rock wall, pointing back the way he had come, then slipped the canister away and walked slowly on, counting each step, all the time turning his head from side to side, scanning the walls and floor ahead of him.

After a moment he stopped again and took his notebook from his pocket, quickly marking down how many paces he had come before checking his compass again to see if the tunnel had diverged from its slow descent.

It was a narrow passageway, one they had not explored the first time he had been here. Overhead it tapered to a crack that seemed to go some way into the rock, but it was barely wide enough to walk down, and it was slowly narrowing. Up ahead, however, it seemed to emerge into a larger space—a small cavern, perhaps—and so he persevered, hoping he might squeeze through and investigate.

The rock was silent. There were no waterflows here, no steady drip from unseen heights, only the absence of sound. He was the intruder here, the noise of his own breathing loud in his ears. It was warm in the rock and he felt no fear. Since he'd been a child and his father had first taken him deep inside the rock, he had felt no fear. What he felt, if anything, was a tiny thrill of anticipation.

There was hidden beauty in the rock. Locked deep within the earth were caverns of such delicate, shimmering beauty that, to step out into them, was a joy beyond all measuring.

Taking his sack from his shoulders, he dropped it softly onto the floor of the passage, then turned and began to squeeze into the narrow space. Breathing in, he found he could just slip through.

He turned, then grabbed hold of the rock beside him. Just below him the rock fell away into a narrow chasm. To his left it climbed to meet a solid wall of rock. But to his right . . .

Aitrus grinned. To his right, just beyond the gap, the cavern opened out. Points of shimmering crystal seemed to wink back at him as he turned his head. The roof of the cavern was low, but the cave itself went back some way, a huge, pillarlike outcrop of rock concealing what lay at the far end.

Aitrus turned and, squeezing back through, retrieved his sack. By the timer on his wrist he had been gone from the base-node almost three hours, but there was still plenty of time. Securing the strap of the sack about his wrist, he edged through the gap again, standing on the lip of the entrance hole.

The gap seemed deep, but he could jump it at a stride. The trouble would be getting back, as the floor of the cave was much lower than where he stood. It would not be so easy leaping up onto this ledge.

Taking a length of rope from his sack, Aitrus hammered a metal pin into the rock beside him and tied one end of the rope fast about it. He uncoiled the rope, letting two or three spans of it hang down, then jumped down.

For a moment he looked about him, his eyes searching for a chunk of loose stone to lay upon the end of the rope to keep it in place, but there was nothing. The rock was strangely fused here and glassy. Aitrus coiled the end of the rope and rested it on the rock, trusting that it would not slip into the gap. Then, straightening up, he turned to face the cavern.

For a moment Aitrus held himself perfectly still, the beam of light from his lamp focused on the pillar at the far end of the cavern, then he crouched and, again taking his notebook from his pocket, rested it on his knee, and began to sketch what he saw.

Finished, he began to walk across. The floor was strangely smooth and for a moment Aitrus wondered if he were in a volcanic chamber of some kind. Then, with a laugh, he stopped and crouched.

"Agates!" he said softly, his voice a whisper in that silent space. "Agates in the rock!"

Taking a hammer and chisel from his tool belt, Aitrus chipped at the smooth surface of the rock just to his left, then, slipping the tools back into their leather holsters, he reached down and gently plucked his find from the rock.

The agate was a tiny piece of chalcedony no bigger than a pigeon's egg. He held it up and studied it, then, reaching behind him, popped it into the sack on his back. There were others here, and he quickly chipped them from the rock. Some were turquoise, others a deep summer blue. One, however, was almost purple in color and he guessed that it was possibly an amethyst.

Aitrus smiled broadly, then stood once more. Such agates were hypabyssal— small intrusive bodies from deep in the earth's crust that had been thrust up with the lava flow to cool at these shallow depths. In a sense they were no more than bubbles in the lava flow; bubbles that had been filled with heated groundwater. Long eons had passed and this was the form they had taken. Polished they would look magnificent.

Aitrus began to walk toward the distant pillar of rock, but he had taken no more than two paces when the floor beneath him began to tremble. At first he thought they had perhaps begun drilling again, for the source of the vibrations seemed quite distant, but then he recalled what Master Telanis had said.

We'll do no work today . . .

As if to emphasize the point, the ground shuddered. There was a deep rumbling in the rock. He could hear rock falling in the passage behind him.

Aitrus walked across. If the passage collapsed, he would be trapped here, and it might be days before anyone knew where he was. He had told no one that he was off exploring.

The rope, at least, was still where he had left it. He swung across and pulled himself up onto the ledge.

There was the faintest trembling in the rock. A trickle of dust fell from a crack above him. He looked up. If there was to be a proper quake, that rock would come down.

Calming himself, Aitrus squeezed through the gap and began to walk back along the narrow rock passage. He was halfway along when the rock shook violently. There was a crashing up ahead of him, dust was in his mouth suddenly, but the passage remained unblocked.

He kept walking, picking up his pace.

The luminous arrows he had left to mark his way shone out, showing him the direction back to the node. Coming to one of the smaller caverns near the node, he found his way blocked for the first time. A fall of rock filled the end of the cavern, but he remembered that there was another way around, through a narrow bore-

hole. Aitrus went back down the tunnel he'd been following until he found it, then crawled through on his
hands and knees, his head down, the sack pushed
before him. There was a slight drop on the other side.
Aitrus wormed his way around and dangled his feet
over the edge. He was about to drop, when he turned
and looked. The slight drop had become a fall of three
spans—almost forty feet. Hanging on tightly, he
turned his head, trying to see if there was another way
out. There wasn't. He would have to climb down the
face, using metal pins for footholds.

It took him a long time, but eventually he was
down. Now he only had to get back up again. He could
see where the tunnel began again, but it was quite a
climb, the last two spans of it vertical. There was nothing he could do; he would have to dig handholds in the
rock face with a hammer.

The ascent was slow. Twice the ground shook and
almost threw him down into the pit out of which he
was climbing, but he clung on until things were quiet
again. Eventually he clambered up into the tunnel.

If he was right, he was at most fifty spans from
the gate.

Half running, he hurried down the tunnel. Here
was the tiny cavern they had called The Pantry, here
the one they'd called The Steps. With a feeling of great
relief, he ducked under the great slab of stone that

marked the beginning of the cave system and out into the D'ni borehole.

Glancing along the tunnel, Aitrus could see at once that it had been badly damaged. The sides had been smooth and perfectly symmetrical. Now there were dark cracks all along it, and huge chunks of rock had fallen from the ceiling and now rested on the tunnel's floor.

Ignoring the feeling in the pit of his stomach Aitrus walked slowly on. He could see that the gate was closed. It would have closed as soon as the first tremor registered in its sensors. All the gates along the line, in every node, would be closed. If he could not open it he would be trapped, as helpless as if he'd stayed in the cavern where he'd found the agates.

There was a rarely used wheel in the center of the gate, an emergency pressure-release.

Bracing himself against the huge metal door, Aitrus heaved the wheel around, praying that another tremor wouldn't come.

At first nothing, then, the sound making him gasp with relief, there was a hiss of air and the door opened, its two halves sliding back into the collar of rock.

Aitrus jumped through, knowing that at any moment another quake might come and force the doors to slam shut again.

After the tunnel, the node was brightness itself. Aitrus blinked painfully, then turned to look back into the borehole. As he did, the whole of the ceiling at the end came crashing down. Dust billowed toward him. At the sudden noise, the sensors in the gate were activated and the doors slammed shut, blocking out both noise and dust.

Aitrus whistled to himself, then turned, looking about him. The walls of the great sphere in which he stood were untouched—it would take a major quake to affect the support walls—but both node-gates were shut.

He would have to wait until the tremors subsided.

Aitrus sat and took his notebook from his pocket, beginning to write down all that had happened.

It was important to make observations and write down everything, just in case there was something important among it all.

Small tremors were quite common; they happened every month or so, but these were strong. Much stronger, in fact, than anything he had ever encountered.

He remembered the agates and got them out. For a while he studied them, lost in admiration. Then, with a cold and sudden clarity, he realized they were clues.

This whole region was volcanic. Its history was volcanic. These agates were evidence of countless millennia of volcanic activity. And it was still going on. They had been boring their tunnels directly through the heart of a great volcanic fault.

Stowing the agates back in the sack, Aitrus wrote his observations down, then closed the notebook and looked up.

It was at least an hour since the last tremor.

As if acknowledging the fact, the node-gates hissed and then slid open.

Aitrus stood, then picked up his sack and slung it over his shoulder. It was time to get back.

AS AITRUS STEPPED OUT FROM BENEATH THE node-gate, he frowned. The base camp was strangely silent.

The two excavators remained where he had last seen them, but there was no sign of the frenetic activity he had expected after the quakes. It was as if the site had been abandoned.

He walked across, a strange feeling in the pit of his stomach, then stopped, hearing noises from the tunnel; the faintest murmur of voices, like a ritual chant.

Coming to the tunnel's entrance, he saw them: the whole company of both ships lined up in ranks, together with the four Observers, who stood off in a tiny group to one side. The assembly stood at the far end, where the accident had happened, their heads bowed.

At once Aitrus knew. This was a ceremony to mark Efanis's passage. He could hear the words drift back to him, in Master Telanis's clear and solemn tones.

"In rock he lived, in rock he rests."

And as the words faded, so Master Telanis lay the dead guildsman's hand upon the open linking book, moving back as the body shimmered in the air and vanished. It was now in the great burial Age of Te'Negamiris.

Aitrus bowed his head, standing where he was in the tunnel's mouth, mouthing the words of the response, along with the rest of the company.

"May Yavo, the Maker receive his soul."

Everyone was silent again, marking Efanis's passage with respect, then individual heads began to come up. Master Telanis looked across; seeing Aitrus, he came across and, placing a hand on Aitrus's arm, spoke to him softly.

"I'm sorry, Aitrus. It happened very quickly. An adverse reaction to the medication. He was very weak."

Aitrus nodded, but the fact had not really sunk in. For a time, in the tunnels, he had totally forgotten about his friend.

"Are you all right?"

"I'm fine," Aitrus answered. "I went back to the cave system. There's a lot of damage there. The quakes . . . "

Telanis nodded. "Master Geran seems to think it is only a settling of the surrounding rock, but we need to make more soundings before we proceed. There may be some delays."

"Guild Master Kedri will not be pleased."

"No, nor his fellows. But it cannot be helped. We must be certain it is nothing critical." Master Telanis paused, then. "It might mean that Master Kedri will require your services for slightly longer than anticipated, Aitrus. Would that worry you?"

Master Telanis had said nothing about Aitrus not letting anyone know where he had gone. That, Aitrus knew, was his way. But Aitrus felt guilty about the breach, and it was, perhaps, that guilt that made him bow his head and answer.

"No, Guild Master."

AS MASTER KEDRI CLIMBED UP INTO THE messenger, he turned, looked back at Aitrus, and smiled.

"Thank you, Aitrus. I shall not forget your kindness."

Aitrus returned the smile.

"And I shall not forget to deliver your letter," Kedri added, patting the pocket of his tunic, where the letter lay.

"Thank you, Guild Master."

Kedri ducked inside. A moment later the door hissed shut and the turbines of the craft came to life.

Aitrus stepped back, rejoining the others who had gathered to see off the Observers.

"You did well, Aitrus," Master Telanis said quietly, coming alongside as the Messenger turned and slowly edged into the tunnel, heading back to D'ni.

"Yet I fear it was not enough," Aitrus answered.

Telanis nodded, a small movement in his face indicating that he, too, expected little good to come of the Observers' report.

Unexpectedly, Master Kedri and his fellows had chosen not to wait for tunneling to recommence, deciding, instead, to return at once. All there read it as a clear sign that the four men had made up their minds about the expedition.

Efanis's death, the quakes——these factors had clearly influenced that choice—— had, perhaps, pushed them to a decision.

Even so, the waiting would be hard.

"What shall we do, Guild Master?" Aitrus asked, seeing how despondent Telanis looked.

Telanis glanced at him, then shrugged. "I suppose we shall keep on burrowing through the rock, until they tell us otherwise."

PROGRESS WAS SLOW. MASTER GERAN TOOK many soundings over the following five days, making a great chart of all the surrounding rock, then checking his findings by making test borings deep into the strata.

It was ten full days before Master Telanis gave the order to finish off the tunnel and excavate the new node. Knowing how close the Council's meeting now was, everyone in the expedition feared the worst.

Any day now they might be summoned home, the tunnels filled, all their efforts brought to nothing, but still they worked on, a stubborn pride in what they did making them work harder and longer.

The advance team finished excavating and coating the sphere in a single day, while the second team laid the air brackets. That evening they dismantled the platforms and moved the base camp on.

Efanis's death had been a shock, but none there had known quite how it would affect them. Now they knew. As Aitrus's team sat there that evening in the refectory, there was a strange yet intimate silence. No one had to speak, yet all there knew what the others were feeling and thinking. Finally, the old cook, Jerahl, said it for them.

"It seems unfair that we should come to understand just how important this expedition is, only for it to be taken from us."

There was a strong murmur of agreement. Since Efanis's death, what had been for most an adventure had taken on the aspect of a crusade. They wanted now to finish this tunnel, to complete the task they had been given by the Council. Whether there was anyone up there on the surface or not did not matter now; it was the forging of the tunnel through the earth that was the important thing.

Aitrus, never normally one to speak in company, broke habit now and answered Jerahl.

"It would indeed seem ill if Efanis were to die for nothing."

Again, there was a murmur of assent from those seated about Aitrus. But that had hardly died when Master Telanis, who now stood in the doorway, spoke up.

"Then it is fortunate that the Council see fit to agree with you, Aitrus."

There was a moment's shocked silence, then a great cheer went up. Telanis grinned and nodded at Aitrus. In one hand he held a letter, the seal of which was broken.

"A special courier arrived a moment ago. It appears we have been given a year's extension!"

There was more cheering. Everyone was grinning broadly now.

"But of much greater significance," Telanis continued as the noise subsided, "is the fact that we have been given permission to build a great shaft."

"A shaft, Master?"

Telanis nodded, a look of immense satisfaction on his face. "It seems the Council are as impatient as we to see what is on the surface. There is to be no more burrowing sideways through the rock. We are to build a great shaft straight up to the surface. We are to begin the new soundings in the morning!"

THE MOON WAS A PALE CIRCLE IN THE STAR-spattered darkness of the desert sky. Beneath it, in a hollow between two long ridges of rock, two travelers had stopped and camped for the night, their camels tethered close by.

It was cool after the day's excessive heat, and the two men sat side by side on a narrow ridge of rock, thick sheepskins draped over their shoulders; sheepskins that had been taken from the great leather saddles that rested on the ground just behind them.

They were traders, out of Tadjinar, heading south for the markets of Jemaranir.

It had been silent; such a perfect silence as only the

desert knows. But now, into that silence, came the faintest sound, so faint at first that each of the travelers kept quiet, thinking they had imagined it. But then the sound increased, became a presence in the surrounding air.

The ground was gently vibrating.

The two men stood, looking about them in astonishment. The noise intensified, became a kind of hum. Suddenly there was a clear, pure note in the air, like the noise of a great trumpet sounding in the depths below.

Hurrying over to the edge of the rocky outcrop, they stared in wonder. Out there, not a hundred feet from where they stood, the sand was in movement, a great circle of it trembling violently as if it were being shaken in a giant sieve. Slowly a great hoop of sand and rock lifted, as if it were being drawn up into the sky. At the same time, the strange, unearthly note rose in intensity, filling the desert air, then ceased abruptly.

At once the sand dropped, forming a massive circle where it fell.

The two men stared a moment longer, then, as one, dropped onto their hands and knees, their heads touching the rock.

"Allah preserve us!" they wailed. "Allah keep us and comfort us!" From the camp behind them, the sound of the camels' fearful braying filled the desert night.

MASTER GERAN SAT BACK AND SMILED, HIS blind eyes laughing.

"Perfect," he said, looking to where Master Telanis stood. "I intensified the soundings. Gave the thing a real blast this time! And it worked! We have clear rock all the way to the surface!"

Telanis, who had been waiting tensely for Geran's analysis of the sounding, let out a great sigh of relief.

"Are you saying this is it, Master Geran?"

Geran nodded. "We shall need to cut test holes, naturally. But I would say that this was the perfect site for the shaft."

"Excellent!" Telanis grinned. For three months they had pressed on, burrowing patiently through the rock, looking for such a site. Now they had it.

"I should warn you," Geran said, his natural caution resurfacing. "There is a large cave off to one side of the proposed excavation. But that should not affect us. It is some way off. Besides, we shall be making our shaft next to it, not under it."

"Good," Telanis said. "Then I shall inform the Council at once. We can get started, excavating the footings. That should take us a month, at least."

"Oh, at least!" Geran agreed, and the two old friends laughed.

"At last," Telanis said, placing a hand on Geran's shoulder and squeezing it gently. "I was beginning to think I would never see the day."

"Nor I," Geran agreed, his blind eyes staring up into Telanis's face. "Nor I."

THE PREPARATIONS WERE EXTENSIVE. FIRST they had to excavate a massive chamber beneath where the shaft was to be. It was a job the two excavators were not really suited to, and though they began the work by making two long curving tunnels on the perimeter, heavier cutting equipment was swiftly brought up from D'ni to carry out this task.

While this was being organized, Master Geran, working with a team of senior members of the Guild of Cartographers, designed the main shaft. This was not as simple a job as it might have appeared, for the great shaft was to be the hub of a network of much smaller tunnels that would branch out from it. Most of these were service tunnels, leading back to D'ni, but some extended the original excavation to the north.

As things developed, Master Telanis found himself no longer leading the expedition but only one of six Guild Masters working under Grand Master Iradun himself, head of the Guild of Surveyors. Other guilds, too, were now steadily more involved in the work.

Aitrus, looking on, found himself excited by all this frenetic activity. It seemed as though they were suddenly at the heart of everything, the very focus of D'ni's vast enterprise.

By the end of the third week the bulk of the great chamber had been part-cut, part-melted from the rock, a big stone burner—a machine of which all had heard but few had ever seen in action—making the rock drip from the walls like ice before a blowtorch.

The chamber needed supporting, of course. Twenty massive granite pillars supported the ceiling, but for the walls the usual method of spray-coating would not do. Huge slabs of nara, the hardest of D'ni stones—a metallic greenish-black stone thirty times the density of steel—were brought up the line. Huge machines lifted the precast sections into place while others hammered in the securing rivets.

A single one of those rivets was bigger than a man, and more than eight thousand were used in lining the mighty walls of the chamber, but eventually it was done.

That evening, walking between the pillars in that vast chamber, beneath the stark, temporary lighting, Aitrus felt once again an immense pride in his people.

Work was going on day and night now—though such terms, admittedly, had meaning only in terms of their waking or sleeping shifts—and a large number of guildsmen had been shipped in from D'ni for the task. The first of the support tunnels, allowing them to bring in extra supplies from D'ni, had been cut, and more were being excavated. The noise of excavation in the rock was constant.

To a young guildsman it was all quite fascinating. What had for so long been a simple exploratory excavation had now become a problem in logistics. A temporary camp had been set up at the western end of the chamber and it grew daily. There were not only guildsmen from the Guild of Surveyors here now but also from many other guilds—from the Guild of Miners, the Messengers, the Caterers, the Healers, the Mechanists, the Analysts, the Maintainers, and the Stone-Masons. There were even four members of the Guild of Artists, there to make preliminary sketches for a great painting of the works.

Food, of course, could have been a problem with so many suddenly congregated there in the chamber, but the Guild of Caterers brought up two of their Books, linked to the great granary worlds of Er'Duna and Er'Jerah, and the many were fed.

Not everything, however, was quite so simple. With the chamber cut and supported, they had begun to bring in the big cutting machines.

For five full days the tunnels were closed to any other traffic as these huge, ancient mechanisms were brought up one by one from D'ni. Dismantled in the lower caverns ready for the journey, they were transported on massive half-tracked wagons and reassembled in the base chamber, beneath the eyes of the astonished young guildsmen.

There were four of these machines in all, and with their arrival, there was a sense that history was being made. Only rarely was more than a single one of these monolithic cutters brought into use; to have all four at a single site was almost unprecedented. Not since the breakthrough to the lower caverns and the opening of the Tijali Mines, eighteen centuries before, had they been found together.

The machines themselves were, in three of the four cases, much older than that. Old Stone Teeth, as it was known, was close on four thousand years old, while Rock-Biter and The Burrower were contemporaries at three thousand years—both having been built for the broadening of the Rudenna Passage. The youngest, however, was also the biggest, and had been fashioned especially for the opening of the new mines. This was Grinder, and it was to Grinder that Aitrus and the rest of the young explorers were assigned.

Grinder arrived in stages. First to arrive was the Operations Cabin—the "brain" of the beast—itself four times the size of one of the excavators. Yet this, as it turned out, was the least impressive of its parts—at least, physically. In the days that followed, two giant, jointed legs arrived, and then, in a convoy that took several hours to enter the great chamber, the eighteen sections that made up its massive trunk.

Aitrus watched in amazement as trailer after trailer rolled in, filling the whole of the northern end of the chamber. Then, when he thought no more could possibly arrive, the cutting and grinding arms turned up— six massive half-tracks bearing the load.

The job of reassembly could now begin.

For much of the following weeks, the young guildsmen found themselves playing messenger for the thousands of other guildsmen who had suddenly appeared at the site—running about the great chamber, taking endless diagrams and maps and notes from guild to guild. The rest of the time they found themselves idle spectators as slowly the big machines took form.

It was a lengthy and painstaking process.

By the end of the third week, Grinder was complete. It crouched there, its matt black shape still and silent beneath the ceiling of the chamber, like some strange cross between a toad and a crab, its huge cutting arms lowered at its sides. Like all the great machines, it was constantly updated and modified, yet its outer form was ancient.

Standing before it, Aitrus felt, for the first time in his life, how small he was compared to the ambitions of his race. Though the D'ni were long-lived, the rock in which they had their being was of an age that was difficult to comprehend; yet with the use of such machines they had challenged that ancient realm, wresting a living from its bare, inhospitable grip.

Grinder was not simply a machine, it was a statement—a great shout into the rock. This was D'ni! Small, temporary creatures they might be, yet their defiance was godlike.

Turning from it, Aitrus walked out across that vast, paved floor, stepping between the massive pillars that stretched up into the darkness, then stopped, looking about him.

Grinder lay behind him now. The Burrower and Rock-Biter lay to his left, like huge black scarabs. Ahead of him was the dull red shape of Old Stone Teeth, squatting like a mantis between the pillars and the ceiling. As a child he had had an illustrated book about Old Stone Teeth, and he could vividly recall the pictures of the great machine as it leaned into the rock, powdered rock spraying from the great vent underneath it into a succession of trailers.

And now, as an adult, he stood before it. Aitrus nodded to himself. It was only when you were up close to such machines that you could appreciate their true size and power. No illustration could possibly do justice to such machines. They were truly awesome.

That night Aitrus barely slept. Soon it would begin, and he would live to see it! This was a tale to tell one's children and one's children's children: how, in the days of old, his people had cut their way up from the depths and made a great shaft that had reached up from the darkness to the light.

The next morning Aitrus was up early, keen to start. But his masters were, as ever, in no hurry. There were test boreholes to be drilled, and rock analyses to be made. For the next few days the Guild of Analysts took over, their temporary laboratories filling the center of the chamber, their "samplers"—a dozen small, bullet-shaped, autonomous drilling machines—boring their way into the rock overhead.

For Aitrus the next few weeks were pure frustration. Much was done, yet there was still no word of when the main excavation would begin. Letters from home spoke of the excitement throughout D'ni, yet his own had waned. And he was not alone in feeling thus.

Returning to the excavator after a day of running messages, Aitrus was about to pass the Guild Master's cabin when he noted Telanis seated at his desk, his head slumped forward, covered by his hands. A single sheet of paper was on the desk before him.

"Master? Are you unwell?"

Telanis looked up. He seemed tired, his eyes glazed and dull.

"Come in and close the door, Aitrus."

Aitrus did as he was told.

"Now take a seat."

Aitrus sat, concern growing in him. Telanis was looking at him now.

"To answer your question, Aitrus, no, I am not unwell, at least, not physically. But to be true to the spirit of your question, yes. I feel an inner fatigue, a sense of . . . "

"Disappointment?"

Telanis's smile was weary. "I thought it would not concern me, Aitrus. I knew that at some stage the whole thing might be taken from my hands. After all, we are but servants of the Council. Yet I had not expected to feel so useless, so peripheral to events. Great things are happening, Aitrus. I had hoped . . . well, that perhaps it would be we few who would be the ones to make the breakthrough."

Aitrus stared at the Guild Master in astonishment. He had not even suspected that Telanis felt this way.

"It seems we were merely the pathfinders, Aitrus. Yet I, for one, had grander visions of myself. Yes, and of you crewmen, too. I saw us as explorers."

"And so we were, Master."

"Yes, and now we are redundant. Our part in things is done."

"So why do they not simply send us home to D'ni?"

In answer Telanis handed him the paper. Aitrus quickly read it then looked up, surprised. "Then it is over."

"Yes," Telanis said quietly, "but not until the day after the capping ceremony. They want us there for that. After all, it would hardly be right for us not to be there."

The slight edge of bitterness in Telanis's voice again surprised Aitrus. He had always viewed Guild Master Telanis as a man wholly without desire; a loyal servant, happy to do whatever was required of him. This tiny fit of pique—if pique it was—seemed uncharacteristic. Yet Telanis clearly felt hurt at being brushed aside.

"They will surely recognize your contribution, Guild Master."

"Maybe so," Telanis answered distractedly, "but it will not be you and I, Aitrus, who step out onto the surface. That honor will be given to others."

For a moment Telanis was silent, staring down at the letter on the desk between them. Then he looked back at Aitrus.

"Forgive me. I did not mean to unburden myself on you, Aitrus. Forget I ever said anything."

Aitrus bowed his head. "As you wish." Yet as he stood, he felt compelled to say something more. "It was not your fault, Guild Master. You led us well. None of us will ever forget it."

Telanis looked up, surprised, then looked back down again, a dark shadow appearing in his eyes. Clearly he was thinking of Efanis.

"The excavation begins tomorrow. The capping ceremony will take place a week from now. Use the time well, Aitrus. Observe what you may. It may be some time before you return here."

THE NEXT MORNING THE MAJOR EXCAVATION work began. first into action was Old Stone Tooth, the picture-book illustrations coming to life for Aitrus as he watched the huge jaws of the machine lean into the ceiling, gnawing hungrily at the dark surface, a great fall of fine-ground rock cascading from three vents in its long, segmented underside into a massive open trailer that squatted beneath the ancient machine, the gray-black heap in its giant hopper neither growing nor diminishing as the minutes passed.

The noise was deafening.

For three long hours it labored, its long legs slowly stretching, its shoulders gradually disappearing into the great hole it was making in the roof of the chamber. Finally, with a deafening hiss, the great hydraulic legs began to fold back down. It was Grinder's turn.

As the grand old machine backed slowly into the shadows at the north end of the chamber, its massive chest stained black, its great cutting jaws still steaming, Grinder eased forward.

As the huge machine hissed violently and settled into place beneath the hole, its maintenance crew hurried across, Aitrus among them, small half-tracks bringing up the six massive stone brackets that would secure Grinder to the floor of the chamber.

In an hour it was ready. The crew moved back behind the barriers as the five-man special excavation team——their stature enlarged by the special black protective suits they wore——crossed the massive floor of the great chamber, then climbed the runged ladder that studded Grinder's huge curved back.

Another five minutes and Grinder's great engines roared into life. Grinder raised itself on its mighty hydraulic legs, like a toad about to leap, its four circular, slablike grinding limbs lifted like a dancer's arms. Then, without warning, it elbowed its way into the rock.

If Old Stone Tooth had been loud, the noise Grinder made was almost unbearable. Even through the thick protective helmet and ear-mufflers he was wearing, Aitrus found himself grimacing as the high-pitched whine seemed to reach right inside him.

Slowly the jointed arms extended as the rock was worn away, until they formed a giant cross that seemed to be holding up the roof of the chamber even as it ground away at its edges. Reaching a certain point it stopped and with a huge hiss of steam the arms retracted inward.

The relief from that constant deafening noise was sweet, but it was brief. In less than a minute it started up again, as Grinder lifted slightly, repositioning its limbs, then began to cut another "step" just above the one it had already made.

And so it went on, until the great hole Old Stone Tooth had made had been extended to form a massive vault. Not that it was finished even then: There was a great deal more rock to be cut from the walls before the shaft could be clad with nara and supported with cross-struts. Before Rock-Biter and The Burrower were brought in, they had first to build a platform two-thirds of the way up the partly completed shaft. Once that was in place, Old Stone Tooth and Grinder would be lifted up onto it by means of massive winches.

And then it would begin again, the two main excavating machines taking turns carving out the main channel, while below them the two slightly smaller machines finished the job they had begun, polishing the shaft walls and cutting the steps that would spiral up the walls of the giant well.

As guildsmen from the Guild of Engineers moved into place, ready to construct the platform, the young Surveyors began to drift away, their part in things finished for a time.

Aitrus was the last to go, looking back over his shoulder as he went. Their camp was a long way down the line, and walking back, through node after node crammed with guild tents and equipment, past endless troops of guildsmen coming up from D'ni, and units of the City Guard, whose job it was to keep the traffic flowing down the tunnels, Aitrus found himself sharing Master Telanis's feeling of disappointment that things had been taken from their hands. In the face of such awesome preparations, he saw now just how peripheral they really were to all of this.

Yes, and in six days they would be gone from here.

Aitrus sighed. His fellow Surveyors were now some way ahead of him; the murmur of their talk, their brief but cheerful laughter, drifted back to him down the tunnel. They, he knew, were keen to go home. Whether it was they or someone else who made the break-through to the surface did not trouble them; at least, not as it troubled Master Telanis and himself.

Yet Master Telanis was right. One ought to finish what one had begun. It seemed only fitting. And though their whole culture was one of finely drawn guild demar-cations and task specialization, there had to be some areas in which pure, individual endeavor survived—and if not in the Guild of Surveyors, where else?

Stepping out under the node-gate and onto the platform where their camp was situated, Aitrus looked across at the excavators where they were parked against the north wall and smiled fondly. He was almost of a mind to ask to serve on an excavator crew again. That was, if there were to be any new explorations after this.

Seeing Aitrus, Master Telanis summoned him across, then quickly took him into his cabin. He seemed strangely excited.

"Aitrus," he said, even before Aitrus had had a chance to take his seat, "I have news that will cheer you greatly! The Council have reconsidered their decision. They have permitted a small contingent from the exploration team to accompany the Maintainers for the breakthrough!"

Aitrus grinned broadly. "Then we shall get to fin-ish the job!"

Telanis nodded. "I have chosen six guildsmen to accompany me. You, of course, shall be among their number."

Aitrus bowed his head. "I do not know how to thank you, Guild Master."

"Oh, do not thank me, Aitrus. Thank your friend Veovis. It seems it was his intervention that swayed them to reconsider."

"Veovis?" Aitrus shook his head in amazement. He had written to Veovis weeks back, thanking him for the gifts, but there had been nothing in his letter about the Council's decision. "I do not understand."

Telanis sat, then took a letter from the side of his desk and handed it to Aitrus. "It appears that your friend and benefactor, Veovis, has been an active member of the Council these past two months, since his father's illness. It seems that he has the ear of several of the older members. His suggestion that a token body of men from the Guild of Surveyors should be included was apparently unopposed." Telanis smiled. "It seems we have much to thank him for."

"I shall write again and thank him, Master."

"There is no need for that," Telanis said, taking the letter back. "Veovis will be here in person, six days from now. Indeed, we are to be honored by the presence of the full Council for the capping ceremony. I am told that every last cook in D'ni has been engaged to prepare for the feast. It should be some occasion! And all from the seed of our little venture!"

THE NEXT FEW DAYS PASSED SWIFTLY, AND on the evening of the sixth day, at the very hour that the Guild of Surveyors had estimated, the great shaft was completed, the last curved section of nara lining bolted into place, the eighty great ventilation fans, each blade of which was thrice the length of a man, switched on.

It was an awesome sight. Standing on the floor of the great chamber, Aitrus felt a tiny thrill ripple through him. The great floor stretched away on all sides, its granite base paved now in marble, a giant mosaic depicting the city of D'ni at its center, the whole surrounded by a mosaic hoop of bright blue rock that was meant to symbolize the outer world that surrounded their haven in the rock. Yet, marvelous as it was, the eyes did not dwell on that but were drawn upward by the great circle of the walls that climbed vertiginously on every side, the spiral of steps like a black thread winding its way toward the distant heights.

Aitrus turned full circle, his mouth fallen open. It was said that some twenty thousand fire-marbles had been set into the walls. Each had been placed within a delicately sprung lamp that was agitated by the movement of the fans. As the great blades turned, the fire-marbles glowed with a fierce, pure light that filled the great well.

He lowered his eyes and looked across. Already the Guild of Caterers was hard at work, whole troops of uniformed guildsmen carryed into the chamber massive wooden tables that would seat twenty men to a side, while others tended the ovens that had been set up all along the southern wall, preparing for the great feast that would take place the next day.

Old Stone Tooth had been dismantled and shipped back down the line to D'ni two days back. Grinder had followed a day later. While the guildsmen set up the tables and began constructing the massive frames that would surround the central area where the feast was to be held, members of the Guild of Miners were busy dismantling Rock-Biter and Burrower on the far side of the great chamber. By tomorrow they, too, would be gone.

Aitrus, freed from all official duties, spent his time wandering on the periphery of all this activity, watching what was happening and noting his observations in his notebook. He was watching a half-track arrive, laden high with fine linen and chairs, when two strangers approached.

"Aitrus?"

He turned. A tall, cloaked man was smiling at him. Just behind was a second, smaller man, his body partly hunched, his features hidden within the hood of his cloak.

"Forgive me," said the taller of the two, "but you are Aitrus, no? I am Veovis. I am pleased to meet you again after all these years."

Veovis was a head taller than Aitrus remembered him and broad at the shoulder. His face was handsome but in a rather stark and monumental manner—in that he was very much his father's son. As Aitrus shook the young Lord's hand, he was surprised by the smile on Veovis's lips, the unguarded look in his eyes. This seemed a very different person from the one he'd known at school all those years ago.

"Lord Veovis," he said, stowing his notebook away. "It seems I have much to thank you for."

"And D'ni has much to thank you for." Veovis smiled. "You and your fellow guildsmen, of course." He turned slightly, introducing his companion, who had now thrown back his hood. "This is my friend and chief adviser, Lianis. It was Lianis who first brought your papers on pyroclastic deposits to my attention."

Aitrus looked to Lianis and nodded, surprised to find so ancient a fellow as Veovis's assistant.

"Lianis was my father's adviser, and his father's before him. When my father fell ill, it was decided that I should keep him on as my adviser, so that I might benefit from his experience and wisdom." Veovis smiled. "And fortunately so, for he has kept me from many an error that my youth might otherwise have led me into."

Aitrus nodded, then looked to Lianis. "My paper was but one of many submitted from the expedition, Master Lianis, and hardly original in its ideas. I am surprised it attracted your attention."

Lianis, it seemed, had a face that did not ever smile. He stared back at Aitrus with a seriousness that seemed etched deep into the stone of his features. "Good work shines forth like a beacon, Guildsman. It is not necessarily the originality of a young man's work but the clarity of mind it reveals that is important. I merely marked a seriousness of intent in your writings and commented upon it to the young Lord's father. That is my task. I claim no credit for it."

Aitrus smiled. "Even so, I thank you, Master Lianis, and you Lord Veovis. I have found good use of the equipment you were so kind in giving me."

"And I am glad it has found good use . . . though I never doubted that for an instant."

The two men met each other's eyes and smiled.

"And now I am afraid I must go. My father's guildsmen await me. But I am glad I had a chance to speak with you, Aitrus. I fear there will be little time tomorrow. However, when you are back in D'ni you must come and visit me."

Aitrus bowed his head. "My Lord."

Veovis gave the faintest nod, then, with a glance at Lianis, the two walked on, their cloaked figures diminishing as they crossed the great floor.

Aitrus stared a moment, then, with a strange sense of something having begun, took his notebook from his pocket and, turning to that day's entries, wrote simply:

Met Veovis again. He has changed. The man is not the child he was. He asked me to visit him in D'ni. He paused, then added. *We shall see.*

Closing the book, he slipped it back into his pocket, then, turning on his heel, hurried across, heading for the bright circle of the exit tunnel.

THE GREAT FEAST TO CELEBRATE THE CUTTING of the great shaft was almost over. Young guildsmen from the Guild of Artists looked on from the edge of events, hurriedly sketching the scene as the great men said their farewells to each other.

It had been an extraordinary occasion, with speeches and poems in honor of this latest venture of the D'ni people. A year from now a whole series of new canvases and tapestries would hang in the corridors of the Guild House back in D'ni, capturing the occasion for posterity, but just now the Grand Masters talked of more mundane affairs. Matters of State stopped for no man and no occasion—even one so great as this—and there was ever much to be discussed.

It was not often that one saw all eighteen major Guilds represented in a single place, and the colorful sight of their distinctive ceremonial cloaks—each Guild's color different, each cloak decorated with the symbols that specified the rank and status of the guildsman who wore it—gave Aitrus an almost childish delight. Such things he had only glimpsed in books before now.

Aitrus's own cloak, like those of all young guildsmen without rank, had eight such symbols, four to each side, beneath the lapels, whereas those of the great Lords had but a single one.

Looking on from where he sat on the far side of the feasting circle, Aitrus saw Veovis rise from his seat to greet one of the Great Lords, his friendly deference making the old man smile. Four of the Five were here today, the fifth—Veovis's father—being too ill to come. All eighteen of the Grand Masters were also here, to represent their guilds, along with several hundred of their most senior Masters, every one of them resplendent in their full Guild colors.

To a young guildsman, they seemed an impressive host. Lord Tulla, it was said, was 287 years old, and his three companions—the Lords R'hira, Nehir, and Eneah—were all well into their third century. Veovis, by comparison, was a babe—a glint of sunlight against dark shadow. Lord Tulla, in particular, looked like something carved, as if, in the extremity of age, he had become the rock in which he had lived all his life.

One day, perhaps, Aitrus too might become a Grand Master, or perhaps even one of the Five, yet the road that led to such heights was long and hard, and some days he wondered if he had the temperament.

If this expedition had proved one single thing to him it was that he was of essence a loner. He had thought, perhaps, that such close proximity to his fellows, day in, day out, might have brought him out of his shell—rounding off the hard edges of his nature—but it had not proved so. It was not that he did not get on with his fellow cadets—he liked them well enough and they seemed to like him—it was simply that he did not share their pursuits, their constant need for small distractions.

You were born old, Aitrus, his mother had so often said. Too old and too serious. And it had worried him.

But now he knew he could not change what he was. And others, Master Telanis among them, seemed to value that seriousness. They saw it not as a weakness but a strength.

Even so, he wondered how well he would settle back into the life of the Guild House. It was not the work— the studying and practicals—that concerned him but the personal element. Watching the great men at the feast had reminded him of that, of the small, personal sacrifices one made to be a senior Guildsman.

Given the choice, Aitrus would have spent his whole life exploring; drilling through the rock and surveying. But that, he understood, was a young man's job, and he would not be a young man all his life. In time he would be asked to take charge; of small projects at first, but then steadily larger and larger tasks, and in so doing he would have to deal not with the dynamics of rock— the certainties of weight and form and pressure—but with the vagaries and inconsistencies of personality.

He looked across, catching Telanis's eye. The Guild Master smiled and raised the silver goblet he was holding in a toast. Aitrus raised his own uncertainly but did not sip. Many of his companions were drunk, but he had not touched even a drain of the strong wine he had been served.

Indeed, if the choice had been given him, he would have left an hour back, after the last speech, but it was not deemed polite for any of them to leave before their Masters. And so they sat, amid the ruins of the feast, looking on as the old men went from table to table.

"Look!" someone whispered to Aitrus's right. "The young Lord is coming over here!"

Aitrus looked up to see Veovis making his way across. Seeing Aitrus, Veovis smiled, then turned to address Telanis. "Master Telanis, might I have a word in private with Guildsman Aitrus?"

"Of course," Telanis answered, giving the slightest bow of respect.

Aitrus, embarrassed by the sudden attention, rose and made his way around the table to where Veovis stood.

"Forgive me, Aitrus," Veovis began, keeping his voice low. "Once more I must rush off. But Lord Tulla has given me permission to stay on an extra day. I thought we might talk. Tomorrow, after the breaching."

The "breaching" was a small ceremony to mark the commencement of the breakthrough tunnel.

Aitrus nodded. "I'd welcome that."

"Good." Briefly Veovis held his arm, then, as if he understood Aitrus's embarrassment, let his hand fall away. "Tomorrow, then."

THAT EVENING THEY WINCHED THE EXCAVATOR up onto the platform at the very top of the great shaft. Aitrus, standing beside Master Telanis, watched as it was lowered onto the metal grid, feeling an immense pride at the sight of the craft. Its usefulness as a cutter was marginal now—other machines, much larger and more efficient were already in place, ready to cut the final tunnel from the rock—yet it would serve as their quarters in this final leg of their journey.

Earlier, Master Telanis had given a moving speech as he said farewell to those cadets who would be returning to D'ni in the morning. Only Master Geran, Aitrus, and five others remained; their sole task now to represent their Guild when finally they broke through to the surface.

"How long will it take?" he asked, looking to Telanis.

The Guild Master's attention was on the excavator, as strange hands removed the winch chains and began to lift the craft so they could extricate the great cradle from beneath it. His eyes never leaving that delicate task, Telanis answered Aitrus quietly.

"A week. Maybe less. Why? Are you impatient, Aitrus?"

"No, Master."

"Good. Because I would hate you to be disappointed."

"I do not understand, Master."

Telanis glanced at him. "The tunnel will be cut. But whether we shall ever step out onto the surface is another matter. There will be one final meeting of the Council to decide that."

Aitrus felt a strange disturbance—a feeling almost of giddiness—at the thought of coming so close and never actually stepping out onto the surface of the world.

"I thought it had been decided."

Telanis nodded vaguely. "So did I. Yet it is an important matter—perhaps the most important they have had to debate for many centuries. If they are wrong, then D'ni itself might suffer. And so the Council deliberate until the last. Why, even today, at the feast, they were still discussing it even as they congratulated one another!"

"And if they decide not to?"

Telanis turned and met his eyes. "Then we go home, Aitrus."

"And the tunnel?"

"Will be sealed. At least, this top part of it. It is unlikely that the surface-dwellers have the technology to drill down into the shaft, even if they were to locate it."

"I see."

"No, Aitrus. Neither you nor I see, not as the Great Lords see. Yet when their final word comes, whatever it may be, we shall do as they instruct."

"And what do *you* think, Master? Do you think they will let us contact the surface-dwellers?"

Telanis laughed quietly. "If I knew that, Aitrus, I would be a Great Lord myself."

THAT NIGHT AITRUS WOKE TO FIND THE platform trembling, as if a giant gong had been struck in the depths. All about him people slept on drunkenly, unaware of the faint tremor. After a while it subsided and the platform was still again. For a moment Aitrus wondered if he had imagined it, but then it came again, stronger this time, almost audible.

Aitrus shrugged off his blanket and stood, then walked across until he stood close to the edge of the great drop. The whole shaft was vibrating, and now there was the faintest hum—a deep bass note—underlying everything.

For close on three months, the earth had been silent. Now, even as they prepared to leave it, it had awoken once again.

Aitrus turned, looking back to where the guildsmen were encamped beside the excavator, but they slept on, in a dead sleep after the feast. He alone was awake.

Hurrying across, he bent down beside Master Geran and gently shook him. At first the old man did not wake, but then his blind eyes flicked open.

"Aitrus?"

Aitrus did not know how the old man did it, but his senses were infallible.

"There's movement," he said quietly. "The shaft was vibrating like a great hollow pipe."

Master Geran sat up, then turned to face the center of the tunnel. For a moment he was perfectly still, then he looked up at Aitrus again. "Help me up, boy."

Aitrus leaned down, helping him up.

"How many times?" Geran asked as he shuffled over to the edge of the shaft.

"Three so far. That is, if the one that woke me was the first."

Geran nodded, then dropped into a crouch, the fingertips of his right hand brushing gently against the surface of the platform.

For two, maybe three minutes they waited, Aitrus standing there at his side, and then it came again, stronger—much stronger—this time and more prolonged. When it had subsided, Geran stood and shook his head.

"It's hard to tell the direction of it. The shaft channels its energy. But it was powerful, Aitrus. I wonder why I was not woken by it."

Aitrus looked down, a faint smile on his lips, but said nothing. He had seen how much of the strong D'ni wine Master Geran had drunk. The only real surprise was that he had woken when Aitrus had shaken him.

"Should we wake the others, Master?" he asked. But Geran shook his head.

"No. We shall leave it for now. The final survey will show whether there is any risk. Personally I doubt it. We have come far to the north of the isopaches we identified earlier. If there is any volcanic activity, it is far from here. What we are hearing are merely echoes in the rock, Aitrus. Impressive, yes, but not harmful."

Geran smiled, then patted his arm. "So get some sleep, eh, lad? Tomorrow will be a long day."

REASSURED BY MASTER GERAN, AITRUS SETTLED back beneath his blanket and was soon asleep once more. If the ground shook, he did not notice it. Indeed, he was the last to wake, Master Telanis's hand on his shoulder, shaking him, returning him from the dark stupor into which he seemed to have descended.

"Come, Aitrus. Wash now and get dressed. The ceremony is in half an hour!"

They lined up before the cutter, alongside men from the Guild of Maintainers, whose task it would be to oversee this final stage of the journey to the surface.

The Maintainers were one of the oldest guilds, and certainly one of the most important, their Grand Masters—alongside those of the Guild of Writers, the Miners, the Guild of Books and the Ink-Makers—becoming in time the Lords of D'ni, members of the Five. Yet this was a strange and perhaps unique task for them, for normally their job was to ensure that the D'ni Books were kept in order, the Ages correctly run, and that the long-established laws, laid down countless generations before, were carried out to the letter. They had little to do with excavations and the cutting of tunnels. Indeed, guildsmen from some of the more physical guilds—those who dealt constantly with earth and rock and stone—would, in the privacy of their own Guild Halls, speak quietly of them, in a derogatory fashion, as "clean-handed fellows." Yet these guildsmen had been specially trained for this purpose and had among their number guildsmen drafted in from the Guild of Miners, and from the Surveyors.

They now would carry out the final excavation, and if any surface dwellers were found, it would be the

Maintainers who would first establish contact, for this was a most delicate matter and it was held that only the Maintainers could be vouchsafed to undertake that task properly.

Few of the Guild Masters who had been at the feast the day before had remained for this final little ceremony; yet in the small group who now stepped forward were no less than two of the Great Lords, Lord Tulla and Lord Eneah. Standing just behind them, among a group of five Grand Masters, was Veovis.

Lord Tulla said a few words, then stepped forward, pulling down the lever that would set the great cutter in motion. As he did, Veovis looked across at Aitrus and gave the tiniest nod.

Were these, Aitrus wondered, the faction in the Council who were in favor of making contact with the surface-dwellers? Or was that a misreading of things? Had the rest, perhaps, simply been too busy to attend?

As Lord Tulla stepped back, the engines of the cutter thundered into life and the circular blade began to spin, slowly at first, then, as it nudged the rock, with increasing speed.

The simple ceremony was concluded. The great men turned away, ready to depart. At a signal from Master Telanis, the Surveyors fell out.

Aitrus could see that Veovis was busy, talking to the Grand Master of the Guild of Messengers. Content to wait, he watched the machine, remembering the noises in the night.

Master Geran had been up early, he had been told, making a new survey of the rock through which this final tunnel was to be dug. His soundings had shown nothing unusual, and the vibrations in the earth had ceased. Both Geran and Telanis were of the opinion that the quakes had not been serious, but were only the settlement of old faults. Aitrus himself had not been quite so sure, but had bowed to their experience.

"Aitrus?"

He turned, facing Veovis.

The young Lord smiled apologetically. "You must forgive me, Aitrus. Once again I must be elsewhere. But I shall return, this evening, after I have seen Lord Tulla off. I did not think he would stay for the ceremony, but he wished to be here."

"I understand."

"Good." And without further word, Veovis turned and hurried across to where Lord Tulla was waiting.

Aitrus watched the party step into the special carriage that had been set up on a temporary track down the wall of the shaft, then stepped up to the edge, following its progress down that great well until it was lost to sight.

It was strange. The more Veovis delayed their talk, the more uncomfortable Aitrus found himself at the thought of it. Veovis wanted to be his friend, it seemed. But why? It made little sense to him. Surely Veovis had friends enough of his own? And even if that were not so, why him? Why not someone more suited to his social role?

Perhaps it would all come clear. Yet he doubted it. The rock was predictable. It had its moods, yet it could be read, its actions foreseen. But who could say as much of a man?

Aitrus turned, looking back across the platform. Already the cutter was deep in the rock, like a weevil burrowing its way into a log. Crouching, he got out his notebook and, opening it, laid it on his knee, looking about him, his eyes taking in every detail of the scene.

This evening, he thought. Then, dismissing it from his mind, he began to sketch.

AITRUS WAS REACHING UP, HIS HANDS BLINDLY feeling for the scales, when the shock wave struck. He was thrown forward, his forehead smacking against the bulkhead as the whole craft seemed to be picked up and rolled over onto its side.

For five long seconds the excavator shook, a great sound of rending and tearing filling the air.

And then silence.

Struggling up, Aitrus put a hand to his brow and felt blood. Outside, on the platform, a siren was sounding. For a moment the lights in the craft flickered dimly, then the override switched in and the emergency lighting came on. In its sudden light, he could see that the excavator had been completely overturned. It lay now on its back.

Pulling himself hand by hand along the tilted corridor, he climbed out onto the side of the craft and looked about him.

Guildsmen were running about, shouting urgently to one another. On the far side of the platform a huge section of the metal grid had buckled and slipped from its supports and now hung dangerously over the shaft. Behind it a dark line snaked up the wall of the shaft.

Aitrus's mouth fell open in surprise. *The shaft was breached! The nara stone torn sheet from sheet!*

The quake must have been directly beneath them.

Looking across, he saw that the mouth of the new tunnel was cracked. A large chunk of rock had fallen from the arch and now partly blocked the tunnel. The cutter, deep inside the tunnel, was trapped.

As he stood there, Master Telanis came over to him and, grasping his arm, turned Aitrus to face him.

"Aitrus! Get on protective gear at once, then report back to me. We must secure this area as soon as possible. If there's another quake, the platform could collapse."

Too shocked to speak, Aitrus nodded, then ducked back inside, making his way to the equipment room. In a minute he was back, two spare canisters of air and a breathing helmet lugged behind him. If the air supply to the shaft had been breached, breathing might soon become a problem, particularly if any of the great ventilation fans had been damaged.

Seeing him emerge, Telanis beckoned him across. Several of the guildsmen were already gathered about him, but of Master Geran there was no sign.

Calmly, the simple sound of his voice enough to steady the frayed nerves of the young men, Master Telanis organized them: sending some to bring power-drills, others to sort out protective clothing. Finally, he turned, looking to Aitrus.

"Master Geran has gone, Aitrus," he said quietly. "He was standing near the edge when it hit. I saw him go over."

The news came like a physical blow. Aitrus gave a tiny cry of pain.

"I know," Telanis said, laying a comforting hand on his shoulder. "But we must look after the living now.

We do not know the fate of the cutter's crew yet. And there were Maintainers with them. If the tunnel came down on them we may have to try to dig them out."

Aitrus nodded, but he was feeling numb now. Geran gone. It did not seem possible.

"What should I do?" he said, trying to keep himself from switching off.

"I have a special task for you, Aitrus. One that will require an immense amount of courage. I want you to go down and make contact with whoever is in the lower chamber. I want you to let them know how things are up here: that the shaft wall is cracked, the cutting team trapped. And if they can send help, then I want it sent as soon as possible. You have that, Aitrus?"

"Master."

But for a moment he simply stood there, frozen to the spot.

"Well, Aitrus?" Telanis coaxed gently.

The words released him. Strapping one of the cylinders to his back, he pulled on the helmet, then hurried across to the head of the steps.

They were blocked. A great sheet of nara had fallen across the entrance. He would have to find another way down.

He went back to where the temporary track began. With the steps blocked, there was only one way down, and that was to climb down the track, hand over hand, until he reached the bottom.

For a moment he hesitated, then, swinging out over the gap, he grabbed hold of the metal maintenance ladder that ran between the broad rails of the track. Briefly his eye went to the metal clip at the neck of his uniform. If another big quake struck, he would have to clip himself to the ladder and pray it did not come away from the shaft wall.

And if it did?

Aitrus pushed the thought away and, concentrating on the task at hand, began the descent.

AITRUS WAS ALMOST HALFWAY DOWN WHEN the second quake struck.

Clipping himself to the metal strut, he locked both arms about the ladder, then dug his toes into the gap between the rung and the wall.

This time it went on and on, the whole shaft shaking like a giant organ pipe, things falling from the platform overhead.

The metal track beside him groaned and for a while he thought it was going to prize itself from the wall as

the metal studs strained to come away from the rock—
if he wasn't shaken from the ladder first!

How long it was he could not tell, but it seemed a
small eternity before, with an echoing fall, the shaking
stopped.

The sudden silence was eerie. And then something
clattered onto the marble far below.

Aitrus opened his eyes. Across from him the shaft
wall gaped. Cracks were everywhere now. The great molded sections were untouched, yet there were huge gaps
between them now, as if the tunnel wall behind them had
slipped backward. The outer wall of the spiral steps had
fallen away in many places, and several of the huge securing rivets had jiggled their way out of the rock.

The sight made his stomach fall away. It had all
seemed so sound, so permanent, yet one more quake
and the whole shaft could easily collapse in upon itself.

Unclipping himself, Aitrus resumed his descent,
ignoring the aches in his calves and shoulders, pushing
himself now, knowing that time was against him. But
he had not gone far when he stopped dead.

There had been a shout, just below him.

He leaned out, trying to see where it had come
from, and at once caught sight of the carriage.

Some forty, maybe fifty spans below him, the track
bulged away from the shaft wall, pulled outward by the
weight of the carriage.

As Aitrus stared, the shout came again. A cry for help. "Hold on!" he shouted back. "Hold on, I'm coming!"

The floor of the shaft was still a good five hundred spans below, and looking at the way the track was pulled away from the wall, he knew he would have to climb along the track and over the top of the carriage if he was to help.

A length of rope would have come in handy, but he had none. All he had was a canister of air.

Making sure his grip on the ladder was good, Aitrus reached across and grabbed hold of the rail.

Just below where he had hold of it, the bolts that had pinned the track to the shaft wall had been pulled out. The question was: Would his extra weight bring a further length of track away from the wall and send the carriage tumbling down to the foot of the great shaft?

He would have to take a chance.

The outer edge of the track was grooved to match the teeth in the track that ran up one side of the carriage. The great guide wire that ran through the carriage had snapped, so that tooth-and-groove connection was all that prevented the carriage from falling. If *that* went . . .

There was the faintest rumble, deep in the earth. Things fell with a distant clatter onto the marbled floor below. The metal of the carriage groaned.

Now, he told himself. *Now, before there's another quake.*

Counting to five, he swung over onto the track, his fingers wrapped about the toothlike indentations in the rail, then he began to edge backward and down, his feet dangling over the abyss.

The track creaked and groaned but did not give. He moved his hands, sliding them slowly along the rail, left hand then right, his eyes all the while staring at the wall just above him, praying the bolts would hold. And then his toes brushed against the roof of the carriage.

He swallowed deeply, then found his voice again. "Are you all right?"

There was a moment's silence, then, in what was almost a whisper. "I'm badly hurt. I've stopped the bleeding, but . . ."

Aitrus blinked. That voice.

"Veovis?"

There was a groan.

It was Veovis. He was certain of it.

"Hold on," Aitrus said. "It won't be long now."

There was a hatch underneath the carriage. If he could climb beneath it and get into it that way, there was much less chance of him pulling the carriage off its guide track.

Yes, but how would he reach the hatch? And what if he could not free the lock?

No. This once he had to be direct. He would have to climb over the top of the carriage and lower himself in, praying that the track would bear the extra weight.

Slowly Aitrus lowered himself onto the roof, prepared at any moment for the whole thing to give.

He was breathing quickly now, the blood pounding in his ears. The straps from the cylinder were beginning to cut into his shoulders and for a moment he wondered if he should slip it off, together with the helmet, and let it fall, but it seemed too much effort. If he was going to die, the cylinder would make no difference. Besides, he was almost there now. He had only to slip his legs down over the edge of the roof and lower himself inside.

It was easier said than done. With his legs dangling out over the roof, he realized that he was just as likely to fall out into the shaft as he was to slip inside, into the relative safety of the carriage. Yet even as he thought it, he lost his grip and slipped. With a cry, he reached out and caught hold of the metal bar above the carriage door. His whole body was twisted violently about and then slammed against the side of the carriage.

The pain took his breath for a moment. For a full second his feet kicked out over the gap as he struggled to hold on. Then, with a grunt of effort, he swung himself inside.

The carriage creaked and groaned as it swung with him. There was the sound of bolts tearing from the wall. One by one they gave with a sharp pinging sound. With a sudden jolt the carriage dropped, throwing Aitrus from his feet, then, with another jolt, it held.

Aitrus lay on his back, the cylinder wedged under him. He felt bruised all over, but he was alive. Turning his head, he looked across the narrow floor of the carriage.

Veovis lay there, not an arm's length from him, his eyes closed, his breathing shallow. His flesh, which had seemed pale before, was now ash white, as if there were no life in him.

Moving slowly, carefully, Aitrus got himself up into a sitting position, then edged across to where Veovis lay.

Veovis looked badly hurt. There was a large bruise at his temple, and blood had seeped through the makeshift bandage he had wrapped about his upper arm, but that would have to wait. His breathing had become erratic. Even as Aitrus leaned over him to listen to his chest, Veovis's breath caught and stopped.

For a moment Aitrus wasn't sure. Then, knowing that every second counted, he reached behind him and pulled the cylinder up over his head, laying it down at Veovis's side before removing his helmet.

Precious seconds were wasted making sure the airflow was working properly; then, satisfied, he lifted

Veovis's head and slipped the helmet on, before rolling him over onto his back.

The carriage swayed then settled.

Nothing was happening . . .

Aitrus blinked, then felt down at the wrist for a pulse. Veovis's heart had stopped.

Leaning over him, Aitrus pressed into his chest, leaned back, then pressed again. Veovis groaned, then sucked in air.

Aitrus sat back, knowing that he had done as much as he could. Veovis was in no condition to help himself, and on his own, Aitrus knew that he would not be able to lift the deadweight of Veovis out of the carriage and back down to the floor of the shaft.

There was a faint rumble. Again the carriage shook.

Slowly the rumbling grew, stronger and stronger until Aitrus was sure that the carriage would shake itself free from the restraining track. Slowly the light faded, as if a great shadow had formed about them. Then, with a sound of rending metal, the carriage was torn from the track.

It tilted sharply forward. Aitrus caught his breath, waiting for the fall, but the carriage had stopped in midair. Slowly, the walls on either side of him began to buckle inward.

"Noooo-oh!"

The buckling stopped. With a hiss of hydraulics the carriage jerked forward, then began slowly to descend with a strange jogging motion.

Aitrus began to laugh. Relief flooded him.

It was a cutter. A cutter had climbed the shaft walls and plucked them from the track. Now, holding them between its cutting arms, it was slowly carrying them down.

Aitrus leaned across, checking that Veovis was breathing steadily, then sat back, closing his eyes, his head resting against the buckled wall.

Safe.

THE COUNCIL ORDERED THE SHAFT REPAIRED, the top tunnel completed, and then they sealed it. There was to be no breakthrough, no meeting with the surface-dwellers. That was decided within the first ten minutes of the meeting. Whether the quakes had happened or not, they would have decided thus. But there was the matter of D'ni pride, D'ni expertise to be addressed, hence the repairs, the drive toward completion.

It would not be said that they had failed. No. The D'ni did not fail. Once they had decided upon a course of action, they would carry it through. That was the D'ni way, and had been for a thousand generations.

In the future, perhaps, when circumstances differed, or the mood of the Council had changed, the tunnel might be unsealed, a form of contact established, but for now that was not to be.

And so the adventure ended. Yet life went on.

IT WAS TWO WEEKS AFTER THE COUNCIL'S decision, and Aitrus was sitting in the garden on K'veer, the island mansion owned by Lord Rakeri situated to the south of the great cavern of D'ni.

Rakeri's son, the young Lord Veovis, was lounging on a chair nearby, recuperating, his shoulder heavily bandaged, the bruising to his head still evident. The two young men had been talking, but were quiet now, thoughtful. Eventually, Aitrus looked up and shook his head.

"Your father's offer is kind, Veovis, and well meant, yet I cannot accept it. He says he feels a debt of gratitude to me for saving your life, yet I did only what any other man would have done. Besides, I wish to make my own way in the world. To win honor by my own endeavors."

Veovis smiled. "I understand that fully, Aitrus, and it does you credit. And if it helps make things easier, I, too, would have turned down my father's offer, though be sure you never tell him that."

Aitrus made to speak, but Veovis raised a hand.

"However," he went on, "*I* owe you a debt, whatever you may say about this mythical 'anyman' who might or might not have helped me. Whether that is so or not, you *did* help me. And for that I shall remain eternally grateful. Oh, I shall not embarrass you with gifts or offers of patronage, dear friend, but let me make it clear, if there is ever anything you want—*anything*—that is in my power to grant you, then come to me and I shall grant it. There, that is my last word on it! Now we are even. Now we can both relax and feel less awkward with each other, eh?"

Aitrus smiled. "You felt it, too?"

"Yes. Though I don't know which is harder, owing a life or being owed one."

"Then let us do as you say. Let us be friends without obligations."

"Yes," Veovis said, rising awkwardly from his chair to grasp both of Aitrus's hands in his own in the D'ni fashion. "Friends, eh?"

"Friends," Aitrus agreed, smiling back at the young Lord, "until the last stone is dust."

PART TWO: OF STONE AND
DUST AND ASHES

A NNA STOOD AT THE CENTER OF THE strange circle of rock and dust and looked about her, her eyes half-lidded.

She was a tall, rather slender girl of eighteen years, and she wore her long auburn hair, which had been bleached almost blond by the sun, tied back in a plait at her neck. Like her father, she was dressed in a long black desert cloak, hemmed in red with a broad leather tool belt at the waist. On her back was a leather knapsack, on her feet stout leather boots.

Her father was to the left of her, slowly walking the circle's edge, the wide-brimmed hat he wore to keep off the sun was pulled back, a look of puzzlement on his face.

They had discovered the circle the previous day, on the way back from a survey of a sector of the desert southwest of the dormant volcano.

"Well?" she asked, turning to him. "What is it?"

"I don't know," he answered, his voice husky. "Either someone spent an age *constructing* this, sorting and grading the stones by size then laying them out in perfect circles, or . . . "

"Or what?"

He shook his head. "Or someone shook the earth, like a giant sieve." He laughed. "From *below*, I mean."

"So what *did* cause it?"

"I don't know," he said again. "I really don't. I've never seen anything like it in over fifty years of surveying, and I've seen a lot of strange things."

She walked over to him, counting each step, then made a quick calculation in her head.

"It's eighty paces in diameter, so that's close on eight hundred square feet," she said. "I'd say that's much too big to have been made."

"Unless you had a whole tribe working at it."

"Yes, but it looks natural. It looks . . . well, I imagine that from above it would look like a giant drop of water had fallen from the sky."

"Or that sieve of mine." He narrowed his eyes and crouched a moment, studying the pattern of stones by his feet, then shook his head again. "Vibrations," he said quietly. "Vibrations deep in the earth."

"Volcanic?"

"No." He looked up at his daughter. "No, this was no quake. Quakes crack stone, or shatter it, or deposit it. They don't grade it and sort it."

"You're looking tired," she said after a moment. "Do you want to rest a while?"

She did not usually comment on how he looked, yet there was an edge of concern in her voice. Of late he had tired easily. He seemed to have lost much of the vigor he had had of old.

He did not answer her. Not that she expected him to. He was never one for small talk.

Anna looked about her once more. "How long do you think it's been here?"

"It's sheltered here," he said after a moment, his eyes taking in every detail of his surroundings. "There's not much sand drift. But judging by what there is, I'd say it's been here quite a while. Fifty years, perhaps?"

Anna nodded. Normally she would have taken samples, yet it was not the rocks themselves but the way they were laid out that was different here.

She went over to her father. "I think we should go back. We could come here tomorrow, early."

He nodded. "Okay. Let's do that. I could do with a long, cool soak."

"And strawberries and cream, too, no doubt?"

"Yes, and a large glass of brandy to finish with!"

They both laughed.

"I'll see what I can rustle up."

THE LODGE HAD BEEN NAMED BY HER FATHER
in a moment of good humor, not after the hunting
lodge in which he had spent his own childhood, back
in Europe, but because it was lodged into a shelf
between the rock wall and the shelf below. A narrow
stone bridge—hand-cut by her father some fifteen
years ago, when Anna was barely three—linked it to the
rest of the rocky outcrop, traversing a broad chasm that
in places was close to sixty feet deep.

The outer walls of the Lodge were also of hand-cut
stone, their polished surfaces laid flush. A small, beautifully carved wooden door, set deep within the white stone
at the end of the narrow bridge, opened onto a long, low-
ceilinged room that had been hewn from the rock.

Four additional rooms led off from that long room:
three to the right, which they used as living quarters,
and another, their laboratory and workshop, to
the left.

Following him inside, she helped him down onto
the great sofa at the end of the room, then ducked
under the narrow stone lintel into the galley-kitchen at
the front.

A moment later she returned, a stone tumbler of
cold water held out to him.

"No, Anna. That's too extravagant!"

"Drink it," she said insistently. "I'll make a special
journey to the pool tonight."

He hesitated, then, with a frown of self-disapproval, slowly gulped it down.

Anna, watching him, saw suddenly how pained he was, how close to exhaustion, and wondered how long he had struggled on like this without saying anything to her.

"You'll rest tomorrow," she said, her voice brooking no argument. "I can continue with the survey on my own."

She could see he didn't like the idea; nonetheless, he nodded.

"And the report?"

"If the report's late, it's late," she said tetchily.

He turned his head, looking at her. "I gave my word."

"You're ill. He'll understand. People are ill."

"Yes, and people starve. It's a hard world, Anna."

"Maybe so. But we'll survive. And you *are* ill. Look at you. You need rest."

He sighed. "Okay. But a day. That's all."

"Good. Now let's get you to your bed. I'll wake you later for supper."

IT WAS DARK WHEN SHE HEARD HIM WAKE she had been sitting there, watching the slow, inexorable movement of the stars through the tiny square of window.

Turning, she looked through to where he lay, a shadow among the shadows of the inner room.

"How are you feeling now?"

"A little better. Not so tired anyway."

Anna stood, walked over to where the pitcher rested in its carved niche, beside the marble slab on which she prepared all their meals, and poured him a second tumbler of cold water. She had climbed down to the pool at the bottom of the chasm earlier, while he slept, and brought two pitchers back, strapped to her back, their tops stoppered to prevent them from leaking as she climbed the tricky rock face. It would last them several days if they were careful.

He sipped eagerly as she held the tumbler to his lips, then sank back onto his pallet bed.

"I was dreaming," he said.

"Were you?"

"Of mother. I was thinking how much you've come to look like her."

She did not answer him. Six years had passed, but still the subject was too raw in her memory to speak of.

"I was thinking I might stay here tomorrow," she said, after a moment. "Finish those experiments you began last week."

"Uhuh?"

"I thought . . . well, I thought I could be on hand then, if you needed me."

"I'll be okay. It's only tiredness."

"I know, but . . . "

"If you want to stay, stay."

"And the experiments?"

"You know what you're doing, Anna. You know almost as much as I do now."

"Never," she said, smiling across at him.

The silence stretched on. After a while she could hear his soft snoring fill the darkened room.

She moved back, into the kitchen. The moon had risen. She could see it low in the sky through the window.

Setting the tumbler down, Anna sat on the stone ledge of the window and looked out across the desert. What if it wasn't simple tiredness? What if he was ill?

It was more than a hundred miles to Tadjinar. If her father *was* ill, there was no way they would make it there across the desert, even if she laid him on the cart. Not in the summer's heat.

She would have to tend him here, using what they had.

Her head had fallen at the thought. She lifted it now. It was no good moping.

Flowers. She would paint him some flowers and place the canvas in the doorway so he would see them when he woke in the morning.

The idea of it galvanized her. She got up and went through to the workroom, lighting the oil lamp with her father's tinderbox and setting it down on the stone tabletop on the far side of the room.

Then, humming softly to herself, she took her mother's paintbox down from the shelf and, clearing a space for herself, began.

ANNA?

"Yes, father?"

What do you see?

"I see . . . " Anna paused, the familiar litany broken momentarily as, shielding her eyes, she looked out over the dusty plain from the granite outcrop she stood upon. She had been up since before dawn, mapping the area, extending her father's survey of this dry and forlorn land, but it was late morning now and the heat had become oppressive. She could feel it burning through the hood she wore.

She looked down, murmuring her answer. "I see stone and dust and ashes."

It was how he had taught her. Question and answer, all day and every day; forcing her to look, to *focus* on what was in front of her. Yes, and to make those fine distinctions between things that were the basis of all knowledge. But today she found herself stretched thin. She did not *want* to focus.

Closing the notebook, she slipped the pencil back into its slot, then crouched, stowing the notebook and her father's compass into her knapsack.

A whole week had passed, and still he had not risen from his bed. For several nights he had been delirious, and she had knelt beside him in the wavering lamplight, a bowl of precious water at her side as she bathed his brow.

The fever had eventually broken, but it had left them both exhausted. For a whole day she had slept and had woken full of hope, but her father seemed little better. The fever had come and gone, but it had left him hollowed, his face gaunt, his breathing ragged.

She had tried to feed him and look after him, but in truth there seemed little she could do but wait. And when waiting became too much for her, she had come out here, to try to do something useful. But her heart was not in it.

The Lodge was not far away, less than a mile, in fact, which was why she had chosen that location, but the walk back was tiring under the blazing desert sun. As she climbed up onto the ridge overlooking the Lodge, she found herself suddenly fearful. She had not meant to be gone so long. What if he had needed her? What if he had called out to her and she had not been there?

She hurried down the slope, that unreasonable fear growing in her, becoming almost a certainty as she ran across the narrow bridge and ducked inside into the cool darkness.

"Father?"

The pallet bed was empty. She stood in the low doorway, breathing heavily, sweat beading her brow and neck and trickling down her back. She turned, looking out through the window at the desert.

What if he'd gone out looking for her?

She hurried through, anxious now, then stopped, hearing a noise, off to her right.

"Father?"

As she entered the workroom, he looked around and smiled at her. He was sitting at the long workbench that ran the full length of the room, one of his big, leather-bound notebooks open in front of him.

"This is good, Anna," he said without preamble. "Amanjira will be pleased. The yields are high."

She did not answer. Her relief at seeing him up and well robbed her of words. For a moment she had thought the very worst.

He had the faintest smile on his lips now, as if he knew exactly what she was thinking. Anna wanted to go across to him and hug him, but she knew that was not his way. His love for her was distant, stern, like an eagle's love for its chicks. It was the only way they had survived out here without her mother.

"Anna?"

"Yes?"

"Thank you for the painting. How did you know?"

"Know what?"

"That those flowers were my favorites."

She smiled, but found she could not say the words aloud. *Because my mother told me.*

HE CONTINUED TO IMPROVE THE NEXT FEW days, doing a little more each day, until, a week after he'd got up from his bed, he came out from the workroom and handed Anna the finished report.

"There," he said. "Take that to Amanjira. It's not precisely what he asked for, but he'll welcome it all the same."

She stared at the document, then back at her father. "I can't."

"Why not?"

"You're not strong enough yet. The journey would exhaust you."

"Which is why I'm not going. You know the way. You can manage the cart on your own, can't you?"

Anna shook her head. She could, of course, but that wasn't what she meant. "I can't leave you. Not yet."

He smiled. "Of course you can. I can cook. And I don't need much water. Two pitchers should see me through until you return."

"But . . ."

"No buts, Anna. If Amanjira doesn't get that report, we don't get paid. And who'll pay the traders then? Besides, there are things we need in Tadjinar. I've made a list."

Anna stared at him a moment, seeing how determined he was in this. "When do you want me to go?"

"This evening, immediately after sundown. You should reach the old volcano before dawn. You could take shelter in the cleft there. Sleep until the evening."

It was what they always did, yet in reiterating it like this it almost seemed as if he were coming with her.

"Aren't you worried?"

"Of course I am," he answered. "But you're a tough one, Anna. I always said you were. Just don't let those merchants in Jaarnindu Market cheat you."

She smiled at that. They were always trying to cheat them.

"I'll fill the pitchers, then."

He nodded, and without another word returned inside.

"To Tadjinar, then," she said quietly, looking down at the report in her hands. "Let's hope Lord Amanjira is as welcoming as my father thinks he'll be."

AMANJIRA WAS IN GOOD HUMOR. HE BEAMED A great smile at Anna, gestured toward the low chair that rested against the wall on one side of the great room, then he returned to his desk and sat, opening her father's report.

As Amanjira leaned forward, his dark eyes poring over the various maps and diagrams, Anna took the chance to look about her. This was the first time she had been inside the great man's house. Usually her father came here while she stayed at the lodging house in the old town.

The room was luxuriously decorated in white, cream, reds, and pinks. Bright sunlight filled the room, flooding in through a big, glass-paneled door that opened out onto a balcony. There was a thick rug on the floor and silk tapestries on the wall. And on the wall behind Amanjira was a portrait of the Emperor, given to him by the Emperor himself.

Everything there spoke of immense wealth.

Anna looked back at the man himself. Like herself, Amanjira was a stranger in this land, a trader from the east who had settled many years ago. Now he was one of the most important men in the empire.

Amanjira's skin was as dark as night, so black it was almost blue, yet his features had a strangely Western cast; a well-fleshed softness that was very different from the hawkish look of these desert people.

As if a dove had flown into a nest of falcons.

But looks deceived sometimes. This dove had claws. Yes, and a wingspan that stretched from coast to coast of this dry and sandy land.

Amanjira made a tiny noise—a grunt of satisfaction—then looked across at her, nodding to himself.

"This is excellent. Your father has excelled himself, Anna."

She waited, wondering what he would say next; what he would give her for this information.

"I shall instruct the steward to pay you in full, Anna. And tell your father that, if his findings prove correct, I shall reward him with a bonus."

She lowered her head, surprised. So far as she knew, Amanjira had never offered them a bonus before.

"You are too kind, Lord Amanjira."

Anna heard him rise and come across to her. "If you wish," he said softly, "you might stay here tonight, Anna. Share a meal, perhaps, before you return home."

She forced herself to look up. His dark eyes were looking at her with a surprising gentleness.

"Forgive me," she said, "but I must get back. My father is not well."

It was not entirely the truth. She wanted to stay this once and explore the alleys of the old town, but duty had to come first.

"I understand," he said, moving back a little, as if sensitive to the sudden defensiveness in her attitude. "Is there anything I can do for him? Potions, perhaps? Or special foods? Sheep's brain is supposed to be especially nutritious."

Anna laughed at the thought of her father eating sheep's brain, then grew serious again, not wanting to hurt Amanjira's feelings. "I thank you for your concern, Lord Amanjira, and for your kind offer of help, but we have all we need."

Amanjira smiled, then gave a little bow. "So be it. But if you change your mind, do not hesitate to come to me, Anna. Lord Amanjira does not forget who his friends are."

Again the warmth of his sentiments surprised her. She smiled. "I shall tell him what the Lord Amanjira said."

"Good. Now hurry along, Anna. I am sure I have kept you far too long."

THE JOURNEY HOME WAS UNEVENTFUL. MAKING good time, Anna arrived at the Lodge just after dawn. She had been away, in all, seven days.

Leaving the cart in the deep shadow by the ridge, she climbed up onto the bridge and tiptoed across, meaning to surprise her father, but the Lodge was empty.

Anna returned to the doorway and stood there, looking out over the silent desert.

Where would he be? Where?

She knew at once. He would be at the circle.

Leaving the cart where it was, she headed east across the narrow valley, climbing the bare rock until she came out into the early sunlight. It made sense that he would go there at this hour, before the heat grew unbearable. If she knew him, he would be out there now, digging about, turning over rocks.

Her father's illness had driven the circle from her mind for a time, but coming back from Tadjinar, she had found herself intrigued by the problem.

It seemed almost supernatural. But neither she nor her father believed in things that could not be explained. *Everything* had a rational reason for its existence.

Coming up onto the ridge, Anna saw her father at once, in the sunlight on the far side of the circle, crouched down, examining something. The simple physical presence of him there reassured her. Until then she had not been sure, not *absolutely* sure, that he was all right.

For a time she stood there, watching him, noting how careful, how methodical he was, enjoying the sight of it enormously, as if it were a gift. Then, conscious of the sun slowly climbing the sky, she went down and joined him.

"Have you found anything?" she asked, standing beside him, careful not to cast her shadow over the place where he was looking.

He glanced up, the faintest smile on his lips. "Maybe. But not an answer."

It was so typical of him that she laughed.

"So how was Amanjira?" he said, straightening up and turning to face her. "Did he pay us?"

She nodded, then took the heavy leather pouch from inside her cloak and handed it to him. "He was pleased. He said there might be a bonus."

His smile was knowing. "I'm not surprised. I found silver for him."

"Silver!" He hadn't told her. And she, expecting nothing more than the usual detailed survey, had not even glanced at the report she had handed over to Amanjira. "Why didn't you say?"

"It isn't our business. Our business is to survey the rocks, not exploit them."

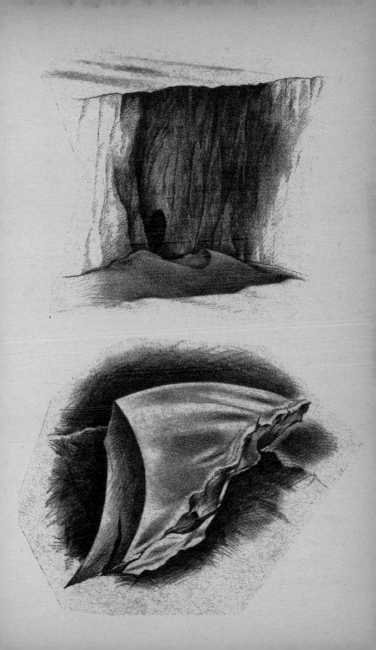

She nodded at the pouch. "We make our living from the rock."

"An honest day's pay for an honest day's work," he answered, and she knew he meant it. Her father did not believe in taking any more than he needed. "Enough to live" was what he always said, begrudging no one the benefit from what he did.

"So how are you?" she asked, noting how the color had returned to his face.

"Well," he answered, his eyes never leaving hers. "I've come out here every morning since you left."

She nodded, saying nothing.

"Come," he said suddenly, as if he had just remembered. "I have something I want to show you."

They went through the gap between two of the converging ridges, then climbed up over a shoulder of rock onto a kind of plateau, a smooth gray slab that tilted downward into the sand, like a fallen wall that has been half buried in a sandstorm.

Across from them another, larger ridge rose up out of the sand, its eroded contours picked out clearly by the sun. The whiteness of the rock and the blackness of its shadowed irregularities gave it the look of carved ivory.

"There," he said, pointing to one of the larger patches of darkness near the foot of the ridge.

"A cave?" she asked, intrigued.

"A tunnel."

"Where does it lead?"

"Come and see."

They went down, crossing the hot sand, then ducked inside the shadowed entrance to the tunnel. They stopped a moment, letting their eyes grow accustomed to the darkness after the brilliant sunlight outside, then turned, facing the tunnel. Anna waited as her father lit the lamp, then held it up.

"Oh!"

The tunnel ran smoothly into the rock for fifteen, twenty paces, but that was it. Beyond that it was blocked by rock fall.

Undaunted, her father walked toward it, the lamplight wavering before him. She followed, examining the walls as she went.

"It looks lavatic," she said.

"It is," he answered, stopping before the great fall of rock. "And I'd say it runs on deep into the earth. Or would, if this rock wasn't in the way."

Anna crouched and examined a small chunk of the rock. One side of it was smooth and glassy—the same material as the walls. "How recent was this fall?" she asked.

"I can only guess."

She looked up at him. "I don't follow you."

"When I found no answers here, I began to look a bit wider afield. And guess what I found?"

She shrugged.

"Signs of a quake, or at least of massive earth settlement, just a few miles north of here. Recent, I'd say, from the way the rock was disturbed. And that got me thinking. There was a major quake in this region thirty years back. Even Tadjinar was affected, though mildly. It might explain our circle."

"You think so?"

"I'd say that the quake, the rockfall here, and the circle are all connected. How, exactly, I don't yet know. But as I've always said to you, we don't know everything. But we might extend our knowledge of the earth, *if* we can get to the bottom of this."

She smiled. "And the surveys?"

He waved that away. "We can do the surveys. They're no problem. But this . . . this is a once-in-a-lifetime opportunity, Anna! If we can find a reason for the phenomena, who knows what else will follow?"

"So what do you suggest?"

He gestured toward the fallen rock. "I suggest we find out what's on the other side of that."

AFTER THEY HAD EATEN, ANNA UNPACKED THE cart. She had bought him a gift in the Jaarnindu

Market. As she watched him unwrap it, she thought of all the gifts he had bought her over the years, some practical—her first tiny rock hammer, when she was six—and some fanciful—the three yards of bright blue silk, decorated with yellow and red butterflies that he had brought back only last year.

He stared at the leather case a moment, then flicked the catch open and pushed the lid back.

"A chess set!" he exclaimed, a look of pure delight lighting his features. "How I've missed playing chess!" He looked to her. "How did you know?"

Anna looked down, abashed. "It was something you said. In your sleep."

"When I was ill, you mean?"

She nodded.

He stared at the chessboard lovingly. The pieces—hand-carved wood, stained black and white—sat in their niches in two tiny wooden boxes.

It was not a luxury item by any means. The carving was crude and the staining basic, yet that did not matter. This, to him, was far finer than any object carved from silver.

"I shall begin to teach you," he said, looking up at her. "Tonight. We'll spend an hour each night, playing. You'll soon get the hang of it!"

Anna smiled. It was just as she'd thought. *Gifts*, she recalled him saying, *aren't frivolous things, they're very neces-*

sary. They're demonstrations of love and affection, and their "excess" makes life more than mere drudgery. You can do without many things, Anna, but not gifts, however small and insignificant they might seem.

So it was. She understood it much better these days.

"So how are we to do it?"

He looked to her, understanding at once what she meant. Taking one of his stone hammers from the belt at his waist he held it up. "We use these."

"But it'll take ages!"

"We have ages."

"But . . ."

"No buts, Anna. You mustn't be impatient. We'll do a little at a time. That way there'll be no accidents, all right?"

She smiled and gave a single nod. "All right."

"Good. Now let me rest. I must be fresh if I'm to play chess with you tonight!"

IN THE DAYS THAT FOLLOWED, THEIR LIVES fell into a new routine. An hour before dawn they would rise and go out to the tunnel, and spend an hour or two chipping away at the rockfall. Anna did most of this work, loathe to let her father exhaust himself so soon after his illness, while he continued his survey of the surrounding area. Then, as the sun began to climb the desert sky, they went back to the Lodge and, after a light meal, began work in the laboratory.

There were samples on the shelves from years back that they had not had time to properly analyze, and her father decided that, rather than set off on another of their expeditions, they would catch up on this work and send the results to Amanjira.

Late afternoon, they would break off and take a late rest, waking as the sun went down and the air grew slowly cooler.

They would eat a meal, then settle in the main room at the center of the Lodge to read or play chess.

Anna was not sure that she liked the game at first, but soon she found herself sharing her father's enthusiasm—if not his skill—and had to stop herself from playing too long into the night.

When finally he did retire, Anna stayed up an hour or so afterward, returning to the workroom to plan out the next stage of the survey.

No matter what her father claimed, she knew Amanjira would not be satisfied with the results of sample analyses for long. He paid her father to survey the desert, and it was those surveys he was interested in, not rock analysis—not unless those analyses could be transformed somehow into vast riches.

In the last year they had surveyed a large stretch of land to the southwest of the Lodge, three days' walk away in the very heart of the desert. To survive at all out there they needed to plan their expeditions well. They had to know exactly where they could find shelter and what they would need to take. All their food, water, and equipment had to be hauled out there on the cart, and as they were often out there eight or ten days, they had to make provision for sixteen full days.

It was not easy, but to be truthful, she would not have wanted any other life. Amanjira might not pay them their true worth, but neither she nor her father would have wanted any other job.

She loved the rock and its ways almost as much as she loved the desert. Some saw the rock as dead, inert, but she knew otherwise. It was as alive as any other thing. It was merely that its perception of time was slow.

On the eighth day, quite early, they made the breakthrough they had been hoping for. It was not much—barely an armhole in the great pile of rock—yet they could shine a light through to the other side and see that the tunnel ran on beyond the fall.

That sight encouraged them. They worked an extra hour before going back, side by side at the rock face, chipping away at it, wearing their face masks to avoid getting splinters in their eyes.

"What do you think?" he said on the walk back. "Do you think we might make a hole big enough to squeeze through, then investigate the other side?"

Anna grinned. "Now who's impatient?"

"You think we should clear more of it, then?"

"I don't know," she answered, walking on. "I think we should think about it."

That afternoon, in the workshop, he talked about it constantly and, come the evening, rather than debate it further, she gave in.

"All right," she said, looking up from her side of the chessboard. "But only one of us goes through at a time. And we use a rope. We don't know what's on the other side. If there's more quake damage it might be dangerous."

"Agreed," he said, moving his Queen. "Check." Then, smiling up at her. "Checkmate, in fact."

IT TOOK THEM TWO MORE DAYS TO MAKE THE gap wide enough. It would be a squeeze, but to make it any bigger would have meant another week's work at the very least.

"We'll prepare things tonight," he said, holding his lamp up to the gap and staring through. "You won't need much."

Anna smiled at that "you." She had thought she might have to fight him over it. "So what am I looking for?"

He drew the lamp back and turned to face her. "Anything unusual. A volcanic funnel, perhaps. Vents. Any pyroclastic deposits."

"You still think this is part of a larger volcanic system?"

"Almost certainly. These vents and boreholes are only part of it. There would have been a great basin of lava—of magma—deep down in the earth. In fact, the deeper it was, the wider spread these surface manifestations will be. The super heated lava would have found all of the weakest routes through the rock, fault lines and the like. That's all this is, really."

"Like the roots of a tree?"

He nodded, smiling faintly at her. Anna had never seen a tree. Not a *proper* tree, anyway. Only the shallow-rooted palms of Tadjinar. Most of what she knew of the world had come out of books, or had been told to her. That was the worst of living here—the narrowness of it.

Walking back with her, he raised the subject, the two of them speaking, as they always did, with their heads down, not even glancing at each other.

"Anna?"

"Yes?"

"Do you regret living here?"

"Do you?"

"I chose it."

"And you think if I had a choice, I'd chose differently?"

"Sometimes."

"Then you're wrong. I love the desert."

"But you don't know anything else."

"I'd still want to be here."

"Are you sure?"

"I'm sure."

"MIND THE ROPE, ANNA, IT'S GETTING snagged."

Anna paused, edging slightly to one side, then tugged gently at the rope. It came free. She was halfway through the gap in the rockfall and finding it a tighter squeeze than she'd imagined. She had managed to shrug her shoulders through the narrow hole, but her hips were another matter altogether. Nor could she see anything properly. The tiny slivers of light that peeped through the narrow gaps between her and the wall served more to emphasize how stuck she was than help her.

She could always try and heave herself through, of course, but then she'd most likely tumble down onto the floor on the other side, and it was quite a drop.

Besides, only her left arm was free; the other was still wedged between her and the wall.

"Turn yourself about, Anna. Until you're facing the ceiling. The channel's wider than it's tall."

"We should have waited another week," she said, trying to do what he said.

"Maybe. But you're almost there now. Try and edge back a little. Yes . . . that's it."

Slowly, very slowly, she wriggled her way back, until she could feel that her head and shoulders were out over the gap. Now she had to try and free her arm. She tried to bring it up, but there wasn't room. She'd have to turn again.

"Hold my feet," she said.

Anna felt his hands grip the ankles of her boots firmly.

"Good. I'm going to try to turn onto my front now. At the same time I'm going to try to free my right arm."

"All right."

It was difficult. It felt as if the rock was trying to crush her—to pop her bones—but slowly she managed to turn herself, until she was facing the floor.

Anna could not see anything. The darkness in front of her seemed absolute. Not that the darkness itself worried her; she simply did not want to fall onto anything sharp.

"All right," she said, as she finally freed her arm. "Now lower me slowly."

The rock seemed to come up to touch her hands. Above her, light slowly spilled into the tunnel.

"That's it," she said. "Slowly now."

She began to take her own weight, reaching forward slightly with her hands.

"All right. You can let go now. I'm down."

Anna felt his fingers relent, his hands move back, away from her ankles. There was a faint noise from him, a grunt.

She scrambled up, then turned, brushing herself down. "Are you okay?"

He made a small noise of assent. "Just winded a little. Just give me a moment to get my breath."

Anna went to the hole and looked back through. The lamp was on the floor by his feet where he had left it. He himself was leaning against the wall, slumped slightly, one hand on his chest.

"Are you sure you're all right?"

He nodded and looked up at her. "I'll be okay. I didn't realize how heavy you are, that's all."

"You're sure?"

"Yes. Now get on. Tie the rope about your waist. I'll pass you through the lamp."

She stooped and picked up the rope, fastening it tightly about her waist. It was a thin, strong rope, and they had some five hundred feet of it. That should be plenty for this preliminary exploration. Satisfied, she turned and, leaning through the gap, took the lamp from him.

"This, too," he said, handing her his protective hat.

She put the lamp down, then tried on the hat, expecting it to be too big for her, but it was a perfect fit. She fastened the leather strap under her chin, then turned, lifting the lamp so that he could see her.

"Good," he said, his eyes shining in the lamplight. "I'll give you an hour, then I'll call you back. But keep your eyes open, Anna. And don't take chances."

"I won't."

"You've got the notebook?"

Anna patted her top pocket.

"All right. Then get going. It's cold here."

She smiled then turned, facing the darkness, the lamp held up before her.

THE LIBRARY OVERLOOKED THE DARKENED lake, its long, latticed windows giving a distant view of D'ni, the city's lamplit levels climbing the great wall of the cavern.

A fire had been lit in the great fireplace. In its flickering light four men could be seen, sitting in huge armchairs about the fire, their faces thrown into sharp contrasts of gold and black. They had eaten an hour ago, now, as it grew late, they talked.

"I don't know how you can say that, Veovis. Not with any certainty, anyway. Where's your proof?"

Veovis turned to face his friend, his wineglass cradled in both hands, the light from the fire winking at its ruby heart.

"But that's just it, Fihar. I need no proof. The matter is axiomatic. You argue that those races we have knowledge of, on those Ages to which we have linked, behave morally. I agree. But they do so because we have made it our business to encourage them to do so. Their morality is not innate, but taught. And we, the D'ni, were the ones who taught it to them. So much we have known for *thousands* of years."

Veovis turned slightly, looking to another of them. "You, Suahrnir. You are a Maintainer. Is it not so? Is it not one of your prime duties to encourage a stable and moral social framework among the natives of the worlds to which we link?"

Suahrnir was in his middle years and a senior member of his guild. He had already served as Keeper of the Prison Ages and was currently in charge of disposing of all failed or unstable Ages. He pondered Veovis's words a moment, then shrugged.

"It is, yet even so I have some sympathy with Fihar's view. We cannot say with certainty until we have seen for ourselves. That, surely, is the scientific method?"

"Nonsense!" Veovis said, leaning forward, his face suddenly animated. "Without D'ni influence and D'ni guidance, those Ages would, without a shred of doubt, be nasty little backwaters, peopled by savages! Have you not instances enough in your own experience, Suahrnir, of such backsliding? Do we not need to be constantly vigilant?"

"We do," Suahrnir agreed.

"Imagine then, up there on the surface. If there *are* people living up there, then they have developed now for several thousand years without any moral guidance. They will, most certainly, be savages, little more than animals, subservient to their most basic needs. And we have seen, all of us on many Ages, how wild animals behave!"

Aitrus, who had been listening silently, now spoke up. "Unless, like the D'ni, they have an innate morality."

Veovis smiled and turned to his friend. "I would say that the chances of that were exceedingly small, wouldn't you agree, Aitrus?"

"I . . . guess so."

"There!" Veovis said, as if that capped it. "You know, it makes me shudder to think of it. A whole society governed by lust and violence!"

"And the threat of violence," Fihar added, clearly half-convinced now by the argument.

"Exactly! And where, in such a society, would there be room for the development of true intelligence? No. The most we might expect from the surface-dwellers is a surly, grunting species, a pack of jackals who would as soon bay at the moon as hold a decent conversation!"

There was laughter at that.

"Then you think the Council should reaffirm their decision?" Aitrus asked, returning the conversation to the place where it had begun. "You believe we should have nothing to do with the surface-dwellers?"

"I do indeed," Veovis said emphatically. "And to be honest with you, I would not have simply sealed the end of the tunnel, I would have destroyed the whole thing altogether!"

"I see."

"Oh, Aitrus," Veovis said, leaning toward him. "I realize what sentimental feelings you have toward that expedition, and I admire you for it, but the venture was a mistake. The Council were wrong even to consider it!"

Aitrus said nothing. He merely sipped his wine and stared into the fire.

"And now I've hurt your feelings." Veovis stood. "Look, I apologize. It was, perhaps, insensitive of me."

Aitrus looked up at him, smiling sadly. "No, Veovis. You spoke as you saw, and I admire you for that.

Besides, I have come to feel that maybe you were right after all. Maybe it *was* a mistake."

Veovis smiled back at him. "Then you will vote with me in Council this time?"

Aitrus shrugged. "Who knows?"

LESS THAN A HUNDRED PACES DOWN, THE tunnel was blocked again, a second rockfall making it unpassable. Yet to the left of the fall, like a grinning dark mouth, was a crack in the tunnel wall, large enough for Anna to step into, if she wished.

Anna stood on the rim, her left hand holding the edge of the wall, and she leaned into it, the lamp held out.

The crack was deep. Its floor went down steeply into the dark, from which a faint, cold breeze emanated. She could hear the sound of water, muted and distant, far below, and something else—a kind of irregular knocking. A tap, tap, tap that was like the weak blow of a chisel against the rock.

Anna turned, looking back the way she had come, then, deciding that the slope was not *too* steep, she clipped the lamp to the top of her hard hat and stepped down, steadying herself against the walls with both hands and digging her heels in, so that she would not fall.

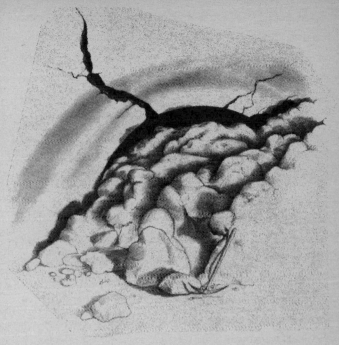

The crack was not as long as she'd imagined. After twenty paces it leveled out. For a moment she thought it was a dead end, for the rock seemed to fill the crack ahead of her, but just before that it twisted to the side again, almost at ninety degrees. As she turned that corner, she gave a little cry of surprise.

"It's a cavern!" she yelled, not knowing whether he could hear her or not. "A huge cavern!"

That tapping noise was close now and the sound of flowing water much stronger.

Stepping out onto the floor of the cavern, Anna turned, looking about her. The lamp illuminated only a small part of space, yet she could see, at the edge of the light, what looked like a tiny stream, its surface winking back at her.

Water. The most precious thing of all here in the desert. More precious than the silver her father had found for Amanjira.

Anna walked over to it, conscious of the rope trailing out behind her. The stream was crystal clear. She stooped down beside it, dipping her hand into the flow, then put her fingers to her lips.

Ice cold, it was, and pure. Much better than the water in the pool.

She grinned, looking forward to telling her father of her discovery, then she turned and looked up at the ceiling, twenty yards or so overhead.

There it was! The source of the tapping noise. It looked like a bright red hanging of some kind, marble smooth yet thin, the tip of it swollen like a drop of blood. And where it hung in the breeze it tap-tap-tapped against the roof of the cavern.

Anna frowned, then turned, looking for the source of the breeze. The cavern narrowed at its near end, becoming a kind of funnel. The breeze seemed to come from there.

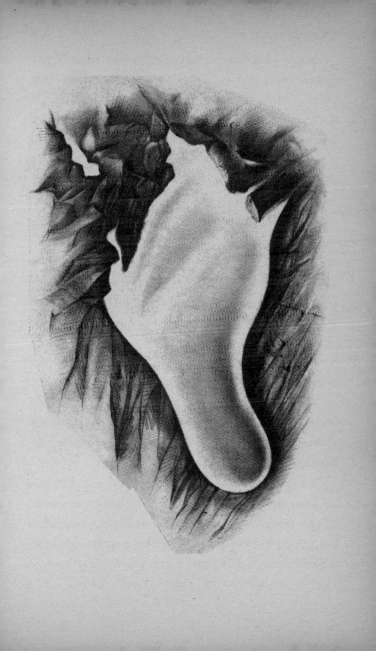

She sniffed the air, surprised by how fresh it was. Usually there was a stale, musty smell in these caverns. A smell of damp and stone. But this was different.

Unclipping the lamp again, she held it up, trying to make out what the red stuff was. It seemed to be trapped in the rock overhead, or to have squeezed through the rock and then congealed.

She took out her notebook; settling it on her knee, she began to write, noting down not merely what she could see but her first notions about the cavern. Such, she knew from experience, could prove important. One might notice something that one afterward overlooked, or simply forgot. It was best to jot down *everything*, even if most of it proved subsequently to be ill-founded.

Putting the notebook away, she took hold of the rope and pulled a length of it toward her, making sure it was not snagged in the crack. It came easily. Reassured, she walked on, toward the near end of the cavern, toward the "funnel," glancing from side to side, keen not to miss anything.

Thirty paces from it, she stopped, the slight sense of wrongness she had felt earlier now welling up in her.

There, facing her, filling the whole of one end of the narrowed cavern, was a huge sheet of the red stuff. It looked like a thick, stiff curtain, except that it jutted from the rock like a lava flow.

But it wasn't lava. Not of any kind she knew, anyway.

It made her think of the circle on the surface. Somehow these two things were connected, but just how she didn't know.

She could not wait to tell her father of it.

Anna walked over and stood before it, lifting the lamp. It was blood red, but within that redness was a faint vein of black, like tiny worm-threads.

Perhaps it *was* a kind of lava.

Clipping the lamp to her hat again, she took one of the hammers from her belt and, kneeling beside the wall, tried to chip a small chunk of the stuff away.

After a moment she looked up, puzzled. The hammer had made no impression. The stuff looked soft and felt soft. It *gave* before the hammer. But it would not chip. Why, it wouldn't even mark!

Not lava, then. But what precisely *was* it? Unless she could get a piece for analysis, there was no way of telling.

Anna stood back a couple of paces, studying the wall, trying to see if there might not, perhaps, be a small piece jutting from the rest that would prove more amenable to the hammer, but the stuff formed a smooth unvarying surface.

She turned, looking about her, then laughed. There, only a few paces from her, lay a line of tiny red beads, like fresh blood spots on the gray rock floor. She looked up, seeing how the red stuff formed a narrow vein overhead, as if, under great pressure, it had been squeezed between the lips of the rock.

And dripped.

Anna crouched and, chipping this time into the rock *beneath* the red stuff, managed to free four samples of it, the largest of them the size of her fist.

As she went to slip the last of them into her knapsack, she turned it beneath the light, then squeezed it in her hand. It was almost spongy, yet it was tougher than marble. Not only that, but it seemed to hold the light rather than reflect it.

It was time to get back. They would need to analyze this before they investigated any further.

Anna slipped the sack onto her shoulder, then, taking the rope in her right hand, began to cross the cavern again, coiling it slowly as she headed for the crack.

THE OTHERS WERE GONE. ONLY VEOVIS AND Aitrus remained. They stood in the broad hallway of the Mansion, beneath the stairs, the great stone steps and the tiny harbor beyond, visible through the glass of the massive front door.

"Stay the night, Aitrus. You can travel back with me in the morning. The meeting does not start until midday."

"I would, but there are some people I must see first thing."

"Put them off. Tell them you have to prepare for the meeting. They'll understand. Besides, I'd really like to talk to you some more."

"I, too. But I must not break my word."

Veovis smiled. "I understand. Your word means much to you, and rightly so. But try and come to me before the meeting. I shall be in my office in the Guild Hall. I would feign speak with you again before you cast your vote."

Aitrus smiled. "I have decided already, old friend. I shall abstain."

"Abstain?"

"I feel it would be for the best. I am not convinced by either argument. It may be as you say, and that my hesitancy is only sentiment, yet I still feel as if I would be betraying Master Telanis should I vote *against* the motion."

"Then so be it. Take care, dear friend."

The two men clasped each other's hands.

"Until tomorrow."

"Until tomorrow," Aitrus echoed, smiling broadly. "And thank you. The evening was a most pleasant one."

"As ever. Now go. Before I'm angry with you."

"I'VE NO IDEA," HE SAID, LIFTING HIS EYE from the microscope.

"I've never seen anything like it. It looks . . . *artificial.*"

"Impossible," Anna said, stepping up beside him and putting her own eye to the lens.

"So tell me what it is, then. Have you ever seen stone with that kind of structure before? There's not a crystal in it! That wasn't formed. At least, not by any *natural* process. That was *made!*"

She shrugged. "Maybe there are processes we don't know about."

"And maybe I know nothing about rock!"

Anna looked up and smiled. "Maybe."

"Well?" he said, after a moment. "Don't you agree?"

"I don't see how you could make something like this. The temperatures and pressures you'd need would be phenomenal. Besides, what would the stuff be doing down there, in the cavern? It makes no sense."

"No . . . "

She saw the doubt creep back into his face. He looked tired again. They had been working at this puzzle now for close on ten hours.

"You should rest now," she said. "We'll carry on with this in the morning."

"Yes," he said, but it was clear his mind was still on the problem. "It has to be obvious," he said, after a moment. "Something we've completely overlooked."

But what *could* they have overlooked? They had been as thorough with their tests as anyone could be. Had they had twice the equipment and ten times the opportunity to study it, they would still have come up with the same results. This stuff was strange.

HE HAD BEEN CHEERFUL THAT NIGHT. MORE cheerful than he'd been in quite some time. He had laughed and joked. And in the morning he was dead.

She had woken, remembering the dream she'd had of flowers. Blue flowers, like those she had painted for him. Getting up, she had gone through into the galley kitchen and set out their bowls and tumblers, staring out of the window briefly, conscious of how different everything looked in the dawn light. It was only then that she found him, slumped on the floor beside the workroom bench. She knew at once that he was dead, yet it was only when she actually physically touched him that it registered on her.

His flesh was cold, like stone.

For a moment she could not turn him over. For a

moment there was a blankness, a total blankness in her mind. Then she blinked and looked down at him again, where he lay.

He must have come here in the night. Unheard by her. And here he had died, silently, without a word to her.

She groaned and closed her eyes, grief overwhelming her.

THE FRONT LOBBY OF THE GREAT GUILD HALL was in turmoil. Aitrus, arriving late, looked about him, then, seeing Veovis to one side of the crowd of senior guildsmen, hurried over to him.

"Veovis. What's happening?"

"It is Lord Eneah. He was taken ill in the night."

Lord Eneah was Lord Tulla's replacement as head of the Council. Without his presence, or the appointment of a Deputy, the business of the Council could not be carried out.

"Then there will be no vote today."

"Nor for a week or two if the rumors are correct. It seems the Great Lord is at death's door."

"Ill tidings, indeed," said Aitrus.

While none of the D'ni elders could be considered jovial in any way that the young could recognize, Lord

Eneah had maintained a sense of humor well into his third century and was wont to control the Council by means of wit rather than chastisement. If he were to die, the Council would indeed lose one of their finest servants.

"What are we to do?" Aitrus asked, looking about him at the crowded vestibule.

"Disperse, eventually," Veovis answered, "but not until our business here is done. Now, if you would excuse me, Aitrus, I would like to take the chance to talk to one or two waverers."

Aitrus nodded, letting Veovis go. Unlike Veovis, he had no strong political ambitions, and though he had been appointed to the Council young—as the junior representative of his Guild—it was not because he had pushed for that appointment.

He had moved swiftly through the ranks, becoming a Master in his thirty-eighth year—the youngest in almost seven centuries—and then, three years ago, he had found himself elected to the Council by his fellow guildsmen; an unexpected honor, for there were men almost twice his age, which was fifty five, who had been put up as candidates against him.

And so here he was, at the very center of things. And though his word meant little yet, and his vote was but a tiny weight on the great scales of D'ni government, he was not entirely without influence, for he was a friend of Lord Veovis.

Watching Veovis from across the pillared hallway, seeing how easily the young Lord moved among his peers, how relaxed he was dealing with the high and mighty of D'ni society, Aitrus found it strange how close they had grown since their reunion thirty years ago. If you had asked him then who might have been his closest friend and confidant in later years, he might have chosen anyone but Lord Rakeri's son, but so it was. In the public's eyes they were inseparable.

Inseparable, perhaps, yet very different in their natures. And maybe that was why it worked so well, for both had a perfect understanding of who the other was.

Had they been enemies, then there would have been no late-night debates, no agreements to differ, no grudging concessions between them, no final meeting of minds, and that would, in time, have been a tragedy for the Council, for many now recognized that in the persons of Veovis and Aitrus were the seeds of D'ni's future.

Their friendship had thus proved a good omen, not merely for them but for the great D'ni State.

"Aitrus? How are you? How is your father these days?"

Aitrus turned to greet his interrogator, smiling at the old man, surprised—ever surprised—to find himself in such high company.

"He is well, Grand Master Yena. Very well, thank you."

ALL WAS DONE. THE CART WAS PACKED, HER last farewells made. Anna stood on the far side of the bridge, tearful now that the moment had come, looking back into the empty Lodge.

This had been her home, her universe. She had been born here and learned her lessons in these rooms. Here she had been loved by the best two parents any child could have wished for. And now they were gone.

What remained was stone. Stone and dust and ashes.

Those ashes——her father's——were in a tiny sealed pot she had stowed carefully on the cart, beside another that held her mother's ashes.

She turned away, knowing she could not remain. Her future lay elsewhere. Tadjinar, perhaps, or maybe back in Europe. But not here. Not now that he was dead.

Her heart felt heavy, but that, too, she knew, would pass. Not totally, for there would be moments when she would remember and then the hurt would return, yet the grief she now felt would lessen. In time.

She clambered down. The cart was heavy and Tadjinar was far, yet as she leaned forward, taking the strain, beginning to pull it up the shallow slope, the harness ropes biting into the leather pads on her shoulders, she recalled her father's words:

A journey of a thousand miles begins with a single step.

That much remained of him, at least. The memories, the words, and the great wisdom of the man.

She wiped the wetness from her cheeks and smiled. He was in there now, in her head, until she, too, was dust or ashes.

What do you see, Anna?

As she climbed the narrow slope that led out of the valley, she answered him, her voice clear in the desert's stillness.

"I see the endless desert, and before me the desert moon, rising in the last light of the dusk. And I see you there, everywhere I look. I see *you* there."

THE WAY TO TADJINAR DID NOT TAKE HER past the circle, yet she felt compelled to see it. If her future path lay elsewhere, she would at least take the memory of it with her.

Leaving the cart hidden in a narrow gully, she set off across the sand toward the circle, the full moon lighting her way. In the moonlight it seemed more inexplicable than ever. What on earth could have caused it?

Or what *in* earth.

Anna crouched at the center of the circle, thinking of what her father had said that first time. It was indeed as if the earth beneath had been not just shaken but *vibrated*. And what could do that? Sound was pure vibration, but what sound—what mighty echo in the rock—could possibly account for this?

Perhaps the answer was in the cavern. Perhaps it was there and she had simply not seen it.

It was madness even to think of exploring again, especially alone, yet the thought of walking away, of never having tried to find an answer, was impossible. She had to go and look.

In the knapsack on her back she had all she needed. In it were her father's hard hat, his lamp and tinderbox, the rope. As if she'd known.

Anna smiled. Of course she'd known. It was compulsion. The same compulsion to know that had driven her father all his life.

And if you find nothing, Anna?

Then she would know she had found nothing. And she would go to Tadjinar, and wherever else afterward, and leave this mystery behind her.

The tunnel was dark—a black mouth in the silvered face of the ridge. The very look of it was daunting. But she was not afraid. What was there to fear, after all?

Anna lit the lamp then walked into the tunnel. The rock fall was where they had left it, and the gap.

She studied it a moment, then nodded to herself. She would have to douse the lamp then push the knapsack through in front of her. It would not be easy in the dark, but she had done it once before.

Taking the hard hat from the sack, she pulled it on, tying the straps securely about her chin, then snuffed the lamp. The sudden darkness was intense. Stowing the lamp safely at the bottom of the sack, she pulled the drawstrings tight, then pushed it through the gap, hearing it fall with a muffled clatter.

Remembering how difficult it had been, this time she went into the gap face down, her arms out before her. Her problem last time was that she had misjudged how wide the gap was. With her arms outstretched it was much easier. The only problem now was lowering herself on the other side.

Emerging from the gap, she let her hands feel their way down the irregular surface of the rock face, her feet hooked about the edges of the gap. Then, when she was confident that the drop was not too great, she pulled herself forward, letting her legs slide into the gap, her head tucked in to her shoulders as she rolled.

In the dark, the drop seemed a lot farther than she remembered it. There was a moment's inner panic, and then she hit the floor hard, the impact jolting her badly.

She lay there a moment, the knapsack wedged uncomfortably in her lower back. Her wrists ached from the impact and the back of her head and neck felt bruised, but there seemed to be no serious damage.

Anna sat up, reaching behind her for the bag, then winced as a sudden pain ran up the length of her left arm from the wrist to the elbow. She drew the arm back, then slowly rotated the wrist, flexing her fingers as she did so.

"Stupid," she said, admonishing herself. "That was a very stupid thing to do."

Yes, but she had got away with it.

Only just, a silent voice reminded her.

She turned herself around, organizing herself, taking the lamp from the knapsack and lighting it.

In its sudden glow, she looked back at the blockage and saw just how far she had fallen. It was four, almost five feet in all. She could easily have broken her wrists.

She had been lucky.

Clipping the lamp onto the hat, Anna slung the bag over her shoulder then eased herself up into a standing position.

She would have one good look around the cavern, and that was it.

And if she found something?

Anna turned, facing the darkness of the borehole, noticing the faint breeze in the tunnel for the first time.

She would decide that if and when. But first she had to look.

of that great flattened mass of redness that protruded from the ordinary rock, was a gap. Eight feet wide and two high, it was like a scowling mouth, hidden from below by the thick, smooth lip of the strange material.

Anna had found it late in her search, after scouring every inch of the cavern, looking for something that clearly wasn't there. Only this—this *made* lavatic rock—was different. Everything else was exactly as one would have expected in such a cave.

Unclipping the lamp from her hat, she leaned into that scowling mouth, holding it out before her. Inside, revealed by the glowing lamp, was a larger space—a tiny cave within a cave—its floor made entirely of the red material, its ceiling of polished black rock, like the rock in the volcanic borehole. Seeing that, she understood. Whatever it was, it had once been in a molten state, like lava, and had *flowed* into this space, plugging it. Or almost so.

She squeezed through, crawling on her hands and knees, then stood. The ceiling formed a bell above her. She was in a pocket within the rock.

It was like being inside the stomach of some strange animal.

At the far end, the ceiling dipped again, yet did not entirely meet the floor. There was another gap.

Anna walked across, then crouched, holding out the lamp.

The gap extended into the rock, ending some ten yards back in a solid wall of the red material.

Yet there was a breeze, a definite breeze, coming from the gap. She sniffed. It was air. Pure, unscented air.

It had to lead up again, to the surface. Yet that didn't quite make sense, for this did not smell like desert air. She knew the smell of the desert. It left a scorched, dry taste in the mouth. This air was moist, almost sweet in its lack of minerals.

And there was something else. The light was wrong.

Dimming the lamp almost until it guttered, she set it down behind her, then looked back. Despite the sudden darkness, the wall in front of her still glowed. That glow was faint and strangely dim, as if the light itself was somehow *dark*, yet she was not mistaken.

There was light somewhere up ahead.

Picking up the lamp again, Anna raised the wick until the glow was bright. Then, getting down on her hands and knees, she crawled into the gap, pushing the lamp before her. Sure enough, the red stuff filled the tunnel's end, yet just before it, to the left, another crack opened up. She edged into it, following its curving course about the swollen wall of red to her right. That curve ended abruptly, yet the crack continued, veering off at ninety degrees to her left. She followed it.

The breeze was suddenly stronger, the scent of sweet, fresh air overpowering. And there was a noise now, like the hiss of escaping gas.

The crack opened up, like the bell of a flower. To her right the red wall seemed to melt away. Ahead of her was a cave of some sort.

No, not a cave, for the floor was flat, the walls regular.

She climbed up, onto her feet, then held the lamp up high, gasping with astonishment at the sight that met her eyes.

ALONE IN HIS ROOMS, AITRUS PULLED OFF his boots, then sat down heavily in his chair. It was a typical guild apartment, like all of those given to unmarried Masters. Sparsely furnished, the walls were of bare, unpolished stone, covered here and there with guild tapestries; thick woven things that showed machines embedded in the rock. Broad shelves in alcoves covered three of the four walls, Aitrus's textbooks—specialist Guild works on rock mechanics, cohesion, tacheometry, elastic limit, shear strength and permeability, as well as endless works on volcanology—filling those shelves.

There were a few volumes of stories, too, including an illustrated volume of the ancient D'ni tales. This latter lay now on the small table at Aitrus's side, where he had left it the previous evening. He picked it up now and stared at the embossed leather cover a moment, then set it down.

He was in no mood for tales. What he wanted was company, and not the usual company, but something to lift his spirits. *Someone*, perhaps.

It seemed not a lot to ask for, yet some days he felt it was impossible.

Aitrus sighed then stood, feeling restless.

Maybe he should take a few days off to visit his family's Age. It was some while since he had been there and he needed a break. It would be several days at least before the Council met again and his work was up straight. No one would blame him for taking a small vacation.

He smiled. Pulling on his boots again, he went over to the door and summoned one of the house stewards. While the man waited, he scribbled a note, then, folding it, handed it to him.

"Give this to Master Telanis."

The steward bowed, then turned and disappeared along the corridor.

Aitrus turned, looking back into the room, then, without further ado, pulled the door closed behind him.

THE CAVERN, WHICH HAD AT FIRST GLANCE seemed small, was in fact massive. What Anna had first taken as the whole of it was in fact only a kind of antechamber. Beyond it was a second, larger chamber whose walls glowed with a faint, green light.

And in that chamber, dominating its echoing central spaces, rested two massive machines, their dark, imposing shapes threatening in the half-dark. Like sentinels they stood, their huge limbs raised as if in challenge.

Indeed, it had been a moment or two before she had recognized them for what they were. Her first irrational thought had been that they were insects of some kind, for they had that hard, shiny, carapaced look about them. But no insect had ever grown *that* large, not even under the blazing desert sun. Besides, these insects had no eyes; they had windows.

Anna walked toward them, awed not merely by their size but by the look of them. She had seen steam-driven machines in her father's books—massive things of metal plate, bolted together with huge metal studs—but these were very different. These had a smooth, sophisticated look that was quite alien to anything she had ever seen before. These were sleek and streamlined, the way animals and insects were, as if long generations of trial and error had gone into their design.

There were long flanges running along the sides of the nearest craft and studded oval indentations. Long gashes in its underside—vents of some kind?—gave it a strange, almost predatory air.

The closer she got to them, the more in awe she felt, for it was only this close that she came to realize the scale on which their makers must have worked. The dark flank of the nearest machine, to her left, rose up at least five times her height. While the second, tucked back a little, was bigger yet.

She also saw now just how different the two were. As if each had a separate purpose. The nearest was the simpler of the two, its four great limbs ending in cone-shaped vents. The other was much more sinister and crablike, its segmented body heavily armored.

Standing beneath the first of them, she reached out and touched its dark, mirror-smooth surface. It was cool, rather than cold. Unexpectedly her fingers did not slip lightly over its surface, but caught, as if they brushed against some far rougher, more abrasive material.

Anna frowned and held the lamp close. Instead of reflecting back her image, the strange material seemed to hold the light, to draw it into its burnished green-black depths.

Out of the corner of her eye she noted something, down low near the floor of the right-hand machine. She crouched, reaching out to trace the embossed symbol with her finger.

Symbol, or letter? Or was it merely decoration?

Whichever, it was not like any written language she had ever seen.

Taking the notebook from her sack, she quickly sketched it, placing the finished sketch beside the original.

Yes. Just so.

She slipped the notebook away, then lifted the lamp, turning slowly to look about her. As she did, she tried to place the pieces of the puzzle together.

What did she have so far? The circle of rock and dust. The strange red "sealing" material. This other, green-black stone, which gave off a dim but definite light. And now these machines.

Nothing. Or, at least, nothing that made sense. Were these the remains of an ancient race that had once inhabited these parts? If so, then why had nothing else been unearthed? So great a race as this would surely have left many more traces of its existence. And why, if these were long-lost relics, did they look so new?

She stared up the huge, smooth flank of the machine toward what seemed to be a control room of some kind. There was a long, slit window up there, certainly, the upper surface of that window flush with the roof of the craft, the lower part of it forming part of the craft's nose.

The rope was in her pack. If she could throw it up over the top of the machine and secure it on the other side, perhaps she could climb up there and look inside?

Anna slipped off her pack and took out the rope. Walking around to the front of the machine, she crouched down, holding the lamp out as she studied the chassis. Some ten, fifteen feet in, there were several small teatlike protuberances just beneath what looked like an exhaust vent. She would tie the rope to one of those.

She walked back, slowly uncoiling the rope in one hand. She really needed a weight of some kind to tie about the end of it, but the only suitable objects she had were the lamp and the tinderbox, and both were much too valuable to risk breaking.

Her first throw merely glanced against the side of the machine and fell back to the floor. Her second was better but had the same result.

Taking the end of the rope she knotted it time and time again, until there was a palm-sized fist of rope at the end of it. Satisfied, she tried again.

This time the rope sailed over the machine, the lightweight cord whistling through the air as it fell to the other side.

Laying her pack on the remaining coil, Anna walked around and collected the other end of it, then got down and crawled under the machine, winding the rope around and around one of the small protuberances until the thick end of it was wedged tightly against the machine.

Edging back, she stood, then tested the rope, tugging at it hard, leaning her full weight back on her heels. It held.

So far, so good. But the most difficult part was next, for the rope was far from secure. If it were to slip to the side as she was climbing, she could easily find herself in trouble.

Pulling the rope taut, she placed one booted foot against the hull of the craft and leaned back, taking the strain, feeling the sudden tension in the muscles of her calves and upper arms.

She began, leaning slightly to her right as she climbed, away from the front of the strange craft, keeping the rope taut at all times, ready at any moment to let go and drop back to the floor if it were to start slipping. But the rope held, almost as if it were glued in place. Perhaps some quality of the material, that abrasiveness she had noticed, helped, but as she continued to climb her confidence grew.

As she came up onto the broad back of the craft, she relaxed. The top of the great slit window was just in front of her now, some ten or twelve feet distant.

Beyond it the nose of the craft tapered slightly, then curved steeply to the floor.

Getting down onto her hands and knees, Anna crawled slowly toward the front of the craft, until the edge of the window was just in front of her. Leaning forward carefully, she looked down, through the thick, translucent plate, into the cabin of the craft.

In the oddly muted light from the oil lamp, the cabin seemed strangely eerie, the wavering shadows threatening.

She frowned, trying to understand exactly what she was looking at. There were two seats—or, at least, they looked like seats; tubular, skeletal things with a kind of netting for the seats—and there was a control panel of some kind just in front of that, but she could make neither head nor tail of the controls, if controls they were.

The panel itself was black. There were indentations in that blackness, and more of the strange symbols, but nothing in the way of levers or buttons, unless such things were hidden.

Anna eased forward a little, trying to see into the back of the cabin, but there was only a bulkhead there, not even a door. Whoever, or whatever, had operated this must have entered the cabin through this window.

That sudden thought, that the makers of this machine might have been other than human—might have been strange, alien creatures of the rock—sent a tiny ripple of fear through her. Until that moment her awe at her discovery had kept her from thinking what these machines might mean. But now her mind embraced that thought.

What if those strange webbing seats were designed not for two, but for a single creature: one huge, grotesque being, multilimbed and clawed, like the machines it made?

No, she told herself. *Whoever made this is long dead and gone. It only looks new.* But that moment of fear, of vivid imagining, had left its shadow on her.

She edged back slowly, then, taking hold of the rope again, climbed down.

Retrieving the rope, Anna stowed it away, then turned to face the second machine. If the function of the first machine was masked from her, this one was self-evident. The great drills at the end of each huge, jointed limb gave it away. This was a cutter.

Anna walked over, stopping just in front of it.

A question nagged at her. Why would someone go to such trouble to cut tunnels in the earth and then seal them? Had they found something down there?

Or was it a tomb?

The thought of a tomb—a royal tomb, surely, for why else go to all this bother?—excited her. Maybe she had stumbled onto the burial vault of some great ancient emperor. If so, then who knew what was down here? If they could build machines like these, then what riches—what curiosities—might lay buried with him?

She walked slowly to the right, circling the machine, her eyes going up, searching its massive flanks, taking in every aspect of its brutal yet elegant form. It had the look of a living thing: of something that had been bred in the depths of the rock. Here and there the material of which it was made seemed folded in upon itself, like the wing-casing of an insect. Yet if it had been based on any insect that existed, it was of a strange, muscular, hydraulic kind. And there were blisters—large swellings on the hull, two or three feet in length—that had no apparent purpose.

Anna stopped. Just beyond the machine, low in the great wall of the chamber, was a hole: a perfect circle of blackness in the green-black material of the wall. She walked another few paces. Just beyond the first hole was another, and a third. Tunnels. Undoubtedly tunnels.

But leading where?

Her heart pounding, she went over to the first of them. It was a small tunnel, barely large enough to walk within, but made, not natural. The same green-black stone lined the walls. It went down, into darkness.

The second tunnel was the same. The third, to her surprise, was not a tunnel at all, but a storeroom of some kind. Broad, empty shelves lined both sides of that excavated space.

Anna stepped out then looked across.

So which was it to be? The first tunnel or the second?

Neither, she decided. Or not now, anyway. Not without first preparing for the journey. That was the proper way of going about things: the way her father had taught her.

But that would mean squeezing through the tiny gap in the rock fall once again, then walking across the desert to where the cart was hidden. That last part alone was a two-hour journey, which was fine in the moonlight, but would be an ordeal under the desert sun.

And for what? She wasn't going to go that far in. She only wanted to see if they led anywhere.

Five hundred paces. That was all she would allow herself. And if it did not look to be leading anywhere, she would come straight back.

Okay. But which?

Without making a conscious decision, her feet led her into the right-hand tunnel.

One, two, three, she counted, her left hand steadying her against the wall as she began the steady descent. *Seven, eight, nine.*

Five hundred. It wasn't far.

Ahead of her the darkness stretched away, running deep into the rock, forever just beyond the bright reach of her lamp.

Eighty-two, eighty-three, eighty-four . . .

HAVING TRAVELED MUCH FARTHER THAN HER
planned five hundred paces, Anna found that she was
lost. She did not want to admit it to herself, but she
was lost. After that last left-hand turn she had doubled
back, but she had come out in a place she hadn't been
before. Or, at least, she couldn't remember having been
there. It was a kind of cavern, only it was small and
perfectly spherical.

She had lost count an hour ago. Two hours, maybe.
Who knew down here? All she knew was that the map
she had been following in her head had let her down.
She had made one wrong turn and everything had
seemed to slip away.

It was a labyrinth—a perfect maze of interlinked
tunnels, all of which looked the same and seemed to
lead . . . nowhere.

A tomb. It had to be a tomb. And this was part of
it, this maze in which she was now inextricably lost.

She would die down here, she was certain of it now.

The thought made her stop and put her hand out
to steady herself. Her head was pounding.

Think, Anna. Think what you're doing.

Anna looked up. The voice was clear in her head,
almost as if he had spoken.

"I can't think," she answered. "I'm frightened."

Fear's the enemy of thought. Think, Anna. Consider what you ought to do.

She let her head clear, let the fear drain from her mind. Slowly her pulse normalized. She took one of the hammers from her belt and held it up.

"I need to mark my way."

Slipping the hammer back into its holster, she slipped the pack from her shoulder and took out the notebook.

"I'll make a map."

It was what she should have done to begin with, but it was too late now. The best she could do now was to slowly chart her way back to that first straight tunnel, before the way had branched. How long that would take she did not know, but if she was methodical, if she marked each tunnel wall, each branch of it with a letter and a number, then maybe, after a while, she would see the pattern of it on the page.

It was a slender chance, but her best.

Anna turned, looking about her. The tunnel sloped down. Just beyond her it forked. She walked across and, slipping her notebook into her tunic pocket, took the hammer and chisel from her belt.

The first blow was solid—she could feel the way the hammer hit the handle of the chisel squarely and firmly—but the wall was unmarked. She stared at it in astonishment, then repeated the blow. Nothing. There was not even a scratch on the green-black surface.

It was just as before, when she had tried to take the sample.

Anna groaned. It had been her only hope. Now she really was lost.

Paper wraps stone. So use paper. Squares of paper.

Of course! She could tear pages from her notebook and leave tiny squares of paper on the floor beside each entrance. It would have exactly the same effect. At once she tore a page from the book and tore it in half, then in half again. Four pieces. It wasn't enough. She'd soon work her way through her stock of paper. She would have to leave much smaller pieces. She tore them in half again, and then a fourth time.

There. That should do it. She had about fifty pages—that ought to be enough.

Crouching, she began to write on them—AI to AI6. She would allocate two pages to each letter, and then move on to the next. That way she would hopefully chart "areas" of the labyrinth. And if she came back to one of them, say C, she would know exactly where she was on her map, and be able to turn away in a different direction, until she knew exactly how it all fit together.

Anna looked up, smiling grimly. She wasn't beaten yet.

THE GUILD HOUSE WAS IN THE OLDEST PART of town, surrounded by the halls of all the major guilds. From its steps one could look out over the great sprawl of D'ni to the harbor and the great arch named after the legendary prince Kerath.

Turning from the steps through a row of fluted marble pillars, one entered a massive vestibule of irregular shape. Here, set into the floor, was a great mosaic map of the main cavern of D'ni, while the floors of the smaller rooms, leading directly off the vestibule, displayed similar mosaic maps of the lesser caverns.

The ceiling of the vestibule was not high—barely twice the height of a standing man—yet it had a pleasant look to it. Great arching beams of pale mauve stone thrust out from the walls on every side, thinning to a lacelike delicacy as they met overhead.

On the right-hand side of the main room was a great arched door. The carved stone fanned about the doorway had the look of trees, forming a natural arch in some woodland glade. Beyond it was the great Council chamber.

It had long been a standing joke that the D'ni would never excavate to the east of the main cavern, lest they had to redesign the Guild House, but the truth was that the rock to the east was home to a stable reservoir of magma, slowly cooling over the millennia, from which they had long tapped energy.

Stepping through the massively hinged doors—each door a great slab of stone three feet thick and ten high—one entered the most impressive of D'ni's many chambers. The great dome of the ceiling seemed far overhead, eighteen huge pillars reaching up like massive arms to support it. Broad steps, which also served as seats, led down into a circular pit, in the midst of which were five huge basalt thrones.

The great shields of the guilds hung on the outer walls, along with their ancient banners.

Today the thrones were occupied, the great steps filled with seated members, here to debate whether the edict banning contact with the "outsiders," the "surface-dwellers" as they were otherwise known, should be lifted.

For six hours they had sat, listening to the arguments for and against, but now the debate was finally coming to a close. The young Lord Veovis was speaking, standing at his place on the second steps, just before the thrones, summing up the case for maintaining things as they were, his confident eloquence making many of the older members nod their heads and smile.

As Veovis sat, there was the sound of fists drumming on the stone—the D'ni way of signaling approval. He looked about him, smiling modestly, accepting the silent looks of praise.

Across from him, just behind the thrones and to the right, some six steps up, Aitrus looked on, concerned now that the time had almost come. Veovis still thought he was going to abstain. Indeed, he was counting on it, for the matter was so finely poised that a vote or two might well decide it. But he could not abstain, and though he knew it might well damage their friendship, he had to do what he believed was right.

But knowing that made it no easier.

There was a brief murmur in the chamber, and then Lord Eneah slowly raised himself up out of his throne, his frail figure commanding the immediate attention of all. Silence fell.

Lord Eneah had been gravely ill, and his voice now as he spoke seemed fatigued; yet there was still a strength behind it.

"We have heard the arguments, Guildsmen, and many among you will have already decided what you think. Yet this is a grave matter, and before we take the irrevocable step of a vote, I feel there should be the opportunity for a more *informal* debate of the matters raised. We shall come to a vote in an hour, but first we shall adjourn this sitting and retire to the vestibule."

If some were disappointed by this, they did not
show it, while others nodded, as if the decision were
wisdom itself. The D'ni were a patient race, after all,
and many matters that might have been decided "hastily"
in the chamber had been resolved in the more informal
atmosphere of the vestibule.

The remaining Lords rose to their feet and made
their way out, followed a moment later by the other
members of the great Council.

If the great chamber had been all solemnity and
dignity, the vestibule was buzzing with talk, as members went from group to group, attempting to persuade
others to their cause.

Rarely in recent years had a single issue raised so
much heat and passion, and now that a vote was but an
hour off, both camps made great efforts to win last-
minute converts to their causes.

Aitrus, who had drifted into the vestibule alone,
stood beneath the great arch a moment, looking across
to where Veovis stood beside Lord Eneah, who sat in
a chair that had been brought out especially for him.
Veovis was addressing a small crowd of elder members, undaunted by the fact that many there were a
century or two older than he. Such confidence
impressed Aitrus, and he knew for certain that Veovis
would one day sit where Lord Eneah had sat today, in
the central throne.

It was not the right time, not just now, when Veovis was among such company, yet he would have to speak to him, to tell him of his change of mind, before they returned to the great chamber.

Aitrus made his way across, smiling and greeting other guildsmen as he went. Yet he was barely halfway across when he noticed a disturbance on the far side of the vestibule.

He craned his neck, trying to see. The door guards were arguing with someone. Then, abruptly, it seemed, they stood back, allowing the newcomer to pass. It was a senior guildsman from the Guild of Messengers. In one hand he clutched a sealed letter.

As the Council members began to realize that there was an intruder among them, the noise in the vestibule slowly died. Heads turned. Guildsmen turned to face the newcomer as he made his way between them, heading directly to where Lord Eneah sat.

The vestibule and chamber were normally sacrosanct. To permit a Messenger to enter while they were in session was almost unheard of. This had to be a matter of the greatest urgency.

By the time the Messenger stepped out before Lord Eneah, a complete silence had fallen over the vestibule. Kneeling, the man bowed his head and held the letter out.

At a gesture from Lord Eneah, Veovis took the letter and, breaking the seal, handed it to the elder. Eneah slowly unfolded the single sheet, then, lifting his chin and peering at it, began to read. After a moment he looked up, a faint bemusement in his eyes.

"Guildsmen," he said, "it appears the decision has been made for us. We have a visitor. An outsider from the surface."

There was a moment's stunned silence, followed by a sudden uproar in the chamber.

PART THREE: FAULT LINES

F OR THE REST OF THAT DAY THE HIGH-
council—the five Great Lords and the eighteen
Grand Masters—sat in special session to decide what
should be done.

While they were meeting, rumors swept the great
city in the cavern. Many concerned the *nature* of the
intruder, speculating upon what manner of creature
had been taken by the Maintainers. While most agreed
that it was humanoid in form, some claimed it was a
cross between a bear and an ape. Other rumors were
wilder yet. One such tale had it that a whole tribe of
outsiders—heavily armed savages, intent on trouble—
had come far down the tunnels, trying to force entry
into D'ni, and that it had taken the whole garrison of
Maintainers, backed up by the City Guard, to fight
them off.

Such "news," Aitrus was certain, was completely
unfounded, yet in the absence of hard fact even he
found himself caught up in the games of speculation—so much so, that as evening fell and the lake
waters dimmed, he left his rooms and set out through
the narrow alleyways of the upper town, intending to

visit the Hall of the Guild of Writers where his friend Veovis dwelt.

If anyone outside that central group of Lords and Masters knew what was happening, Veovis would.

Arriving at the gate of the ancient hall, Aitrus waited in the tiny courtyard before the main doors while a steward was sent to notify Veovis of his presence.

Several minutes passed, and then the steward returned.

Aitrus followed him through, between high, fluted pillars and along a broad mosaic path that bisected Ri'Neref's Hall, the first of five great halls named after the greatest of the guild's sons. Like most of the ancient Guild Halls, the Hall of the Guild of Writers was not a single building but a complex of interlinked buildings and rooms, some of them cut deep into the face of the great cavern. As Aitrus ventured farther into the complex, he climbed up narrow flights of ancient steps, the stone of which seemed almost to have been melted over time, like wax, eroded by the passage of countless feet over the six millennia of D'ni's existence.

Here, in this great sprawl of ancient stone, two thousand guildsmen lived and ate and slept. Here they were educated, here went about the simple daily business of the guild. Here also were the book rooms and great libraries of the guild, the like of which could be found nowhere else in D'ni.

Walking through its ancient hallways, Aitrus felt the huge weight of history that lay behind the Writers Guild. Though the Writers claimed no special privileges, nor had a greater voice than any other on the Council, it was held to be the most prestigious of the Eighteen, and its members had a sense of that.

To be a Writer, that was the dream of many a D'ni boy.

The steward slowed, then stopped before a door. Turning to Aitrus, he bowed again. "We are here, Master."

Aitrus waited while the steward knocked.

A voice, Veovis's, called from within. "Enter!"

The steward pushed the door open a little and looked inside. "Forgive me, Guild Master, but it is Master Aitrus, from the Guild of Surveyors."

"Show him in."

As the steward pushed the door back, Aitrus stepped forward. Veovis was in his chair on the far side of the big, low-ceilinged study. Books filled the walls on every side. A portrait of Rakeri, Veovis's father, hung on the wall behind a huge oak-topped desk. In tall-backed chairs close by sat two other men—one old, one young. The elder Aitrus recognized as Lianis, Veovis's tutor and chief adviser, the younger was Suahrnir, Veovis's Maintainer friend.

"Ah, Aitrus," Veovis said, getting up, a broad smile lighting his features. "Welcome, dear friend."

Aitrus heard the door close quietly behind him. "Forgive me for intruding, Veovis, but I wondered if you had any news."

Veovis came over and took his hands, then, stepping back, gestured toward the chair beside his own. "It is curious that you should arrive just at this moment. Suahrnir has just come from the Guild House. It seems the High Council has finished deliberating. A notice is to be posted throughout the city within the hour."

"So what *is* the news?"

Veovis sat. The smile had gone from his face. "There are to be special Hearings, before the Council."

Aitrus sat, looking to his friend. "Hearings? What kind of Hearings?"

Veovis shrugged. "All I know so far is that the outsider is to be interrogated, and that we, as Council members, will be allowed to witness the interrogation. My assumption is that the questions will have to do with the nature of life on the surface."

"He speaks D'ni?"

"Not a word. And it is not a he, Aitrus. The outsider is a female."

Aitrus blinked with surprise. "A woman?"

"A girl. A young girl, so I am told, barely out of infancy."

Aitrus shook his head. It was difficult to believe that anyone, let alone a young girl, could have made her way down from the surface. He frowned. "But if she speaks no D'ni, then how are we to question her?"

"Who can say?" Veovis answered, the slightest hint of irony in his voice. "But it appears she is to be handed over to the Guild of Linguists. They are to try to make sense of her strange utterances. That is the idea, anyway. Personally, I would be surprised if she does more than grunt for her food when she wants it."

"You think so?"

"Oh, I am quite certain of it, Aitrus. Word is that she is a rather large-boned animal, and totally covered in hair."

"In *hair*?"

Veovis nodded. "But I guess that, too, is to be expected, no? After all, one would need some kind of special covering to protect the body against the elements, wouldn't one?"

"I suppose so."

"And besides, some creatures find that *attractive*, or so I am told."

There was laughter, but Aitrus was silent, wondering just what circumstances would force a young girl—

whatever her species—to venture down the tunnels. It was not, after all, what one would expect.

"Is there any way I could see her?" Aitrus asked.

"I doubt it," Veovis answered. "Word is she is being kept on an island in the cavern of Irrat. The Linguists will have her locked away for months, no doubt. You know how *thorough* they are!"

"Besides," Veovis went on, "it is unlikely any of us will get a glimpse of her before the Hearings. If what Suahrnir says is true, almost half of the High Council were in favor of shipping her out to a Prison Age straight away, and having done with the matter. Only Lord Eneah's personal intervention prevented such a course."

"But she's only a girl."

"Sentiment, Aitrus," Suahrnir chipped in. "Pure sentiment. A girl she may be, but she is not D'ni. We cannot attribute her with the same intelligence or sensitivity we D'ni possess. And as for her being *only* a girl, you cannot argue that. Her mere existence here in D'ni has thrown the people into turmoil. They talk of nothing else. Nor will they until this matter is resolved. No. Her arrival here is a bad thing. It will unsettle the common people."

Aitrus was amazed by Suahrnir's vehemence. "Do you really think so, Suahrnir?"

"Suahrnir is right, Aitrus," Veovis said quietly. "We might joke about it, but this issue is a serious one, and had my own opinion been sought, I, too, would have advocated placing her somewhere where she can trouble the public imagination as little as possible."

Aitrus sighed. "I hear what you are saying. Maybe it *will* unsettle people. Yet it would be a great shame, surely, if we did not attempt to discover all we can about conditions up there on the surface?"

"We know now that it is inhabited. Is that not enough?"

Aitrus looked down. He did not want to be drawn into an argument with his friend over this issue.

"Still," Veovis added, when he did not answer, "the matter is out of our hands, eh, old friend? The High Council have decreed that there shall be Hearings and so there shall, whether I will it or no. Let us pray, then, that the Linguists—good men though they are—fail to make sense of the creature this one time."

Aitrus glanced up and saw that Veovis was smiling teasingly. Slowly that smile faded. "Nothing but trouble can come of this, Aitrus, I warrant you. *Nothing* but trouble."

the cell, then turned, facing his pupil. She sat there behind the narrow desk, quiet and attentive, the light blue robe they had put her in making her seem more like a young acolyte than a prisoner.

"And how are you, this morning, Ah-na?"

"I am well, Master Haemis," she answered, the slight harshness in her pronunciation still there, but much less noticeable than it had been.

"Thoe kenem, Nava," she said. How are you, Master?

Haemis smiled, pleased with her. They had begun by trying simply to translate her native speech, to find D'ni equivalents for everyday objects and simple actions, but to his surprise she had begun to turn the tables on them, pointing to objects and, by means of facial gesture, coaxing him to name them. The quickness of her mind had astonished them all. By the eighth week she had been speaking basic D'ni phrases. It was baby-talk, true, but still quite remarkable, considering where she came from.

Twenty weeks on and she was almost fluent. Each day she extended her vocabulary, pushing them to teach her all they knew.

"Is it just you today, Master Haemis?"

Haemis sat, facing her. "Grand Master Gihran will be joining us later, Ah-na. But for the first hour it is just you and I." He smiled. "So? What shall we do today?"

Her eyes, their dark pupils still disturbingly strange after all this time, stared back at him. "The book you mentioned . . . the *Rehevkor* . . . Might I see a copy of it?"

The question disconcerted him. He had not meant to tell her about the D'ni lexicon. It was their brief to tell her as little as possible about D'ni ways. But she was such a good pupil that he had relaxed his guard.

"That will not be easy, Ah-na. I would have to get permission from the Council for such a step."

"Permission?"

Haemis looked down, embarrassed. "I should not, perhaps, tell you this, but . . . I should not have mentioned the existence of the *Rehevkor* to you. It was a slip. If my fellow Masters should discover it . . . "

"You would be in trouble?"

He nodded, then looked up. Anna was watching him earnestly.

"Then I will say nothing more, Master Haemis."

"Thank you, Ah-na."

"Not at all," she said softly. "You have been very kind to me."

He gave a little nod, embarrassed once more, not knowing quite what to say, but she broke the silence.

"Will you answer me one thing, Master Haemis?"

"If I can."

"What do they think of me? Your fellow Masters, I mean. What do they *really* think of me?"

It was a strange and unexpected question. He had not thought it would have bothered her.

"To be honest, most of them saw you at first as some kind of grinning primitive animal."

Haemis glanced at her and saw how she digested that fact; saw how thoughtful it made her look.

"And you, Master Haemis? What did *you* think?"

He could not look at her. Even so, there was something about her that compelled his honesty. "I thought no differently."

She was quiet a moment, then, "Thank you, Master Haemis."

Haemis swallowed, then, finding the courage to look at her again, said quietly. "I do not think so now."

"I know."

"I . . . I will speak for you at the Hearings, if you wish."

Anna smiled. "Once more, your kindness does you great credit, Master Haemis. But I must speak for myself when the time comes. Else they, too, will think me but an animal, no?"

Haemis nodded, impressed by her bearing, by the strength that seemed to underlie every aspect of her nature.

"I shall ask," he said quietly.

"Ask?" She stared at him, not understanding.

"About the *Rehevkor*."

"But you said . . . "

"It does not matter," Haemis said, realizing that for once it mattered very little beside her good opinion of him. "Besides, we cannot have you going unprepared before the Council, can we, Ah-na?"

ANNA STOOD BY THE WINDOW OF HER CELL, looking out across the cavern she had been told was called Irrat. The bleakness of the view did little to raise her spirits. The sill into which the great iron bars were set was four feet thick, the view itself of rock and yet more rock, only one small, rust red pool creating a focal point of contrast in that iron gray landscape.

Master Haemis had been kind to her today, and she sensed that maybe he was even her friend, yet he was only one among many. For all his small kindnesses, she was still alone here, still a prisoner in this strange, twilight world where the days were thirty hours long and the seasons unchanging.

Anna sighed, a rare despondency descending upon her. She had tried her best to learn their language and find out something that might help her—she had even enjoyed that task—yet where she was or who these people were she still did not know.

She turned, looking across at the door. Like all else here it was made of stone. Her bed was a stone pallet, cut into the rock of the wall. Likewise, a small shelf-table had been cut from the stone. On the bed was a thin blanket, folded into squares, and a pillow; on the table was a jug of water and a bowl.

Anna walked across and sat on the edge of the stone pallet, her hands clenched together between her knees. For a time she sat there, staring blankly at the floor, then she looked up.

The door had opened silently, unnoticed by her. An elderly man now stood there; tall, dignified, in a long dark cloak edged with the same shade of burgundy the guards who had captured her had worn.

His eyes, like theirs, were pale. His face, like theirs, was tautly fleshed, the bone structure extremely fine, as if made of the most delicate porcelain. His long, gray-white hair, like theirs, was brushed back neatly from a high, pale brow.

But he was old. Far older than any of those she had so far seen. She could see the centuries piled up behind that thin-lipped mouth, those pale, cold eyes.

She waited, expecting him to talk, but he merely looked at her, then, as if he had seen enough, glanced around the cell. Behind him, in the half shadows of the passageway, stood Master Haemis and one of the guards. He took a step toward the door. As he did, Anna stood, finding her voice.

"Forgive me, sir, but might I draw you?"

He turned back, a look of surprise in those pale, clear eyes.

"My sketch pad," she said. "It was in my knapsack, together with my charcoal sticks. It would help me pass the time if I had them."

There was the slightest narrowing of his eyes, then he turned and left the cell. The door swung silently shut.

Anna sat again, feeling more depressed than ever. She had seen the unfeeling coldness in the old man's face and sensed that her fate had been sealed in that brief moment when he had looked at her.

"So what now?"

She spoke the words quietly, as if afraid they would be overheard, yet she had little more to fear now. She let her head fall, for an instant or two sinking down into a kind of stupor where she did not need to think. But then the image of the old man's face returned to her.

She recalled his surprise, that narrowing of the eyes, and wondered if she had somehow made a brief connection with him.

"Miss?"

Anna looked up, surprised to be spoken to after so lengthy a silence. Again there had been no warning of the woman's presence before she had spoken.

"Here," the woman said, stepping across and placing a tray onto the table at Anna's side. The smell of hot soup and fresh-baked bread wafted across to Anna, making her mouth water.

As the woman stepped back, Anna stood, surprised to see that instead of the usual sparse fare, this time the tray was filled with all manner of foods; a tumbler of bright red drink, another of milk, a small granary loaf. And more.

Anna turned to thank the woman, but she was gone. A guard now stood there in the doorway, expressionless, holding something out to her. It was her sketch pad and her charcoals.

Astonished, she took them from him, nodding her head in thanks. She had asked a hundred times, but no one had listened to her. Until now.

The door closed behind the woman.

Anna put her things down, then, taking the tray onto her lap, began to eat.

He listened, yes, but what does that mean?

Was this simply the courtesy they extended to every prisoner? And was this to be her life henceforth, incarcerated in this bleak stone cell?

And if so, could she endure that?

At least she had the sketch pad now. She could use the back of it, perhaps, to write down all her thoughts and observations, something she had sorely missed these past six months. And then there were always the sessions with Master Haemis to look forward to—her struggles with that strange, delightful language.

For a moment she sat there, perfectly still, the food in her mouth unchewed. That face—the old man's face. If she could draw *that*, then maybe she would begin to understand just who he was and what he wanted of her. For the secret was there, in the features of a man, or so her mother had once said.

Stone-faced, he'd seemed. Yet if she could chip the surface stone away and see what lay behind.

Anna set the tray back on the table, then yawned, feeling suddenly tired, in need of sleep.

She would make the sketch later, when she woke.

Unfolding the blanket, Anna stretched out on the pallet and lay it over her, closing her eyes. In a moment she was asleep.

THE CAPTAIN PAUSED A MOMENT, STUDYING the sketch, impressed despite himself that she had

captured the old man's face so perfectly. Then, closing
the sketch pad, he turned and handed it to her, before
pointing toward the open doorway.

"Come. It's time to go."

Gathering up her charcoals, Anna tucked them into
her pocket, then looked across at him. "Where are you
taking me?"

He did not answer, merely gestured toward the door.

Anna stepped outside, letting the guards fall in, two
to the front of her, two just behind. This time, however, no one bound her hands.

As the captain emerged, they came smartly to attention, then set off at a march, Anna in their midst, hurrying to keep pace.

A long stairway led down through solid rock, ending in a massive gateway, the stone door of which had
been raised into a broad black slit in the ceiling overhead. They passed beneath it and out onto a great slab
of rock, still within the cavern yet outside the stone
keep in which Anna had been kept. She looked back at
it, surprised by the brutality of its construction.

They slowed. Just ahead, the rock fell away almost
vertically into a chasm on three sides, a chain bridge
spanning that massive gap, linking the fortress to a circular archway carved into the far wall of the cavern.
Stepping out onto the bridge, Anna looked down, noting the huge machines that seemed to squat like black-

limbed fishermen beside dark fissures in the earth.
Machines, no doubt, like those she had found up near
the surface. There were buildings down there, too, and
chimneys and huge piles of excavated rock, like a giant's
building blocks, all far below the narrow, swaying
bridge. She was not afraid of heights, nor of falling,
but even if she had, the guards would have paid no
heed. They moved on relentlessly, nudging her when
she was not quick enough.

The arch in the far wall proved to be ornamental.
Just beyond the great carved hoop of stone lay a wall
of solid rock; black marble, polished smooth. She
thought perhaps they would stop, but the captain
marched on, as if he would walk straight through the
rock itself.

As they passed beneath the arch, however, he turned
abruptly to the right, into deep shadow. More steps led
down. At the foot of them was a door. As he unlocked
it, Anna looked to the captain, wanting to ask him
where they were taking her and what would happen
there, but he was like a machine, distant and imperson-
al, programmed to carry out his tasks efficiently and
silently, his men mute copies of himself, each face
expressionless.

She understood. They did not like her. Nor did
they wish to take the chance of liking her.

Beyond the door the passage zigzagged through the rock, small cresset lamps set into the stone. And then they were "outside" again, in another cavern.

Anna stepped out, looking about her. A great bluff of rock lay to her right, obscuring the view. To her left, just below her and about a hundred yards or so away, a broad coil of water cut its way through a steep-sided chasm. It was not as dark here as in the first cavern. She did not understand that at first. Then, to her surprise, she saw how the water gave off a steady glow that underlit everything.

They went down the bare, rocky slope, then along a path that led to a stone jetty. There, at the foot of a flight of steep, black basalt steps, a long, dark, elegant boat was anchored, the chasm walls towering above it. Four burgundy-cloaked oarsmen waited patiently on their bench seats, their oars shipped. A burgundy-colored banner hung limply from the stern of the boat, beside the ornamental cabin, a strangely intricate symbol emblazoned in gold in its center. Anna stared at it as she clambered aboard, intrigued by its complexity.

"Where are we?" she asked.

The captain turned to her, giving her a cold, hard look, his eyes suspicious of her. For a moment she thought he would not answer her, then, curtly, he said:

"We are in D'ni. This is the main cavern."

"Ah . . ." But it did not enlighten her. *Duh-nee.* That was what it had sounded like. But where was *Duh-nee?* Deep in the earth? No, that simply wasn't possible. People didn't *live* deep in the earth, under the rock. Or did they? Wasn't that, after all, what she had been staring at every day for these past six months? Rock, and yet more rock.

The securing rope was cast off, the oarsmen to her left pushed away from the side. Suddenly they were gliding down the channel, the huge walls slipping past her as the oars dug deep in unison.

Anna turned, looking back, her eyes going up to the great carved circle of the arch that had been cut into the massive stone wall of the cave; a counterpart, no doubt, to the arch on the far side. The wall itself went up and up and up. She craned her neck, trying to see where it ended, but the top of it was in shadow.

She sniffed the air. Cool, clean air, like the air of the northern mountains of her home.

Outside. They *had* to be outside. Yet the captain had said quite clearly that this was a cavern.

She shook her head in disbelief. No cavern she had ever heard of was this big. It had to be . . . *miles* across. Turning, she looked to the captain. He was standing at the prow, staring directly ahead. Beyond him, where the channel turned to the right, a bridge had come into view—a pale, lacelike thing of stone, spanning the chasm, the carving on its three, high-arched spans as delicate as that on a lady's ivory fan.

Passing under the bridge the channel broadened, the steep sides of the chasm giving way to the gentler, more rounded slope of hills, the gray and black of rock giving way to a mosslike green. Ahead of them lay a lake

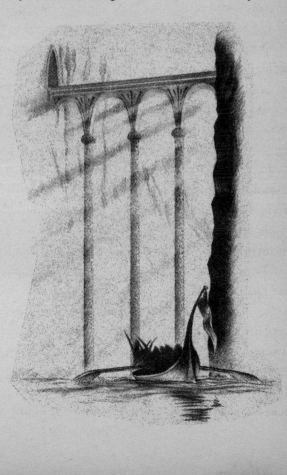

of some kind, the jagged shapes of islands visible in the distance, strangely dark amid that huge expanse of glowing water.

At first Anna did not realize what she was looking at; then, with a start, she saw that what she had thought were strange outcrops of rock were, in fact, buildings; strangely shaped buildings that mimicked the flowing forms of molten rock. Buildings that had no roofs.

That last made a strange and sudden sense to her. So they *were* inside. And the water. Of course . . . Something must be in the water to make it glow like that.

As the boat glided out onto the lake itself, Anna took in for the first time the sheer scale of the cavern.

"It's magnificent," she said quietly, awed by it.

The captain turned, glancing at her, surprised by her words. Then, as if conceding something to her, he pointed to his right.

"There. That is where we are headed. See? Just beyond the bluff. It will come into sight in a moment."

There was pillar of some kind—a lighthouse maybe, or a monument—just beyond the great heap of rock that lay directly to their right, the top of it jutting up above the bluff. Yet as they rounded the headland, she saw, with astonishment, that the pillar was not as close as she had presumed. Indeed, it lay a good two or three miles distant.

"But it's . . . "

"Over three hundred and fifty spans high."

Anna stared at the great column of twisted rock that lay at the center of the glowing lake. Three hundred and fifty spans! That was over a mile by her own measure! Somehow it didn't seem natural. The rock looked as if it had been shaped by some giant hand. Looking at it, she wasn't sure whether it was hideous or beautiful; her eyes were not trained to appreciate so alien an aesthetic.

"What is it called?"

"The ancients called it Ae'Gura," he answered, "but we simply call it The Island. The city is beyond it, to its right."

"The city?"

But it was clear that he felt he had said too much already. He looked away, falling silent once again, only the swish of the oars in the water and the creak of the boat as it moved across the lake breaking the eerie silence.

VEOVIS SAT IN THE CORRIDOR OUTSIDE LORD Eneah's study, waiting, while, beyond the door, the elders finished their discussion.

He had been summoned at a moment's notice, brought here in the Great Lord's own sedan. That alone said much. Something must have happened—something that the elders wished urgently to consult him about.

Veovis smiled. He had known these men since childhood. He had seen them often with his father, in both formal and informal settings. They ate little and spoke only when a matter of some importance needed uttering. Most of what was "said" between them was a matter of eye contact and bodily gesture, for they had known each other now two centuries and more, and there was little they did not know of each other. He, on the other hand, represented a more youthful, vigorous strain of D'ni thinking. He was, as they put it, "in touch" with the living pulse of D'ni culture.

Veovis knew that and accepted it. Indeed, he saw it as his role to act as a bridge between the Five and the younger members of the Council, to reconcile their oft-differing opinions and come up with solutions that were satisfactory to all. Like many of his class, Veovis did not like, nor welcome, conflict, for conflict meant change and change was anathema to him. The Five had long recognized that and had often called on him to help defuse potentially difficult situations before push came to shove.

And so now, unless he was mistaken.

As the door eased open, Veovis got to his feet. Lord Eneah himself stood there, framed in the brightly lit doorway, looking out at him.

"Veovis. Come."

He bowed, his respect genuine. "Lord Eneah."

Stepping into the room, he looked about him, bowing to each of the Great Lords in turn, his own father last of all. It was exactly as he had expected; only the Five were here. All others were excluded from this conversation.

As Eneah sat again, in the big chair behind his desk, Veovis stood, feet slightly apart, waiting.

"It is about the intruder," Eneah said without preamble.

"It seems she is ready," Lord Nehir of the Stone-Masons, seated to Veovis's right, added.

"Ready, my Lords?"

"Yes, Veovis," Eneah said, his eyes glancing from one to another of his fellows, as if checking that what he was about to say had their full approval. "Far more ready, in fact, than we had anticipated."

"How so, my Lord?"

"She speaks D'ni," Lord R'hira of the Maintainers answered.

Veovis felt a shock wave pass through him. "I beg your pardon, Lord R'hira?"

But R'hira merely stared at him. "Think of it, Veovis. Think what that means."

But Veovis could not think. The very idea was impossible. It had to be some kind of joke. A test of him, perhaps. Why, his father had said nothing to him of this!

"I . . ."

"Grand Master Gihran of the Guild of Linguists visited us earlier today," Lord Eneah said, leaning forward slightly. "His report makes quite remarkable reading. We were aware, of course, that some progress was being made, but just how much took us all by surprise. It would appear that our guest is ready to face a Hearing."

Veovis frowned. "I do not understand . . . "

"It is very simple," Lord Nehir said, his soft voice breaking in. "We must decide what is to be done. Whether we should allow the young woman to speak openly before the whole Council, or whether she should be heard behind closed doors, by those who might be trusted to keep what is heard to themselves."

"The High Council?"

His father, Lord Rakeri, laughed gruffly. "No, Veovis. We mean the Five."

Veovis went to speak then stopped, understanding suddenly what they wanted of him.

Lord Eneah, watching his face closely, nodded. "That is right, Veovis. We want you to make soundings for us. This is a delicate matter, after all. It might, of course, be safe to let the girl speak openly. On the other hand, who knows what she might say? As the custodians of D'ni, it is our duty to assess the risk."

Veovis nodded, then, "Might I suggest something, my Lords?"

Eneah looked about him. "Go on."

"Might we not float the idea of *two* separate Hearings? The first before the Five, and then a second—possibly—once you have had the opportunity to judge things for yourselves?"

"You mean, promise something that we might not ultimately grant?"

"The second Hearing would be dependent on the success of the first. That way you have safeguards. And if things go wrong . . . "

Eneah was smiling now, a wintry smile. "Excellent," he said. "Then we shall leave it to you, Veovis. Report back to us within three days. If all is well, we shall see the girl a week from now."

Veovis bowed low. "As you wish, my Lords."

He was about to turn and leave, when his father, Rakeri, called him back. "Veovis?"

"Yes, father?"

"Your friend, Aitrus."

"What of him, father?"

"Recruit him if you can. He's a useful fellow, and well liked among the new members. With him on your side things should prove much easier."

Veovis smiled, then bowed again. "As you wish, father." Then, with a final nod to each of them in turn, he left.

ENEAH SAT AT HIS DESK LONG AFTER THEY had gone, staring at the open sketch pad and the charcoal image of his face. It was some time since he had stared at himself so long or seen himself so clearly, and the thought of what he had become, of the way that time and event had carved his once familiar features, troubled him.

He was, by nature, a thoughtful man; even so, his thoughts were normally directed outward, at that tiny, social world embedded in the rock about him. Seldom did he stop to consider the greater world within himself. But the girl's drawing had reminded him. He could see now how hope and loss, ambition and disappointment, idealism and the longer, more abiding pressures of responsibility, had marked his flesh. He had thought his face a kind of mask, a stone lid upon the years, but he had been wrong: It was all there, engraved in the pale stone of his skin, as on a tablet, for all who wished to read.

If she is typical . . .

The uncompleted thought, like the drawing, disturbed him deeply. When he had agreed to the Hearings, he had thought, as they had all thought, that the matter was a straightforward one. The savage would be brought before them, and questioned, and afterward disposed of—humanely, to a Prison Age—and then, in time, forgotten. But the girl was not a simple savage.

Eneah closed the sketch pad, then sighed wearily.

"If she is typical . . . "

"VEOVIS?"

Veovis looked up, no sign of his normal cheeriness in his face. He looked tired, as if he had not slept.

"Ah, Aitrus. I'm glad you've come."

Veovis gestured to the chair facing him. They were in the great Common Room in the Writers Guild Hall. The huge, square room was filled with big, tall-backed armchairs. It was a favorite place for guildsmen to come and talk, but few of the chairs were filled at this early hour of the day.

Veovis smiled faintly, then looked at him. "Lord Eneah summoned me last night."

"And?"

Veovis lowered his voice. "And they want me to help them."

"In what way?"

"They want to cancel the Hearings."

Aitrus sat forward. "But Lord Eneah announced the Hearings before the full Council. He cannot simply *cancel* them!"

"Exactly. And that is why he hopes I can persuade individual members to let the matter drop."

"Is that why I am here? To be persuaded?"

"No, old friend. You will decide as you decide. But my father wanted me to speak to you, and so here you are."

"I don't follow you, Veovis."

"He wants you to help me. He thinks you might."

"And what did you say to him?"

"I said I would speak to you. No more."

Aitrus laughed. "Come now. No games. Do you want my help or don't you?"

Veovis smiled. "I'd welcome it. If you'd give it."

"Then you had better tell me everything."

THAT EVENING AITRUS DID NOT RETURN TO his rooms in the Guild Hall, but went back to the family home in the Jaren District, which was in the upper northeast of the city, overlooking the Park of the Ages. His mother was delighted to see him, but it was his father, Kahlis, he had come to see.

Stepping back from her embrace, Aitrus looked toward the polished stone stairway that led up to the second floor.

"Is Father in his study?"

"He is, but he is very busy, Aitrus. He has a report to finish for the morning."

Kahlis looked up as Aitrus entered the big, book-lined room, and smiled wearily at him from behind a great stack of papers he was working on. "Ah, Aitrus. How are you?"

"Can I speak with you, Father?"

Kahlis glanced at the paper before him, then, setting his pen back in the inkstand, sat back.

"It is important, I take it?"

Aitrus stepped across and took a seat, facing him. "This matter with the intruder bothers me."

"How so?"

"I went to see Veovis early this morning. He asked me to call on him at his Guild Hall. His mood was . . . strange. I asked him what it was, and he said he had been asked to undertake a task, on behalf of the Five, and that he needed my help."

"And you promised you would help him?"

"Yes."

"So what exactly is the problem?"

"I do not like what I am doing, Father. I gave my word before I understood what was involved."

"That is most unlike you, Aitrus."

"Perhaps. But Veovis is my friend. To refuse him would have been difficult."

"I understand. But what exactly is it that you find so difficult about the 'task' the Five have given you?"

Aitrus stared at his father. "You have heard nothing, then?"

"What ought I to have heard?"

"That the girl now speaks fluent D'ni."

Kahlis laughed. "You jest with me, Aitrus. Word was she could barely grunt her own name!"

"Then word was wrong."

Kahlis took that in, his expression sober suddenly. "I see. Then the Hearings will be soon, I take it."

"That is just it," Aitrus said. "The Five no longer want to hold such hearings—not before the full Council, anyway. They want the sessions to be held in private, with only themselves in attendance. And they have charged Veovis and myself with the job of persuading members of the Council to that viewpoint."

Kahlis stared at him. "I am glad you came to me, Aitrus, before any damage could be done. Lord Eneah made a promise to the full Council, and that promise must be upheld."

Kahlis stood and came around his desk. Aitrus also stood, turning to face his father. "So what will you do?"

"I will go and see Lord Eneah, now, before this matter goes any further. I will tell him that I have heard rumors and that I want his confirmation that they are untrue."

"Then you will say nothing of my part in this?"

"Of course." Kahlis held his son's arms briefly. "Do not worry, Aitrus. I understand the delicacy of your predicament. If Veovis thinks you came to me, he will blame you for whatever trouble follows. But I shall make sure that Lord Eneah does not get that impression."

"Yet he might guess . . . "

Kahlis smiled. "Between guessing and knowing is a long dark tunnel. I know it is not in your nature to deceive, Aitrus, but it might be kinder on your friend—yes, and on yourself—if you kept this meeting with me to yourself."

Aitrus bowed. "I had best go, then."

"Yes. And Aitrus, thank you. You did the right thing."

LORD ENEAH WAS ALREADY IN BED WHEN HIS servant knocked on the door.

"Yes, Jedur, what is it?"

A face only a degree or two less ancient than his own poked around the door and stared at him.

"It is Grand Master Kahlis, my Lord. He knows the hour is late, but he begs a meeting. He says it is of the gravest importance."

Eneah sighed, then slowly sat up. "Ask Master Kahlis to allow me a moment to refresh myself, then I shall come and speak with him."

"My Lord." The wizened face disappeared.

Eneah slid his legs around and, throwing back the single cotton cover, put his feet down on the cold stone of the floor. There had been a time when he had enjoyed the luxuries his post had brought him, but nowadays he embraced simplicity in everything.

He walked across to the washstand in the corner of his spartanly-furnished bedroom and, pouring water from a jug into a bowl, washed his face and hands, drying himself with a small cloth.

His cloak of office hung on a peg behind the door. He took it down and pulled it on, buttoning it to the neck.

"There!" he said, smoothing one hand over what remained of his ash white hair, staring at his face in the small mirror he had had placed on the wall only two days ago. "Now let us see what Master Kahlis wants."

Kahlis was waiting in the study. As Lord Eneah entered the room, he stood hastily, bowing low.

"Forgive me, Lord Eneah . . . "

Eneah waved the apology away. "What is it, Kahlis? Has it to do with the plans for the new cavern?"

He knew it wasn't. Kahlis would hardly have got him from his bed for such a matter. No. He knew already what it was. In fact, he had half expected one or other of them to come to see him. The only surprise was that it was so soon.

As Eneah sat, Kahlis stepped forward, standing at the edge of his desk.

"No, my Lord, it has nothing to do with the plans for the new cavern. Rather, it is to do with certain rumors that have been circulating throughout the day."

"Rumors?" For a moment longer he played innocent, staring back at Kahlis hawkishly. "You wake me to talk of *rumors*, Master Kahlis?"

"I would not have bothered you with such, Lord Eneah, were they not concerned with a matter of the gravest importance."

"And what matter would this be?"

"The matter of the hearings." Kahlis hesitated, then. "Word is that the Five wish to hold the hearings in secret, behind locked doors. Is that so, my Lord?"

For the first time, Eneah smiled. "It is so."

Kahlis, who had clearly steeled himself for a denial, blinked. Then, "Might I ask why, my Lord?"

Eneah gestured to a chair. "Take a seat, Master Kahlis, and I shall try to explain. It might indeed help us were you to understand our thinking on this matter."

AITRUS WAS SEATED AT HIS DESK IN THE corner of his study, trying to catch up on his work before he left for the Guild House, when there was a sharp rapping on his door. He stood, then went across and opened it. It was Veovis. Brushing past him, Veovis stormed across and threw himself down on the padded bench, his face dark with suppressed anger.

"Have you heard?"

"Heard? Heard what?"

"The Hearings. They are to go ahead, after all. The Five have changed their minds. They will take place a week from now."

"Before full Council?"

Veovis nodded, but he was not looking at Aitrus; he was staring straight ahead of him, as if recalling the meeting he had just come from. "It is a mistake. I told Lord Eneah it was a mistake. And they will rue it. But he was adamant. A promise is a promise, he said. Well, I would not argue with that, yet circumstances change."

"You think it might be dangerous, then, to let the girl speak?"

Veovis glanced at him. "Is there any doubt? No, the more I think of it, the more certain I am. The girl has a natural cunning. It is that, more than anything, that has allowed her to master our tongue."

"You think so?"

"Oh, I know it. And I fear that she will use that same native cunning to try to manipulate the Council. Why, I have heard that she has beguiled several of those who were sent to study her, weedling information from them when they least suspected it. And her audacity!"

Aitrus sat, facing Veovis. "Go on."

Veovis sat forward, staring down at his hands where they were clenched in his lap. "It seems one of the Linguists, thrown off-guard by her act of youthful innocence, mistakenly mentioned the existence of the *Rehevkor* to her. She, it seems, elicited from him a promise to show her a copy of it."

"But that is not allowed."

"Precisely. Which is why a certain Guild Master Haemis has been removed from the study team."

"Why did you not mention this to me before now?"

"Because I did not know until this morning."

Aitrus sighed, then shook his head. "You must feel . . . let down."

Veovis looked up at him, then nodded.

"So what will you do now?"

"Do?" There was a bitterness now in Veovis's face that had not been there before. "I can do nothing. I must act the perfect son and sit upon my hands and bite my tongue."

"Has your father instructed you so?"

"Not in so many words. But how else am I to interpret this?" He shook his head. "But they will rue it, I guarantee you, Aitrus. The girl is cunning."

"You have seen her?"

"No. And yet I know her by her work. She is a savage, after all, and savages have no morality, only cunning. Her words, I fear, will poison many ears, persuading them to courses they would otherwise have shunned."

"Then you must set your voice against hers."

Veovis stared at Aitrus a moment; then, smiling, he nodded. "Yes. Yes, of course. It *must* be so. My voice against hers. Truth against trickery." And now he grinned. "As ever, you are wisdom itself, Aitrus, yes, and a pillar to me in my despair!"

Veovis stood and came across, and embraced Aitrus, "Here, let me hug you, old friend. I came here despondent and you have filled me with new hope. It shall be as you said. I shall be the voice of reason, a fierce, strong light shining in the darkness."

Veovis stood back, smiling into Aitrus's face. "And you, my friend? Will you speak out with me?"

"I shall speak the truth as I see it," Aitrus said. "I can promise you no more."

"Then let that be enough. For you will see, Aitrus, I promise you. Do not be blinded by her seeming innocence; think rather of the cunning that lies behind that mask. And as you see, so speak."

"I shall."

"Then good. I'll leave you to your work. And Aitrus?"

"Yes?"

"Thank you. You are the very best of friends."

THE NARROW ALLEYWAYS OF THE LOWER CITY were crowded with onlookers as the procession made its way up that great slope of fashioned rock toward the Great Hall of the Guilds. A small troupe of the City Guard forced a way through, keeping the more curious from the huge palanquin that eight young guildsmen—Maintainers all—carried between two long poles.

From within the partly curtained palanquin, Anna sat in her chair, looking out at the sea of faces that had gathered to see the so-called outsider taken to the Hearings. Some called out to her in their strange tongue that she had yet to fully master, yet few of them seemed hostile. It was more as if she were a curio, an exotic beast captured in some foreign clime and brought back to be displayed before the court.

Anna looked about her, at the men, women, and children that had gathered simply to stare. There were thousands of them, yet every face had that same strange elongation of the features, that almost-human fineness to the bones that she had slowly grown accustomed to these past six months. Indeed, looking in a mirror last night, it had been her own face she had found strange, and looking now she wondered how they saw her. Did they find her nose and mouth too thick and coarse, her cheekbones much too heavy, too *pronounced*, in her face?

Beyond the gate the crowds thinned out. This was a richer district, the citizens who stood outside their doors dressed opulently now, their curiosity if anything much fiercer than the people of the lower city. And the path, too, was suddenly much broader. A marble path, worn by a million feet to a melted smoothness, winding its way between huge roofless houses that were as different from one another as the houses of the lower city were similar.

Anna noted those differences and nodded inwardly. So it was with societies. For the poor uniformity, of dress and housing, for the rich . . . well, *anything*. So her father had pointed out to her years ago when she was still a child, his disillusionment with empires at its darkest ebb.

And today she would face the might of this small empire head on. It was a daunting thought, yet the days alone in her cell on the island had prepared her well for this. They could do their worst and she would still be herself, unbroken and unrepentant. For what *should* she repent, except that she lost her way? No, it was as her father had always taught her: If she believed in herself then it did not matter what the greater world thought of her. If she could square her conscience with herself then all was well.

And, thinking that, she heard his voice clearly for the first time in long months, encouraging her; saying what he had always said to her:

Be brave, Anna, but before all, be true to yourself.

She would not flinch away from what lay ahead. Whatever was said, whatever they decided, she would bear herself with pride, no matter what.

A welcoming party of senior guild officials waited before the next gate, a massive pile of stone with flanking guard towers and huge, twenty-foot doors.

Anna recognized few of them, but the three who stood at the front of the party were well known to her by now.

"Step down, Ah-na," Lord Eneah said, approaching the palanquin and putting out a hand to her courteously, "you must walk from here on."

She let herself be helped down, then stepped between the elderly Gihran and his fellow guildsman,

Jimel. Now that she had to trust to her own legs she felt suddenly less confident. Her pulse had noticeably quickened; her heart fluttered briefly in her chest. They were almost there now. She sensed it.

Beyond the gate the street opened out into a square, the ground tilted steeply, as everywhere here in D'ni. Anna looked about her, realizing that she had seen this open space from her cell window many times but never understood its significance—until now.

The Guild House lay ahead of her now, a massive building fronted by huge, six-sided basalt pillars, its massive, tiered roof reaching up toward the ceiling of the great cavern. Standing before it she did not need to be told what it was, for the shields of the different guilds betrayed its function. Guildsmen crowded the covered paths surrounding the great square, young and old, all of them wearing the various-colored cloaks— burgundy, yellow, turquoise, crimson, emerald green, black, pale cream, and royal blue—of the guilds.

As Lord Eneah came alongside, she glanced at the old man, noting how hard and expressionless his face was. Yet she knew him now to be fair if not kind. If anyone would save her, it was he. Master Gihran, she knew, did not like her, and Master Jimel had as good as told her that he thought she should be locked away for good. Only Master Haemis had been kind, and he had been replaced.

At a gesture from Lord Eneah, the party walked on, Anna in their midst.

At least they have not shackled me again.

But then, why should they? What would she have done? Run away? No. For there was nowhere to run to. She stood out, like a goat in a sheep pen.

As they came to the great marble steps that led up into the hall, Gihran leaned close and whispered to her:

"You must keep absolutely silent, unless you are directly requested to speak, you understand, Ah-na? If you speak out of turn, Lord Eneah will order you gagged."

Anna turned, astonished, to look at him, but the old man merely nodded.

"Our codes of behavior must not be flouted," he continued, his words almost inaudible as they began to climb the steps. "You must do precisely what you are told, and you must answer every question as it is put. All right?"

Anna nodded, but she suddenly felt anything but all right. The tension that had been in her stomach all the while now threatened to unnerve her. She fought against it; fought against the instinct to let her knees buckle and her head go down.

Her throat was dry now. Her hands trembled.

She stopped dead, straightening her head and clenched her fists into tight balls, controlling the nervous spasm. It was only a hearing, after all, not a trial.

She would speak clearly and answer every point, exactly as Master Gihran said. And maybe they would see that she was telling them the truth. For why should she lie?

The Great Hall was huge, much bigger than she would have guessed from the outside of the building. A series of steps followed the contours of the walls, at the top of which was a broad marble plinth. On the plinth was a line of massive basalt thrones. Cloaked guildsmen, more than a hundred in number, sat in those great chairs, thick golden chains of office hung about their necks.

There were only two breaks in that great square of thrones: the entrance she had come through and a second door set deep into the rock on the far side of the hall. Lord Eneah led the party on, across that great mosaic floor, then stopped, turning to face Anna.

"You will stand there, Ah-na," he said commandingly.

She nodded, then watched the old man walk across and take his place on the great throne facing her. Tense now, she looked about her. Most of the seated guildsmen were old—graybeards like Lord Eneah, if not as ancient—but one or two seemed young by D'ni standards. Two in particular caught her eye. They sat side by side, just to the left of Lord Eneah, the first's black cloak trimmed in bright red, the second's in a pale blue.

She glanced at their faces, expecting to see there the same indifference that was on Lord Eneah's features, then looked again, surprised to see how intently each of them looked at her: one curious and one with clear hostility.

Seeing that look, Anna shivered, her blood suddenly cold. There was no mistaking it; whoever he was, the young guildsman clearly hated her.

But why?

"Ah-na!" Lord Eneah said, his voice booming in that great space between the pillars.

"Yes, my Lord."

"You know why you are here?"

She spoke out clearly, letting her voice fill with a confidence she did not entirely feel. "To answer questions, Lord Eneah."

"Good. But you will keep to the point. You will not stray from the question you are asked. You understand?"

"I understand, my Lord."

"Good. Then let us begin. We have many questions to get through before we have finished here today."

AS SHE CLIMBED UP INTO THE SEDAN AND pulled the curtain across, Anna felt a great weariness descend on her. For almost five hours she had stood there, without a break, answering their questions.

She sat down heavily in the cushioned seat, remembering.

Who was she? Where was she born? Who were her parents? What did her father do? To whom did he make his reports? What was Tadjinar like? What form of government did it have? Were there wars where she came from? Did they have machines? What power sources did they use? Were the men of her race honest?

Some of the questions were easy to answer. Others, like the last, were far more difficult. *Were* men honest? Some, like her father, were. But what of the traders in Jaarnindu Market? What of the inspectors and middlemen who worked for Lord Amanjira? She could hardly claim that *they* were honest. But the guildsman seemed to want a single answer to the question.

It was the young Guild Master, the one who had glared at her at the outset, who had been so insistent on this matter.

"Well, girl? *Are* all men honest?"

"No, my Lord. Not all men are honest."

"Then men are dishonest by nature?"

"Not all men."

"Come. You cannot have it both ways. Either they are—by nature—or they are not. Which is it?"

"Are all men in D'ni honest by nature, my Lord?"

There had been a sudden tension in the chamber. Lord Eneah stood, seeming suddenly a figure of great power.

"You are here to answers questions, not pose them."

She had bowed her head, and Lord Eneah, glaring at her, had signaled to his fellow Lords, ending the session. But there was to be another, tomorrow, and a further one if necessary—until she was bled dry of answers.

Anna slumped back against the cushion and closed her eyes as the sedan lifted and began its gentle rocking motion.

With her eyes closed she could see the young man vividly. Veovis, his name had been. He was a handsome, princely man, yet she had noted just how closely he had watched her throughout, the light of suspicion in his eyes at all times.

The other, who sat beside him, had often leaned toward Veovis, to catch a whispered word and sometimes nod. He seemed an ally of Veovis's, yet his eyes had never once held even the smallest hint of criticism of her. Nor had he asked a single question.

How strange, she thought, seeing his face clearly. A long, severe-looking face; not unattractive, yet not as obviously handsome as Veovis's. He seemed a studious type. But then, weren't all the D'ni studious?

The movement of the carriage lulled her. For a moment she dozed, then woke again, not knowing for an instant where she was.

Remembering, she found herself for the first time wondering just what use they would make of the answers she had given. She had seen the tunnels to the surface, and knew they were interested in what went on up there, but she could not make out just what they planned to do with the information she had given them. Some things seemed to have interested them more than others. For instance, they had seemed extremely interested in her answer as to whether her people were warlike or not. Did that mean they planned, perhaps, to invade the surface? Was that why the tunnels were there?

More to the point, did she really care? Lord Amanjira aside, she did not feel close to anyone in Tadjinar—no, nor in the entire empire. Those she had loved were dead. So did it matter?

Of course it matters, the voice inside her answered. *The weight of your words could determine the fate of empires. Besides, war of any kind is bad. Think of the suffering, Anna.*

The thought of it troubled her. Ought she, perhaps, to refuse to say anything more? Or had she said too much already?

The trouble was, she knew so little about these people. Whereas she had answered every question, they had taken great care to keep as much as possible from her. As if she were a spy.

Anna let out a long, sighing breath. Was that what they thought? That she had come to spy on them?

Were it not so serious a matter, she might have laughed. A spy! Why, the idea of it!

Yet even as she thought of it, she recalled the hostility in the young guildsman's face and wondered whether that might not be the cause.

They think I threaten them.

The thought was sobering. And suddenly, for the first time since those early days on Irrat, Anna began to wonder if her life was not possibly in danger.

"WELL?" LORD ENEAH ASKED LATER THAT evening when the five were finally alone together, "Do you still think she is a threat, Nehir?"

Nehir, who had just taken a seat on the far side of the desk to Eneah, looked up, his pale eyes challenging.

"Not her, Eneah, but what she says. Personally, I think we have heard enough."

"I agree," Rakeri said, leaning forward in his chair. "What she is in herself does not concern us here; it is the threat that contact with her people might entail."

"You feel there is a genuine threat, then?"

Rakeri met Eneah's eyes and gave a single nod. "As you know, I did not agree with Veovis at first, but I feel my son's views have been fully vindicated. If what the girl says is true—and I believe it is—then the surface-dwellers are a backward, warlike, immoral race, whose every action is motivated by greed."

"You read that much into her words?"

"I did indeed. Why, her every utterance spoke of a deep corruption in their natures!"

"I agree," R'hira said quietly, speaking from his seat in the corner of the room. "I think we need hear no more. It would be folly even to think of establishing contact with the outsiders."

"And you, Sajka?"

Sajka, the most recently appointed of the Five, simply nodded.

"Then, so we shall propose." Eneah looked about him. "I shall summon the full Council to session tomorrow at tenth bell. There is, however, one small matter that still needs to be settled, and that is what to do with the girl."

"Send her back," Rakeri suggested.

"Far too risky," R'hira countered. "It is unlikely, I admit, but someone might believe her tale and come looking for us."

"Then maybe we should place her on a Prison Age," Nehir said. "It need not be a harsh one. Somewhere pleasant, possibly. We could even make a new one for her, if need be."

"Pleasant or otherwise, do you think that would be

just reward for her honesty with us, Nehir?" Eneah's eyes went from one to another of their faces, silently questioning each in turn, then he nodded.

"So it is. The girl will stay here, in D'ni. We shall find a home for her, temporarily, until it is decided fully. Agreed?"

"Agreed."

"Agreed."

"Agreed."

Sajka, who had not spoken until then, looked about him, a wintry smile on his thin lips, and nodded. "Agreed."

VEOVIS WAS ECSTATIC. THAT EVENING HE threw a celebratory party at an inn down by the harbor. Aitrus, who had never found time to visit such places, tried hard to make his excuses, but Veovis would have none of it.

And so Aitrus found himself wedged into a corner of a huge dining room packed with busy tables, while all about him a dozen young guildsmen—some familiar to him, others only "faces"—dipped their goblets into the great central vat that rested at the table's center and drank to the young Lord's success.

"It was that final question that did it," Suahrnir said, his face glowing with excitement. "After that, it was a mere formality."

"Maybe so," Veovis said, standing up and looking to Aitrus across the table, "but let me say one thing that has not been said. I was wrong about the girl."

"Wrong?" several voices said as one.

Veovis raised his hands, palms out. "Hear me out, gentlemen! Before the hearing I was quite clear in my mind what kind of creature she would prove to be, and if you recall I was not hesitant in saying so!"

There was laughter at that and a great deal of nodding.

"However," Veovis went on, "I *was* wrong, and I am not too proud to admit it. Whatever the merits or otherwise of her race, the girl spoke well. Yes, and honestly, I warrant. I think we all sensed that."

There was a murmur of agreement and more nodding of heads.

"Word is," Veovis continued, "that she is to stay in D'ni. Now, whether that is for the common good or not remains to be seen, but so our Masters have decided, and I feel we should, this once, wait and see. That said, we must remain vigilant."

"What do you mean?" Veovis's constant companion, Lianis asked from where he sat to the left of the young Lord.

"I mean we ought not to let the girl become a focus for any movement to reverse today's decision. No contact ought to mean exactly that. No contact."

"And if she proves such a focus, Veovis?" Suahrnir asked.

Veovis smiled and looked about him confidently. "Then we should act to have her removed from D'ni to some more suitable place."

Aitrus, who had been listening closely, frowned. A Prison Age, that was what Veovis meant. Yet he could not deny that his friend was being as fair as he could be, considering his views.

Aitrus reached out and took his goblet, cradling it to his chest. He was pleased that Veovis was so happy, yet he could not share their jubilation at today's decision. Perhaps it was as Veovis said, that he was letting sentiment cloud his better judgment, but part of him was still back there in the rock, making his way up to the surface, with Master Telanis and Jerahl and all the others who had gone on that youthful venture. Whatever he had become these past thirty years, he could not shed that earlier self.

Watching the girl speak, it had finally crystallized in him. He knew now that he wanted contact: wanted, more than anything, to stand up there and see, with his own eyes, what the surface was like.

But how could he say that to Veovis and remain his friend? For to Veovis the very idea of it was anathema.

"Guild Master Aitrus?"

The voice cut through the general babble of voices at the table. Aitrus looked up, expecting it to be one of the young guildsmen, then saw, just behind Lianis, a cloaked guildsman from the Guild of Messengers.

Silence fell around the table. Aitrus set down his goblet, then stood. "What is it?" he asked.

"An urgent message, Master," the Messenger answered, drawing off one of his gloves, then taking a sealed letter from his tunic pocket. "I was told to ensure that you act upon its contents immediately."

With a smile, Veovis put out a hand. "Here. I'll hand it to my friend."

The Messenger looked to Aitrus, who nodded. With a small bow to Veovis, he handed the letter to him, then stood back, pulling on his glove again.

Veovis turned back, then handed the letter across. "Urgent business, eh, old friend? That looks like Lord Eneah's seal."

Aitrus stared at the envelope a moment. Veovis was right. It was Lord Eneah's seal. But when he opened it, the note was not from Lord Eneah, but from his father.

He looked up. "Forgive me, Veovis, but I must leave at once."

"Is there trouble?" Veovis asked, genuinely concerned.

Aitrus swallowed. "It does not say."

"Then go," Veovis said, signaling to the others about the table to make way. "Go at once. But let me know, all right? If there is anything I can do . . ."

Aitrus, squeezing past his fellow guildsmen, gave a distracted nod. Then he was gone.

Veovis sat, staring across the crowded room, his face briefly clouded. Then, looking back at the others about the table, he smiled and raised his goblet. "To D'ni!" he exclaimed.

A dozen voices answered him robustly. *"To D'ni!"*

KAHLIS STOOD IN THE ENTRANCE HALL, PACING up and down, awaiting his son. It was midnight and the city bell was sounding across the lake.

As the last chime echoed into silence, he heard the outer gate creak back and hurried footsteps on the stone flags outside. A shadow fell across the colored glass of the door panels.

Kahlis stepped across and drew the bolt, pulling the door open.

Aitrus stood there, wide-eyed and breathless. From the look of him he had run the last half mile.

"What's happened?" he said, looking past his father.

Kahlis closed the door. "Come upstairs, Aitrus."

They went up, into his study. Closing the door quietly, Kahlis turned to him.

"I have been asked to look after the outsider for a time. Lord Eneah summoned me this evening and asked me if I would take the girl, Ah-na into my household, as a temporary measure. Until better arrangements can be made. He asked me because he understood my concern for the young woman."

"And you want me to agree to this?"

"Yes."

"Then I agree."

Kahlis went to speak again, then realized what his son had said. "You agree?"

"I take it Mother has agreed. And you must have, else you would not be asking me."

In answer Kahlis went over to the door and opened it, then called down the steps. "Tasera!"

His mother's head and shoulders appeared at the foot of the stairs.

"Tasera," Kahlis said, "bring the young lady. I wish to introduce her to our son."

AS SHE STEPPED INTO THE BOOK-FILLED
study, Anna looked about her warily.

"Aitrus," Kahlis said, "this is Ah-na. She is to be our
house guest for a time."

Aitrus bowed his head respectfully. "I am glad you
will be staying with us."

"Thank you," she said, their eyes meeting briefly as
he lifted his head again. "I am grateful for your kindness in letting me stay."

"You are welcome," Tasera interrupted, coming
across to take Anna's arm. "Now if you would excuse
us, I must see Anna to her room."

The brevity of the welcome surprised her; yet she
turned and followed the woman out and down the
corridor.

"Here," Tasera said, opening a door and putting out
an arm. "This will be your room."

Anna stepped inside, surprised. Compared to the
Lodge, it was luxurious. Anna turned and bowed her head.

"You are too kind, Tasera. Much too kind."

AITRUS WAS WALKING ACROSS THE OPEN
space between the main Guild House and the Great

Library when Veovis stepped from a group of guildsmen and made to intercept him. It was more than
a week since they had last met, in the inn beside
the harbor.

"Aitrus! Did you get my note?"

Aitrus stopped. "Your note . . . Ah, yes. I have
been busy."

Veovis smiled, putting out his hands to Aitrus who
took them in a firm grip.

"So what is she like?"

"She seems . . . polite. Well mannered."

"Seems?"

Aitrus found himself oddly defensive. "It's my
impression."

"Then you think she is genuine?"

"Didn't *you*? I thought you said as much?"

Veovis smiled, defusing the situation. "That was *my*
impression, I grant you. But then, I am not living with
her—day in, day out. If there are any cracks in that
mask of hers, you would see them, no?"

"If there were."

"Oh, I am not saying that there *are*. It's just . . . "

"Just what?"

"Just that we ought to be totally certain, don't you
think?"

For some reason the idea of checking up on the girl
offended Aitrus.

"She seems . . . unsettled," he said, after a moment, wanting to give Veovis something.

"Unsettled? How?"

"Maybe it is just the strangeness of everything here. It must be hard to adapt to D'ni after living under an open sky."

"Does she miss her home?"

"I am not sure. To be honest, I have not asked her."

Veovis laughed. "What you really mean is that you have not spoken to her yet."

"As I said, I have been busy. Helping my father, mainly."

Veovis stared at Aitrus a moment, then reached out and held his arm. "You should take a break some time, Aitrus. And when you do, come and visit me, on K'veer. And bring the girl."

"That would be nice."

"Soon, then," Veovis said, and without another word, he turned and walked away.

Aitrus watched Veovis a moment—saw him return to the group he had left earlier, greeting them again, at ease among them—then smiled to himself as he walked away. To be honest, he had dreaded meeting Veovis again, knowing how Veovis felt about the "outsider." He had thought, perhaps, that his friend would be angry that the girl was staying with his family, but his fears, it seemed, had been illusory.

His smile broadened as he hastened his pace, knowing he was late now for his meeting.

K'veer. It would be nice to take the girl to see K'veer.

THE ROOM WAS A WORKROOM OR LAB OF SOME kind. Anna hesitated, looking behind her at the empty corridor, then slipped inside, pulling the door closed.

You should not be in here, Anna, she told herself, yet that old familiar compulsion to explore was on her. Besides, she would not stay long, and she would not disturb anything.

There was a long, stone-topped bench along the left-hand side of the room, a big low table in the middle, complete with sinks and gas taps. On the far wall a number of small shelves held all manner of jars and bottles. To the right of the room, in the far corner, was a desk and a chair, and on the wall above a set of shelves on which were many notebooks.

She put her hand out, touching the cool, hard surface of the bench. It had been scrubbed clean and when she lifted her hand, she could smell a strange scent to it. What was that? Coal tar? Iodine?

Slowly she walked about the room, picking things up then placing them back. Most of the equipment was familiar, yet there were one or two things that were strange to her. One in particular caught her attention. It was a small bronze jar with eight lips, beneath each of which was a tiny bowl. A bronze ball sat on a tiny stand at the very center of the jar, balanced above all else.

Anna crouched down, onto its level, staring at it for a time, then walked on, over to the far corner of the room.

Only two things were on the surface of the desk; an elaborately decorated inkstand made of fine blue jade and, just beside the stand, a pair of glasses.

Anna picked them up and studied them. The lenses were thick and seemed to be constructed of several very fine layers that acted as light filters of some kind. About each of the lenses was a tight band of expandable material which, in turn, was surrounded by a thick leather band, studded with tiny metal controls. She adjusted them, noting how they changed the opacity of the lenses, and smiled to herself. Then, on a whim, she tried them on. Strange. They were very tight. Airtight, probably, on the person for whom they were designed. And, wearing them, it became very dark.

Again she adjusted the controls, varying the light.

Taking them off, she set them down again, wondering what precisely they were used for. Mining? To protect the eyes against chips of rock? But if so, then why the varying opacity?

Anna half-turned toward the door, listening for a moment, then, turning back to face the shelves, she reached up and took one of the journals down. Inside the pages were filled with strange writing, totally unlike any script she had ever seen before. Flicking through a few pages she stopped, staring in admiration at a diagram on the right-hand page. There were more farther on, all of them intricately drawn, the lines fine yet dark, the shading subtle. They spoke of a highly organized mind.

She closed the journal and set it back in its place, then, with a final look about her, hurried from the room.

It was no good. She would have to do something or she would die of boredom.

Distracted, she almost bowled into Aitrus.

"Come," he said quietly. "We need to speak."

Anna followed him, surprised. He had barely said a word to her all week. She was even more surprised when he led her along the corridor and into the workroom she had been exploring.

Did he know? Was that what this was about?

Inside, Aitrus closed the door, then gestured for her to take the chair beside the desk. He seemed awkward.

"Here," he said, turning to reach up and take down one of the books that were on the topmost shelf. He offered it to her. "That is a history of D'ni. It is a child's book, of course, but . . ."

Aitrus stopped. She was staring at the pages blankly. "What is it?"

She looked up at him, then, closing the book, handed it back to him. "I cannot read this."

"But I thought . . ." He shook his head, then. "You mean, you learned to *speak* D'ni, but not to read it?"

Anna nodded.

Aitrus stared at the book a moment, then set it down and turned, searching among the bottom shelves until he found something. It was a big, square-covered book with a dark amber leather cover. He pulled it out from among the other books; turning, he offered it to Anna.

"Here. This is the key to all."

Anna took it, studying the beautifully tooled leather cover a moment before opening it. Inside, on heavy vellum pages, were set out columns of beautifully intricate figures—more like designs than letters.

She looked up at him and smiled. "Is this what I think it is? Is this the D'ni lexicon?"

"The *Rehevkor*," he said, nodding.

She looked back at the page, smiling sadly now. "But I do not know what they mean."

"Then I shall teach you," Aitrus said, his pale eyes watching her seriously.

"Are you sure that is allowed?"

"No," he answered, "but I will teach you anyway."

ANNA SAT AT THE PROW OF THE BOAT AS IT approached the island, Aitrus just behind her, standing, his right hand resting lightly on the rail.

"So that is K'veer," she said quietly. "I saw it once before, when they brought me from Irrat."

Aitrus nodded. "It has been their family home for many years."

"I remember thinking how strange it was. Like a great drill bit poking up from the bottom of the lake."

He smiled at that.

"So who is this Veovis?"

"He is the son of Lord Rakeri, Grand Master of the Guild of Miners."

"And he, too, is a Miner?"

"No. Veovis is a Master of the Guild of Writers."

"You have a Guild of Writers? Are they important?"

"Oh, very much so. Perhaps the most important of all our guilds."

"Writers?"

He did not answer her.

She looked back at him surprised. Slowly the island grew, dominating the view ahead of them.

"Has Veovis many brothers and sisters?"

"None. He is an only child."

"Then why so huge a mansion?"

"Lord Rakeri often entertains guests. Or did before his illness."

Anna was quiet for a time as they drifted slowly toward the island. There was a small harbor directly ahead of them now, and beneath a long, stone jetty, a dark, rectangular opening.

"Does your friend Veovis dislike me?"

The question surprised Aitrus. "Why do you ask?"

"I ask because he stared at me throughout the hearing."

"Is that so unusual? I stared."

"Yes, but not as he did. He seemed hostile toward me. And his questions . . . "

"What of his questions?"

She shrugged, then. "Did he ask you to bring me?"

"He invited you specifically."

"I see."

Yet she seemed strangely distant, and Aitrus, watching her, wondered what was going on in her head. He wanted Veovis and her to be friends. It would be so easy if they were friends, but as it was he felt awkward.

"Veovis can be outspoken sometimes."

"Outspoken?"

"I thought I ought to warn you, that's all. He can be a little blunt, even insensitive at times, but he is well meaning. You should not be afraid of him."

Anna gave a little laugh. "I am not afraid, Aitrus. Not of Veovis, anyway."

THEY SPENT HOURS, IT SEEMED, JUST GOING from room to room in the great mansion that was built into the rock of K'veer, Veovis delighting in showing Anna every nook and cranny.

At first Anna had been wary, but as time went on she seemed to succumb to the young Lord's natural charm, and Aitrus, looking on, found himself relaxing.

As they climbed the final flight of steps that led onto the veranda at the top of the island, Aitrus found himself wondering how he could ever have worried about these two not getting along.

"The stone seemed fused," Anna was saying, as they came out through the low arch and into the open again. "It is almost as if it has been melted and then molded."

"That is *precisely* what has happened," Veovis answered her with an unfeigned enthusiasm. "It is a special D'ni process, the secret of which is known only to the guilds concerned."

They stepped out, into the center of the veranda. There was a tiled roof overhead, but the view was open now on all four sides. All about them the lake stretched away, while in the distance they could see the great twisted rock of Ae'Gura and, to its right, the city.

They were high up here, but the great walls of the cavern stretched up far above them, while overhead there were faint clouds, like feathered cirrus. Anna laughed.

"What is it?" Veovis asked.

"It's just that I keep thinking I am outside. Oh, the light is very different, but . . . well, it's just so big."

Veovis looked to Aitrus and smiled, then gestured toward a group of lounging chairs that rested at one end of the veranda.

"Shall we sit here for a while? I can have the servants bring us something."

"That would be nice," Anna said, looking to Aitrus and smiling.

As Veovis went to arrange refreshments, Anna and Aitrus sat.

"He's very pleasant," she said quietly. "I can understand why he is your friend."

"So you've forgiven him?"

"Forgiven him?"

"For scowling at you."

"Ah . . . " Anna laughed. "Long ago."

Aitrus smiled. "I'm glad, you know."

"Really?"

"Yes. I wanted you to be friends. It would have been hard otherwise."

Anna frowned. "I didn't know."

"I . . ."

He fell silent. Veovis had returned. The young lord came across and, taking the chair between them, looked from one to another.

His eyes settled on Anna. "Can I be honest with you, Ah-na?"

Anna looked up. "Honest? In what way?"

Veovis grinned. "We are alike, you and I. We are both straightforward people." He looked pointedly at Aitrus. "*Blunt*, some call it. But let me say this. I was not disposed to like you. Indeed, I was prepared to actively *dislike* you. But I must speak as I find, and I find that I like you very much."

She gave the smallest little nod. "Why, thank you, Lord Veovis."

"Oh, do not thank me, Ah-na. I did not *choose* to like you. But like you I do. And so we can be friends. But I must make one or two things clear. I am D'ni. And I am jealous of all things D'ni. We are a great and proud people. Remember that, Ah-na. Remember that at all times."

Anna stared at him a moment, surprised by that strange and sudden coldness in him, then answered him.

"And I, my Lord, am human, and proud of being so. Remember *that*," she smiled pointedly, "at all times."

Veovis sat back, his eyes studying Anna thoughtfully. Then, more cheerfully than before, he smiled and slapped his knees. "Well . . . let us forget such somber stuff. Aitrus . . . how go the plans for the new cavern?"

ON THE JOURNEY HOME ANNA WAS SILENT, locked in private thoughts. Aitrus, sitting across from her, felt more than ever how alien their worlds were. What, after all, did they really know about each other?

"Ah-na?"

She looked up, a deep melancholy in her eyes. "Yes?"

"What would you like to do?"

Anna turned her head, staring out across the lake. "I'd like to understand it all, that's what. To know where all the food comes from. It mystifies me. It's like something's missing and I can't see what it is."

"And you want me to tell you what it is?"

She looked to him. "Yes, I do. I want to know what the secret is."

He smiled. "This evening," he said mysteriously, sitting back and folding his arms. "I'll take you there this evening."

AITRUS UNLOCKED THE DOOR, THEN STOOD
back.

"You want me to go inside?"

He nodded.

Anna shrugged. She had noticed the door before
now. It had always been locked, and she had assumed it
was a store cupboard of some kind. But inside it was a
normal room, except that in the middle of the floor
was a marble plinth, and on the plinth was an open
book—a huge, leatherbound book.

Anna looked to Aitrus. "What is this room?"

Aitrus locked the door then turned to her again.
"This is the Book Room."

"But there is only one book."

He nodded, then, with a seriousness she had not
expected, said, "You must tell no one that you
came here. Not even my mother and father. Do you
understand?"

"Are we doing something wrong?"

"No. Yet it may be forbidden."

"Then perhaps . . . "

"No, Ah-na. If you are to live here, you must
understand. You have too simple a view of who we
are. It . . . *disfigures* your understanding of us."

Disfigures. It was a strange word to use. Anna stared at him, then shook her head. "You frighten me, Aitrus."

Aitrus stepped up to the plinth and stared down at the book fondly.

Anna stepped alongside him, looking down at the open pages. The left-hand page was blank, but on the right . . .

Anna gasped. "It's like a window."

"Yes," he said simply. "Now give me your hand."

ANNA FELT THE SURFACE OF HER PALM TINGLE, then, with a sudden, sickening lurch, she felt herself drawn into the page. It grew even as she shrank, sucking her into the softly glowing image.

For a moment it was as if she were melting, fusing with the ink and paper, and then, with a suddenness that was shocking, she was herself again, in her own body.

Only she was no longer in the room.

The air was fresh and heavy with pollen. A faint breeze blew from the shelf of rock just in front of her. And beyond it . . .

Beyond it was a vividly blue sky.

Her mouth fell open in astonishment, even as Aitrus shimmered into solidity beside her.

He put his hand out, holding her arm as a wave of giddiness swept over her. She would have fallen but for him. Then it passed and she looked at him again, her words an awed whisper.

"Where are we?"

"Ko'ah," he said. "This is my family's Age."

ANNA STOOD ON THE TOP OF THE ESCARPMENT, looking out over a rich, verdant landscape that took her breath away, it was so beautiful. Flat, rolling pasture was broken here and there by tiny coppices, while close by the foot of the hill on which she stood, a broad, slow-moving river wound its way out across the plain, small grassy moundlike islands embedded like soft green jewels in its sunlit surface.

To her right a line of mountains marched into the distance, birds circling in the clear blue sky above them.

Sunlight beat down on her neck and shoulders; not the fierce, destructive heat of the desert but a far softer, more pleasant warmth.

"Well?" Aitrus asked, from where he sat, just behind her, staring out through the strange, heavy glasses that he now wore. "What do you think of Ko'ah?"

Anna turned, looking back at him. "I think you have enchanted me. Either that or I am still in bed and dreaming."

Aitrus reached out and plucked a nearby flower, then handed it to her. She took the pale blue bud and lifted it to her nose, inhaling its rich, perfumed scent.

"Are your dreams as *real* as this?"

She laughed. "No." Then, more seriously, "You said you would explain."

Reaching into his pocket, Aitrus took out a small, leather-bound book. He stared at it a moment, then handed it to her.

"Is this another of those books?" she asked, opening it and seeing that it contained D'ni writing.

"It is. But different from the one we used to come here. This book links back to D'ni. It is kept here, in the small cave we went to.

"The words in that book describe the place to which we link back—the study in my family's mansion in D'ni. It was *written* there. Without it we would be trapped here."

"I see," she said, staring at the thin volume with new respect. "But where exactly are we? Are we in the pages of a book, or are we actually *somewhere?*"

His smile was for her quickness. "There is, perhaps, some way of calculating precisely where we are—by the night-time stars, maybe—but all that can be said for certain is that we are elsewhere. In all likelihood, we are on the other side of the universe from D'ni."

"Impossible."

"You could say that. But look about you, Anna. This world is the Age that is described in the book back in the room in D'ni. It conforms *precisely* to the details in that book. In an infinite universe, all things are possible—within physical limits, that is—and any book that *can* be written *does* physically exist. Somewhere. The book is the bridge between the words and the physical actuality. Word and world are linked by the special properties of the book."

"It sounds to me like magic."

Aitrus smiled. "Maybe. But we have long since stopped thinking of it as such. Writing such books is a difficult task. One cannot simply write whatever comes into one's head. There are strict rules and guidelines, and the learning of those rules is a long and arduous business."

"Ah," she said. "I understand now."

"Understand what?"

"What you said about Writers. I thought . . . " Anna laughed. "You know, Aitrus, I would never have guessed. Never in a thousand years. I thought you D'ni were a dour, inward-looking people. But this . . . well . . . you are true visionaries!"

Aitrus laughed.

"Why, the great cavern in D'ni is like a giant skull, filled with busy thoughts, and these books—well, they are like the dreams and visions that comes from such intense mental activity!"

Aitrus stared at her a moment, then shook his head. "You are amazing, Ah-na. Why, I have lived in D'ni more than fifty years and never once have I thought of such a thing!"

"Different eyes," she said, looking pointedly at him, "that's all it is. Sometimes it takes a total stranger to see the obvious."

"Perhaps so."

"But tell me, Aitrus. You spoke of the book's special properties. What exactly did you mean?"

He looked away. "Forgive me, Ah-na, but perhaps I have already said too much. Such things are great secrets. Grave and greatly guarded secrets, known to only the Guilds."

"Like the Guild of Ink-Makers?"

Aitrus glanced at her, then smiled. "Yes, and the Guild of Books who manufacture the paper . . . and, of course, the Guild of Writers."

"And the writing in the books . . . is it different from the writing you have been teaching me?"

"Yes."

For a moment Anna stared at the book in her hands; then, closing it up, she handed it back to him.

She turned, looking about her once again, savoring the feel of the cool and gentle breeze on her arms and neck. Her hand went to her neck, drawing back the fine silk of her long, lustrously dark hair.

"It must have been cruel for you," Aitrus said, watching her, a strange expression coming to his eyes, "being locked up."

"It was." She glanced around at him, then smiled—a bright smile, full of the day's sunlight. "But let's forget that now. Come, Aitrus. Let us go down to the river."

THAT EVENING NEITHER AITRUS NOR ANNA spoke a word about their visit to Ko'ah. But later, in her room, the impossibility of it struck Anna forcibly. She sat on the edge of the bed, her mouth open in astonished recollection.

In that instant after she had "linked," she had never felt more scared. No, nor more exhilarated. And the world itself. *Ko'ah.* Sitting there, she could scarcely believe that she had really been there. It had seemed so strange and dreamlike. Yet in a small glass vase on the table at her side was the pale blue flower Aitrus had given her.

Anna leaned close, inhaling its scent.

It had been real. As real as this. The very existence of the flower was proof of it. But how could that be? How could simple words link to other places?

On their return from Ko'ah, Aitrus had shown her the Book, patiently taking her through page after page, and showing her how such an Age was "made." She had seen at once the differences between this archaic form and the ordinary written speech of D'ni, noting how it was not merely more elaborate but more specific: a language of precise yet subtle descriptive power. Yet seeing was one thing, believing another. Given all the evidence, her rational mind still fought against accepting it.

Beside the Book itself, Aitrus had gone on to show her the books of commentary—three in all, the last containing barely a dozen entries. All Books, he said, were accompanied by such commentaries, which were notes and observations on the Ages. Some of the more ancient Ages—like Nidur Gemat—had hundreds of books of commentary.

She had asked him about it.

"Nidur Gemat?"

"It is one of six worlds belonging to Veovis's family."

"Ah, I see. And do all the D'ni own such Ages?"

"No. Only the older families own such Ages. The rest—the common people of D'ni—use the Book Rooms."

"You mean, there are common worlds, that everyone can visit?"

"Yes. In fact, until my father became Grand Master of our guild, we did not have our own Age. Ko'ah was written for my father twenty years ago."

"And before that?"

"We would visit the Guild Ages. Or Ages owned by friends."

Anna had smiled at that. "That is some incentive."

"Incentive?"

"To work hard and make one's way in the guild. Is there no resentment among the common people?"

Aitrus had shrugged. "Not that I know of. The Common Ages are free to everyone. It is not as if they are denied."

"No, but . . . " She had let the matter drop, returning her attention to the first of the books of commentary. "What is this?" she had asked after a moment, looking up at him, again.

There had been a stamped impression on the page, beneath a paragraph of small, neat writing in a bright green ink.

"That is an inspection. By the Guild of Maintainers. They ensure that all Ages are maintained according to Guild laws."

"And if they are not?"

"Then the Book can be confiscated and the owner punished."

"Does that happen often?"

"Not often. All know the penalty for misdemeanors. To own an Age is an immense responsibility. Few are trusted."

"And yet you took me there."

He had hesitated, then looking at her directly, he had nodded. "Yes, I did," he said.

ANNA SLEPT WELL THAT NIGHT, AND IF SHE dreamed she did not recall it when she woke. Refreshed, she sat up, looking across at the delicate blue flower in its vase beside her bed, her mind at once filled with the wonder of what she had witnessed the day before.

Aitrus was not at breakfast, and at first she thought that maybe he had left early to go to the Guild Hall, but then, at the last moment, as she was finishing her meal, he rushed into the room in a state of immense excitement.

"Anna! Wonderful news! Veovis is to be given a *Korfah V'ja!*"

She stared at him uncomprehendingly.

He laughed. "I'm sorry. The Korfah V'ja is a special ceremony to mark the Guild's acceptance of his Book—his first Master work, that is. It is a momentous event. Few guildsmen are ever given one, and Veovis is immensely young to have been granted such an honor!"

"And Veovis . . . he *wrote* this Book? Like the Age we went to?"

Aitrus nodded. "Only much better. Incomparably better."

The thought of that made her reassess Lord Veovis. She had thought him merely a rich man's son, a politician. She had not even considered that he was also a "creator," let alone a great one.

"Then it will be a great occasion, no?"

"The greatest for many a year. All of D'ni society will be there. And you must come with us, Anna!"

She looked down. Usually she hated social occasions, but the thought of seeing all of D'ni society—and of meeting Lord Veovis once again—filled her with a strange excitement.

"When is to be?" she asked, looking back at Aitrus.

"A week from now," he answered. "On the anniversary of Kerath's homecoming."

IT WAS A SMALL CEREMONY. THE SIX ASSISTANT
grand masters and the Grand Master, Lord Sajka himself, stood in a half circle on the great platform, while
the celebrant, Veovis, stood before them, his Book, the
work of sixteen long years, on the podium before him.

The day was bright and springlike, the blue sky dot-
ted with clouds. In the distance, snow-capped mountains marched toward the south and the great ocean.
Below them the great plains stretched away to east and
west and south, while to the north the ancient settlement of Derisa was tucked into a fold of hills.

This was the oldest of the guild's many Ages—the
Age of Yakul, made by the first great Writer of the
Guild, Ar'tenen, and here, traditionally, the first official
ceremony took place.

There would be a second, more public, ceremony
later, on Veovis's own world of Ader Jamat, at which
this moment would be reenacted for all to see, but this
seemingly low-key event was by far the more important.

Each of the seven senior members of the guild had
read the great work that was today accepted into the
guild's own canon, and each had given their separate
approval for this ultimate recognition of the young
Guild Master's talent. It was 187 years since the last

Korfah V'ja and it would be many years before another. Only ninety-three Books had been accepted into the canon in the whole of the long history of the guild—among them the Five Great Classics of D'ni—and only four guildsmen had ever received this honor younger than the man who now stood before them. Among those four was the legendary Ri'Neref.

A faint breeze gusted across the open space, rustling their cloaks, as Lord Sajka, Grand Master of the Guild of Writers, stepped forward and, in a tongue as distinct from the common speech of D'ni as that of the surface-dwellers, pronounced the Words of Binding.

And then it was done. As Veovis bowed his head to his peers, Lord Sajka smiled and, in the common speech, said:

"Well done, Veovis. We are all immensely proud of you."

Veovis looked up and smiled, conscious of the great honor being accorded him.

"My Lord, Guild Masters . . . I hope to prove worthy of your approval. It is a great privilege to be a member of the Guild of Writers, and I count myself blessed the day I chose to enter it."

And so it was done.

As, one by one, the elders linked back to D'ni, Veovis turned and looked about him at the ancient world of Yakul, and wondered if, one day, several thousand years hence, some other guildsman would stand on an Age he had written and wonder, as he now wondered, what kind of man it was whose imagination had wrought the connections to such a world as this.

He turned and walked over to the linking book. It was time to return to D'ni, to pause and reflect before beginning the next chapter in his life. For his next work would be something other, he was determined on it; not just a great work but a classic.

But before all, celebration. For today was his day. Today he became a great man, honored before all D'ni.

Veovis placed his hand against the glowing panel and linked, a smile appearing on his lips even as his figure shimmered and then faded into the air.

ON THE BOAT ACROSS TO K'VEER, ANNA BEGAN to have second thoughts about meeting so many strangers at the ceremony.

With Aitrus it was fine, for it was only the two of them, as it had been with her father, but with all others, even with Aitrus's parents, she felt ill at ease. She was not by any means a social creature. How she should act and what she should say, these things were a complete mystery to her.

It does not matter, Aitrus had said to her. *They do not expect you to behave as they behave.*

Now, as the island grew nearer and she could see the great host of boats queuing to enter the tiny harbor, she felt her nervousness return.

Last night, before her conversation with Aitrus, there had been a strange little scene in Kahlis's study. Knowing that his father knew nothing of their ventures into Ko'ah, Aitrus had had his father "explain" about Books to Anna, and she, schooled by Aitrus in what to say and how to react, had pretended that it was all completely new to her.

Kahlis had clearly been concerned; not only at Anna's possible reaction but by the problem of just how *much* to tell her. Aitrus, however, had convinced him that had Lord Eneah not meant her to know, then he would have given explicit instructions to that effect. Kahlis would, indeed, have gone to see Lord Eneah had the great man not taken to his bed again with a recurrence of his illness.

And so Kahlis had "prepared" her, telling her that she must expect a great surprise, and that she was not to be afraid, for all that she would experience was quite normal. And she, prompted by Aitrus, had feigned that she understood, even though she would barely have recognized the process of "linking" from the description

Aitrus's father had given her. It had been vague almost to the point of willfulness.

As their boat joined the great queue of boats, Anna could see, on the decks, endless guildsmen and their wives and sons and daughters, all of them dressed in their best finery. Looking at them, Anna felt her spirits sink again. She should never have come. Then her father's voice sounded clearly in her head.

Don't worry, Anna. Just be yourself.

IT WAS ALMOST AN HOUR BEFORE THEIR BOAT drew up alongside the stone jetty and they climbed the dark granite steps, up onto the marble-flagged forecourt. Facing them was the carved stone gate that surrounded the massive doorway.

Anna had seen K'veer by day and it had seemed a strange yet pleasant edifice, but at night it seemed a wholly forbidding place. As they approached the doorway, Aitrus came alongside her.

"Forgive me, Ah-na," he said quietly, "but we must conform to certain formalities. When we are inside, you will draw back and wait a moment while my father and I are greeted. Then it will be your turn."

Inside the great atrium, Anna did as she was told, holding back beside Tasera as Aitrus and his father stepped forward and were presented by the Chief Steward to Rakeri and his son.

Anna saw once more that curious taking of both hands that was the D'ni way of greeting, the fingers linked; witnessed the smiles, the easy banter between the two sets of men, and knew that this was a world she would never enter, book or no book.

As Kahlis turned, Tasera nudged her gently. "Ah-na."

Veovis was smiling pleasantly, his attention half on what was being said, half on greeting the next guests. As he looked across and his eyes met hers, the smile faded. There was a moment's consideration and then he turned to Kahlis.

"Forgive me, Master Kahlis, but might I have a word with you, in private?"

Kahlis looked to his son, then shrugged. "Of course, Veovis."

Veovis turned and bowed to Rakeri. "If you would forgive us a moment, Father? I shall not be long."

Tasera and Anna had stopped, yards distant of Lord Rakeri. As Veovis and Kahlis walked away, Aitrus stared after them, perturbed. Rakeri himself was simply mystified.

There was an embarrassed silence. Rakeri looked to Tasera and smiled weakly. Aitrus simply stared at the door through which Veovis and his father had passed. A moment later the two men returned, his father clearly embarrassed by something. Coming over to Aitrus, he drew him aside.

"It seems there has been a misunderstanding," he began. "I took the invitation to include our house guest, Ah-na, but it was not meant so."

Aitrus, who had been listening to his father's words, glanced over at Veovis, who stood beside his father, wearing a determined look.

"A misunderstanding?" Aitrus tried to keep calm, tried not to let his anger show.

"Yes," Kahlis said. "Ah-na can stay here, in the house. Veovis has promised that his servants will make sure she has everything she wants. But she cannot go through into Ader Jamat."

"Why not?"

Kahlis raised a hand, bidding him be silent. "Because she is not D'ni."

Aitrus felt the anger boil up inside him. Keeping his voice low, he leaned close to Kahlis. "This is not right, Father."

"Maybe," Kahlis conceded, "but it is Lord Veovis's decision who enters his Age, not ours, and we must respect that."

"I see."

"I'm glad you do. Now will you tell her, Aitrus?"

Aitrus stared back at him a moment, then looked down. "You must forgive me, Father. I respect you deeply, and love you, but in this I must disobey you. This is wrong."

"Aitrus . . . "

But Aitrus turned and walked across to where Rakeri and Veovis stood. "Forgive me, Lord Rakeri, but I have been suffering from an illness these past few weeks. It has left me feeling rather weak . . . light-headed." He glanced at Veovis, who was watching him hawkishly now. "I feel it coming on now, and beg you to excuse me."

Rakeri, who had no idea what was going on, gave a tiny bow of his head. "I commiserate, Aitrus, but maybe my house surgeon could help?"

"That is kind of you, my Lord, but I really ought to go home."

Rakeri shook his head, a look of disappointment in his eyes. "I am sorry about that. I had hoped to talk with you."

Aitrus bowed low, then turned to Veovis. "And may good fortune shine down on you, Veovis. I am sorry that I cannot be there for the celebration of your Korfah V'ja."

There was a black anger now behind Veovis's eyes, yet if he felt like saying something, he kept it well in check. He nodded curtly.

Aitrus stood there a moment longer, wondering whether something more ought to be said; then, knowing that the situation was irreparable, he turned on his heel and walked across to where Anna stood beside his mother.

"Aitrus," Tasera said, her curiosity almost overwhelming her by now, "what is going on?"

"Ah-na and I are leaving," he said, making no attempt to explain how things were. "Ask Father."

Anna was staring at him now, bemused. "Aitrus? What's happening?"

"Later," he said, then took her arm and turned her, leading her out through the gathered ranks of guildsmen and their families, heading back toward the boat.

AITRUS WAS STANDING AT THE STERN OF THE boat, chewing on a thumbnail and staring back at the great rock of K'veer as it slid into the darkened distance.

"You do not want to know."

Anna, sitting just below him, let out an exasperated sigh. "I am not blind, Aitrus. I saw how Veovis looked at you."

"There was a misunderstanding."

Anna waited, conscious of how pained he was by all
this. After a moment he spoke again.

"He said you were not invited."

"Ah . . . I see."

"He said it was because you were not D'ni."

"That much is undeniable."

Aitrus was silent a moment, then, "It was an impossible situation, Ah-na. He made me choose."

"And you chose me?"

"Yes."

"Why?"

"Because he was not right to make me choose."

ANNA WAS DRESSING THE NEXT MORNING
when there was a hammering on the door downstairs.
It was still very early and it was unusual for anyone to
call at this hour. Going over to her door, she opened it
a crack, listening.

There was a murmured exchange between Kahlis
and his steward. Then,

"Here? Are you sure?"

There was silence for a moment, then:

"Lord Veovis! Welcome! To what do we owe this
most pleasant surprise?"

"I have come to see your son, Master Kahlis. Is he at home?"

"He is. I shall go and see if he has risen. If you would take a seat, meanwhile. I'll not be long."

A hand briefly brushed her arm. She turned, her heart thumping, and found herself staring into Aitrus's face.

"Aitrus!"

"Will you come down with me, Ah-na?"

She hesitated, then shook her head. "This is between you two."

"No. This is about *you*, Ah-na. You ought to be there."

VEOVIS STOOD AS THEY STEPPED INTO THE ROOM.

"Aitrus," he said, coming across the room, both hands extended. "Will you forgive me?"

Aitrus took his hands, tentatively at first, then with a greater firmness.

"That depends."

"I understand. I handled things badly. I know that, and I am sorry for it." He looked past Aitrus to where Anna stood. "And you, Ah-na. I owe you an apology, too."

"You do, indeed," Aitrus said sternly.

Veovis nodded, accepting the rebuke. "Yes. And that is why I have brought you a present. To try to make amends."

He turned and, going back across, picked up a box and brought it back, handing it to Anna. It was a small, square box with tiny airholes in one side of it.

She stared at it a moment, then untied the bright red ribbon and lifted the lid . . . and then looked up at Veovis, laughing.

"Why, it's beautiful! What is it?"

Carefully, cupping it in one hand, she lifted out a tiny creature—a veritable fur ball, its long silky coat the dark, brown-black of rich loam. Its large, cobalt-colored eyes stared up at her.

"It is a reekoo," Veovis said. "It comes from Ader Jamat."

Aitrus, who had turned to look, now smiled. "Thank you. It was a kind thought."

Veovis sighed, then, somberly. "I am sorry you were not there last night, Aitrus."

"And I. Yet we must resolve this matter, no?"

Anna, who was stroking the rippled, leathery neck of the tiny creature, looked up, glancing from one to the other. So it was not settled, even now.

Veovis took a long breath, then nodded. "Tonight," he said. "Come to my rooms. We'll talk about it then."

IT WAS VERY LATE WHEN HE CAME BACK THAT night. Anna waited up, listening as his footsteps came up the stairs. As he made to pass her room, she opened the door and stepped out.

"Aitrus?" she whispered.

Aitrus turned. He looked weary.

"Is everything all right now?"

He stared at her, then, "You had better come to my study, Ah-na. We need to talk."

The words seemed ominous. Anna nodded, then followed him down the long corridor and into his room.

"Well?" she asked, as she took a chair, facing him.

Aitrus shrugged. "I am afraid Veovis is intractable."

"Intractable? In what way? You are friends again, are you not?"

"Perhaps. But he will not bend on one important matter."

"And that is?"

Aitrus looked down glumly. "He says that as you are not D'ni, he will not countenance you going into an Age, no, nor of learning *anything* about D'ni books. He claims it is not right."

"Then you said nothing of our visit to Ko'ah?"

Aitrus hesitated, then shook his head.

"Can I ask why? It is unlike you to be so indirect."

"Maybe. But I had no will to fight Veovis a second time."

"So did you promise him anything?"

"No. I said only that I would consider what he said."

"And was that enough for him?"

"For now."

She stared at him a moment, then, "So what *have* you decided?"

His eyes met hers again. "Can I hide nothing from you, Ah-na?"

"No. But then you have had little practice in hiding what you feel from people, Aitrus."

Aitrus stared at her for a long time, then sighed. "So you think I should abandon my plan?"

"Your plan?"

In answer, he opened the top right-hand drawer of his desk and took out a big, leather-bound book. It was a *book*—a D'ni book—she could see that at a glance. But when he opened it, there was no box on the front right-hand page, and the inside pages were blank.

She stared at it. "What is it?"

"It is a *Kortee'nea*," he said. "A blank book, waiting to be written."

Anna looked up, her mouth falling open slightly.

"I have had it for a year now," he answered. "I have been making notes toward an Age. One I myself am writing. And I thought . . . well, I thought that perhaps you might like to help me. But now . . . "

She saw what he meant. There was a choice. Defy

Veovis and lie about what they were doing, or go along with Veovis's wishes and deny themselves this.

"And what do you want, Aitrus?" she asked quietly, her dark eyes probing his. "What do you *really* want?"

"I want to teach you everything," he said. "Everything I know."

IN THE MONTHS THAT FOLLOWED, THE RELA-tionship between Aitrus and Veovis was strained. As if both sensed that all was not well between them, they kept much to themselves. It was a situation that could not last long, however, and a chance remark to Veovis by a young man from the Guild of Maintainers brought things to a head once more.

Aitrus was in his rooms at the Guild Hall, when Veovis burst in upon him unannounced.

"Is it true?" Veovis demanded, leaning across the desk.

Aitrus stared at his old friend in amazement. Veovis's face was suffused with anger. The muscles stood out at his neck.

"Is *what* true?

"The girl . . . the outsider . . . are you teaching her to Write? How could you, Aitrus! After all you promised!"

"I promised nothing. I said only that I would consider your words."

"That's pure sophistry, and you know it! You lied to me, Aitrus. You lied and deceived me. And not only me, but D'ni itself!"

"Now come," Aitrus said, standing.

"You are a traitor, Aitrus! And you can be sure I shall be taking this matter before the Council!"

And with that Veovis turned and stormed from the room. Aitrus stood there a moment, half in shock, staring at the open doorway. Since the Maintainers inspection two weeks back he had feared this moment. Veovis wouldn't go to the Council, surely? But he knew Veovis. His friend was not one to make idle threats.

ANNA SAT IN THE WINDOW OF HER ROOM, THE tiny reekoo asleep in her lap as she gazed out over the ancient city and the harbor far below.

They had come that morning—six uniformed guards from the Guild of Maintainers and the great Lord R'hira himself. Kahlis and Aitrus had greeted them at the door, then stood back as Guild Master Sijarun, walked through and opened the door to the

Book Room, removing both the Book of Ko'ah and the new, uncompleted book that had no name.

The decision of the Council had been unanimous— Kahlis and his son were given no voice in the matter. It had been ruled that there had been a serious breach of protocol. In future, no one who was not of D'ni blood would be allowed to see a Book or visit an Age. It was, Veovis had argued, important that they set a precedent. And so they had.

Anna sighed. It was all her fault. And now Aitrus was in despair. Even now he sat in his study, wrestling with the question of whether to resign his seat on the Council.

She had seen Kahlis's face, and Tasera's. To lose a Book, Aitrus had once told her, was a matter of the gravest importance, but to have one taken forcibly, by order of the Council, was far, far worse. And she had brought that upon them. She groaned softly.

There was no way she might make amends. No way, unless . . .

THE OLD MAN LOOKED ACROSS AT ANNA, staring at her through half-lidded eyes, then, pulling his cloak about him, he answered her.

"I do not know," he said, shaking his head sadly. "I really do not know. Even if we find something . . ."

"They will listen. They *have* to listen."

Kedri, Master of the Guild of Legislators, lifted his shoulders in a shrug. Then, with a sad smile. "All right. I shall try my best, young Ah-na. For you, and for my dear friend Aitrus."

He sat there for a long time after she had gone, staring straight ahead, as if in a trance. It was thus that his assistant, Haran, found him.

"Master? Are you all right?"

Kedri slowly lifted his head, his eyes focusing on the young man. "What? Oh, forgive me, Haran. I was far away. Remembering."

Haran smiled and bowed his head. "I just came to say that the new intake of cadets is here. A dozen keen young students, fresh from the academy. What shall I do with them?"

Normally, Kedri would have found them some anodyne assignment—an exercise in dust-dry law, overseen by some bored assistant or other—but the arrival of this new intake coincided perfectly with his need.

If he *was* to search back through the records, he would need help—and what better help that a dozen keen young men, anxious to impress him? At the same time, he needed to be discreet. If word of his activities got back to the Council, who knew what fuss might ensue, particularly if young Lord Veovis got wind of it? By assigning these cadets to the Guild Age of Gadar—to search among the legal records stored in the Great Library there—he could split two rocks with a single blow, as the old saying went.

"Take them to the Book Room," he said. "I'll address them there. I have a task for them."

Haran stared back at him a moment, surprised, then, recollecting himself, he bowed low and quickly hurried away.

It was strange that the girl, Ah-na, had come to him this morning, for only the evening before he had dreamt of the time he had spent with the Surveyors thirty years ago. It was then that he had first come to know young Aitrus. Aitrus had been assigned to him—to show him how things worked and answer his every query. They had got on well from the start and had been friends ever since.

As far as Ah-na was concerned, he had met her only once before, when Aitrus brought her to his house, but he had liked her instantly, and saw at once why Aitrus was fascinated by her. She had a sharp intelligence and an inquisitive mind that were the match of any guildsmen. It had crossed his mind at once that, had she been D'ni, she would have made young Aitrus the perfect bride.

Even so, it surprised him still that she had come and not Aitrus, for he had half-expected Aitrus to pay him a call.

Kedri sat back, stretching his neck muscles and then turning his head from side to side, trying to relieve the tension he was feeling.

What he had agreed to do would not make him a popular man in certain circles, yet it had been a simple choice: to help his young friend Aitrus or abandon him.

Kedri sighed heavily. The Great Library of Legislation on Gadar contained a mass of information stretching back over six thousand years—the handwritten minutes of countless Council meetings and hearings, of guild committees and tribunals, not to speak of the endless shelves of private communications between Guild Masters. It would be like digging for one specific tiny crystal in the middle of a mountain.

And he had two weeks and a dozen keen young men to do it.

LORD ENEAH SAT AT HIS DESK, AITRUS'S cloak of office lay folded on the desk before him. It had come that morning, along with that of Aitrus's father, Kahlis. Eneah had dealt with Kahlis, sending the cloak back to the Grand Master of the Surveyors.

Whatever the rights or wrongs of the issue, Kahlis was clearly not to blame. But Aitrus's conduct was a different matter entirely.

It was fairly simple, really. Either he accepted Aitrus's resignation now and ended the rumors and speculation, or he left matters to the Guild of Surveyors, who, so he understood, had already instigated investigations into the conduct of their representative.

Whatever happened now, the damage was already done. The vote in Council had betrayed the mood of the guilds. In teaching the outsider D'ni, and in showing her an Age, Aitrus had not merely exceeded his brief, but had shown poor judgment. Some even claimed that he had been bewitched by the young girl and had lost his senses, but Eneah doubted that. Those who said that did not know Aitrus.

Yet Aitrus had been injudicious.

Eneah straightened slightly. He had not slept at all last night and every joint ached as if it had been dipped in hot oil, but that was not unusual. These days he lived in constant pain.

With a small, regretful sigh, he drew a sheet of paper to him and, taking a quill pen from the inkstand, quickly wrote an acceptance letter then signed his name. Once the remaining Lords had set their names to it, the letter would be sealed and incorporated into the

public record. In the meantime, a notice would be posted throughout D'ni, advising the citizens of this news.

And so ended a promising career.

Eneah reached across and rang his summons bell.
At once a secretary appeared at the door.

"Take this to Lord R'hira at once.

ANNA STOOD BEFORE THE THREE OF THEM.

"So you wish to leave?" Kahlis asked.

"No," she answered. "You have all been kind to me.
Yet I feel I ought to. I have brought so much trouble to
this household."

"The choice was mine," Aitrus said. "If anyone
should leave, it should be me."

"That would be wrong," Anna said. "Besides, I shall
be comfortable enough at Lord Eneah's mansion."

"Nonsense!" Tasera said, speaking for the first time
since Anna had summoned them to this meeting. "I
will not hear of it! Lord Eneah is an old man! No. You
will stay here!"

Anna stared at Tasera, astonished. She had thought
Tasera most of all would have wanted her gone. Since the
Council's meeting she had been practically ostracized. Yet
Tasera seemed by far the most indignant of the three.

"Then it is settled," Kahlis said, smiling proudly at his wife, "Ah-na stays here, as family."

IT WAS AN ANCIENT BOOK, GREAT WHORLS OF faded color dotting the pale gray of its musty leather cover like dusty jewels. Looking down at it, Guild Master Kedri found himself smiling. Until yesterday it had remained unread upon its shelf for close on nineteen hundred years.

Kedri looked up at Anna, who sat to one side of the desk, then addressed the young man. "Forgive me, Guildsman, but how exactly did you find this? It is not as if this lay directly on the path of our main search."

The young man bowed his head nervously, then spoke. "It was something you said, Master Kedri. Last night, at supper. You know, about trying to identify possible factors in the search."

"Go on."

"It got me thinking, Master, asking myself just what kind of person might be granted access to an Age. That is, what kind of non-D'ni person, naturally."

"And?"

"Well . . . my first thought was that such a person would have to have the ear of someone important—

someone very important, indeed, perhaps even one of the Five. And so I went to the list of clerks . . . "

"Clerks?"

"To the Five."

"Ah . . . and what did that give you?"

The young man smiled. "Six names."

Already Kedri was ahead of him. "Names that were not D'ni, I presume."

"Yes, Master. There was a time when some of the more talented natives—from Guild Ages and the like—were permitted to come here, into D'ni itself."

Kedri raised an eyebrow. "Now *that* I did not know."

"No, Master, for it was a very long time ago, very shortly after the Council was first set up in its present form, not long after the Age of Kings."

"I see. And these clerks . . . were they restricted to D'ni, or were they granted access to other Ages?"

The guildsman nodded at the book before Kedri. "I have marked the relevant passages, Master. I am sure there are further entries in the other books."

There was a small pile of books on the floor behind the young guildsman.

Anna felt a tingle of excitement pass through her. She stood and, crouching, lifted one of the books and opened it, sniffing in the scent of great age as it wafted up to her off the page.

It was an old script, different in several ways from its modern counterpart, yet easily decipherable. In several places the ink had faded almost to nothing, yet the meaning of the text was quite clear.

Anna looked across at Kedri and nodded, a feeling of deep satisfaction flooding her at that moment.

"It is not too old then, Master?" the young guildsman asked. "I thought, perhaps, that its age might possibly invalidate it."

"A precedent is a precedent," Kedri said, looking to Anna, then reading the passage once again. "We shall find further sources to verify this, no doubt—and further instances, I warrant."

He closed the book, then nodded. "You have done well, guildsman."

"Thank you, Master," the young man answered, bowing low, a great beam of a smile on his face.

"Thank *you*, Guildsman . . . "

"Neferus, Master. Guildsman Neferus."

WHAT HAD TAKEN THE FULL VOTE OF THE Council to decide, took but a single signature to revoke.

As Lord Eneah pushed the document away, he felt a great weight slip from him. He was glad Master Kedri had found what he had found, for he had never felt quite at ease with the decision, yet looking up, he saw in his mind the closed face of Lord Rakeri, and knew that all the Five were not as pleased as he.

The Books would be returned to Master Kahlis, and Ah-na would be free to travel in them. Yet all was not quite as it had been. Aitrus still refused to take up his vacated role as representative of the Guild of Surveyors. He said he had had enough of votes and meetings, and maybe he was right. And as for Veovis . . .

Eneah dropped the pen back into the inkstand and leaned back, weary now that it was all over.

Young Veovis had called on him earlier that day, determined to have his say. He had not been rude, nor had he challenged in any way the validity of Master Kedri's discoveries, yet it was clear that he resented the Legislator's intrusion in Council matters, and was dead set against allowing Ah-na entry into any D'ni Age. He had ended by begging Lord Eneah to set the ancient precedent aside and endorse the Council's decision, but Eneah had told him he could not do that.

The law *was* the law, after all. Precedent was precedent. It was the D'ni way and had been for a thousand generations.

And so Veovis had left, under a cloud, angry and resentful, and who knew what trouble would come of that?

But so it is, Eneah thought, *looking about him at the empty study. No single man, however great or powerful, is more important than D'ni.*

He smiled, knowing that soon he would be little more than a name, another statue in the Great Hall of the Lords.

"So it is," he said quietly. "And so it must be. Until the end of time."

And with that he stood, walked across the room and out, moving slowly, silently, like a shadow on the rock.

PART FOUR: GEMEDET

A NNA WAITED, CROUCHED JUST IN FRONT of Aitrus in the narrow tunnel, looking out into the bottom of the well. Just below her, the surface of the tiny, circular pool was black. Slowly, very slowly, sunlight crept down the smooth, black wall facing her, a pure light, almost unreal it seemed so bright, each separate shaft a solid, shining bar in that penumbral darkness.

It was cool and silent, yet overhead, far above the surface, the sun approached its zenith.

"Wait . . . " Aitrus said softly. "Just a moment longer."

The sunlight touched the still, curved edge of the water. A moment later the water's depths were breached, the straight beam bent, refracted by the clear liquid.

Anna gasped. It was beautiful. The well had a solid wooden lid, but Aitrus had cut an intricate design into the wood. As the sun climbed directly above the well, so each part of that design was slowly etched upon the dark circle of the pool, until the whole of it could be seen, burning like shafts of brilliant fire in the cool, translucent depths of the water.

The D'ni word Shorah. *"Peace."*

Anna smiled and turned to look at Aitrus, seeing how the word was reflected in the black centers of his pupils.

"So that's what you were doing," she said quietly. "I wondered."

She turned back, knowing, without needing to be told, that its beauty was transient, would be gone just as soon as the sun moved from its zenith and the sunlight climbed the wall again.

"I made it for you," he said.

I know, she thought. Aloud, she said, "Thank you. It's beautiful."

"Isn't it?"

They watched, together in the silence, until, with a final, glittering wink, the brightness in the pool was gone.

Anna stared into the blackness and sighed.

"What are you thinking?" he asked, after a moment.

"I was thinking of my father."

"Ah . . . " He was silent a long while, then. "Come. Let's go back up."

Anna turned and followed, half-crouched as she walked along the tiny tunnel, then straightening to climb the twisting flight of steps that had been cut from the rock. Aitrus had worked weeks on this. And all for that one small instant of magic.

A tiny shiver passed through her. She watched him climb the steps ahead of her, noticing how neatly his hair was clipped at his neck, how strong his back and arms were, how broad his shoulders, and realized just how familiar he had become these last few years.

As familiar almost as this Age they had slowly built together.

Stepping out into the sunlight beside Aitrus, Anna smiled. It was so green. All she could see was green. Forest and grasslands, wood and plain. Why, even the slow, meandering rivers were green with trailing weed.

Only the sky was blue. A deep, water-heavy blue. In the distance a great raft of huge white clouds drifted slowly from right to left, their movement almost imperceptible, casting deep shadows on the hills and valleys below.

It had all seemed strange at first, after the desert landscape she had known all her life. So strange, that she had spent hours simply staring at the clouds, fascinated by them.

She looked to Aitrus. He was wearing his D'ni glasses now, to protect his eyes against the glare of the sun. They all wore them when not in D'ni. Only she did not have to.

"We should go north next," she said. "To the mountains. I could map that area beyond the lake."

Aitrus smiled. "Perhaps. Or maybe that long valley to the northeast of here."

She looked down, smiling, knowing exactly why he

was interested in that area. They had passed through it several weeks ago on their way back from the peninsula and had noticed signs of long-dormant volcanic activity. She had seen the tiny gleam of interest in his eyes.

"If you want."

They walked on, talking as they went, continuing the discussion they had begun earlier that day. Wherever they went, they talked, making observations on the physical signs of this world, and debating which small changes to the words and phrasing might have caused this effect or that.

Sometimes Aitrus would stop, crouch down with the notepad balanced on his knee, and would write down something he or she had said, wanting to capture it, ready to enter it in the book of commentary they had begun six months back. Already they had filled half the great ledger with their observations, and each day they added to it, with words and maps and drawings.

A long slope led to the encampment, which was sighted at the head of a verdant valley. To one side of that grassy plateau, the earth had folded and a great slab of smooth black rock jutted from the green. Just above it a slow-moving river pooled, then fell sheer two hundred feet to the valley floor in a clear, narrow curtain.

The sound of the falls was ever-present, a counter-point to the exotic, echoing cries of birds from the wood that climbed the steep slope behind them. To the north were mountains, to the south the great ocean.

It was a beautiful place.

Aitrus's tent was to the left of the camp, its long frame of green canvas blending with the background. A smaller, circular tent, its canvas a vivid yellow, stood just beside and was used for stores. Until a week ago there had been a third tent, the twin of Aitrus's, but now that the cabin was habitable, Anna had moved in. It was not finished yet—Aitrus had yet to cut and fit the wooden floor—but the roof was on and it was dry. Beside Anna's section, which was screened off, Aitrus had set up a temporary lab, which they planned to use until they had built a proper, permanent laboratory a little way farther up the slope.

They walked across. A trestle table stood just outside Aitrus's tent, in the shadow of the canvas awning. On top of it, its corners held down by tiny copper weights, was the map Anna had been working on earlier, a clear thin cover of D'ni polymer laid over it in case of rain.

The map was remarkably detailed, a color key on the right-hand side of the sheet making sense of the intricate pattern of colors on the map itself. Areas of the sheet were blank, where they had not yet surveyed the land, but where they had, Anna had provided a vivid guide to it—one that not only made sense of its essential topography but also gave a clue to the types of soil and thus vegetation that overlay the deeper rock formations. It was all, she said, using one of her father's favorite terms, "a question of edaphology."

Maybe it was because she was from the surface, but her grasp of how the kind of rock affected the visible features of the land was far more refined than his, almost instinctive. Often she did not have to analyze a rock sample but knew it by its feel, its color and its texture. His instinct was for the pressures and stresses within the rock that provided what one saw with its underlying structure.

At first it had astonished Aitrus that she had known so much of rocks and minerals and the complex art of mapping the rock, and even when he learned more of her father and how she had helped him, he was still amazed that she had grasped quite so much in so brief a time. Yet as the weeks went on, his surprise had turned to delight, knowing that here at last was someone with whom he might share his lifelong fascination with the rock.

It was not long before he had begun to teach her the D'ni names for the different types of rock and the terms his people used to describe the various geological processes. Anna learned easily and was soon fluent enough to hold those conversations which, through to today, had never ceased between them. After a while Aitrus had begun to push her, testing her, as if to find the limits of her intelligence, but it seemed there were no bounds to what she was capable of.

Right now, however, the two of them stood beside the trestle table. Aitrus studied the half-completed map a moment then tapped an area in the top left corner with his forefinger.

"We could start here, Ah-na, where the river bends and drops. It would give us the opportunity to map all of this area to the west of the river. That would take, what? Two days?"

Anna studied the blank area on her map and nodded. "Two. Three at most."

"Three it is. We could take the tent and camp there. Then we could spend a day or two exploring the valley. There are cave systems there. Did you see them?"

Anna smiled. "I saw."

"Good. And once we've finished there, we could come back here and spend a couple of days writing things up."

"Can the guild spare you that long?"

"If they need me urgently, they'll send someone. But I doubt it. Things are slow at present, and until the Guild of Miners present their report on the new excavation, that is how it will remain. We might as well use the time fruitfully."

"Aitrus?"

"Yes?"

"Can we set out a little later tomorrow? In the afternoon, perhaps?"

"You want to see the well again?"

Anna nodded.

"All right. I guess it will take most of the morning to pack what we need, anyway."

She smiled. That was so like Aitrus. Rather than admit to indulging her, he would always find some excuse to let her have her way.

"And Aitrus?"

He turned, clearly distracted. "Yes?"

"Oh, nothing . . . Nothing important, anyway."

THAT EVENING IT RAINED: A WARM, HEAVY
rain that thundered on the roof of the cabin and
filled the valley like a huge, shimmering mist of silver.

Anna stepped out into the downpour, raising her
arms, her head back, savoring the feel of the rain
against her skin.

Just across from her, Aitrus peeked out from his
tent and, seeing what she was doing, called out to her.

"Ah-na! What are you doing? You'll be soaked to
the skin!"

Laughing, she turned to face him, then, on whim,
began to dance, whirling around and around, her bare
feet flying across the wet grass.

"Ah-na!"

She stopped, facing him, then put a hand out.

"Come, Aitrus! Join me!"

Aitrus hesitated, then, reluctantly, yet smiling all the
same, he stepped out. Almost instantly he was soaked,
his hair plastered to his head.

He took her hand.

"Come!" she said, her eyes shining brightly, excit-
edly, "let's dance!" And without warning, she began
to whirl him around and around beneath the open
sky, the light from the hanging lanterns in front
of the cabin turning the fall of rain into a cascade
of silver.

Exhilarated, Aitrus whooped loudly, then stopped dead. He was laughing, his whole face alive as she had never seen it before.

"Isn't it *wonderful?*" she asked, almost shouting against the noise of the downpour.

"Marvelous!" he shouted back, then, unexpectedly, he grabbed her close and whirled around and around again, until, giddy from their circling, he stopped, swaying and coughing and laughing.

Anna, too, was laughing. She put her head back, drinking in the pure, clean water from the sky. Rain! The wonder of rain!

ANNA STOOD BEHIND THE WOODEN PARTITION, toweling her hair. Outside, the rain still fell, but now it could be heard only as a gentle, murmuring patter against the roof. Soon the storm would pass.

She had changed into a dry, woolen dress of cyan blue, her favorite color, fastened at the waist with a simple cord.

Folding the towel, she dropped it onto the end of her pallet bed then turned full circle, looking about her. There were books wherever she looked, on shelves and surfaces, and, on the narrow wooden table in the corner, scientific equipment, the polished brasswork gleaming in the lamplight.

Anna sighed, feeling a real contentment. For the first time in a long, long while, she was happy.

To be honest, she had never worked so hard, nor felt so good. Before Aitrus had asked her to work with him on the creation of this Age, she had felt useless, but now . . .

Now she had a problem.

Anna sat on the edge of her low bed, staring at the bare earth floor. Perhaps it was the dance. Perhaps it was that glimpse of Aitrus, happy just as she was happy. Was that an illusion? Was it a transient thing? Or could it last?

And besides . . .

There was a knock on the door of the cabin. Anna looked up, startled. It was Aitrus's habit to spend an hour at this time writing up his journal for the day.

"Come in."

Aitrus stepped inside, his right hand drawing his dark hair back from his brow.

"I wondered if you were all right."

She smiled up at him. "I'm fine. It was only rain."

Aitrus stood there a moment, hesitant, not sure just what to say, then: "Would you like a game of *Gemedet?*"

"All right."

He grinned, then nodded and turned away, returning to the tent to bring the grid. Smiling, Anna stood, then went across to clear a space on the table.

Gemedet, or six-in-a-line, was the most popular of D'ni games. She had seen a close variant of the game in Tadjinar, played by the Chinese merchants, but the D'ni version was played not on a two-dimensional board but on a complex three-dimensional grid, nine squares to a side.

It was, she thought, the perfect game for a race embedded in the rock, whose thinking was not lateral but spatial.

Aitrus returned a moment later, setting the grid down on the table. It was a beautiful thing, of hand-carved lilac jade, as delicate-looking as a honeycomb yet strong. Strong enough to have survived a thousand games without a single chip or blemish.

The base of the grid was a polished hemisphere of topaz on which the grid revolved smoothly. Long, silver tweezers, called *re'dantee*, were used to slip the playing pieces into place, while the pieces themselves were simple polished ovoids of green tourmaline and dark red almandine.

Both the re'dantee and the "stones" were kept in a velvet-lined box, which Aitrus now opened, placing it on the table beside the grid, so that both of them could easily reach it.

Anna smiled. She had fallen in love with the set at first sight.

They sat, facing each other across the table. As ever, Anna went first, slipping her first "stone" into place, deep in the heart of the grid, giving herself the maximum of options.

For an hour or more they played, in total silence, each concentrating on the pattern of the stones. After a while the patter of rain on the roof stopped. Night birds called in the darkness of the woods outside. Inside the game went on, beneath the lantern's light.

Finally, she saw that she had lost. Aitrus had only to place a single stone in the bottom left-hand corner and there was no way she could stop him making six.

Anna looked up and saw, by his smile, that he knew.

"Another game?"

She shook her head. Was now the time to speak? To tell him what she had been thinking earlier?

"What is it?" he asked gently.

Anna looked down. "I'm tired, that's all."

"Are you sure?"

She gave a single nod. It had been a good day—an almost perfect day—why spoil it?

"Shall I pack the game away?" he asked, after a moment.

"No," she said, looking up at him and smiling; content now that she had decided. "I'll do that in the morning. Besides, I want to see how you managed to beat me."

Aitrus grinned. "Experience, that's all."

At that moment, there did not seem to be so many years' difference in their ages. In human terms, Aitrus was old—as old, almost, as her father—but in D'ni terms he was still a very young man. Why, it was quite likely that he would live another two centuries and more. But was that also why she was afraid to speak of what she felt?

"I'll leave you, then," he said, standing, the lamp-light glinting in his fine, dark hair. "Good night. Sleep well, Ah-na."

"And you," she said, standing.

He smiled. And then he left, leaving her staring at the door, the words she wanted so much to say unsaid, while outside the night birds called, their cries echoing across the darkness of the valley.

THE VALLEY WAS A DEEP GASH IN THE surounding land, cut not by a river but by older, far more violent processes. Bare rock jutted from the slopes on either side, the folded pattern of its strata long exposed to the elements so that the softer rocks had been heavily eroded, leaving great shelves of harder rock. At one end of the valley, in the shadow of a particularly long shelf, were the caves. It was there that they began their survey.

Anna knew what Aitrus was looking for, and it was not long before he found it.

"Ah-na! Come here! Look!"

She went across to where Aitrus was crouched in the deep shadow of the overhang and looked.

"Well?" he said, looking up at her triumphantly.

It was old and worn, but there was no doubting what it was. It was the puckered mouth of a diatreme—a volcanic vent—formed long ago by high pressure gases drilling their way through the crustal rocks.

For the past two days they had kept coming upon signs that there was a volcano somewhere close by. Volcanic deposits had been scattered all about this area, but this was the first vent they had found.

From the look of it the volcano was an old one, dormant for many centuries.

"I thought we'd made a stable world."

He smiled. "We did. But even stable worlds must be formed. Volcanoes are part of the growing process of an Age. Even the best of worlds must have them!"

"So where is it?" she asked.

He stood, then turned, pointing straight through the rock toward the north.

"There, I'd guess."

"Do you want to go and look for it?"

Aitrus shrugged, then. "If you wouldn't mind."

Anna laughed. "Why should I? It's a volcano. *Our* volcano. Our first!"

He grinned, as if he had not thought of that, then nodded. "Come then. If I'm right, it can't be far."

THE CALDERA WAS STILL VISIBLE, BUT TIME and weather had worn it down. Trees covered its shallow slopes and filled the great bowl of the volcano, but here and there the thin covering of soil gave way to fissures and vents whose darkness hinted at great depths.

It was old. Far older than they had first thought. Not thousands, but millions of years old.

It was this part that Anna had taken a little while to grasp. The Ages to which they linked were not made by them, they already existed, for the making of worlds was a process that took not months but long millennia. Aitrus, trying to make things absolutely clear to her, had summed it up thus:

"These Ages are worlds that do exist, or have existed, or shall. Providing the description fits, there is no limitation of time or space. The link is made regardless."

And so, too, this world of theirs, their Age, which they had called Gemedet, after the game. It, too, existed, or had existed, or would. But where it was or when they did not know.

Not that it mattered most of the time, but on occasion she did wonder just where they were in the night sky, and when—whether at the beginning of the universe or somewhere near the end of that vast process.

The very thought of it humbled her, made her understand why her father had believed in a Maker who had fashioned it all. Having "written," having seen the great skill and subtlety involved merely in creating a *link* to these worlds, she now found herself in awe of the infinite care that had gone into the making of the originals to which their templates linked.

Personally, she could not believe that blind process had made it all. It was, for her, quite inconceivable, bearing in mind the complexity and variety of life. Yet in this, if nothing else, Aitrus differed from her. His was, or so he claimed, a more rational approach, more *scientific*—as if understanding the product of such processes were a key to understanding the why of them existing in the first place.

Aitrus had walked down the tree-strewn slope, making his way between the boulders, until he stood beside one of the larger vents. Resting his chest against the sloping wall of the vent, he leaned out, peering into the darkness. For a moment he was perfectly still, then he turned his head, looking back at her through his D'ni glasses.

"Shall we go in?"

Anna smiled. "All right, but we'll need to bring a rope from the camp."

Aitrus grinned. "And lamps, and . . . "

". . . your notebook."

A look of perfect understanding passed between them. It was time to explore the volcano.

THEY GOT BACK TO THE ENCAMPMENT THREE days later than they had planned, to find that a message had been delivered from D'ni. It lay upon the map table in its dark blue waterproof wrapping.

While Anna began to stow away their equipment, Aitrus broke the seal of the package and took out the letter. He knew it was not urgent—they would have sent a Messenger into the Age to find him if it was— but it was unusual. Unfolding the letter, he squinted at it through the lenses of his glasses. It was from his old friend Kedri, and concerned a query Aitrus had put to him the last time they had met for supper.

He read it through quickly, then, smiling, he slipped the paper into his tunic pocket.

"Well?" Anna asked, coming alongside him. "Anything important?"

"No, but I need to go back."

"Should we pack?"

He shook his head. "No. I only need to be away an hour or two. I'll go later tonight. You can stay here. I'll come back as soon as I can."

Anna smiled. "You should have a bath when you get back to D'ni."

"A bath?" He looked mock-offended. "Are you saying I smell, Ti'ana?"

"You positively reek of sulphur!" she said, grinning now. "Like Old Beelzebub himself!"

He smiled at that. In the caves beneath the caldera, she had taught him much about the mythology and gods of the surface, including the demons whom, according to many religions, lived in the regions beneath the earth.

"If only they knew the reality of it," she had said. "They'd be amazed."

It was then that he had given her her new name— *Ti'ana*, which in D'ni meant "story-teller," as well as punning on her surface name. "Do you need me to cook you something before you go?"

"I'd rather you helped me sort those samples."

"All right," she said, her smile broadening. "I'll do the tests, you can write up the notes."

AITRUS LOOKED ABOUT HIM AT THE TENT. ALL was neat and orderly. His notebook was open on the small table by his bed, the ink of the latest entry not yet dry. It was time to link back.

Anna was in her cabin. He would say goodnight to her, then go.

Aitrus went outside and stepped across to the cabin, knocking softly on the door. Usually she would call out to him, but this time there was nothing. Pushing the door open a little, he saw that she was not at her desk.

"Ti'ana?" he called softly. "Are you there?"

As if in answer he heard her soft snoring from behind the thin, wooden partition. Slipping inside, he tiptoed across and, drawing back the curtain, peered in.

Anna lay on her side on the pallet, facing him, her eyes closed, her features peaceful in sleep. The long journey back from the valley had clearly exhausted her. He crouched, watching her, drinking in the sight of her. She was so different from the women he had known all his life—those strong yet frail D'ni women with their pale skin and long faces.

It had been more than two months ago, when they had made their first, and as yet only, journey to the mountains north of the camp. On the way Anna had collected samples of various native flowers for later study. Yet, coming upon the wonder of a snow-covered slope—the first she had ever seen or touched or walked upon—she had taken the blooms from her pocket and scattered their petals over the snow. He had asked her what she was doing, and she had shrugged.

"I had to," she had said, staring at him. Then, pointing to the scattered petals, she had bid him look.

Aitrus closed his eyes, seeing them vividly, their bright shapes and colors starkly contrasted against the purity of the whiteness—like life and death.

It was then that he had decided, and every moment since had been but a confirmation of that decision— an affirmation of the feeling he had had at that moment, when, looking up from the petals, he had seen her face shining down at him like the sun itself.

Aitrus opened his eyes and saw that same face, occluded now in sleep, like the sun behind clouds, yet beautiful still. The most beautiful he had ever seen. At first he had not thought so, but time had trained his eyes to see her differently. He *knew* her now.

Aitrus stretched out his hand, tracing the contours of that sleeping face in the air above it, a feeling of such tenderness pervading him that he found his hand trembling. He drew it back, surprised by the strength of what he felt at that moment. Overwhelming, it was, like the rush of water over a fall.

He nodded to himself, then stood. It was time to go back to D'ni. Time to face his father, Kahlis.

"I CANNOT SAY THAT I HAVE NOT HALF-expected this," Kahlis was saying, "but I had hoped that you would, perhaps, have seen sense in time."

"I am sorry that you feel so, Father."

"Even if it is as you say, Aitrus, have you thought this through properly? Have you thought out the full implications of such a union? She is an outsider. A surface-dweller. And you, Aitrus, are D'ni—a Guild Master and a member of the Council. Such a marriage is unheard of."

"Maybe so. Yet there is no legal impediment to it." Aitrus took the letter from his tunic pocket and placed it on the desk before his father. "I asked Master Kedri to look into the matter, and that is his expert opinion."

Kahlis took the sheet of paper and unfolded it. For a moment he was silent, reading it, then he looked up, his eyes narrowed.

"And the age difference, Aitrus? Have you considered that? Right now you are the elder, but it will not always be so. Your life span is thrice hers. When you are still in your prime she will be an old woman. Have you thought of that?"

"I have," he answered. "Yet not to have her—to have never had her by my side—that would be death indeed."

"And what if I said I was against the marriage?"

Aitrus merely stared at him.

Kahlis stood, then came around his desk.

"You will not accept my advice, Aitrus. But I shall give you my blessing. That, I hope, you *will* accept."

"Gladly!" Aitrus said, then, reaching out, he took his father's hands in the D'ni way. "You will be proud of her, Father, I promise you!"

AITRUS LINKED BACK INTO THE CAVE ABOVE the encampment. Stepping out, he saw that nothing had changed. In the moonlight the camp looked peaceful, the tents to the left, the cabin to the right. Beyond and to the right the waterfall was like a sheet of silver, its constant noise lulling him.

Walking down between the trees he found that he was whistling softly, an old D'ni song his mother had once sang to him. He stopped, his eyes going to the cabin. There she slept. Ti'ana. His love.

"It cannot be wrong," he said quietly.

Aitrus felt a light touch on his shoulder and started. Turning, he found Anna standing there behind him. She was smiling, as if pleased by her little trick.

"What cannot be wrong?"

He swallowed. Now that the moment had come, he was afraid of it. Yet that fear was natural, it was there to be overcome.

"You and I," he answered, taking her hands.

Her eyes went down to where their hands met, then looked up to meet his own again. "What do you mean?"

"I mean I wish to marry you."

Her eyes slowly widened. She stared at him silently, as if in wonder.

"Well?" he asked, when the waiting grew too much. "*Will* you marry me, Ti'ana?"

"I will," she said, her voice so soft, so quiet, that he felt at first he had imagined it.

"You will?"

Anna nodded, the faintest trace of a smile coming to her lips.

"You *will!*" He whooped, then drew her close and, for the first time, embraced her. Her face was suddenly close to his, less than a hand's width away. The sight of it sobered him.

"I will be a good husband to you, Ti'ana, I promise. But you must promise me something."

"Promise what?"

"That you will be my partner in all things. My helpmate and companion, by my side always, in whatever I do."

Slowly the smile returned to her face. Then, leaning toward him, she gently kissed him. "I promise."

VEOVIS STORMED INTO THE ROOM, SLAMMING the door behind him. He grabbed an inkwell from the desk beside him and hurled it across the room, shattering it into tiny fragments.

"Never!" he said, glaring across the empty room. "Not while there's breath left in my body!"

His father, Rakeri, had broken the news to him an hour back. Aitrus was to be betrothed. At first, if anything, he had been indifferent to the news. He had not even heard that Aitrus was seeing anyone. Then, abruptly, he had understood. The girl! The surface-dweller!

Veovis stomped across the room and threw himself down into his chair, gnawing on a thumbnail.

"Never!" he said again, the word hissing from him with a real venom.

His father had explained how the Five had been approached, the documents of precedent laid before them. Again that was Kedri's fault, the traitor! Aitrus need only go before the full Council now to receive their blessing, and that was a formality.

Or had been, in the past.

Veovis took a long, calming breath, then turned his head, staring at the shattered fragments of glass as if he did not recognize the cause, then shuddered.

Never.

AITRUS STOOD BEFORE THE FIVE, AT THE center of the great chamber. All were present. Lord R'hira had read out the formal request; now, all that remained was for the Council to ratify the document.

R'hira stared at Aitrus a moment, then looked beyond him, his eyes raking the levels of the chamber.

"All those in favor?"

There was a chorus of "Ayes," some reluctant, others enthusiastic. For six thousand years the question had been asked and answered thus.

Lord R'hira smiled.

"And those against?" he asked, the question a formality.

"Nay."

R'hira had already turned the paper facedown. He had been about to congratulate young Aitrus. But the single voice brought him up sharp. He stared at Veovis, where he sat not two spans behind where Aitrus was standing.

"I beg pardon, Guild Master Veovis?"

Veovis stood. "I said 'Nay.'"

R'hira's wizened face blinked. All five Lords were leaning forward now, staring at Veovis. This was unheard of.

"Could I possibly have your reasons, Master Veovis?"

Veovis's face was a mask, expressionless. "I need give no reason. I am simply against." And he sat, as if that was that.

As indeed it was. The verdict of Council had to be unanimous in this matter. R'hira looked to Aitrus. The young man had his head down, his own expression unreadable; yet there was a tension to his figure that had not been there before.

"Master Aitrus . . . " he began, embarrassed. "It would seem . . . "

Aitrus looked up, his pale eyes hard like slate. "I understand, Lord R'hira. The Council has turned down my request."

R'hira, marking the immense dignity with which Aitrus bore this disappointment, gave a reluctant nod. "So it is."

"Then I will trouble you no more, my Lords."

Aitrus bowed to each of the Five in turn, then, turning on his heel, walked from the chamber, his head held high, not even glancing at Veovis as he passed.

"AITRUS! COME NOW, OPEN THE DOOR!"

Tasera stood before the door to her son's room, her husband just behind her in the shadows of the corridor.

When there was no answer, Tasera turned and looked to her husband. "Why did you not say something in Council, Kahlis?"

"I did," Kahlis said quietly, "but it made no difference."

"And is that *it*, then?" she asked, incredulous. "One man says nay and nay it is?"

There was the grating metallic noise of the latch being drawn back, and then the door eased open an inch.

"Forgive me, Mother," Aitrus said from within the darkness of the room. "I was asleep."

"I heard what happened in Council," she said. "We need to discuss what should be done."

"There's nothing can be done," he said. "The Council has given their answer."

No word, then, of Veovis. No individual blame. As if this were the genuine will of Council.

"Nonsense!" she said, angry now. Pushing past him, she went over to the table and lit the lamp.

Tasera turned, looking at him in the half light. Aitrus's face seemed gaunt, as if he had been ill, but he was still, beneath it all, the same strong man she had bred.

"I know you, Aitrus. You are a fighter. I also know how much Ti'ana means to you. Now, will you bow before this decision, or will you fight?"

"Fight? How can I fight? And what can I fight with? Can I force Veovis to change his mind? No. Neither he nor the Council would allow it! And as for persuasion . . ."

"Then beg."

"Beg?"

"If Ti'ana means that much to you, go to Lord Veovis and beg him to change his mind and grant you what you want. Go down on your knees before him if you must, but do not simply accept this."

"On my knees?" Aitrus stared at his mother, incredulous.

"Yes," she said, standing face-to-face with him. "What matters more to you, Aitrus? Your pride or your future happiness?"

"You want me to beg?"

Tasera shook her head. "You said yourself: He will not be forced or persuaded. What other course is open to you?"

"Aitrus is right."

Both turned. Anna was standing in the doorway.

"Ti'ana, I . . . " Aitrus began, but she raised a hand to bid him be silent. "I know what happened. Your father just told me."

"Then you must agree," Tasera said, appealing to her. "Aitrus must go to Veovis."

"Maybe," Anna said, nodding to her. Then she turned slightly, looking to Aitrus lovingly. "You know how proud I would be to be your wife, Aitrus. Prouder than any woman in the whole of D'ni. Yet I would not have you go down on your knees before that man, even if it meant we must spend our lives apart. It would be a violation, and I could not bear it. But there is, perhaps, another way . . . "

Aitrus raised his eyes and looked at Anna. For a long time he simply studied her, and then he nodded. "So be it, then," he said, "I will go to him. But I do not hold much hope."

VEOVIS AGREED TO MEET WITH AITRUS IN HIS father's study, Lord Rakeri a silent presence in his chair, there to ensure that things were kept within due bounds.

"So what is it that you want, Guildsman?" Veovis said, standing six paces from where Aitrus stood facing him, his hands clasped behind his back.

Aitrus met Veovis's masklike stare with his own. "I seek an explanation for your vote this morning."

"And I decline to give it."

"You do not like her, do you?"

Veovis shrugged. "As I said . . . "

". . . you decline to give your reasons."

Veovis nodded.

"You recall our meeting in the shaft all those years ago?"

"What of it?"

"You recall what happened . . . afterward? How I helped save your life?"

Veovis blinked. He took a long breath, then: "I was very grateful for your actions. But what of it? What bearing has it on this matter?"

"You made me a promise. Remember? You said then that if there was anything I wanted—*anything*—that was in your power to grant, then I should come to you and you would grant it."

Veovis stood there like a statue, his eyes like flints, staring back at Aitrus.

"*Do* you remember?"

"I remember."

"Then I ask you to keep your word, Lord Veovis, and give me your permission, before the full Council, to marry Ti'ana."

Veovis was silent for a long time. Finally he turned, looking to his father. Rakeri stared back at his son a moment, his eyes filled with a heavy sadness, then gave a single nod.

Veovis turned back. "I am a man of my word, and so your wish is granted, Aitrus, son of Kahlis, but from this day forth I wish neither to speak with you nor hear from you again. Whatever once existed between us is now at an end. All promises are met. You understand?"

Aitrus stared back at him, his face expressionless. "I understand. And thank you."

"You *thank* me?" Veovis laughed bitterly. "Just go, for I am sick of the sight of you."

PART FIVE: THE PHILOSOPHER

THE VESTIBULE WAS PACKED WITH GUILDS-men—Grand Masters and their assistants, great Lords, and other, humbler members of the central D'ni Council—all waiting to enter the great chamber for the debate. As ever before any momentous occasion, the place was buzzing with talk as small groups of cloaked members gathered between the fluted marble pillars to indulge in informal discussion of the new proposal.

At the center of one of the larger groups stood Aitrus, whose proposal it was. In the fifteen years since he had returned to Council, he had established himself as the unofficial leader of the more liberal faction in the House, and was often consulted by the Five on matters of policy. Today, however, he was distracted.

"Any news?" his friend Oren of the Guild of Chemists asked as he joined the group.

"Nothing yet," Aitrus answered.

"She'll be all right," Penjul, another close friend and a Master of the Guild of Legislators, said, laying a hand briefly on Aitrus's shoulder.

"I guess so," Aitrus said, but his concern was clear.

"So how will it go today?" Oren asked, looking about him at the dozen or so Masters who formed the core of their faction. "Does anyone have a clear idea?"

There were smiles. Oren, as a Chemist, always wanted a certain answer.

"Whichever way it goes, it will be close," Hamil, the eldest of their group and Grand Master of the Guild of Messengers, said, pulling at his long white beard. "Much will depend upon the eloquence of our friend here."

Oren looked to Aitrus. "Then we are lost," he said, a faint smile at one corner of his mouth. "Master Aitrus has but a single thing in his head today."

Aitrus smiled. "Do not fret, Master Oren, I shall be all right. Having to speak will distract me from more important matters."

All nodded at that. Though the proposal was important to them all there, Ti'ana's health was tantamount.

Indeed, without Ti'ana there would have been no proposal, for it was she who had taken them down to the lower city to see conditions for themselves; she who, in the main part, had drafted the proposal.

"They say Veovis is to speak for our opponents," Penjul said, looking across the vestibule to where Veovis stood, beneath the great arched doors to the main chamber, surrounded by the old men of his faction.

"Then the debate will be long and hard," Tekis of the Archivists said wryly.

"Long-winded, certainly," Penjul added, to general laughter.

"Maybe," Aitrus said, "yet I understand Lord Veovis's objections even so. He fears that this change is but the thin end of the wedge, and he is not alone in fearing this. Our task is to allay such fears, if not in Veovis, then in others who might vote with him. They must see that we mean exactly what we say and no more. Only then might we win."

There were nods all around at that.

"And if we lose?" Oren asked.

Aitrus smiled. "Then we find other ways to help the lower city. As Ti'ana has often said to me, there is always more than one way to skin a reekoo."

THE CHAMBER WAS SILENT AS VEOVIS ROSE from his seat on the lowest level and, turning, looked about him at the gathered members.

"Guildsmen, my Lords . . . as you know, my task is to persuade you not to adopt this rash proposal. I do not think I need say much. As the present system of governing our city has worked for more than five thousand years, then one might argue that it *has* worked well."

Veovis paused, his eyes resting briefly on Aitrus, who sat not five spans from where he stood, watching him intently.

"Yet there is another issue here, and that is the question of who runs D'ni. Such measures as are proposed might seem innocuous, yet they are guaranteed to encourage restlessness among the common people, for having tasted power—if only of this limited kind—then would they not want greater power? Would they be content to remain thus limited?

"Besides, as we who were bred to it know to our great cost, power is but one side of the equation; responsibility is the other. Power can be given overnight, but responsibility must be taught. Long years go into its making. Do we not, then, ask a great deal of these common men, however good their intentions, in expecting them to shoulder the burden of responsibility without due preparation? Of course we do. Is it not unfair to ask them to be as wise and knowing as ourselves, when all they have known until this time is service? It is."

Veovis smiled. "And that is ultimately why I say nay to this proposal. Because of the unhappiness it would bring to those who presently are happier than us. Why give them such care? Why burden them with it? No, fellow guildsmen, let us be content and leave things as they are. Say nay as I say nay and let us be done with it. Guildsmen, my Lords, thank you."

Veovis sat, to a murmur of approval. At a signal from Lord R'hira, Aitrus stood.

"Guildsmen, my Lords . . . As you may know, my wife, Ti'ana is in labor, and so I, too, ought to be brief."

There was laughter. Even Veovis gave a grudging nod.

"However, let me just say a word or two in answer to my fellow member's comments. I understand how busy Lord Veovis is, yet if he had read my proposal thoroughly, he would see that what I am proposing falls far short of the kind of *power* he suggests we would be relinquishing. Not only that, but I find myself in profound agreement with Veovis. Power is not a thing to be given lightly. And yes, responsibility is a grave and heavy burden and ought to be something one is schooled to bear. That is the D'ni way, and I would not have it changed."

Aitrus paused, looking about him, his eyes going from face to face among the circular levels of the great chamber.

"Let me therefore say it clearly, for the benefit of all, so that there is no mistaking what I am asking you to agree to today. I am as one with Lord Veovis. All matters of policy and funding *must* remain the prerogative of this chamber. I do not contest that for a moment. My proposal is designed to give, not take—

to *empower* the common people of D'ni and give them a degree of control over their lives that at present they do not have."

Aitrus smiled. "I see that some of you shake your heads at that, but it is true, and some of you have seen it with your own eyes. Our people—D'ni, like ourselves—are not poor, nor are they hard done by. They have food and shelter, sanitation and medicines if need be, but—and this is the vital point—their lot could be improved. Greatly improved."

He looked about him once again, scrutinizing face after face.

"I know what some of you are thinking. Why? Why should we be concerned about improving their lot? Well, let me give you two good reasons. First, just think of whom we speak. We are not talking of idlers and spendthrifts and good-for-nothings, but of good, hardworking people, men and women both. All of us here know a good dozen or more such people. We meet them daily and depend on them for many things. And they depend on us.

"Second, it is often said, with justifiable pride, that D'ni rules ten thousand Ages, yet a society ought to be judged not merely by the extent of its empire but by the quality of life of *all* its citizens. We are a rich people. We can afford to be generous. Indeed, I would argue that it is our moral duty to be generous, especially to our own. And that is why I ask you, fellow guildsmen, to say 'aye' to this proposal. For D'ni, and so that we might in future look ourselves squarely in the mirror and be proud of what we have done here today. Guildsmen, my Lords, thank you."

As Aitrus sat, Lord R'hira signaled to the stewards at the back of the hall. Veovis and Aitrus had been the last two speakers; now it was all down to the vote.

R'hira waited as the eight stewards took their places. It was their job to count the hands raised both for and against the proposal. When they were ready, R'hira looked to his fellow Lords, then spoke again.

"All those in favor of the motion raise your hands."

The stewards quickly counted.

"And those against."

Again the stewards made their tally.

"Thank you, Guildsmen."

The stewards turned, making their way down, forming an orderly queue before Lord R'hira. As each gave his tally, R'hira wrote it down in the great ledger before him. As the final steward turned away, Lord R'hira quickly added up the two columns of figures, then looked to either side of him. It was a protocol that the Five Lords did not vote unless a decision was so close—within three votes, usually—that their opinion could decide the matter.

"Guildsmen," he said, looking back at the rank after rank of members seated around and above him. "It appears that you are divided on this issue. One hundred and eighty-two members for, one hundred and eighty against. In the circumstances, the Five speak *for* the proposal."

Veovis was on his feet at once. "But you cannot, my Lord! For what good reason . . . "

He fell silent, then bowed his head.

R'hira stared at the young Lord a moment, then stood, signaling to all that the proceedings were over. "The Council has spoken, Master Veovis. The proposal is carried."

SUAHRNIR CLOSED THE DOOR QUIETLY BEHIND HIM, then turned, looking across the lamplit room to where his friend Veovis sat in the corner chair, lost in thought.

It was some time since he had seen Veovis quite so agitated, and even though he had calmed down considerably since the Council meeting, there was still a brooding intensity to him that did not bode well.

"Would you like a drink?" he asked, going over to the great stone cupboard beneath the window and picking up one of the three crystal decanters he kept there.

Veovis glanced up, then shook his head.

Suahrnir shrugged, then poured himself a large drink. He took a swig from the glass, then turned, facing Veovis again as the warmth of the liquor filled his throat.

"There must be something we can do," Veovis said quietly, as if speaking to himself.

Suahrnir smiled. "Maybe there is."

Veovis's eyes widened with interest. "Go on."

"There is a man I know," Suahrnir said, taking the seat beside Veovis. "They call him the Philosopher. He writes pamphlets."

"Pamphlets!" Veovis made a sound of disgust. "Really, Suahrnir, I thought you were being serious."

"I am. This Philosopher is a very influential man in the lower city. People read his writings. Lots of people. And they listen to what he has to say. More so than Ti'ana and the reformers."

"And just what does he say?"

Suahrnir sat back. "That would take too long. You ought to read one or two of them for yourself. You would like them, Veovis."

Veovis stared at his friend skeptically, then reached out and took the glass from him, taking a sip from it before he handed it back.

"And what name does this Philosopher go by?"

"A'Gaeris."

Veovis roared with laughter. "A'Gaeris! The fraudster?"

"It was never proved."

But Veovis waved that away. "The guilds do not expel their members on the strength of rumor, Suahrnir. Besides, I was there when A'Gaeris was ripped of his Guild cloak. I heard the charges that were on the roll."

"That was fifty years ago."

"It does not matter if it was five hundred years ago. The man is untrustworthy."

"I think you are wrong. I think he could help you."

"Help me? How? By writing a pamphlet about it?"

Suahrnir looked down. He had never heard Veovis sound quite so bitter. The defeat today had clearly hit him hard; more so perhaps because of who it was had swung the vote against him.

"The Philosopher has no love of outsiders," Suahrnir said, staring into his glass. "Indeed, he argues that the mixing of bloods is an abomination."

Suahrnir looked up. Veovis was watching him now. "He says that?"

"That and much more. You should meet him."

Veovis laughed sourly. "Impossible."

"Then you will just sit here and brood, will you?"

"No," Veovis said, standing, then reaching across for his cloak. "I will go home to K'veer and brood, as you clearly do not want my company."

Suahrnir put his hand out, trying to stop his friend. "Veovis . . ."

"Tomorrow," Veovis said, brushing his hand off. "I will be in a better mood tomorrow."

Suahrnir watched him go, then sighed. Veovis was in a bad mood right now and closed to all suggestions, but maybe in a day or two . . .

He smiled, then, going over to his desk, began to pen a note.

ANNA SAT UP IN BED, A HUGE PILE OF PILLOWS at her back, cradling the newborn; a serene smile, forged out of tiredness and exultation after a difficult twenty-hour labor, on her unusually pale face.

On a chair to one side, Tasera sat forward, her fingers laced together on one knee, her features set in a permanent grin of delight as she studied her grandson. He was small—much smaller than Aitrus had been at birth—but sturdy, and the midwife said he was a healthy child.

They were on Ko'ah, and it was spring on the island. The scent of blossoms was on the air and birdsong filled the morning's sunlit silence.

"Where *is* Aitrus?"

"He will be here soon," Anna said, smiling soothingly at Tasera. "He cannot simply walk away. It *was* his proposal."

"Even so . . . "

Tasera stopped, a grin breaching her face. "Aitrus! So there you are! What took you?"

Aitrus greeted his mother, then stepped past her, looking across the room to where Anna lay, his face, at that moment, filled with wonder.

"A boy," Anna said, smiling back at him.

Aitrus went across, then knelt beside the bed, his face on a level with the sleeping child, his eyes wide at the sight of this, his son.

"Why he's . . . "

". . . like you." Anna laughed softly. "He's beautiful, no?"

Aitrus nodded, then looked up at her. "Thank you," he said quietly, then, leaning carefully across the child, he gently kissed her.

Again he stared, drinking in the sight of his child the same way he had once studied the sleeping form of Anna, that night before he had asked her to be his wife, the two moments joined like links in a chain.

"Well, little Gehn," he said, the first hint of a tender smile on his lips. "How is the world?"

THEY HAD BEEN EXPECTING MASTER OREN FOR some hours. He had said he would be late, but as the time went on it began to look more and more as if he would not make the celebration. And then he arrived, his face dark, his manner withdrawn.

Aitrus, about to greet him, saw how he looked and took him aside.

"What is it, old friend?"

"We are summoned, Aitrus," Oren answered, embarrassed slightly. "All guildsmen must report back to D'ni at once. Two young guildsmen from the Guild of Maintainers have gone missing. We are to search the Ages for them."

Aitrus blinked. "But that's . . . "

". . . a mammoth task, yes, Aitrus, which is why the Maintainers have asked for the help of all the other guilds. The circumstances are . . . suspicious, let us say. They were investigating something important. What it was, we do not know, but Grand Master Jadaris is concerned enough to think that they may have been kidnapped, even killed."

The news stunned Aitrus. "All right," he said. "Come in and greet my family a moment, Oren. I, meanwhile, will gather up our friends and tell them the news. Then we shall go."

Oren nodded. For a moment he gently held Aitrus's arm. "I am sorry to be the bearer of such ill news on so joyous an occasion. I hear you have a son."

A brief smile appeared on Aitrus features once more. "Come see him, Oren. His name is Gehn and he shall be a great guildsman one day."

AN HOUR LATER, AITRUS STOOD BEFORE MASTER Jadaris himself.

"Ah, Master Aitrus. I hear congratulations are in order. A son, eh? That is good news. Very good news indeed!"

"Thank you, Grand Master," Aitrus said, bowing low.

"You have been told what is happening?" Jadaris asked.

"We are to search the Ages."

"Indeed. But not all the Ages. Only those which the two guildsmen were known to have personally investigated in the last five years."

Aitrus frowned. "Master?"

"This must not be known to all, Aitrus," Jadaris said, lowering his voice slightly and sitting forward, "but a number of blank linking books have gone missing from our Halls. We suspect that the guildsmen took them to carry out their investigations."

That news was grave. Aitrus saw at once how difficult things were.

"Do we know what they were investigating, Master Jadaris?"

"We do not. But we think they may have found something on one of the Ages they were sent to look at routinely. Something very important. And they may have gone back to try to get conclusive proof, using the missing linking books."

"How many Ages are involved, Master?"

"More than sixty."

"And you suspect that a senior guildsman might be involved?"

Jadaris nodded. "That is why we are sending in teams, rather than individual guildsmen. We do not want to take the risk of losing any more of our men. I have assigned you to a team of our own Maintainers."

"I see. And where would you like me to go, Grand Master?"

"To K'veer."

"K'veer!"

Jadaris raised a hand. "Before you object, Lord Rakeri himself asked for you, Aitrus. He considers you above reproach and felt that if you were to lead the team investigating his family's Books, no possible taint would fall upon his family. As you might understand, this is a most sensitive matter."

"Of course. Even so . . . "

"It is decided," Jadaris said with a finality that made Aitrus look up at him, then bow.

"As you wish, Master Jadaris."

LORD RAKERI GREETED AITRUS ON THE STEPS above the jetty. Behind the old man, the great spiral rock of K'veer blotted out all else. It was early, and the light in the great cavern was dim, but across the lake D'ni glowed like the embers of a fire.

"Aitrus, I am glad you came. And well done. I hear you have a son."

Aitrus took the old man's hands in his own and smiled. "Thank you, Lord Rakeri. The boy's name is Gehn."

Rakeri returned his smile, squeezing his hands before he relinquished them. "It is a good name. He whom he is named after, his father's father's father, was a great man. Or would have been, if time had been kind to him. But come, let us go through. This is a difficult business yet it must be done, so let us do it with some dignity."

Aitrus nodded, walking beside the old man as they went inside, the other guildsmen—six young Maintainers and one Master of the Guild—following behind.

The great mansion was still and silent. After the laughter of the party on Ko'ah, this seemed a somber, joyless place.

The huge doors to the Book Room were locked. Rakeri took a key from the huge bunch at his belt and unlocked the right-hand door, then pushed it open.

"Will you not come in with us, my Lord?" Aitrus asked, hesitating before stepping inside the room.

"I would rather not, Master Aitrus," Rakeri said, with a tiny sigh. "This whole matter is difficult. Routine inspections one can live with. They are . . . *traditional*. But this . . . this casts a bad light on all, don't you think?"

"I am sure there is an explanation, my Lord." Aitrus smiled consolingly. "We shall work as quickly and as efficiently as we can, and I shall make sure that a copy of my report is placed before you before we leave here."

Rakeri smiled. "That is kind of you, young Aitrus. Very kind."

chamber, and though Aitrus had seen it often before, stepping into it once more he felt again the weight of years that lay upon its shelves.

Shelves filled three of the walls from floor to ceiling—endless books of commentary, numbered and dated on their spines in golden D'ni letters. In one place only, to Aitrus's left as he stood, looking in, were the shelves breached. There, two great windows, paned with translucent stone of varying colors, went from floor to ceiling. Through them could be seen the lake and the far wall of the great cavern.

The whole Book Room was like a giant spur, jutting from the main twist of the rock. There was a drop of ten spans between it and the surface of the lake below.

It was a daunting place for a young guildsman to enter. Rakeri and his family owned six Books in all—six ancient Ages. These massive, ancient books were to be found at the far end of the long, high-walled chamber, resting on tilted marble pedestals, the colors of which matched the leather covers of the Books themselves. Each was secured to the pedestal by a strong linked chain that looked like gold but was in fact made of nara, the hardest of the D'ni stones.

Aitrus walked across, studying each of the Books in turn. Five of them were closed, the sixth—the Book of

Nidur Gemat—was open, the descriptive panel glowing in the half light of the early morning.

He had been to Nidur Gemat often, in earlier days, when he and Veovis had been friends. Standing there now, Aitrus felt a great sadness that they had been estranged, and wished he might somehow bridge the chasm that had developed between them these past fifteen years.

Aitrus turned, calling to the Guild Master. "Master Kura. Post two men on the door. We shall start with Nidur Gemat."

The Guild Master nodded and was about to talk to his guildsmen when the door burst open and Veovis stormed into the room.

"I thought as much!" he cried, pointing directly at Aitrus. "I might have known you would have yourself appointed to this task!"

Kura went to intercede, but Veovis glared at him. "Hold your tongue, man! I am speaking to Guild Master Aitrus here!"

Aitrus waited as Veovis crossed the chamber, keeping all expression from his face, yet a tense combative urge made him clench his right fist where it rested beside his leg.

"Well?" Veovis said, stopping an arm's length from Aitrus. "Have you nothing to say?"

Aitrus shook his head. He had learned long ago that when someone falsely accused you, the best defense you had was silence.

"You couldn't keep yourself from meddling, could you? As soon as you heard . . . "

"Veovis!"

Veovis straightened up, then turned. His father, Rakeri, stood in the doorway. "Father?"

"Leave us now," Rakeri said, the tone of command in his voice one that Aitrus had never heard him use to Veovis before this hour.

Veovis bowed, then turned glaring at Aitrus, an unspoken comment in his eyes. When he was gone, Rakeri came across.

"Forgive my son, Aitrus. He does not understand how things are. I shall speak with him at once. In the meantime, I apologize for him. And I am sure, in time, he will come and apologize in person."

Aitrus gave the tiniest nod of his head. "Thank you, Lord Rakeri, but that will not be necessary. Things are bad enough between us. Your apology is quite enough."

Rakeri smiled and gently nodded. "You are wise as well as kind, Aitrus. Yes, and I regret that my son has lost so good a friend. And no blame to you for that. My son is stubborn, just as his grandfather was."

There was a moment's awkward silence, then the old man nodded once again. "Well, Aitrus, I shall leave you once again. Do what you must. We have nothing here to hide."

Aitrus bowed his head. "My Lord . . . "

A MONTH PASSED WITH NO WORD OR SIGN OF the two missing guildsmen. Slowly the great sweep of the sixty Ages came to a close. Two days after the departure of Aitrus and the Maintainer team from K'veer, Veovis sat on the veranda at the top of the island, reading his father's copy of the report.

Turning the final page, he read the concluding remarks, then set the report down on the low table at his side and sat back, staring thoughtfully into the distance.

Suahrnir, seated just across from him, studied his friend a moment, then, "Well? What does our *friend* Aitrus say?"

Veovis was silent a moment, then he turned his head and looked at Suahrnir. "He was most thorough. But also fair. Scrupulously so. I may have misjudged him."

"You think so?" Suahrnir laughed. "Personally I think he feels nothing but animosity toward you, Veovis."

"Maybe so, but there is nothing in the report."

"In the official report, maybe . . . "

Veovis narrowed his eyes. "What do you mean?"

"I mean that what is written down for all to see is not always what is said . . . in private. What if Master Aitrus gave another, separate report to the Five?"

"Then my father would have heard of such, and he, in turn, would have told me."

"Or to Lord R'hira alone?"

Veovis looked down, then shook his head. "No," he said, but the word lacked certainty.

"What if he found something?"

"*Found?* What could he find?"

"Oh, I don't mean found as in really found. Yet he might *say* he found something."

"And the Maintainers?"

Suahrnir gave an ironic smile. "They could be fooled easily enough. They were, after all, but *apprentice* guildsmen."

The thought of it clearly disturbed Veovis, nonetheless he shook his head once more. "Aitrus does not like me, but that does not make him a cheat, nor a slanderer."

"Who knows what makes a man do certain things? You hurt him badly when you opposed his marriage to the outsider. It is not the kind of thing a man forgets easily. And it is a more than adequate motive to wish to seek revenge."

Veovis looked down, his whole expression dark and brooding. Finally, he raised his head again. "No, I cannot believe it of him."

Suahrnir leaned forward, speaking conspiratorially now. "Maybe not. But there is a way we could be certain."

"Certain? How?"

"I have a friend. He hears things . . . from servants and the like. If something secretive is going on, *he* will have heard of it."

"This friend of yours . . . who is he?"

Suahrnir smiled and sat back. "You know his name."

"A'Gaeris!" Veovis laughed dismissively, then shook his head. "You ask me to take *his* word?"

"You do not have to believe anything he says," Suahrnir answered. "But what harm will it do to listen? You might learn something to your benefit."

"And what does *he* want out of this?"

Suahrnir looked surprised at the suggestion. "Why, nothing. Nothing at all. The man owes me a favor. Besides, I think you will enjoy meeting him. Yes, and he you. You are both strong, intelligent men. I would enjoy watching you lock horns."

Veovis stared at his friend, then, with a grudging shrug of his shoulders, he said. "All right. Arrange a meeting. But no word of this must get out. If anyone should witness our meeting . . . "

Suahrnir smiled, then stood, giving a little bow to his friend. "Don't worry, Veovis. I know the very place."

IT WAS D'NI NIGHT. NOT THE NIGHT OF MOON and stars you would find up on the surface, but a night of intense, almost stygian shadow. The lake was dark, the organisms in the water inactive, their inner clocks set to a thirty-hour biological cycle established long ago and in another place, far from earth.

On the roof garden of Kahlis's mansion, Anna stood alone, leaning on the parapet, looking out over the upper city. Earlier in the evening it had been a blaze of light; now only scattered lamps marked out the lines of streets. Then it had seemed like a great pearled shell, clinging to the dark wall of the cavern; now it looked more like a ragged web, strung across one corner of a giant's larder.

Out on the lake itself the distant wink of lights revealed the whereabouts of islands. Somewhere out there, on one of those islands, was Aitrus. Or, at least, he would have been, were he in D'ni at all.

Anna sighed, missing him intensely, then turned, hearing the child's cries start up again in the nursery below where she stood. For a moment she closed her eyes, tempted to leave things to the nurse, then, steeling herself against the sound, she went across and, bending down, lifted the wooden hatch that was set into the floor. Slipping inside, she went down the narrow stairs and out into the corridor that ran the length of the top of the house.

At once the sound of the crying grew much louder; a persistent, whining cry that never seemed to end; or if it did, it ended but briefly, only to intensify.

Stepping into the room, Anna saw that the nurse had been joined by her male colleague, Master Jura of the Guild of Healers. The ancient looked up from the desk in the corner where he had been writing and frowned at Anna, as if she and not the baby were the cause of the problem.

Ignoring him, Anna walked over to the cot and looked down at her son. Gehn lay on his back, his tiny red face screwed up tight as he bawled and bawled, his mouth a jagged black O in the midst of that redness, his arms and legs kicking in a continuous mechanical movement of distress. The sight of it distressed her. It made her want to pick him up and cuddle him, but that would solve nothing; the crying would go on whatever she did.

"Well . . . " the Healer said after a moment, consulting his notes, "I would say that the matter is a simple one."

Anna saw how he looked at her, his manner cold and unsympathetic, and felt her stomach tighten.

"The child's problems stem from its stomach," the Healer continued. "He cries because he is not receiving adequate sustenance, and because he is in pain."

"In pain?"

The Healer nodded, then looked to his notes again. "If the child were D'ni it would be fairly easy to prescribe something for his condition, but as it is . . . "

"Forgive me," Anna interrupted, "but what difference does that make?"

Master Jura blinked, surprised. When he spoke again, there was a note of impatience in his voice. "Is it not self-evident? The child is unnatural. A hybrid. He is neither D'ni nor human, but some curious mixture of the two, and therein lie his problems. Why, it is astonishing that he is even viable!"

Anna felt the shock of what he had said wash through her. How dare he talk of her son as if he were some strange experiment! She looked down at the bawling child, then back at the old Healer.

"Have you *tested* him, Master Jura?"

The old man laughed dismissively. "I do not have to test him. As I said, it is self-evident. One cannot mix human and D'ni blood. To be perfectly honest with you, the child would be better off dead."

Anna stared at him, her anger rising. Then, with a calmness she did not feel, she spoke.

"Get out."

The old man had gone back to his notes. At her words, he looked up, glancing first at the nurse, to see if it were she whom Anna had addressed, and then at Anna herself.

"Yes," Anna said, her face hard now. "*You*, old man. You heard me. Get out before I throw you out!"

"Why, I . . ."

"Get *out!*" she shouted, focusing her anger on the man. "How dare you come into my house and tell me that my son would be better off dead! How *dare* you!"

Master Jura bristled, then, closing up his notes, he slipped them into his case and stood.

"I will not stay where I am not wanted."

"Good," Anna said, wanting to strike the man for his impertinence. "And you," she said, turning on the nurse. "Pack your things and go. I have no further use for you."

IT WAS A QUIET, FIRST-FLOOR ROOM IN A house in the J'taeri District, overlooking the harbor. As the door closed, Veovis looked about him. It was a staid, respectable room, three large chairs resting against one wall, a large, dark-wood dresser against another. On the third, either side of the huge picture window, were two portraits. He walked across and studied them a moment. Both of the women looked stern and matronly, their clothing dark and austere— the dour uniform of respectable D'ni women for four thousand years and more.

He shook his head, then turned. The city bell was sounding the fourth hour of the afternoon. All was peaceful.

Would A'Gaeris come? And if he did, what would the old fraud have to say?

He could remember how angry A'Gaeris had been, the day of his expulsion—could remember vividly how he had glared at the Grand Master before throwing down his guild cloak and storming from the Hall.

Veovis had been but a student that day, not even a guildsman, let alone a Master. And now here he was, almost fifty years on.

The door behind him creaked open. Veovis turned, to find Suahrnir standing there.

"Has he come?"

Suahrnir nodded, then stood back as A'Gaeris entered the room. He was a tall, broad-shouldered man, but stout in girth and balding, his gray hair swept back from his pate and worn unfashionably long. He wore a simple black tunic and long baggy pants of a similar black cloth. But it was his eyes that drew attention. Fierce eyes that stared intently, almost insolently back at Veovis.

"My Lord," A'Gaeris said, the slightest sneer in the greeting.

"Philosopher," Veovis replied, matching his tone perfectly.

A'Gaeris smiled. "I was not wrong, then."

"Wrong?"

"I said you had fire in you. And I was right."

Veovis smiled sardonically. "That would be praise if from another's lips."

"But not from mine?"

"I do not know you, except by reputation."

"You have read my writings, then?"

"Not a word."

A'Gaeris barely batted an eyelid at the news. "Then that is a joy to come."

"And modest, too?"

"Need I be?"

Veovis smiled, warming to the man. "You are sharp, A'Gaeris, I'll give you that."

"Sharp enough to cut yourself on, I warrant. So why are you here?"

"To be honest, I am not sure. I was persuaded that you might help me."

"Help you?" A'Gaeris laughed, then walked to the window and stared out. "But you are a Lord of D'ni. How can I, a mere common man, help *you*?"

But there was a teasing glint in the Philosopher's eyes that intrigued Veovis.

"I do not know."

"No," A'Gaeris looked back at him and smiled. "But maybe I do."

"Go on."

"I hear things."

"So Suahrnir told me. But are they things worth hearing?"

A'Gaeris shrugged. "What would you know?"

"Something to my benefit?"

"And your foes' disadvantage?"

"Perhaps."

The Philosopher smiled. "We share one important thing, Lord Veovis. A love of D'ni, and a belief in the purity of D'ni blood."

"What do you mean?"

"I speak of your once-friend Aitrus and his ill-chosen wife."

Veovis narrowed his eyes. "What of them?"

"Only last night, it seems, the outsider woman sent Master Jura of the Healers away with his tail between his legs. And the child's nurse."

Veovis looked to Suahrnir again. This was news indeed if it were true.

"Do you know why?"

A'Gaeris grinned broadly. "It seems Master Jura suggested that it might save time and trouble were the half-breed to be peacefully done away with."

Veovis stared back at him a moment, astonished. "And what did Master Aitrus say of this?"

"What could he say? He is away. But he will know soon enough when he is back."

"It is a shame."

"Indeed," A'Gaeris agreed. "Such a union should never have been allowed."

"I did all I could to prevent it."

"I know." The Philosopher was looking at him now with sympathy and understanding.

Veovis looked down. "It seems you know what I want, Philosopher. But what of you? What do you want?"

"To be your friend."

Veovis looked up, smiling, expecting some sardonic look upon A'Gaeris's face, but those eyes were serious and solemn.

"I have missed the company of my peers," A'Gaeris said. "It is all very well preaching to the rabble, but it changes nothing. My life ended when the guild threw me out."

"They had good reason . . . "

"They had none!"

The sharpness of the rejoinder surprised Veovis.

"I was falsely accused," A'Gaeris went on. "There was no missing book. Or if there was, it was not I who took it."

"So you say," Veovis said quietly.

"So I say," A'Gaeris said, fiercely now, challenging Veovis to gainsay him a second time.

There was a moment's silence, then Veovis shrugged. "Give me a day or two to think on this, and then, perhaps, we shall meet again."

"As you wish."

Veovis nodded, then smiled. "You say she threw the Healer out?"

"She threatened him, I'm told."

"Well . . . " Veovis nodded to himself thoughtfully, then walked over to the door. "It was interesting meeting you, Philosopher."

"And you, Lord Veovis."

DARKNESS WAS RISING FROM THE LAKE AS A'Gaeris climbed the back stairs of the lodging house where, for the past fifty years, he had stayed. Corlam, his mute assistant, watched him from the darkened window overhead, turning hurriedly to cross the room and light the lamp.

The Philosopher seemed thoughtful tonight. As he came into the room he barely acknowledged Corlam, but went straight to his desk and sat.

The room was a shrine to the Philosopher's endeavors. Apart from the door and window, there was not a square inch of the walls that was not covered in books, piled two deep on broad stone shelves. Some were reference books, others books of Council minutes and resolutions. Some—almost all of those on the shelves at the far end of the rectangular room—A'Gaeris's own journals.

For fifty years he had labored here, since the day he had been cast out of the guild, making his plans, slowly preparing for the day when he could emerge again from obscurity and become a name again. Someone *everybody* knew, and not just the rabble of the lower city.

All this Corlam knew intimately, for, having "adopted" him as a child—an orphan of the lower alleys—A'Gaeris trusted Corlam as he trusted no one else, using him as a sounding board, rehearsing his ideas and thoughts, refining his theories until Corlam knew them almost as well as he.

Corlam went across and stood behind his master, watching as A'Gaeris took his latest journal from the left-hand drawer and, laying it on the desk, opened it and began to write.

Today had been important. Corlam knew that. His master had been in a state of some excitement for days before this meeting, though why exactly Corlam could not ascertain. Lord Veovis was, he knew, an important man, but why his master should desire to meet him only A'Gaeris himself knew, for he had said nothing on this score to Corlam.

"Real books," A'Gaeris said, after a while, glancing up at Corlam. "If only I could get my hands on some *real* Books."

Corlam stared back at him. There were many Books on the shelves—most of them "liberated" from the guild libraries; for, after all, with so many books, the guildsmen rarely ever noticed one was missing—but he knew what his master meant. He was talking about kortee'nea. Blank D'ni Books. The kind one used to link to the Ages.

"I know," A'Gaeris said, smiling at him, then turning back to his journal. "You cannot help me there, Corlam. But maybe our lordship can. Besides, I have a man on the inside now. A friend who wants to help me. If I can persuade *him* to aid me, who knows?"

Corlam looked closer. His master was practicing again. Writing words in someone else's hand. Corlam squinted at the page, then tapped A'Gaeris's shoulder, nodding vigorously. It was Lord Veovis's writing, as clear as day. He had seen examples only the other day, from the records of the Council.

Corlam watched, openmouthed. Though he had watched A'Gaeris do this many times now over the years, he still found it magical the way his master could so easily copy another's hand. He had only to study it an hour and he had it.

Pushing the journal away from him, A'Gaeris yawned and stretched, then turned to face Corlam.

"You know, I had an idea today, Corlam. While I was waiting for his Lordship to turn up."

Corlam smiled, a look of attention coming to his features.

"It's like this," he went on. "I was asking myself how I could get into a place where I should not be— into a Guild strong room, say, or a well-guarded cell— and then get out again without being caught. The easiest way, of course, would be to write a specific linking book to allow me to link into that place. But to get out again I would need a second linking book, and I would have to leave it there. You follow me?"

Corlam nodded.

"So. Getting in would be easy. Getting out without being followed and tracked down by the Maintainers would be extremely hard. Unless . . . "

A'Gaeris smiled a great smile of self-satisfaction. "Unless, of course, one linked on to another Age, and then another after that. In fact, one might take three separate Linking Books into the cell with one, just to confuse things. But it would be no good having the second and third Linking Books at the place where one linked *to* each time. That would be no good at all. No. One would need to hide the Book a good hour's walk from where one linked to, so that anyone following you would have to search a wide area in order to find that second Book. Indeed, one could have three or four such Books—only one of which you would use. And when one linked the second time, again you would have an hour's walk to get to the next Linking Book. That way no one could follow you. At least, not quickly, and maybe not at all. A little preparation, two hours' walking, and one would be safe."

For a moment A'Gaeris's eyes glowed, then he looked down. "Of course, one would need a masterful writer to create Ages at will, and, say, a mole inside with access to places such as . . . cells, for example."

ANNA WAS IN THE LABORATORY, WORKING ON the latest soil samples from Gemedet, when Aitrus came in. Gehn was in the cot on a bench nearby. As Aitrus came across, he stopped to lean over and smile at his softly cooing son before greeting Anna.

Anna looked up from the lens of the microscope and smiled. "I won't be long."

He nodded. "I have had a letter."

"Who is it from?"

"That is just it. It is not signed and the handwriting is unfamiliar."

He handed it to her, then waited as she read it.

"Destroy it," she said, handing it back to him. "And do not get involved, whatever it is."

"But what does it mean?"

"Does it matter?"

Aitrus shrugged. "It is the tone of it that bothers me. 'Something to your benefit'. And all of the secrecy. What do you think is going on?"

Anna sighed. "If it really worries you, Aitrus, hand it over to the Maintainers. Let them send a man along. But don't you get involved."

"All right," he smiled. "I'll destroy it." And having said it, he reached across and, turning on the gas tap, ignited it, and held the corner of the letter in the fine blue flame. When it was well aflame, he dropped it into the sink. "There," he said.

Behind him, Gehn began to whimper. Aitrus went over, lifted the baby from the cot, and cuddled him in the crook of his arm.

"He must be hungry," Anna said. "I'll finish here."

"No, you work on," he said. "I'll feed him."

She smiled. "Don't overfeed him. That was the trouble last time. The poor little mite could barely cope!"

"I know," he said, then, as if it were an afterthought, he added. "I have to go back to my rooms later on. There's a report I have to finish. I'll only be an hour or two. I can join you for a late supper."

Anna grinned. "That would be nice. And maybe we could get away for a few days soon. To Gemedet."

Aitrus nodded. "I shall ask Master Erafir to stand in for me. It is time he took on more responsibility."

"Then go and see to Gehn. But remember, Aitrus, nothing too heavy for his stomach."

AITRUS HAD MEANT TO GO STRAIGHT TO HIS rooms; his feet had lead him partway there, but then curiosity had overcome him and he found himself descending the steps, then walking beneath the gate and into J'Taeri District.

I do not have to get involved, he told himself. Whatever it was, he did not have to act upon it. He would observe whatever had to be observed, then leave.

The street itself was an ordinary street, the house a staid, respectable dwelling of the kind merchants often bought. The windows were dark, the door locked. Aitrus turned. The house overlooked the harbor and Kerath's arch, the top of which was almost on a level with where he stood. Across the street, between the facing buildings, was a low wall, from which one could look out over the lake. He went across and stood there, his hands resting lightly on the stone.

There was a faint mist in the cavern tonight. In the narrow streets lamps wavered as wagons moved between the houses. There was a shout from somewhere far below, and then laughter. Otherwise the night was peaceful. Aitrus turned, conscious of a faint gurgling sound. Close by a narrow culvert cut across the street, clear water running in a stream from the very top of the huge, scallop-shaped city. He bent down and dipped his hand. It was cool.

He was about to turn away and go when he heard footsteps coming along the far end of the street. Looking about him, he spied a nearby doorway and stepped into its shadows.

The footsteps came on, the slow click of leather boots on stone, then stopped. Aitrus hesitated. He was about to risk a glimpse, when a second set of footsteps could be heard, this time from his left, brisker than the first. They paused, then came on again, slower now. There was a low murmur of greeting.

Aitrus peeked out. Two men stood in the lamplight before the door of the house. One was cloaked and hooded, the other, a heavier-set man, wore nothing on his balding head. He looked familiar, but where Aitrus had seen him he could not say. He ducked back into shadow, listening.

"What do you want?" one of them asked, the voice, again, familiar.

"I have something to show you," the second answered. "Something that will interest you."

It was a deep voice, cultured yet with a strangely common edge to it. Whereas the first . . .

"You want *me* to go in there with you?" the first man asked, and as he did, Aitrus finally recognized the voice.

Veovis!

"Don't you trust me?"

"Alone, at night, in a strange house?" Veovis laughed ironically. "Would *you* trust *me?*"

"Implicitly."

There was a silence, then a huff of resignation.

"All right," Veovis said finally. "I shall trust you. But be warned. I am armed, A'Gaeris."

That name came as a shock to Aitrus. All young guildsmen knew it. No other name attracted quite such infamy. But what was he doing here in J'Taeri, a respectable district? And what was Veovis doing meeting him?

Aitrus peeked out again, in time to see the big, heavyset man place a key in the lock and turn it, then put out his hand, inviting Veovis to step inside.

"You first," Veovis said, standing back a little, his hand on the hilt of his dagger. "And put a light on. Then I shall come inside."

A'Gaeris smiled and shrugged, then stepped inside the house. A moment later a light went on in the hall.

Letting his hand fall from the hilt of his dagger, Veovis glanced to either side, then stepped into the house.

Was that it? Was that what the anonymous writer had meant him to see? And if so, why?

Aitrus was about to leave, to make his way back up to the Guild Hall, when a light went on in the ground-floor room to the left of the front door. Easing back against the wall, Aitrus watched as A'Gaeris entered the room, followed a moment later by Veovis.

Veovis, standing in the doorway, seemed ill at ease. He glanced about him, then, satisfied that it was not a trap, closed the door and walked across to where A'Gaeris was rummaging among the papers on a desk. There were a number of slender books among the papers, and A'Gaeris lifted one and handed it to Veovis.

Veovis hesitated, then opened it. He studied it a moment then looked up, his eyes wide.

A'Gaeris smiled, then gestured toward the chair facing him.

AITRUS WENT STRAIGHT TO HIS ROOMS IN THE Guild Hall. He had work to do, but he found he could not work. What he had seen troubled him greatly. Anna was right, of course; he ought to have gone straight to Master Jadaris and put the matter in the hands of the Maintainers, but he had not, and this was the result. Oh, he could go there now, but what proof would he have? It was his word against Veovis's.

But what was going on? Why were such strange and unlikely companions meeting in a merchant's house?

Aitrus sat still a long while, trying to fathom it, but he could make no sense of it at all.

Anna. Anna would know. Only he could not ask Anna, because he had promised her he would not get involved. He had burned the note, as if it had held no power over him. But it had. And now he had this dilemma.

Veovis. Maybe he ought to go and see Veovis and confront him openly with what he had seen.

Aitrus thought a while, then nodded. It seemed the right thing to do. No skulking about in shadows. That was not his way. He would take a boat to K'veer in the morning and have it out with Veovis, face-to-face. For there had to be an explanation.

Aitrus put away his files, then left the room, locking it behind him. *Tomorrow*, he told himself, making his way down the long, silent corridor toward the great gate. *It will all come clear tomorrow.*

AITRUS ROSE EARLY THE NEXT MORNING. AT supper the previous evening he had said nothing to Anna, nor had he hinted at what he planned. Yet even as he ate a hasty breakfast, a servant brought him in a second letter, the handwriting on the envelope the same as that on the anonymous note the day before.

Aitrus stared at the envelope a long while, then, with a sigh of resignation, slit it open with his finger-nail. Inside was a brief note in the same hand as before, but with it was a letter—a letter from Veovis to one of the two young guildsmen who had gone missing thirty days back.

He read it through, then looked to the date at the top of the page. That was the day before the guildsmen disappeared.

"No," he said quietly, setting the letter aside and picking up the note once more. "It is not possible . . . "

The note read: "Come and see me if you wish to know more" and gave a time and place. That place was the merchant's house in J'Taeri.

Three choices now lay before him: to go to Master Jadaris and lay the matter before him; to go straight to K'veer and confront Veovis; or to wait until tonight and meet the author of the note.

The first was common sense; the second satisfied his sense of honor; but it was the third he would do.

Why? He could not answer why. It was simply how he was.

Forgive me, Anna, he thought, slipping the note and letter into his pocket and rising from his seat.

VEOVIS STOOD BESIDE A'GAERIS ON THE GREAT rock, looking out across the massive plain that stretched away below him and shook his head.

Everything was subtly wrong. The colors were unnatural, the shapes of trees, even the way the hills were formed, all was wrong. Yet it existed.

He turned, looking through his lenses at A'Gaeris. "Who made this?"

A'Gaeris turned, his eyes gleaming beyond the surface of the protective glasses. "Your old friend, Aitrus."

"Impossible," Veovis said dismissively. "Aitrus and his kin own but two Ages—Ko'ah and Gemedet. Both are strictly monitored by the Maintainers. If either were anything like this . . . well, it would not be allowed."

"Yet this *is* his Age," A'Gaeris said, smiling now as he handed Veovis the Linking Book.

"No," Veovis said quietly, disbelief vying with horror as he stared at the handwriting on the pages of the Book. It *was* Aitrus's. He had seen Aitrus's hand too often to be in doubt.

"He is experimenting," A'Gaeris answered, matter-of-factly. "Secretly, of course, for he knows the guilds would frown upon his activities. The woman leads him on, of course. Without her he would never have strayed from the D'ni path. It is her insidious influence we see all about us, Veovis. The wrongness . . . that is her doing."

Veovis looked about him, then nodded, half-convinced.

"Poor Aitrus."

"You pity him?"

Veovis looked up, a flash of anger in his eyes. "He was a good man, once. As you rightly say, the outsider has bewitched him and stolen his senses." He closed the Book and shook it. "If *this* is true . . . "

A'Gaeris put his arm out, indicating their surroundings. "Can you doubt it?"

"No . . . no, it is clear to me now."

Veovis sighed heavily.

A'Gaeris stared at him, as if sympathetic. "Would you like me to leave you for a while?"

Veovis nodded, then, with a small sad smile, opened the Linking Book for the Philosopher. The square on the right-hand page glowed softly, showing a picture of a study back on D'ni.

A'Gaeris met his eyes a moment. "There *is* more."

"More?"

"Yes. This is not the only Age he made. Perhaps you would like to see a few before you make up your mind what to do."

Again Veovis nodded, clearly shocked by this news.

"Well," A'Gaeris said finally, putting out his hand, "I shall leave you now. Farewell."

His hand touched the glowing box. In a moment he was gone.

Veovis closed the Book and pocketed it, then looked up again. There was a curious beauty to this world, yet it *was* wrong.

Aitrus had to be stopped. But how? If he went to the Five with this information, Aitrus would be expelled from the Council, stripped of his guild membership, and possibly even incarcerated on a Prison Age. Such was the penalty for making illicit Ages. It would rid him of his chief opponent in Council, but that was unimportant. Besides, he wondered if he could do it if it meant destroying Aitrus and his family. Maybe the woman *was* a pernicious influence, and maybe the child *was* better off dead, but for Aitrus himself he still felt a great sympathy. Despite all their recent animosity, he could not help but remember how good and kind a friend Aitrus had once been. A true friend, unafraid to say as he saw.

Walking to the edge of the great slab, Veovis sat, his booted feet dangling over the drop. What should he do?

I'll wait, he decided, *and see what other evidence our friend A'Gaeris has to offer. And then I'll take my father's counsel.*

Veovis stood, taking the Linking Book from his pocket and opening it. Then, like a child gently leaping a stream, he jumped out, over the edge of the great rock, putting his hand to the panel as he leapt, linking—vanishing into the air—even as the Book tumbled down into the wilderness of rock and tree below.

"WAIT HERE. MY MASTER WILL SEE YOU IN A moment."

As the boy left the darkened room, Aitrus walked across. What, for the briefest instant, he had taken to be a mirror was in fact a window, looking in to what appeared to be a study. A single wall lamp lit the inner room dimly.

"Strange," he said quietly, surprised to find a window in the middle of a house.

On the far side of the study was a desk. Open upon the desk, recognizable by the tell-tale glow on its right-hand page, was a D'ni book.

Aitrus stared at it, astonished to see it there. Yet even as he looked, a figure formed in the air in front of the desk, until it stood, as solid as everything about it, on the thick, red carpet.

A'Gaeris!

A'Gaeris shook himself, shrugging off the sensation of the link, then went around to the far side of the desk and opened one of the drawers, taking something from within. For a time he sat there, staring down at it, then, sensing a disturbance in the air, he looked up.

As he did, a second figure formed before the desk. Veovis.

A cold certainty swept through Aitrus at the sight. This was ill indeed.

Veovis turned, looking to his seated companion, then nodded.

"All right. You had better show me the others."

A'Gaeris stood. In his hands was another Book. He stepped around the desk and handed it to Veovis.

"There are more," he said. "This is the only one that I have here, but I can bring the others if you wish. Tomorrow night, if that is convenient."

Veovis studied the Book in his hands a while, then handed it back. "Tomorrow," he said. "I shall come tomorrow."

"At this hour?" A'Gaeris asked.

"At this hour," Veovis answered. And then he turned and left, slamming the door behind him.

A'Gaeris stared at the Book a moment, then set it down and turned to face the one-way mirror, looking directly at Aitrus.

"Aitrus. We need to talk."

"YOU DID NOT BELIEVE HIM CAPABLE, DID you?"

Aitrus looked up wearily. For more than two hours

he had worked his way through a stack of letters and documents, all in Veovis's hand.

There was nothing here that was directly incriminating—in almost every case the evidence against Veovis was purely circumstantial—yet the pattern of it seemed conclusive. Enough to convince Aitrus, anyway. He looked back across the desk at the Philosopher. A'Gaeris's brow was beaded with perspiration. In the wavering candlelight he seemed much older than his eighty five-years.

"How long has he been trading in illicit Books?"

"Two, maybe three years now—that is, as far as *I* know. As I said, I was not sure of it at first. After all, he was a great Lord. A man of real substance. It seemed remarkable—unbelievable, almost—that he should be demeaning himself so."

"It still is," Aitrus said, setting the final memorandum aside. "If I had not seen all this with my own eyes." He stared at it a moment, then looked back at A'Gaeris. "Where did you get these?"

"I have sources," A'Gaeris answered. "I bought this here, that there, collecting, all the while collecting, until I had enough to be certain."

"And the Books you are selling him; where did *they* come from? I have heard nothing of missing Books."

"They were from his friend, Suahrnir."

"*Suahrnir!* But . . . "

Aitrus saw it at once. One of the duties of the Guild of Maintainers was to destroy "failed" Books—D'ni Books that, for one reason or another, had not worked, linking to unstable Ages. These were burned in special guild ovens. Or were supposed to be. And the man in charge of that task was . . . Guild Master Suahrnir.

"But why does he not deal with his friend Veovis directly?"

A'Gaeris smiled. "They are friends, yes, but neither trusts the other. Besides . . . " he laughed, "neither knows the other is involved. Suahrnir does not know who buys the Books, and Veovis . . . "

"Does not know who supplies them, right?"

Aitrus sat back, astonished. Then, "So why are you showing *me* all this?"

A'Gaeris sat forward, the fire of indignation in his eyes suddenly. "Because no one would listen to me. But you, Aitrus, *you* could do something. You could even get to Lord R'hira himself."

"But *why?*"

"Because I, who was once an honest man, was barred from the guild for something I did not do, while this Lord's son, this rock-worm, can do as he will and get away with it. That's why!"

A'Gaeris's face was dark with anger. "You must understand. Veovis came to me. And they found out.

They must have been watching him. That is why he killed them."

The room was silent. Aitrus stared at the Philosopher coldly.

"I do not believe you," he said, finally.

"No," A'Gaeris said sadly, "yet it *is* true." He pointed to the last thing in the pile—the Linking Book—his eyes grave. "See for yourself if you do not believe me!"

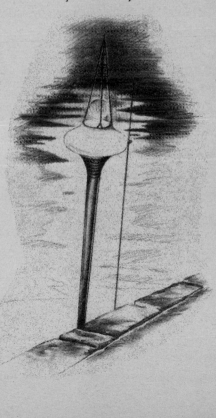

VEOVIS STEPPED FROM THE BOAT ONTO THE bottom step, then turned, looking back across the lake toward the sleeping city. Beneath him, dark as pitch, the water lapped softly against the stone. Above and to his right, beyond the stone lip of the harbor wall, a lamp burned steadily atop its pole, reflected in the water farther out.

The great cavern was silent, as if empty of all other life. Only the faint, dull air-rhythm of the great fans could be heard, distant like a heartbeat.

Veovis stretched and yawned. He had much to think about, yet he was tired now and experience had taught him not to make decisions while in the grip of such lassitude. He would sleep on the matter, and in the morning, fresh, reflect anew upon the problem.

He climbed the steps, up onto the black stone jetty. Lianis was awaiting him there, two servants with him. As Veovis emerged, one brought a cloak and wrapped it about his shoulders, while another held up a lamp to light his way.

"Lianis," he said, greeting his advisor. "You did not have to wait up for me."

Lianis fell in beside him as they walked across the flags toward the mansion. "You have visitors, my Lord."

The news chilled Veovis. He glanced at Lianis, then looked away, troubled. Had he been watched? Had someone witnessed his meetings with A'Gaeris? For if so he would be hard stretched to explain his comings and goings.

"Where are they?" he asked, stopping as they came beneath the arch.

"In your study, my Lord. I thought it best to keep this matter discreet."

"You did well," Veovis answered, touching his arm briefly. They walked on, through the great doors and down the broad, high corridor, the servant hurrying to keep up with them, his lamp throwing their shadows on ahead of them as they approached the great staircase.

Coming to the first step, Veovis turned to Lianis again. "I will take things from here, Lianis. Send one of the servants in with wine in a brief while. I shall send for you if I need you."

"My Lord," Lianis bowed then backed away.

Veovis climbed the stairs alone. At the foot of the steps, the servant held the lamp high, lighting his way as best he could.

His study was to the left. As he stood before the door, Veovis tried to calm himself and still his swirling thoughts. Things looked bad. He had met with a sworn enemy of the D'ni state. And why? To discredit an opponent. It was that simple, and no end of sophistry could cloud the matter. Yet against that was what he now knew of Aitrus and the illicit Ages. Was that enough? Might he claim, perhaps, that he had known before the meetings—had known and wanted confirmation?

Perhaps.

He grasped the door handle and turned it, stepping into the room, a smile forming on his lips.

"Guildsmen . . ."

The smile froze. Facing him, rising from a chair beside his desk, was the outsider woman, Ti'ana. Cradled in her arms was the half-breed child. As the door clicked shut behind Veovis, she took two steps toward him, her dark eyes accusing him.

"Where is he, Veovis? Where *is* my husband?"

AITRUS SAT IN HIS STUDY, THE LINKING BOOK open on the desk before him. If what A'Gaeris said was true, he would find the bodies of the two young guildsmen on the other side. But could he trust A'Gaeris?

Who knew what kind of Age this really linked to? For all he knew it could be deadly, the air poisonous. On the other hand, it was, in all likelihood, the only real piece of evidence he had against Veovis—*if* things were as A'Gaeris claimed.

Aitrus reached out and closed the book. To link was too risky. If he had had a breathing mask and a second linking book to bring him back to D'ni, he *might* have gone . . .

If. Besides, there were Anna and Gehn to think of now.

Taking a sheet of vellum from the side, he took his pen from the inkstand and began to write, penning a note to Grand Master Jadaris of the Maintainers. He would send him the linking book and let him decide what should be done. In the meantime, he would take Anna and the child to Gemedet, away from things.

Aitrus signed the note then stood. He did not feel like sleep—his mind was much too filled with things for rest—yet he felt the need to see Anna and Gehn. Walking through to the bedroom he stopped in the doorway, listening for their breathing in the darkness.

Nothing. There was nothing. Slowly he tiptoed across, then crouched beside the bed, putting out his hand. The bed was empty.

He stood, then went across and lit the lamp. The bed was made. There was no sign of them in the room.

For a moment or two he could not think. When he had left, four hours ago, they had been here, asleep.

Aitrus went out, then knocked on the end door, waking his house steward.

"Were there any callers while I was gone?"

"A Messenger came," he answered, sitting up. "From the Guild House. He brought a message for you from your father. The Mistress—Ti'ana—came down and took it from me. She spoke to the man."

"Did you hear what she said."

"No."

Aitrus thanked him, then went back to his study. There was no sign of the message, but whatever it was, he knew exactly what Anna would have thought. He had told her he was going to the Guild Hall, and any message would have reached him there.

Unless he had not gone to the Guild Hall.

She would have remembered the anonymous note, and, piecing things together, would have gone after him.

Maybe. But why take Gehn? Why not go alone? Unless she had not gone to the house.

Gemedet, then? But again, why, in the middle of the night? Why not wait for him to return?

No, only her fear for him would have made her go out after him. But why should she be afraid? Unless she already knew—knew at some deeper, instinctive level—that Veovis was behind it all.

K'veer!

No sooner had the thought been spawned than it became a certainty in his mind. K'veer! They had gone to K'veer!

Whirling about, he hastened across the room and out, then ran down the corridor, not caring if he woke the house. His booted footsteps thudded on the stairs, yet as he threw open the door, it was to be greeted by the sight of men carrying lamps at his gate and, just beyond them, a dark sedan, suspended between eight uniformed runners. Veovis himself stood beside the carriage, talking to someone within its shadowed interior.

A sudden anger boiled up in Aitrus. Striding down the path, he confronted Veovis even as he turned.

"What are *you* doing here?"

Veovis stared back at him haughtily.

"Come!" Aitrus demanded. "What do you want?"

"Want?" Veovis's face hardened. "Nothing from you, Aitrus. I deal only with men of honor."

Aitrus bristled. "You dare to question *my* honor?"

"Say only that I know who D'ni's friends are, and who its enemies."

Aitrus felt a flash of hatred ripple through him. He wanted to strike Veovis. To break him as one might dash a plate against the ground.

"You had best hold your tongue, *Lord* Veovis, before I rip it from your mouth!"

Veovis's eyes flared. "It is you who should be careful, lest I teach you a lesson in manners!"

Aitrus clenched his fist, then, knowing that violence would solve nothing, forced himself to be calm. "I know to whom *my* loyalty lies well enough, Veovis. Would that I could say the same of you."

"I give my loyalty to those who deserve it," Veovis responded. "It is no *cheap* thing."

Aitrus frowned. If that was a jibe at him he did not understand it. What did Veovis mean? Changing tack, he asked the question he ought to have begun with.

"Where is my wife? Where is Ti'ana?"

Veovis's lips formed a sneer. "Do you not know, Master Aitrus? Surely it is a husband's *duty* to know where his wife is!"

Aitrus took a step closer, so that his face was but a hand's width from Veovis's. He spoke quietly, threateningly.

"Do *you* have her?"

For a moment Veovis simply stood there staring back at him, his eyes yielding nothing, then he turned and, drawing back the curtain of the sedan, reached in and, grasping her roughly by the hand, tugged Anna from her seat.

Anna glared at Veovis, then turned back, reaching in to take the sleeping child from the nurse within the sedan.

"A pretty pair you make!" Veovis said, a heavy sarcasm in his tone now. "Neither knows where the other is!"

Aitrus looked to Anna, his eyes concerned, but she shook her head, as if at some unspoken question.

Cradling Gehn, she moved past Aitrus, then turned, standing at his shoulder.

"Thank you," she said, speaking to Lord Veovis. "I am sorry to have troubled you."

"No trouble," he answered, his cold eyes never leaving Aitrus's face. "No trouble at all."

"MASTER AITRUS. THEIR LORDSHIPS WILL SEE you now."

Aitrus pulled himself up off the bench, then followed the guildsman along the corridor to where two guards stood before a pair of huge double doors.

For a week he had wrestled with his conscience, not knowing what to do. It was A'Gaeris's role in things that worried him most. The man had no love of D'ni, and to bring down D'ni's favorite son, Veovis, would fit in well with any plans he had for vengeance. All well and good, yet Aitrus had seen the Book, and still had the linking book in his possession. That was Veovis's hand and no mistake. And A'Gaeris's indignation, that burning sense of injustice Aitrus had glimpsed the last time they had met, that, too, had seemed genuine.

Anna had begged him to go straight to Master Jadaris and leave the Maintainers to deal with the matter, but that would have meant going behind Lord Rakeri's back, and that Aitrus would not do.

And so, eight days on, he had gone to see Lord Rakeri in his rooms in the Halls of the Guild of Miners. The old man had greeted him warmly. There, over a cup of mulled wine, he had told the old man of his son's activities.

Aitrus could see how torn the old man was. He had always treated Aitrus like a second son, even after the breach in Aitrus's friendship with Veovis, but suddenly there was a coldness, a distance in his manner. The old man had stared long and hard at the linking book, and then he had nodded.

"Leave it with me, Master Aitrus," he said, his voice cold and formal, "I shall make sure that the matter is fully investigated."

A long silence had followed. But now, a full month after that audience with Rakeri, the matter was to be decided.

As the doors swung back, Aitrus looked about him. Beside the five Lords who sat behind the great desk on the far side of the chamber, there were six others, seated at desks to either side of the room. To his left were three guild scribes, to his right two senior guildsmen in the Guild of Maintainers, and, slightly apart from them, their Grand Master, the elderly Jadaris.

There was no sign of Veovis.

Aitrus felt relief flood him. He had been feeling awkward enough about this, but had Veovis been there in person it would have been far more difficult.

"Take a seat, Master Aitrus," Lord R'hira said, looking up from a document.

Aitrus sat, then glanced at Rakeri. The old man was looking down, distracted, it seemed, the fingers of one hand drumming idly on the leather cover of an official-looking file. He did not look well these days, as if the cares of this inquiry had fallen heavily on his shoulders.

R'hira looked directly at Aitrus. "In view of what you told us, a unit of the City Guard was sent to the house in J'Taeri District and a thorough search was made. Unfortunately, no trace of any of the papers you mentioned could be found. This is not to say that they do not exist somewhere, but without them we have only your word. That in itself is no small thing, Guild Master Aitrus, yet it is not evidence, as defined by D'ni law." He paused, then. "It comes down to this. After long consideration we have decided that we cannot possibly risk using the linking book. To risk a third life would be, we felt, a reckless chance, and without the direct evidence of which you speak—that is, the bodies of the two guildsmen—then it is a matter of your word against that of Veovis."

Aitrus blinked, surprised.

"Forgive me, Lord R'hira, but I find this situation intolerable. Either I am a liar or Lord Veovis is. If you will not send another guildsman, I am prepared to go."

There was a moment's silence, then Lord R'hira nodded. "It shall be as you say."

Aitrus stood, then walked across and, taking the Book from Lord R'hira, and a Linking Book, he opened the Book in question, placing his hand against the glowing panel.

There was silence in the room. A few moments later Aitrus reappeared, his face ashen.

"It is true," he said. "There are bodies there."

THAT EVENING A WARRANT FOR VEOVIS'S arrest was issued. Though the day was now advanced, K'veer still blazed with lights. Every room was lit, every lantern burned brightly. Men from both the City Guard and the Guild of Maintainers were everywhere; in every room and every corridor. It was clear that a thorough search of the island had been undertaken.

Climbing the great stairway at the heart of the rock, Aitrus began to wonder just what he had set in motion. It was true what people said about the messenger who brings ill news.

Passing the entrance to the Book Room, Aitrus saw how armed teams of Maintainer guards were waiting there, ready to link into the family Ages. That, as much as anything, told him that they had not yet taken Veovis.

So he is guilty, he thought, surprised despite all, for some small part of him still held that this was all a mistake and that an explanation would be found. But no. If Veovis was missing, then there could be but a single explanation.

Master Jadaris was waiting for him in Lord Rakeri's study, near the very top of the island mansion. It was a regular cave of a room. There were no windows; instead, huge, book-lined shelves filled every inch of the walls.

"Ah, Aitrus," Jadaris said, looking up at him from behind the great desk. The Linking Book lay before him, open, the tiny panel glowing in the half-light of the room. "We have searched high and low, but there is no sign of Lord Veovis in D'ni. In the circumstances I have given the order for the family Ages to be searched. That will happen now. But there is one other matter we must deal with."

Jadaris waved a hand over the Linking Book. "A guildsman ventured in four hours back. He found another Book at the foot of the slope. It linked back to this very room."

Aitrus nodded soberly. There was a moment's silence and then Master Jadaris stood.

"So, Aitrus. Will you link through with me?"

THEY LINKED TO A CAVE ON THE EASTERN slope of a large, mountainous island. A cluster of smaller islands surrounded it, linked by suspended wooden bridges. It was on one of these that they finally found the two guildsmen, lying side by side in a hut beside the cliff's edge, their hands and feet bound tight. They were long dead, their cloaks stiff with their own dried blood, their throats slit from ear to ear. On the floor nearby was the dagger that had been used to kill them, lying beside its sheath as if abandoned.

It was Veovis's weapon. One he had been seen to carry often.

Aitrus saw how Jadaris stared at the dagger; saw the strange flicker in the muscles of his neck, the sudden change in his eyes, and knew that this had finally

convinced him. These were *his* men who had been murdered—his young boys. To see them like this— trussed and butchered—had clearly shocked him deeply.

As a team of Maintainers arranged to bring the bodies back, Aitrus and Master Jadaris linked back to K'veer. There they were greeted by the news that Veovis had been taken in Nidur Gemat and was being held in the Book Room down below.

They went down, Aitrus hanging back as Jadaris walked across to confront Veovis.

Veovis's hands were bound behind his back. Two guards—Maintainers—stood to either side of him, yet Veovis seemed unrepentant. His head was raised defiantly and his eyes burned with indignation.

Jadaris held the sheathed dagger out before him. "Is this yours, Master Veovis?"

"It is," Veovis said. "What of it?"

"You do not deny it, then?"

But Veovis seemed not to hear. He took a step toward Jadaris.

"What have I done to deserve this treatment, Master Jadaris? Am I a common criminal to be bound and herded like an animal?"

"We found the bodies," Jadaris said.

But Veovis did not seem to be listening. "I am not normally an impatient man, but I warn you, Guildsman. Unbind me now or you shall answer to my father!"

A shiver went through Jadaris. "It was your father who ordered it."

Veovis fell silent; the words had taken him aback. "Impossible," he said. "He would never have given such an order."

"Never?" Jadaris seemed to watch Veovis a moment, then: "Do you deny the charges?"

"Charges?" Veovis laughed coldly, then tilted his head slightly. His eyes were hostile now. "I do not understand you, Master Jadaris. Of what precisely am I charged?"

"Of trading in illicit Ages. And of murder."

The look of shock in Veovis's face surprised Aitrus. For a moment Veovis seemed unable to speak, then he shook his head. "But this is ridiculous! I have done nothing."

"We have the proof," Jadaris said coldly. "But I am not your judge, Veovis. At least, not alone."

Jadaris seemed to straighten, taking on his full authority, then spoke again.

"Guild Master Veovis, you will be taken from this place to the Guild Fortress of Irrat where you will be held secure until a date is set for your trial."

"My *trial?*" Veovis's expression was one of sheer disbelief.

Jadaris nodded, yet he seemed far from triumphant. "This is a sad day for the guilds, Lord Veovis. You have brought great shame upon us, and even greater shame upon your father."

"But I have done nothing!"

Jadaris glared at him. "*Nothing?* You will be silent, Guild Master, or I shall have you gagged!"

Veovis blinked, astonished. His mouth opened, then snapped shut.

"Good," Jadaris said curtly. "Now take him from here. Before I am tempted to do to him what he did to those poor boys."

AITRUS RETURNED HOME TO FIND THE BLINDS drawn, doctors hurrying to and fro. His mother, Tasera, greeted him in the hallway, her face gaunt, her eyes troubled. Gehn had worsened, it seemed, and almost died. It was she who had finally called in the Healers, when all else seemed hopeless.

Aitrus went through to the nursery, fearing the worst. Anna was sitting beside the cot, clearly exhausted, staring down at the feverish child as he lay there like a waxwork doll, his eyes closed, his breathing shallow. Nearby, a doctor spoke quietly, urgently to one of his colleagues, then, seeing Aitrus, came across.

"There's little we can do," he said sorrowfully. "We have tried several remedies, but the child seems unable to keep anything in his stomach. I fear it is up to the Maker now."

Aitrus thanked the man, then went over and knelt beside Anna, resting his hand lightly on her knee.

"Ti'ana? . . . Ti'ana? It's Aitrus. I'm back."

She turned her head slowly and looked down at him. "He's dying, Aitrus. Our son is dying."

The desolation in her face was unlike anything he had ever seen. "No," he said softly. "He'll come through."

But she was not to be consoled. "You did not hear him, Aitrus. The sounds he made. Such awful, dreadful sounds. And the spasms. Twice I thought I'd lost him."

"Maybe," he said, "but he's still here."

He took her hands and clenched them, looking up into her face. "Won't you fight for him, Ti'ana? Won't you help our son survive?"

Anna closed her eyes, pained by his words. "I've tried, Aitrus. The Maker knows I've tried my best. But I am so tired now. So very, very tired."

"Then rest, my love. It's my turn now."

Aitrus stood, then, bending down, lifted Gehn from the cot, holding him tightly, securely against his shoulder. The child whimpered a little, then settled against him. He was so light now; there was so very little of him. The lightest breeze would carry him off.

Aitrus shuddered, filled with an ineffable tenderness for his infant son. "Come now, little one," he said softly as he carried him from the room. "Let us see what a little sunlight can do for you."

VEOVIS LOOKED UP FROM THE SUMMARY document and sighed. It was lies, every word of it, yet even he could see how convincing a case Aitrus had made against him. If the Five believed this—and why should they not?—then he would be found guilty, without a doubt.

Suahrnir. Suahrnir was the key, but Suahrnir could not be found.

Veovis's own statement lay on the desk beside his elbow—six pages in his own hand. At best it seemed naive, at worst a tissue of lies and excuses. He knew which his fellow guildsmen would think.

They had let him see the evidence against him; the books and documents and letters, all of it written, or so it appeared, in his hand. Good forgeries they were—the best he had ever seen—but forgeries all the same, for he had not written a single word of what they had shown him.

He had pointed the finger at Aitrus, but they had expected that. It was to be expected, after all. To "humor" him, and perhaps to mollify his father, they had even searched back in the guild records to see whether there might not be some earlier instance of such fraud, one that might be attributable to Aitrus, but there was nothing.

Aitrus was a clever one. None cleverer. He played the honest man. But Veovis knew better. He knew now what a snake Aitrus was.

He heard the cell door open behind him and turned to see a guard bring in a pile of clean clothes and place it on the bed in the far corner of the room. Another guard stood in the door, blocking it. The sight of it almost made him laugh, for it suggested that he might try to escape, and when did a D'ni Lord run from his fate?

Veovis turned back to the copy statement, then pushed it away from him. It was no use. There was no way he could answer this. It was like grasping at phantoms.

He even understood it, now that he had had time to reflect upon it.

How long had Aitrus prepared this? Since he had refused to countenance the wedding, no doubt.

Veovis stood and stretched. Was that all Aitrus wanted? To bring him down? Or was there more? Was there some further part he could not see?

Veovis crossed the room and sat on the edge of the bed, beside the pile of clothes. He felt weary now and in need of sleep. Too much had happened much too quickly.

He reached out and picked up the pile of clothes, meaning to move it so that he could stretch out on the bed, but the pile was heavier than he expected. Strangely heavy, in fact. He put it down, then began to sort through it, his brows knitted.

There! Halfway down the pile his fingers closed on something hard. A book! A leather-covered Book! He drew it out and stared at it, amazed. There was no mistaking it—It was a Linking Book. He opened it. There, on the right-hand page, the tiny panel glowed invitingly.

It was a trap. It had to be, or a test of some kind. He closed the Book and set it down.

A trap. Of course it was.

But what if it was not. What if this was his father's doing? Veovis stood, then closed his eyes, wracked by indecision. This was his chance to prove himself an honest man. If he handed in the Book . . .

He groaned, then sat once more. Who was he fooling? They would find him guilty whatever. The evidence was too strong against him. And what then? Two hundred years, he'd spend, trapped on some hideous, tiny island on a Prison Age, watched every second of the day and night.

The thought was unbearable. Opening the Book again, he placed his hand against the panel . . . and linked.

LORD R'HIRA STEPPED INTO THE EMPTY CELL and looked about him. The Linking Book lay on the bed where Veovis had left it only a moment before. He stared at it, then shook his head. A while later he heard a shout from farther down the hallway—a curse that turned into a groan.

So now you know, R'hira thought sadly. *And what will that knowledge do to you, Veovis?*

The Book had linked to an enclosed room on a different Age, in which was a table. On that table was a second Linking Book and a tank of acid. It was a classic escape maneuver, and Veovis, naturally, had seen exactly what to do.

But that second Book linked right back to D'ni—to the interrogation cell at the end of the hallway, wherein sat Master Jadaris and his guards.

R'hira sighed. Had Veovis known it was a test? Or was this simply some final piece of arrogance on his part?

He turned. Rakeri was standing in the doorway, his eyes dark with the knowledge of what his son had done.

"I'm sorry," he said quietly, but Rakeri shook his head.

"Do what you must," the old man said. "I wash my hands of him."

AITRUS WOKE, NOT KNOWING WHERE HE WAS. It was bright, too bright to fully open his eyes.

Gemedet. I must be on Gemedet.

Squeezing his eyes shut again, he searched about him with his hand until his fingers closed upon his glasses. He pulled them on, then slowly opened his eyes again. The filters in the glass made the brightness bearable.

It was morning. Or maybe afternoon. How long had he slept?

Then he remembered.

"Gehn!"

He sat up, looking about him anxiously, then relaxed. Gehn lay not three feet away from him, swaddled in a blanket where Aitrus had laid him last night. He lay there silently, his tiny glasses shielding his eyes against the light that shone in a broad band through the window just above them.

Aitrus shuffled across, then picked up his baby son, cuddling him for a moment, then putting a hand lightly to his brow.

The fever had passed.

Gehn stared back at him, curiously, his eyes placid, calm. D'ni eyes, for all the doctors said.

"You came through," Aitrus said, smiling at him, proud suddenly of his son. "Look at you, there's nothing of you, Gehn, yet you came through. You *lived!*"

There was a noise outside. Aitrus turned. Was it some forest animal, sniffing about the camp? Then he heard the soft hum of Anna's voice and smiled.

He stood, carrying the child out to her. She was standing with her back to him, looking out across the valley and the mist-wreathed waterfall. For a moment he simply stood there, watching her, conscious of how the sunlight formed a shining wreath about her long, flowing hair, then he spoke.

"Ti'ana?"

She turned, smiling at him. "I wondered when you would wake."

"Look," he said, holding out Gehn to her. "The fever's gone."

"I know," she said, coming across and taking Gehn from him. "I came in earlier and saw. I thought I'd let you both sleep."

He looked up at the sky. The sun was sinking toward the west. "It's late," he said. "How long have we slept?"

"A full day and more," she said, smiling broadly at him. "It clearly did you good."

"Yes," he agreed. Then, as if suddenly recalling something, he laughed. "You know, I had a dream last night."

"A dream?" she looked at him, intrigued. "What kind of dream? A pleasant one I hope."

He smiled. "Oh yes. I dreamed we walked the tunnels to the surface. You and I . . . and Gehn. And you took us to all of those places you have told me of in the past, even to Tadjinar itself."

"And the Lodge?"

"Yes." He nodded, staring out past her as if he really saw it. "I dreamed that we stayed there and that I sat there in the window with you, looking out across the desert. There was a full moon above us and the sky was full of stars. And Gehn . . . I could hear Gehn sleeping in the room behind us."

"Maybe it will happen, one day."

"You think so?"

She was quiet a moment, then, "I heard what happened . . . with Veovis."

"Ah . . . " He nodded, then. "I do not know what to think, Ti'ana. The Veovis I knew would never have acted in such a fashion."

"Yet people change."

Aitrus looked directly at her. "Do they? I am not so sure, my love. What a man is, he is. Though Veovis is no friend, I would yet trust him above many who call themselves my friend. And do you forget . . . he brought you home that time."

"It was but common courtesy."

"Was it? And yet that same man is charged with callously murdering two guildsmen. Do you really think him capable of that?"

Anna looked down, troubled. "Of course . . . you have not heard, have you?"

"Heard what?" Aitrus asked.

"The Five Lords tested him. Secretly gave him a Linking Book, in his cell on Irrat. He took it and tried to escape. No honest man would do that, would they?"

Aitrus stared at her a moment, then looked down. "So it is true, after all."

"It seems so."

"And Lord Rakeri? How has he taken the news?"

"Badly," Anna said, rocking Gehn gently. "It appears he has taken to his bed. Some say he is dying."

Aitrus looked down, touched deeply by the news. "Then it is an ill day for D'ni," he said quietly. "An ill day indeed."

THE NARROW STREETS LEADING TO THE GREAT Guild House were packed as the carriage carrying Veovis rattled through the gates, drawn by two great oxen.

After twenty days of evidence, the Council was to give their verdict. Never before had so high a public figure been on trial, and never for such heinous crimes.

To trade in illicit Books was bad enough, but to kill one's fellow guildsmen, that was unheard of. And that was why they crowded into the narrow spaces between the great houses of the upper city, straining to get a glimpse of the villain of the piece, Veovis.

Some saw him as a greedy man, for whom great riches had never been enough. Others commented on his hypocrisy and saw his protestations of innocence in the face of such a weight of fact as a sure sign of his mental instability.

This was the atmosphere in which Veovis stepped down from the carriage, and, climbing the marble steps of the Guild House, crossed the outer room and entered the great chamber to hear the verdict of his peers.

A temporary gallery had been built at one end of the chamber especially for the occasion—a temporary affair that seated those few dozen guests who had been invited by the Council to bear witness. Among these were the families of the two dead guildsmen, A'Gaeris, and Aitrus's wife, Ti'ana.

Anna was now a D'ni citizen. In a private ceremony, a week earlier, she had become by law what blood nor marriage could make her. It was a precedent, but one the Council approved.

But now the moment had come. As Veovis stepped out between the great doors, a silence fell over the great, circular chamber. From their seats on the various levels, every member turned to look.

Veovis had had his hair cut stubble short. He wore a simple one-piece of rust-red cloth. There were iron manacles about his wrists, linked by a short length of chain, and manacles at both ankles, from which two fine steel chains led back into the hands of a Maintainer guard; a big man, capable, it seemed, of holding back a team of horses.

Even so, Veovis stood there a moment with his head high, his eyes as proud, as unbowed, as an eagle's, then he began to descend the steps, passing between the great pillars.

Below Veovis, in the center of the chamber, stood the five great thrones of the Five Lords of D'ni, but today only four of them were filled. As Veovis came to a halt in the space before them, the great Lords stared at him like living statues, their dignity immense.

There was a moment's silence, tense, expectant, and then Lord R'hira spoke.

"Guildsmen. Have you decided?"

There was a resounding "Aye!" from all sides of the chamber.

"And your verdict?"

"Guilty!" 360 voices said as one.

It was done. Veovis seemed to tremble; yet his head did not waver, nor did his eyes show even a flicker of regret. If anything he seemed even more defiant than before.

R'hira looked to him, his ancient eyes cold, no trace of compassion in them. "Before I come to your sentence, is there anything you would like to say, Guild Master Veovis?"

Veovis met the ancient's eyes, then shook his head.

"Very well. Then it is the decision of this House that you be stripped of all rank and that from henceforth your membership of the guild be annulled. Further, you will be taken from here and on the seventeenth hour fifteen days hence will be transferred to a suitable Prison Age, to be held there for the remainder of your natural life."

All eyes were on Veovis. From her seat in the gallery Anna saw how fine, how dignified he looked in this his final moment and felt the slightest flicker of doubt cross her mind. Yet he *was* guilty. She had heard and seen enough these past twenty days to know that much. Glancing across, she saw how A'Gaeris was leaning forward. What was that gleam in his eyes? Delight that justice had finally been done? Or was it simple gloating?

She looked down briefly, a shiver of distaste running through her, then looked back, her eyes seeking out Aitrus where he sat in the first row, just behind Veovis.

As Veovis turned, preparing to climb the steps again and leave the chamber, he halted briefly, right in front of Aitrus, staring down at his once-friend. Something seemed to be said, then he walked on, his bare, manacled feet climbing the stone, the big Maintainer trailing behind.

Anna waited, as the great Lords ended the session, then, as the members began to stand, a great murmur of talk rising in the chamber, she hurried quickly down the steps.

Aitrus was standing in the midst of a tiny group of other members. As she stepped into their circle they broke off their animated discussion, bowing to her respectfully.

"What did he say?" she asked, looking anxiously to Aitrus.

He hesitated, conscious of the others listening. "Not here, Ti'ana."

She frowned. "Did he threaten you?"

Aitrus shook his head, but he was awkward now. Looking about him apologetically, he stepped across the circle and, taking Anna's arm, led her away.

"Well?" she asked, when they were outside, out of the hearing of the others. "What did he say?"

Aitrus turned from her, as if he could not face her. He seemed pale now, discomfited. "He blames me."

"Is that what he said. That he blames you?"

Aitrus shook his head.

"Well, *tell* me, Aitrus. What *did* he say?"

Aitrus turned, looking directly at her. "'You should have let me fall.' That's what he said."

"But you are not to blame."

"No? I wish I could believe that. At the end there, watching him—even after all that was said and shown—do you know what I thought? I thought he was innocent. *That* is what I thought. And yet I said 'Aye' with all the rest. And sent him to his rock."

"Do you want to do something? To say something, perhaps, to the Five?"

He laughed bitterly. "What could I say? No. I must live with this, Ti'ana. Knowing I might have been wrong. Yes, and knowing that I was the one who set the wheels in motion. Those great wheels of the D'ni state that can crush a man as easily as our great hammers pound the rock."

They stood there a moment, silent, staring at each other, and then Anna took his arm and led him out. Yet even as they stepped out beneath the massive arch at the front of the Guild House, the great bell on Ae'Gura began to sound, sending its sonorous tones across the cavern.

Lord Rakeri was dead.

PART SIX: THE INK IN THE WELL

IT WAS THE FOURTH ANNIVERSARY OF Gehn's naming day and a solemn ceremony was taking place in the family mansion in D'ni. Until today, Gehn had been a child, free to play as a child played, but from this hour onward he would take the first steps toward becoming a guildsman.

Looking on, Anna felt deeply for her son. Standing amid the guild officials, little Gehn looked terrified. His hair had been cut and he was wearing guild clothes—duplicates of those his father, Aitrus, and his grandfather Kahlis wore as they stood on either side of him. In front of them, behind a special trestle table that had been set up in the room, stood Yteru, the Grand Master of the Guild of Books. It was to his guild that Gehn was to be apprenticed, and the boy would join them in their halls two weeks from now.

Two days ago, knowing how much her son was dreading the occasion, Anna had gone to Aitrus in his study and asked him if Gehn really did need to join the guild just then. He was sure to miss home dreadfully, but Aitrus was adamant. It was the D'ni way, and if Gehn was to be considered D'ni and make his eventual way in the world, then he must conform to the ways of the guilds.

And so she was to relinquish him, long before he was ready to be taken from her. It would break his heart and hers, but maybe Aitrus was right. Maybe, in the long run, it *would* be best for him. Yet she had her doubts.

As the Grand Master called the boy forward, she found herself praying silently that he would remember the words she had taught him—the words of the guild oath.

Slowly, stumblingly, Gehn forced them out. As he finished, Master Yteru smiled benevolently down at the child, then, in a slow, sonorous drawl, uttered the words of acceptance.

And so it was done. Her son was now a guildsman.

Afterward, she held him, telling him how proud she was, but she could see the fear of separation in his eyes.

Aitrus had been saying his farewells to the guildsmen; now he came back. He stood in the doorway, looking in at her and Gehn. "Are you angry with me?"

She nodded.

He sighed, exasperated. "I am sorry, Ti'ana, but you know how things stand. It is the D'ni way, and we cannot afford to act differently. That would be self-indulgent. You knew that when you became D'ni."

"I know," she said, as angry at herself as at him, "but I did not think it would be so hard."

"No. But there is one thing we can do. Before Gehn goes, that is."

"You want to go to Gemedet?"

Aitrus shook his head. "I promised you once. Remember?"

At first she did not understand; then her eyes widened.

He nodded.

"Yes, Ti'ana. It's time our son saw where his mother came from."

THE JOURNEY THROUGH THE TUNNELS TOOK two days. On the morning of the third they came to the cavern where the two great digging machines stood silently. As Anna and Gehn came up beside him, Aitrus turned to them and smiled.

"We are almost there." He pointed across at the great red wedge of rock facing them. "There is the seal. The surface must be just above."

Anna nodded. "This is where I came in. I remember it vividly. The machines . . . " She stared at them fondly, then smiled. "Do you know what I thought, Aitrus?"

"No, tell me."

"I thought I had discovered the tomb of a great king. And these . . . I thought these were the remains of some great civilization, a long-lost race of giants, perhaps, or . . . " She laughed. "Little did I know."

Aitrus looked at her fondly. "I am glad you chose to look, Ti'ana. But for that curiosity of yours, I would have been lost."

Anna looked away, a smile on her lips. "Oh, I am sure some young D'ni maiden would have found you."

He laughed. "Maybe. But let us press on now. I am impatient to see the surface."

Gehn, who had been silent until that moment, now spoke up. "Daddy? Why did we not *link* to the surface?"

Aitrus came back and, crouching before his son, began to explain. "If this were a different Age, then we might have linked to it, but the surface is in the same Age as D'ni and one cannot link to a place in the same Age."

"What, *never?*" the boy asked, wide-eyed.

"Never," Aitrus said, smiling patiently.

Gehn frowned, considering that, then looked back up at his father. "But how will we find our way back to D'ni?"

Aitrus took his notebook from his pocket and opened it. Inside, between the tanned leather covers, were page after page of maps and diagrams. Aitrus flicked through it for a while, then, coming to the page, turned the notebook so that Gehn could see.

"Look, Gehn. Here is a map of the tunnels. I have been making notes as we went along. We need only trace our way back."

It seemed to satisfy the boy. He grinned, then went across to his mother, who stood beneath one of the great machines. She put her arm about him, then looked back at Aitrus.

"When I first saw these, I was convinced that whoever had made them must be long dead, for what kind of race would make such wonderful machines then leave them in the rock?"

Aitrus smiled then walked across to her. "Was it this one that you climbed?"

She nodded.

"You climbed it, Mama?" Gehn asked, looking up at his mother in wide-eyed wonder.

"I did. And then I walked down into D'ni. Only I did not know it was D'ni. Not until long after."

They went through the gap, Anna leading the way, Gehn close behind. Reaching the pocket, Aitrus lit the lantern again. He knew what lay ahead—Anna had already told him—but now they were so close, he felt a strange excitement. How many years now had he waited for this?

Fifty years, at least.

Anna was first to climb down. At the bottom she turned, reaching up to take Gehn as Aitrus let him down. Then they were in the cavern, where it had first began for Anna, all those years ago. She looked to him.

"It hasn't changed."

They went on, climbing up into the tunnel and along, until the three of them stood before the rock fall.

Aitrus set the timer, then took them back to a safe distance. There was a huge bang. The whole tunnel shuddered. As the smoke cleared, Anna picked Gehn up and, following Aitrus, walked through, stepping over the rubble.

It was night. A full moon rested like a shining disk of silver in the center of the blue-black velvet sky. Surrounding it, a billion flickering stars shone down.

Aitrus stood there at the entrance to the tunnel, staring up at the moon. Beside him, Anna held Gehn against her side, her face close to his, and pointed.

"Look, Gehn. That's the moon."

"Moon," he said, snuggling in to her, tired now.

Anna smiled then turned her head, looking to Aitrus. He met her eyes and smiled.

"Come," he said, taking her hand, "let's find the Lodge."

THEY SAT ON THE LEDGE OF THE OPEN WIN-
dow, looking out across the narrow bridge toward the
desert. Gehn was asleep in the room behind them.

Anna listened a moment, then smiled. Aitrus sat
just behind her, his arms about her, his chin resting on
the top of her head. It had been her secret dream to
bring him here and sit with him like this, yet now that
it was real it seemed more dreamlike than the dream—
a moment wholly out of time. She pressed back against
him and felt his arms tighten about her.

"Do you still miss him?" he asked softly.

"Sometimes."

She half-turned her head, looking back at him. "He
speaks to me sometimes. In my head."

Aitrus smiled, but she could see he only half-
believed her, or maybe thought she meant that she
thought of her father and remembered his words. But
it was true what she said.

She felt Aitrus sigh, a sigh of pure contentment,
and turned back, letting her eyes go to the descending
moon once more, the smile lingering at the corners of
her mouth.

"Ti'ana?"

"Hmm?" she answered lazily.

"I know how much you loved your father, and how
much you owed to him, but . . . well, what of your
mother? You never speak of her."

"No."

Even the thought of it brought back the pain.

"Ti'ana?" Aitrus sat forward.

"It's all right," she said.

She began again, hunching forward as she spoke, letting the words come haltingly. "It was an accident. We were climbing. In the mountains to the south of here. My father had gone up the cliff face first, and I had followed. Mother was last, all three of us tied on the same rope. Father had walked on a little way, to inspect the cliffs we had glimpsed from below. That was why we were there, you see. We were always exploring."

Anna stopped, catching her breath. Again she saw it, vividly, as if it had happened not thirty-five years ago but yesterday—the staring eyes, the mouth open in surprise.

Anna collected herself, then carried on. "The difficult part of the climb was behind her and she was only six or eight feet from the edge. I could almost have put out a hand and hauled her up. She was smiling. And then her foot slipped. It ought not to have mattered. The rope ought to have held her. I felt a momentary tension on it, then it went, like a rotten vine. And next thing she was falling. And not a sound—just her eyes looking back at me, her mouth open in surprise.

"Father blamed himself, of course. He should have checked the rope, he kept saying, but I could see that he was devastated."

Aitrus was silent a while. "I am sorry, Ti'ana. I did not know. I should not have asked."

She turned to face him, kneeling on the ledge. Her face was streaked with tears, but she was smiling tenderly now. She reached out, her hands gently holding his cheeks. "No, Aitrus. You of all people should have known. We should have no secrets, you and I."

She kissed him then; softly, tenderly, her eyes shining in the moonlight. And as they broke from the kiss, his eyes were wide with wonder.

GEHN WOKE HIM, SHAKING HIM AWAKE. SUNLIGHT blazed in from the room at the front of the Lodge, so strong it stabbed into his pupils, making him shield his eyes then feel about him for his glasses.

"Mama's gone!" Gehn was saying. "Mama's gone!"

Aitrus pulled on the glasses, then sat up, putting out his arms to hold the frightened boy. "No, Gehn. She will be back. I promise you."

But Gehn was sobbing uncontrollably at the thought that he had lost his mother. Aitrus held Gehn tightly until the crying subsided, then, picking him up, he carried him out, through the room at the front until they stood in the doorway, looking out over the valley.

The heat surprised him. It could not be more than an hour since dawn, yet already it was far hotter than the hottest day on Gemedet or Ko'ah. He recalled what Anna had said about the heat; how it was the single factor that determined life here. It was not something he would have written into an Age, but someone, the Grand Master who had written the Book of Earth, had thought of it, and created the conditions for such extremes of cold and heat.

Gehn had fallen silent, yet he still clung to his father's neck as if his life depended on it. Aitrus looked at him and smiled.

"You want a drink, Gehn?"

Gehn nodded.

Aitrus took him back inside, setting him gently down on the window ledge while he poured him a goblet of cool, clear water from the jug Anna had filled the night before.

Turning, he saw how Gehn was staring about him. "Where are we?" he asked, taking the water gratefully.

"This is where your mother lived when she was young," he answered. "This is where she grew up, with her father."

"Here?" Gehn seemed astonished. "But where are the Books?"

Aitrus laughed. "These people are human. They are not like the D'ni. They do not have Books and Ages. This is all they have."

Gehn wiped his mouth with the back of his hand, then looked up at Aitrus. "But how could they live with just this?"

Aitrus looked about him. To be honest, he had asked himself the very same question. Now that he had seen the Lodge, he wondered how Anna had survived out here.

"They made do," he answered, finally. Yet even as he said it he heard Anna's voice. She was singing. A song he had never heard before, in a tongue he did not know.

Quickly he joined Gehn at the window, in time to see Anna come over the crest of the hill, a small cart pushed before her. She was wearing a black cloak trimmed with red, the hood of which was up over her head. Seeing them, she waved, then came on again, finishing her song.

Aitrus went out onto the bridge, Gehn beside him. The heat was fierce but not yet overpowering. As Anna came up onto the bridge, she smiled and held out something for Gehn to take. He ran to her and took the strange box, then scuttled back inside, into the shade. Anna pulled back her hood, then stepped up to Aitrus.

"You should wear something on your head," she said, touching his brow. "Ten minutes in this and you will get sun-stroke."

"Sunstroke?" He did not understand her.

"The heat," she said. "It will affect your brain. You will collapse and be ill."

"You are jesting with me," he said, smiling, as if he understood she was joking, but she was not smiling.

"It is very dangerous out here," she said simply. "Both you and Gehn must keep covered up as much as possible. The desert sun is unforgiving."

He nodded, then. "Where have you been? And that cart . . . "

Anna half-turned, looking across at the cart, then she turned back to Aitrus. "I went to get it. It had all my books and journals on it. And other things. Fortunately I hid it well, and the desert did the rest. It was untouched, as if I'd left it yesterday."

"And that song. What was that?"

Anna smiled. "Did you like it?" She quickly sang a verse. "It's something my mother taught me. I could not sing it before. But now . . . " Again she smiled, then took his arm, leading him back into the shadows of the Lodge.

As they came into the main room, Gehn looked up at them, his eyes wide. "What is this game?" he asked, pointing to the checkered board, the black and white pieces that were laid out beside it.

"It is called chess," she said, squatting beside him. "My father taught me how to play, and I shall teach you."

Gehn beamed. "So I am not going to go to the Guild Hall after all?"

Anna looked down. "No, Gehn. You must go. But not yet. We will stay here for a few days, yes? Just you and I and Father."

Gehn looked away a moment, struggling with his disappointment, then he nodded and, turning back to Anna, picked up the white queen. "So what is this piece and what does it do?"

"THINBLOOD . . . "

"Who-man . . . "

"No-dunny . . . "

The whispers surrounded Gehn in the darkness of the dormitory; endless, taunting whispers that filled the lonely nights. Gehn lay there, facing the bare stone wall, the knuckles of his right hand pressed into his mouth, trying to shut it all out, but still the whispers came.

The mattress was too thin beneath him, the blankets rough and scratchy. But worst of all was the sense of abandonment that came each evening as the great door to the dormitory was closed and absolute darkness fell.

It was awful. More awful than he had ever thought possible. They had heard him crying the first few nights and had laughed at him for it. And then the whispers had begun, playing upon his fears and insecurity, making his life even more of a misery than it already was.

At home he was used to his own room, his own smooth sheets and blankets. There, a night-light rested in the corner, warm and reassuring. And he knew that his mother was always there, next door, in case bad dreams came and disturbed his sleep. But here there was nothing. Nothing but the darkness and the endless hurtful whispers.

Why had they done this to him? Why? Had he been bad? If so, he could not remember what it was that he had done. Or did they no longer love him? For to leave him here, among these awful, spiteful boys, was surely some kind of punishment.

He could remember his father's face, unnaturally stern, as he spoke to him the night before he had come here.

"You must be brave, Gehn. It is the D'ni way. It might seem hard at first, but you will get used to it, I promise you."

So much for promises. But the worst had been the parting from his mother. He had kicked and screamed, refusing to go with them, so that eventually they had had to pick him up and carry him to the waiting carriage.

That had been two weeks ago now. Two weeks of endless homesickness, and the torment of the nights.

Yet even as the whispers multiplied, Gehn found himself thinking of the lesson earlier that day. He had begun to think himself a fool; had begun to believe that the boys were right when they called him "No-dunny" and said he had sand in his head instead of brains. But today he had begun to understand what he was doing here, for today he had seen Master Urren.

Gehn was taught in a group of eight, the eldest aged seven, the youngest himself. Most of it was basic, the kind of stuff his mother had taught him back at home, but some was specific stuff about ink and writing; today's lecture in particular.

Master Urren, the visiting tutor from the Guild of Ink-Makers, was a big, ungainly, birdlike man, with a long, thin face and huge bushy eyebrows that seemed to form a continuous line across his upper face. He had the habit of staring into the air as he spoke, as if in a trance, then looking directly at one or other of his pupils, startling them. But it was not this habit but his words that had woken Gehn this morning.

With his eyes closed, Gehn could see Master Urren now, his right hand clenched into a fist as he spoke the Ink-Maker's litany.

"What binds the Word to the World? The Ink!

"What burns the bridge between the Ages? The Ink!

"What forms the living darkness between two lights? The Ink!"

Then, to the astonishment of them all, he had brought out a great tub of ink—lifting a handful of the fine dark granules so that they could see.

"The manufacture of this is a secret. A very grave and great secret, like the secret of the paper, which in time each of *you* will learn. But you must first prove yourself worthy to be trusted with such a secret, for the making of these two things is the key to immense power—the power to make worlds!"

And there was more, the words issuing thunderously from Urren's lips, so that Gehn had found himself staring at the guildsman openmouthed, amazed by the power of the words. This, he realized, was what his father had been talking about. This was what it meant to be a guildsman. Until that moment he had thought it a senseless thing to want to be, but suddenly, in one single, blazing moment, he understood.

Gehn turned and lay upon his back, letting his hand fall onto his chest. The whispers had stopped now. Soft snoring filled the silent darkness of the narrow room.

Secrets. He was to be the heir to great and wonderful secrets. Twenty years it might take, but then he would know, as Master Urren knew, and maybe then his eyes would burn with that same ferocious knowledge, that same certainty.

Gehn shivered, then, wiping his hand across his face, formed the words silently in the darkness.

It is the D'ni way.

THE INK-WORKS WERE BURNING. GREAT FLAMES curled up into the darkness, lighting the roof of the cavern almost a mile overhead. Gehn stood on the stone ledge, staring out the window across the rooftops of the upper city. Surrounding him, his fellow students jostled to see, but he stood at the very front, both hands tightly grasping the great central bar of the paneless window, looking out across the dark toward the massive blaze.

They had heard the explosion twenty minutes back, but at the time they had not understood just what was happening. Now they knew. Someone had placed a bomb in the very middle of the Ink-Works. Many were dead. Many more were missing.

For the past eight weeks there had been incidents. Senior guildsmen had been mysteriously attacked. Offices had been ransacked. In the worst of the incidents, three Kortee'nea—blank Books—had gone missing, along with a whole stock of smaller Linking

Books. The Maintainers had been placed on constant alert; no one knew yet who was behind the outbreak.

And now this.

There was a shout in the corridor behind them. Gehn turned, along with the others, to see the Duty Master hurrying down the corridor toward them, his hands waving madly.

"Boys! Boys! Get down from there at once!"

They climbed down, obedient to their Guild Master, yet as Gehn went to walk away, he saw how the Master hung back at the window, staring out at the blaze, the glowing orange light reflected in his pale eyes, a look of pure fear etched in his face.

AITRUS DID NOT WAIT TO BE SUMMONED BUT went straight to the Guild House. All but two or three of the Emergency Council were already there, the others arriving very shortly after Aitrus. As Lord R'hira called the meeting to order, a Master from the Guild of Maintainers hurried in and, bowing to R'hira, gave him the latest report from the Ink-Works.

Fifteen had died. Another eight were missing. It was too early to know for certain, but it seemed that a large stock of ink had been taken.

"But how was this possible?" Master Jadaris asked, when his man had finished.

"Someone is linking to places throughout D'ni," Guild Master Jerahl answered him. "Someone with special knowledge of the guilds."

"Some*one*?" R'hira queried, looking about the table. "Or are there several miscreants? Look at the pattern of the attacks. Not one but six separate guilds have now been targeted. And who knows where they will strike next? The only thing these incidents have in common is that they know the intimate workings of the guilds. They know where we are vulnerable. They know precisely where to attack and when."

"Veovis?"

All eyes turned to Aitrus, who had spoken the name.

"Impossible," Jadaris said, after a moment. "He is more than safe where we have put him."

"Is he?" Lord R'hira asked, leaning toward the Grand Master. "When did you last check on him?"

"Three weeks ago. After the first of these incidents."

"But before the remainder, yes?"

Jadaris nodded. Then, shaking his head. "No. I refuse to believe it. But if my fellow guildsmen would like me to check?"

"Do so, Master Jadaris," R'hira said. "And let us know what you discover."

Jadaris bowed to R'hira and left.

R'hira looked about the table. "Whoever this is—and we must not leap to *any* assumptions without full and proper knowledge—they aim to create a climate of fear, and what better way than to engage in a meaningless sequence of violent events?"

"Do you think that is what's happening here?" Master Jerahl asked.

"I do. But there is something none of you know about. Something that has been kept a secret among the Five. In view of this latest outrage, however, we feel you ought to know of it." R'hira paused significantly, then, looking down at his hands, said, "One of the Five great Books has been desecrated. That of Master Talashar. In fact, the structure of the text was so damaged and distorted that the Age has become unstable and we fear it will shortly self-destruct."

There was horror about the table. This was one of their worst fears—that their Ages would be tampered with and destroyed. And here was news that such a thing had happened, and not just to any Age but to one of the five "Classics," those ancient, beautiful Ages made by the greatest of D'ni's Writers.

"Who would do such a thing?" Hajihr of the Stone-Masons asked, his face mirroring the shock everyone felt at that moment.

"I do not know for certain," R'hira answered, "but I am beginning to have my suspicions. If it *is* Veovis, then I'd judge he is not acting alone. And there is one other thing. The new entries were in the same hand as that of Master Talashar."

"But he died more than six thousand years ago," Jerahl said, voicing the thoughts of all.

"That is so," R'hira said. "Yet the ink on the page was barely three weeks old."

There was a stunned silence, then Aitrus spoke again. "I think we should find A'Gaeris and hold him, until his part in this is fully known."

"You think *he* is involved, then?" Hajihr asked.

Aitrus shrugged. "He may be innocent, but I think not. I begin to share my Lord R'hira's doubts."

"And Veovis?" Jerahl asked, looking across at Aitrus.

"Perhaps Lord Veovis was innocent after all."

GUILD MASTER JADARIS PAUSED AT THE OUTER gate, waiting as the Master of the Keys unlocked the ancient door that led down into the earth.

No part of D'ni lay deeper in the rock than this, no part of the great city in the rock was more secure. A sloping tunnel led from the inner gate down to the Gate of Traitors, ten spans into the rock. There, in a cavern that had been hollowed more than three thousand years before, lay the Cells of Entry.

Jadaris walked down the long passage between the cells. All but one were empty. So it was. For though there were fifteen cells beyond the inner gate, few were ever used, for D'ni was an orderly society and transgressions that merited incarceration on a Prison Age were rare indeed.

"He *must* be there," he muttered to himself as, standing before the solid stone door of Veovis's cell, he waited for the Master of the Keys to unlock.

But R'hira's words had rattled him. Lord R'hira did not act on whim. If *he* had a suspicion, then like as not it was the truth. Even so, he could not believe that Veovis was not in the Age.

As the door swung back, he pushed past his Key Master almost rudely, so anxious was he for confirmation one way or another.

The cell was bare, the walls plain rock. A single wooden chair and a table were the only furnishings.

The book, allowing one to monitor the Prison Age, lay on the desk, open, its glowing panel visible.

Jadaris leaned over it. The panel showed no sign of Veovis at his desk in the Prison Age.

He turned, looking back at the squad of guards who had followed him and nodded.

"We go in."

MASTER JADARIS APPEARED IN A ROOM OF metal. The floor of the linking chamber was slatted black metal, the six walls a metallic blue that was almost black, undecorated and windowless, featureless almost, except for one large panel on the far wall facing him. Dim lighting panels in the ceiling gave the room an underwater feel. In the center of the floor was a hexagonal pedestal, on which rested the Linking Book. It appeared untouched.

More men were linking into the room now. Armed Maintainers, wearing sealed masks and carrying air tanks on their backs, ready for any sort of trouble.

As Jadaris stood, the armed men positioned themselves along the walls to either side of him. At Jadaris's signal, his first assistant stepped up to the panel and placed a flat "locking square" against the faint indentation in the panel, then stepped back.

There was a heavy *thunk!* as all six of the steel locking bolts retracted at once. With a hiss the door slid slowly into the floor.

Cold air flooded the room. Beyond the door a metal walkway ran on. Jadaris sniffed again, an expression of acute distaste in his face, then walked toward the doorway.

Stepping out onto the walkway he looked up. The sky was dark and glowering, a wintry sun obscured behind heavy cloud.

Facing him was the island. Jadaris stared at it, wondering what Veovis had thought the first time he had seen it, knowing that this was to be his home henceforth, until he died.

The island was a great block of black volcanic rock, its tapered shape thrusting up from a black and oily sea. Standing on top of that desolate rock was a black tower, its walls smooth and windowless. The walkway was an unsupported length of metal some five or six feet above the surface, joining the linking chamber to the island. A set of steps cut from the rock lead up from the walkway to the great door of the tower.

A cold, bleak wind blew from Jadaris's left, whipping the surface of the water and making him pull his cloak tighter about him.

"Come," he said, half-turning to his men, "let us see what is to be seen."

The great door was locked. As his Chief Jailer took the key from his belt and stepped up to fit it to the lock, Jadaris shook his head. It was not possible. It simply was not possible. Yet as they went from room to room in the tower, his certainty dissolved. In the top room was a table. On it they found a meal set out. Yet the meal had been abandoned weeks ago and lay there rotting. Beside it lay three Linking Books.

Jadaris took the first of the three Books and stared at it. He did not know how it had been done, but Veovis had been sprung.

He shivered. This whole business filled him with profound misgivings. It was hard to know just who to trust.

He opened the Linking Book and read a line or two. This one led straight back to D'ni. Or so it seemed. It would be easy to check—he could send one of his guards through—but that was not the way they normally did things. It was not guild practice to send a man through to any Age without a Linking Book to get them back.

Jadaris sat there a moment, staring at the words, his eyes unseeing, his thoughts elsewhere, then suddenly he stood. Sweeping the rotting meal onto the floor, he lay the Book down in its place and opened it to the descriptive panel. Then, looking about him at his men, Jadaris smiled and placed his hand down firmly on the panel.

THERE WAS THE ACRID TASTE OF SMOKE IN the air as Veovis, cloaked and hooded, made his way along the alleyway toward the gate. The narrow streets of the lower city were strangely crowded for this late hour, as people stood outside their houses to watch the guildsmen fight the great blaze farther up the city. The light from that blaze flickered moistly in Veovis's eyes as he walked along, but no one noticed a single figure passing among them. Great events were happening in the cavern. They had all heard the explosion, and rumor was even now filtering down from the upper city. Guildsmen were dead. Some said as many as a hundred.

Stepping out from under the gate, Veovis glanced up at the blaze. It was still some way above him and to his left. A muscle twitched at his cheek, then lay still. The guard at the gate had barely glanced at him as he passed, his attention drawn to the fire at the great Ink-Works. And so he walked on, passing like a shadow among that preoccupied crowd.

The gate to the upper city lay just ahead.

ANNA PULLED ON HER BOOTS, THEN STOOD, looking about her at the room. A cloak. Yes. She would need to take a cloak for him.

Going over to the linen cupboard, she took down one of Gehn's cloaks. Then, knowing that if she thought too long about it she might change her mind, she quickly left the room, hurrying down the hallway and out the front door.

Outside Anna paused, her eyes going straight to the blaze. It was below her and slightly to the left of where she stood. What it meant for D'ni she did not know, but the sight of it had finally made up her mind. She was going to bring Gehn home, whether Aitrus liked it or not. This had gone on far too long.

She hurried through the streets, yet as she came into the lane that lead to the Guild Hall, she found it barricaded, a squad of Maintainers keeping back a small crowd of bystanders. Even so, she went across, begging to be allowed to pass, but the guards would not let her and eventually she turned, making her way back along the street, wondering if there might not be another way to get to the Hall.

Down. If she went down to the gate and then across, she might come at the Hall by a different way.

She walked on, making for the gate, yet as she did, a man strode toward her. He was cloaked and hooded and kept his head down as he walked, as if heavily pre-occupied. There was something strange about that, and as he brushed past her, she caught a glimpse of his eyes beneath the hood.

She turned, astonished.

Veovis! It had been Veovis!

No. It could not be.

Anna swallowed, then, taking two steps, called out to the man. "Sir?"

But the man did not stop. He went on, hastening his pace, disappearing into a side street.

Anna hesitated a moment, then hurried after.

Turning the corner, she thought for a moment she had lost him; then she glimpsed a shadowy figure at the end of the narrow lane, slipping into the side gate of a darkened mansion.

Anna stopped, looking about her, but the lane was empty. If she was to find out what was happening she would have to do it herself.

Slowly, almost tentatively, she approached the gate. The blaze was at her back now. In its light everything was cast in vivid shadows of orange and black. There was a padlock on the gate, but it had been snapped and now hung loose. Anna leaned her weight gently on the door and pushed.

Inside was a tiny yard, enclosed by walls. A door on the far side was open. Anna went across and stood in the doorway, listening. Again she could hear nothing. She slipped inside, into what was clearly a kitchen. The house was dark, abandoned, or, more likely, boarded up. Only the glow of the distant fire lit the room, giving each covered shape a wavering insubstantiality.

She crossed the room, her footsteps barely audible. A door led onto the great hallway of the mansion. The body of the hall was dark, but on the far side was a huge staircase, leading up to the next floor. A great window on the landing let in the pale red glow of the blaze.

Anna listened a moment, then frowned. Perhaps she had imagined it. Perhaps he had not come in here at all. After all, it was dark, and she had been quite some distance off.

Briefly she wondered whose house this was and why it was abandoned. There were portraits on the walls, but most were in heavy shadow, all detail obscured. Only one, on the landing wall right next to the great window, could be discerned with any clarity, yet even that, in the wavering glow, seemed just a head and shoulders. It could have been anyone. Anyone at all.

Across from her, on the far side of the hallway, were more rooms. She quickly went across and peered inside, into the intense darkness, listening as much as looking. Again there was nothing.

She was about to go, to give up her fruitless search, when there was a distinct noise from the room overhead; a thump of something being put down; a heavy noise of metal and wood.

Anna felt her heartbeat quicken. She should not be here. Not alone, anyway. If it was Veovis, then he had escaped. And if he *had* escaped . . .

She was in danger—she knew that for a certainty—but she could not stop herself. Not now. The spirit of exploration was upon her. She had to know if it really *was* him, and if so, what he was doing.

She went to the foot of the stairs, staring up past the turn. Was there a faint light up there or was she imagining it?

Slowly Anna began to climb the stairs, ready at any moment to rush down and out of the great house. There were more noises now; the sounds of someone taking things and stowing them—in a sack, perhaps, or a bag. At the turn of the stairs she stopped, glancing up at the portrait. She was about to go on, when she looked again at the painting, sudden understanding coming to her.

It was A'Gaeris, or one of his ancestors so like him as to make no difference. The figure had the same querulous eyes, the same long brow and receding hairline, the same swept-back hair.

So this was your mansion once, Philosopher. Before you fell.

The knowledge was a key. She knew now that it *was* Veovis up above, and that A'Gaeris had somehow helped him to escape. How she did not know just yet, but perhaps she would discover that, given time.

Anna climbed the last few stairs, then stopped, her hand on the top rail, listening once more. The noises were coming from a room at the far end of the hallway—to her left as she stood. All the doors to the right of the corridor were shut, so it was not the light of the blaze she had seen from below. It came, in fact, from a room just up the corridor and to the left.

Anna took a long, calming breath then began to walk toward it. But she had only gone two paces when Veovis stepped from the room at the far end of the corridor and placed a backpack down on the floor of the hallway. She stopped dead, certain he would see her, but he did not even glance her way. With a sniff he turned and went back inside.

She quietly let out a breath, then walked on.

In the doorway to the first room she stopped, staring down the hallway to the door of the end room, certain that he would step out at that moment and see her, but then she heard him, whistling softly to himself, his footsteps clearly on the far side of the room.

She turned and looked inside. It was a study. Book-filled shelves were on every wall and a huge desk sat in the far corner. On it was a tiny lamp with a pale rose bulb of glass, lit by a fire-marble. In its glow she could see the outline of a Linking Book, the descriptive panel shining brightly.

For a moment she hesitated, then, walking across, she stood beside the desk and, putting out her hand, placed it on the panel.

VEOVIS CROUCHED, TYING THE NECK OF THE sack, then carried it outside. Lifting the backpack, he slung it over his shoulder then went along the hallway to the study.

All was as he had left it. He glanced about the study, then reached across and slid the catch back on the lamp, dousing the fire-marble. Slowly its glow faded. As the room darkened, the brightness of the panel in the Linking Book seemed to intensify, until he seemed to be looking through a tiny window.

Reaching out, Veovis covered that brightness with his hand, as if to extinguish it. For a moment the room was dark; then, slowly, the vivid square of light reappeared through the melting shape of his hand.

There was silence in the empty room.

ANNA STOOD AT THE WINDOW, LOOKING OUT at a view that was as strange as any she had ever seen. It was not simply that the sky had a heavy purplish hue, nor that the dark green sea seemed to move slowly,

viscously, like oil in a bowl, it was the smell of this Age—
an awful musty smell that seemed to underlie everything.

The chamber into which she had linked had been
cut into the base of the island, forming a kind of cellar beneath it. Knowing that Veovis was likely to link
after her, she had quickly left the room, hurrying up a
flight of twisting metal stairs and into a gallery that
looked out through strong glass windows on an underwater seascape filled with strange, sluggish creatures,
dark-skinned, with pale red eyes and stunted fins.

Halfway along this gallery, facing the windows, was
a large, circular metal hatch—wheel-operated, as on a
ship. Anna glanced at it, then went on.

A second set of steps led up from the gallery into a
spacious nest of rooms, at the center of which was a
six-sided chamber—a study of some kind. Two of the
walls were filled floor to ceiling with shelves, on which
were books. Further piles of ancient, leather-covered
books were scattered here and there across
the wooden floor, as if dumped there carelessly. A
dozen or so large, unmarked crates were stacked against
the bare stone wall on one side, next to one of the three
doors that led from the room. Two large desks had
been pushed together at the center. These were covered
with all manner of clutter, including several detailed
maps of D'ni—street plans and diagrams of the sewers
and service runs. In the far corner of the room a golden

cage hung by a strong chain from the low ceiling. In it was a cruel-looking hunting bird. Seeing Anna it had lifted its night-black, glossy wings as if to launch itself at her, then settled again, its fierce eyes blinking from time to time as it studied her watchfully.

A long, dark corridor led from the nest of rooms to the chamber in which she stood, which lay at a corner of the island. It was a strange room, its outer walls and sloping ceiling made entirely of glass panels. Through the glass overhead she could see even more rooms and balconies, climbing the island, tier after tier.

Like K'veer, she thought, wondering if Veovis had had a hand in its design.

At the very top of the island, or, rather, level with it, she could glimpse the pinnacle of a tower, poking up out of the very center of the rock.

Anna turned from the window. Behind her were three doors. The first led to a continuation of the corridor; the second opened upon a tiny storeroom; the third went directly into the rock—perhaps to the tower itself.

She went across, opening the last of the doors. A twisting stone stairwell led up into the rock. She was about to venture up it when there was a noise from the rooms to her right. There was a thud as something heavy was put down, then the unmistakable sound of Veovis whistling to himself. That whistling now grew louder.

Anna closed the door quietly and hurried over to the middle door. She could explore the stairwell later. Right now it mattered only that Veovis not find her there.

Slipping into the storeroom, she pulled the door closed behind her, even as Veovis's footsteps came along the final stretch of the corridor and into the room beside where she hid.

AITRUS TOOK OFF HIS CLOAK, THEN TURNED to face his mother.

"What is it?" he asked.

"It is Ti'ana," she answered. "I do not know where she is, Aitrus. One of the servants saw her leave an hour back."

"She went out? With things as they are?"

Tasera nodded. "I would have sent a man out after her, if I had known. But she left no message."

Aitrus frowned. "Wait here," he said, "I think I know where she might be."

"You know?"

"Not for certain, but Ti'ana has been unhappy these past few months. She has missed Gehn badly."

"We have all missed him."

"Yes, but Ti'ana has missed him more than anyone. Last week she asked me if he could come home. I think she may have gone to fetch him."

"They would not let her."

"Do you think that would stop Ti'ana if she were determined on it?"

Tasera shook her head.

"Well, I will go and see. Wait here, Mother. If she is not at the Guild Hall I shall return at once. But do not worry. I am sure she is all right."

ONE OF THE GUARDS ON THE BARRICADE remembered her.

"She was most persistent," he said, "but we had strict orders. We were to let no one pass, not even guildsmen, without special notification. She left here, oh, more than an hour ago now."

"Did you notice where she went?"

The young guard nodded, then pointed up the lane. "She went back the way she came, then turned left, under the arch. It looked as if she was heading for the western sector."

Aitrus thanked the guard then turned away. If Anna had been going home, she would have walked straight on and cut through farther up. Unless, of course, she was trying to get through to the Guild Hall by another route.

"Home," he told himself. He would check home first, just in case she had returned. Then, if she was not there, he would go to the Guild House and ask there.

ANNA CROUCHED AGAINST THE WALL, TRYING not to make a sound.

Veovis was just beyond the door. She had heard him stop and sniff the air.

"Strange," she heard him say. "Very strange."

She closed her eyes. At any moment he would pull back the door and see her there. And then . . .

His footsteps went on. She heard the door to the corridor creak open, then close behind him, his footsteps receding.

Anna took a long breath, then pushed the door ajar. The outer room was empty now, filled with the strange mauve light from the sky. She was about to step outside again when she glimpsed, just to her right, two shelves, cut deep into the wall. She had not noticed them before, but now she stepped across, amazed by what was on them.

Books! Linking Books! Dozens of them! She took one down and examined it. D'ni! This linked to D'ni! Quickly she examined another. That, too, appeared to link to D'ni. One after another she flicked through them.

All of them on the top shelf—every last one—seemed to link back to D'ni; each at a separate location: in a specific room in a Guild Hall, or in the cellar of a house; in storerooms and servants' quarters; and one, audaciously, direct into the great Council chamber of the Guild House.

So *this* was how they did it! Veovis was behind the spate of incidents these past few weeks.

Veovis, yes . . . and A'Gaeris.

The Books on the bottom shelf were blanks, waiting to be used. She counted them. There were forty-eight.

Anna stared at them, perplexed. How had they managed to get hold of so many blank Books? Had Suahrnir provided them? And what of Suahrnir? He had disappeared five years ago, presumed dead, but was he here, too?

When she had linked through she had not been quite sure what she meant to do. To take a peek and then get back? But now that she had seen the Books . .

I have to stop this, she thought. *Fifteen dead. That's what the guard said. And more will die, for certain, unless I act. Unless I stop this now.*

But how?

Anna stared at the Books, then nodded to herself, a plan beginning to form in her head.

VEOVIS STOOD AT THE END OF THE STONE jetty, his left hand resting lightly on the plinth as he looked out over the glutinously bright green sea toward a nearby rock that jutted, purest white like an enameled tooth, from its surface. A circular platform rested on that rock, as if fused onto its jagged crown, its gray-blue surface level with where Veovis stood.

Veovis glanced at the timer on his wrist, then slowly turned the dial beneath his fingers, clockwise, then counterclockwise, then clockwise again. He waited a moment, listening as the massive cogs fell into place beneath his feet, then pressed down on the dial.

Slowly a metal walkway slid from the stone beneath his feet, bridging the narrow channel, linking the jetty to the platform. There was a resounding *chunk!* as it locked in place.

Veovis waited, tense now, resisting the temptation to glance at his timer again. Then, shimmering into view, a figure formed in the air above the platform. It was A'Gaeris.

The Philosopher blinked and glanced up at the sky, as if disoriented, then looked across at Veovis and grinned, holding up the Linking Book that both Anna and Veovis had used; that, until five minutes ago, had rested in the study back in the boarded-up house in D'ni.

The two men met in the middle of the walkway, clasping each other about the shoulders like the dearest of friends, while behind them a third figure shimmered into being on the platform.

It was Suahrnir.

HIGH ABOVE THEM, FROM WHERE SHE STOOD at the north window of the tower, Anna looked on, watching the three men greet each other then turn and walk back along the jetty, Veovis and A'Gaeris side by side, Suahrnir following a pace or two behind.

She had been thinking all along of the Linking Book back on D'ni—asking herself why they should leave the back door to this Age open like that. But now she understood. A'Gaeris had come along behind Veovis and gathered up the Book, then used a second Linking Book, hidden elsewhere, no doubt, to link back to the rock.

The walkway had been retracted. If anyone now tried to link through to this Age they would be trapped on the rock, unable to get across to the island.

She stepped back, away from the window, then turned, looking about her. The big circular room seemed to be used as a laboratory of some kind. Three long wooden benches were formed into an **H** at the center, their surfaces scattered with gleaming brass equipment. Broad shelves on the long, curving walls contained endless glass bottles and stoppered jars of chemicals and powders, and, on a separate set of shelves, Books. *Guild* Books, she realized, stolen from the libraries of D'ni.

Anna walked across, picking things up and examining them. Coming to the window on the south side of the room, she looked out. The sea went flat to the horizon, its dark green shading into black, so that at the point where the sea met the pale mauve sky there seemed to be a gap in reality.

Just below the tower, the land dipped steeply away to meet the sea, but in one place it had been built up slightly so that a buttress of dark, polished rock thrust out into the sea. A kind of tunnel extended a little way from the end of that buttress, at the end of which was a cage; a big, man-sized cage, partly submerged.

Looking at it, Anna frowned.

She turned, looking back across the room. There was only one doorway into the room, only one stairway down. The strong wooden door had a single bolt, high up, which could be drawn from inside.

"Perfect," she said quietly, smiling to herself. "Absolutely perfect."

BACK INSIDE THE STUDY, VEOVIS SHUT THE door, then walked across. A'Gaeris and Suahrnir were already deep in conversation, pointing to locations on the map and debating which to strike at next.

Veovis stared at them a moment, then walked around past them and picked up one of the two bags he had brought with him from D'ni.

"Here," he said, handing it to A'Gaeris, "I brought you a few things back this time."

A'Gaeris looked inside the bag, then laughed. Taking out the cloak, he held it up. It was guild cloak, edged in the dark red of the Guild of Writers.

"To think I once valued this above all else!"

A'Gaeris shook his head, making a noise of disgust, then threw the cloak about his shoulders casually, preening himself in a mocking fashion and looking to Veovis as he did.

"So how *are* things in D'ni?"

Veovis smiled. "You were right, Philosopher. The destruction of the Ink-Works has unnerved them. Before now they were able to keep things close. Now all of D'ni knows there is a problem."

"That may be so," Suahrnir said, "but there is another problem: They now know that you are no longer on the prison Age."

Veovis turned to him. "They *know?*"

Suahrnir nodded. "I overheard two guards talking. It seems Master Jadaris himself took an expedition in to check that you were still there. Finding you gone, they will know that someone had to have sprung you." He turned to A'Gaeris and grinned. "And they will not have far to look, will they?"

A'Gaeris turned back to Veovis, concerned. "Then we must escalate our campaign. Until now we have had the advantage of surprise, but they will be vigilant from here on. We must identify our prime targets and hit them."

"Lord R'hira," Suahrnir suggested.

"Naturally," Veovis agreed. "But not first. First we deal with my meddlesome friend."

"Your friend?" A'Gaeris looked puzzled.

"My ex-friend, then. Guild Master Aitrus."

"Aitrus?" Suahrnir frowned. "But surely we can deal with him later?"

"No," A'Gaeris said. "What Veovis suggests makes sense. Cut off the head and the body cannot fight on. And who are the men whom we might call the 'head' of D'ni? Why, the Emergency Council, of course! Aitrus, Jadaris, Yf'Jerrej, R'hira. These are the four who are really running things right now, and so they must be our primary targets. Thus far we have unnerved the guilds. Now we must destabilize them."

"I agree," Veovis said. "But you will leave Aitrus to me."

A'Gaeris smiled. "If you want him, he is yours, my friend. But make no mistakes. And show no pity. Remember that he showed you none."

Veovis nodded. "I will not forget that easily. But come, let us formulate our plans."

ANNA TIPTOED PARTWAY ALONG THE CORRIDOR, then stopped. She could hear the faint murmur of their voices through the door. There was brief laughter, and then the talk went on.

Good. While they were occupied, she would move the Linking Books.

Returning to the room, she gathered up all she could carry at one go, then hurried up the tower steps.

Three trips saw all of the Books removed to the big room at the top of the tower. Satisfied, Anna cleared the surface of one of the benches, then began to pile the Books up in a heap, leaving only one aside.

That done, Anna picked up the Book she had set aside and returned to the door.

The easiest and quickest way was to burn the Books—to set fire to them, then link straight back to D'ni—but the easiest was not always the best. If she was to be sure of damaging their plans, she would need to make certain that there were no more Linking Books elsewhere on the island.

Anna listened a moment, then, satisfied that there was no one on the stairs, slipped out and hurried down. She had been depending on surprise so far, but she would need luck now, too, if she was to succeed.

Her luck held. They were still there inside the study. She could hear their voices murmuring behind the door.

"All right," a voice, Suahrnir's, said angrily. "But I do not know why we cannot just kill him and be done with it!"

Anna stepped back. At any moment the door might open and she would be discovered, yet she stayed there, listening.

"I'll go right now," Veovis said clearly. "Unless you have any further objections?"

"Not I," A'Gaeris said. "But hurry back. There's much to do before the morning."

"Do not worry," Veovis answered sardonically. "I know how best to hook our friend. I shall take no longer than I must."

AITRUS SAT AT HIS DESK IN HIS ROOMS AT the Guild Hall, in despair, his head in his hands. There was no sign of Anna. A search of the upper city had not found her. All inquiries had drawn a blank. And though Master Jadaris had agreed to make a more thorough search, Aitrus knew that they would not find her. Not in D'ni, anyway.

No. Veovis was somehow behind this. He had to be. And this was his revenge—to take Anna.

But what had he done with her?

Aitrus looked up, staring into the air, trying to think.

If he were Veovis, what would he want? Justice? No. It was far too late for justice. Vengeance? Yes, but not simply vengeance; at least, not the blind, uncaring kind that madmen seek, unless the isolation of the prison rock had sent Veovis mad.

No. He could not believe that. Veovis was stronger than that.

Perhaps, but what of A'Gaeris? What was his role in all this? And how had he persuaded Veovis to ally with him against the Guilds?

Betrayal. That was the seed A'Gaeris had planted in Veovis's mind. *Betrayal.* The guilds had betrayed Veovis, as they had once betrayed A'Gaeris. And now the guilds had to be punished.

Punished . . . or destroyed?

Aitrus stood, realizing that there was only one thing to do. They would have to search every inch of D'ni for Linking Books.

"If we can find out where he is linking back to . . . "

Aitrus looked up. Footsteps. There were footsteps farther down the hall.

He went out into the hallway.

"Ti'ana? . . . Ti'ana, is that you?"

Aitrus had barely gone two or three steps when the door at the far end of the hall swung open. He stopped dead.

"Veovis?"

Veovis stood there, smiling, a Linking Book held open in one hand.

"Yes, Aitrus, *dearest* friend. I have your wife. If you want her back, you had better follow me. And no tricks, or Ti'ana will die."

"No! Wait!"

Aitrus started toward him, yet even as he did, Veovis brought his other hand across, touching the glowing panel.

"*Veovis!*"

The Book fell to the floor.

So it was true. His darkest thoughts were thus confirmed. Walking across, he bent down and picked up the Book.

Help. Common sense told him he ought to get help.

But what if Veovis meant what he said?

Then common sense would kill his beloved wife.

"No choice," he said, as if to excuse himself. Then, sensing that only ill could come of it, he lay his hand upon the panel and linked.

DOWNSTAIRS THE DOOR SLAMMED SHUT. There were footsteps on the stairs. A moment later A'Gaeris appeared at the top of the stairs, looking about him. Seeing the Linking Book he smiled, then he went across and bent, picking it up. For a moment he studied the glowing panel, his smile broadening; pocketing the Book, he turned and went back down the stairs.

It was time to link back to the island.

ANNA SLIPPED THROUGH THE OPEN DOORWAY
and into the dimly lit chamber. To her right was the
study. Through its thin, wooden walls she could hear
the low murmur of two voices—those of A'Gaeris and
Suahrnir.

She sighed. It looked as if she was never going to
get the chance to search the study.

Anna turned, looking about her. There was a narrow bed in one corner of the room. Beside it, against
the back wall, were a small desk and chair. A worn silk
coverlet lay over the bed. On the desk were a number of
thin, coverless books, like child's exercise books. She
picked one up and opened it. It was one of A'Gaeris's
pamphlets—one of his endless ranting tirades against
the guilds that had won him notoriety, mainly in the
lower city.

Putting the pamphlet aside, Anna quickly examined
what else was on the surface. There was a small notebook, locked, she noted, with a tiny silver clasp. A D'ni
symbol—a simplification of A'Gaeris's name—was
burned into the leather of the cover. She picked it up
and pocketed it. Beneath it, to her surprise, was a tiny
picture in a gilded frame. It showed a young woman,

barely Anna's own age by the look of her, her dark hair swept back from a stunningly beautiful face.

That, too, she pocketed.

Anna turned, looking about her once more, checking that there was nothing else—no hidden panels and no hatches in the floor. Satisfied, she hurried back across the room again, meaning to make her way back to the tower.

She had delayed too long. Every moment now increased the chance of her being discovered. Best, then, to cut her losses: to go back to the room at the top of the tower and burn the Linking Books she had.

It would be a start. Besides, she knew much now about their plans. If she could reach Master Jadaris with that knowledge . . .

There was a sudden noise behind her, a buzz of voices from the central room. Veovis had returned. She heard his voice giving hasty orders. Then there was a strange grunt and the thud of a body falling to the floor.

There were other noises—scraping and scratching noises that she could make no sense of—and then Veovis spoke again, much louder this time:

"Take him down into the cellar. We'll put him in the cage. I'll use him as bait for another, much more tasty fish."

There was laughter, unwholesome laughter, and then the sound of a body being dragged across the room.

So they had taken another guildsman.

The corridor that led to the cellar was on the other side. For the moment she was in no danger of discovery. But time was running out. It was time to prepare things. Time to bait her own trap.

BACK IN THE TOP ROOM OF THE TOWER, ANNA began to search the shelves. She knew what she wanted: potassium nitrate, sulphur, carbon; some liquid paraffin, a length of wick; a tinderbox.

The bottles were labeled, each with a handwritten D'ni symbol, but she glanced at these only to confirm what her eyes already told her. She took the tiny bottles down, one after another, setting them side by side on the worktop, then took a mixing dish and a metal spoon from the side.

There were wicks in a drawer, and a polished silver tinderbox.

"What else?" she asked, her heart pumping quickly in her chest.

One bottle, set aside from all the others on the worktop, had no label. She had noticed it earlier. Its contents were clear, with a faint bluish tinge. Now, curious, she picked it up and unstoppered it, sniffing its contents.

Sputtering, Anna jerked her head back and replaced the stopper, her eyes watering. It was a horrible, noxious mixture; clearly a sleeping draught of some kind. Even a small sniff of it had taken her breath and made her head go woozy.

Anna shivered, then slipped it into her left-hand pocket, knowing that it might have a use.

A heavy iron file lay on one of the trays nearby. She took that too, tucking it into her belt. It would be useful to have a weapon of some kind.

Just in case . . .

Anna returned to the desk and picked up one of the jars, unstoppering it; yet even as she did, she heard noises from below—a single cry and a splash.

Hurrying to the south window, she looked out. Far below, at the end of the great stone buttress, the cage was now occupied. A man was struggling, spluttering in the water momentarily; then he went still, looking about him, as if coming to a sudden realization of his fate.

As he turned toward her, Anna caught her breath, horrified.

It was Aitrus.

VEOVIS GLANCED AT A'GAERIS AND SMILED.

"Did you hide the Book?"

A'Gaeris pulled the Linking Book from his pocket. "You mean *this?*"

The two men were halfway along the tunnel that led from the cage. They had left Suahrnir on the platform, overlooking the cage. Now it was time to carry out the next part of their scheme.

"Are you sure she will come?" A'Gaeris asked, his eyes half-hooded.

"I am certain of it," Veovis said.

They walked on. Turning a corner, they came to the narrow steps that led up to the gallery. Here they had to go single file.

"Can I ask you something?" A'Gaeris said, as he followed Veovis up.

"Ask," Veovis said, glancing back over his shoulder as he climbed out through the hatch.

"Why do you want her? I mean, she will never love you. Not while you keep Aitrus prisoner. And if you kill him . . . "

"Vengeance," Veovis said, as A'Gaeris ducked out under the rim of the hatch and joined him in the strangely lit gallery.

"Why not simply kill them both?"

"Because I want them to suffer the way I suffered." Veovis's face was hard now, much harder than A'Gaeris had ever seen it. "I dreamed of it, when I was on the Prison Age, night after night. I want them to be tormented the way I was tormented. I want them to feel betrayed the way *I* felt betrayed."

Behind the thick glass of the gallery windows, strange fish swam slowly, menacingly, their pale red eyes unblinking.

A'Gaeris nodded. "I understand."

"Do you?"

"Yes, friend. It was not just my guild membership I lost. I was betrothed. Betrothed to the most beautiful young woman you have ever seen."

"Ah . . . " Veovis had been about to move on, to return straight to the study, but now he changed his mind. "What do you want, A'Gaeris? I mean, what do you *really* want?"

A'Gaeris did not hesitate. "To destroy it all. That is my dream."

"Then the Guilds . . . ?"

"Are only the start. I want to destroy D'ni the way D'ni tried to destroy me." A'Gaeris's whole frame seemed to shudder with indignation. "There! Does that frighten you, Veovis?"

Veovis shook his head. "No. I know now how you feel."

"You do?"

"Yes. Come . . . "

A'GAERIS HAD THOUGHT IT WAS A STORAGE cupboard of some kind, but inside was a long, high-ceilinged room, and lining the walls of that long room were rack after rack of guns and swords. Enough to start a small war.

Veovis turned, staring at the Philosopher thoughtfully. "You once wrote that it is fortunate that the common people are unarmed, for if they were armed, D'ni would fall overnight. Do you still believe that?"

A'Gaeris reached out, taking down one of the swords and examining it. He nodded, impressed. "I do," he said finally, looking to Veovis with a smile.

"Then will this do?"

A'Gaeris grinned. "I see I badly misjudged you, Lord Veovis."

ANNA STOOD AT THE DOOR, LISTENING, THEN opened it and slipped out, into the adjacent room. There were voices coming from just down the corridor. Was there another chamber down there; one she had not noticed?

It seemed so. Recessed into the wall, partway along, was a door. It was open the slightest crack and she could hear Veovis and A'Gaeris talking within. Realizing that she might have only one chance, she hurried past and on into the gallery. To her surprise the hatch halfway down on her left was wide open. She edged over to it and listened, then peeked her head around. A flight of steps went down.

She went inside, hastening down the steps, then stopped. Ahead of her, just around a turn, she could hear Suahrnir murmuring something.

The bottle containing the sleeping draught was still in her pocket, the iron file in her right hand. Taking a cloth handkerchief from her pocket, Anna wrapped it about her mouth, then took the bottle from her pocket.

With more confidence than she felt, she stepped out around the corner. Suahrnir was sitting on a platform at the end of the tunnel, overlooking the cage. He had his back to her. Calming herself, she walked on, trying not to make any noise.

She was right beneath Suahrnir when he turned, realizing that she was there. Yet even as he turned, Anna hit him hard over the head with the file. As he collapsed, she pulled the cloth up over her nose and, unstoppering the bottle, poured its contents over his face.

A cloud of thick, white fumes rose from the platform.

Anna blinked, her eyes stinging furiously, then, closing them tight, she edged around Suahrnir and climbed up onto the cage, not daring to take a breath.

The cage swayed from side to side as she moved around the outside of it, as far as she could get from the stinging white cloud. As the cage steadied, she leaned out and raised the silk, taking in a lungful of air.

"Ti'ana? Is that you?"

Aitrus was just beneath her, blinking up at her as if only half conscious. Only his head and shoulders were above the surface of the vile, dark green liquid and she could see that there was a large, dark bruise on the side of his forehead. Seeing him thus, Anna winced, her love for him making her forget her own danger. His hands were tightly bound. They had hooked them over the massive padlock to keep him from sinking down into the water. It was cruel, but it had also probably saved his life.

"It's all right, my love," she said gently. "I'll get you out. But you must be quiet. We must not alert the others."

"I was stupid," he said, his eyes flickering closed, as if he could not keep them open. His voice was faint and fading. "Veovis said he had you prisoner. I should have known. I should have brought help."

"No," Anna said, pained by the way he blamed himself for this. She took the file from her waist and, leaning across, began to try to force the lock. "You did what you thought best."

Aitrus coughed. Some of the sleeping gas was now drifting across from the tunnel. Anna could sense its stinging presence in the air. She grimaced then leaned back on the file once more, heaving at it, trying to force the lock, but it would not budge. She needed a longer piece of metal, something with more leverage.

A sudden gust of wind, coming in off the surface of the sea, swept back the drift of noxious white gas.

"Aitrus," she said, reaching through the bars, trying to touch his brow, her fingers brushing air. "Aitrus . . . I shall not be long, I promise. I'll come back for you. So hold on."

But he could not hear her. His eyes were closed, and whether it was the gas or whether he had slumped back into unconsciousness she could not tell.

Time. Time was against her now.

Taking a huge gulp of air, she pulled the cloth down over her mouth again, then turned and, scrambling back around the cage, ducked back inside the tunnel, her eyes tightly shut as she stumbled through the choking whiteness.

VEOVIS WAS SITTING AT A TABLE AT THE END
of the armory, fitting together an incendiary device.
Five completed bombs lay in a row just by his elbow;
long red tubes with bulbous silver ends filled with
explosive chemicals. Nearby, A'Gaeris was still working
his way through the racks, looking for the ideal weapon
for himself.

"We should only use guns when we need to," Veovis
said, looking up at him. "For what we plan, a poisoned
dart is best."

"And the incendiaries?" A'Gaeris looked down the
barrel of a hunting gun at Veovis, then set the gun
aside. "I would have thought they would notice one of
those going off."

Veovis continued to fit the device together.
"These are not for use as weapons, my friend, these
are to destroy the Linking Books after we have
used them."

A'Gaeris stared at him. "And the Hidden Linking
books? The ones we already have in place? Did I take
those risks for nothing, Veovis?"

"No, but it might be difficult to use them, now that
the guilds are more vigilant. Besides, we have a whole
store of Books we can use. If time were less pressing I
would be less profligate, but as things are . . . "

A'Gaeris nodded. "You are quite right. And it will,
at least, allow us to slip in and slip out at will." His eyes

gleamed. "Think of it, Veovis! They will not know what has hit them!"

Veovis smiled and nodded, then set the sixth bomb aside, next to the others. "We shall be like shadows," he said, reaching out to take another of the incomplete incendiaries from the rack by his feet. As he set it down on the desk, he glanced across at A'Gaeris again. "Bring the map from the study. We can discuss things while we work."

AS A'GAERIS STEPPED INTO THE ROOM, HE saw her. Ti'ana, Aitrus's wife. She was at the center of the room, beside the table, hunched forward slightly, her back to him. She was very still, as if concentrating on something: reading, perhaps, or studying something.

The map of D'ni . . .

Smiling, A'Gaeris drew his dagger and tiptoed across until he was no more than a couple of feet from her.

"Do not move, Ti'ana," he said, a quiet menace in his voice. "I have a knife and I will not hesitate to use it."

She froze, her shoulders tensed.

"Turn slowly," he said. "Very slowly. Make no sudden movements."

She began to turn, slowly at first, very slowly; then, in a sudden rush her arms came up.

And something else. Something heavy and black that seemed to expand into his face, screeching as it did, its sharp claws digging in deeply.

VEOVIS STOOD, TURNING TOWARD THE DOOR. The first scream had made him drop the incendiary; the second startled him into action.

He ran, out of the room and along the corridor, bursting through the first room and into the study. The screaming was louder here, mixed with the bird's high, screeching call.

A'Gaeris was on the far side of the room, struggling to fend off the ferocious assault of the bird. Blood ran down his face and upper arms. Nearby the golden cage lay on the floor, the chain snapped, the door forced open.

Intruders . . .

"Help me!" A'Gaeris pleaded, putting an arm out toward Veovis. "In the Maker's name, help me!"

Veovis stared at his ally a moment, then, drawing the old, long-barreled gun from his belt, crossed the room quickly, ignoring A'Gaeris and vanishing through the far door, heading for the far room and the corridor beyond.

ANNA SLAMMED THE DOOR BEHIND HER THEN reached up and slipped the bolt into place. Hurrying over to the bench, she took the stoppers from bottles and jars then began to pour things into various containers.

She could hear A'Gaeris's screams, even where she was, through the thickness of stone and wood, and knew that Veovis would be coming after her.

Taking her concoction, Anna poured some of the clear, thick liquid over the door, soaking the wood with it, then laid a trail of it across to the far side of the room, where the Linking Books were piled up. That done, she put the bowl aside and went back to the door, sliding the bolt back once again and pulling the door slightly ajar.

She could hear footsteps now, hurrying up the twist of steps.

Anna scrambled back across the room, setting the Linking Book she was to use to return to D'ni down on the desk to one side, open to the descriptive panel. Then, taking the length of wick, she lit it from the tinder, blowing on the smoldering end of it until it glowed.

The footsteps came to the head of the steps and stopped. There was a moment's hesitation and then the door on the far side of the room was kicked open. Veovis stepped inside, the cocked gun raised, its dark mouth pointed directly at her.

Seeing her, Veovis gave a surprised laugh. "Ti'ana! You were the last person I expected."

Anna stared back at him defiantly, her left hand hovering over the glowing panel, her right holding the smoldering wick.

Noticing the Books, he blinked, reassessing the situation. "What are you doing?"

"I am putting a stop to this. Before things get out of hand."

His face grew hard. "Give me the book, Ti'ana. Give it to me and I shall spare you. You and your son both. The rest will die. They have to. But you and Gehn can live . . . *if* you give me the Book."

Anna smiled and dropped the wick onto the pile of Linking Books, igniting it, at the same moment placing her other hand against the linking panel.

As the Books went up in a great rush of flame, Veovis roared and pulled the trigger. The sound of the detonation filled the room as the bullet hurtled toward her disappearing shape. At the same moment, the trail of liquid chemicals flared, the flame running along it like a trail of magma searing through the rock.

There was a great hiss and then the door behind Veovis exploded into flame, throwing him forward, his hair and cloak on fire.

But Anna did not see it. Anna had already gone.

THE GREAT CHAMBER WAS ALMOST DARK. ONLY at its very center, where the five great thrones were, was there a small pool of light, where a single flame flickered between the pillars. Beneath its scant illumination the five great Lords of D'ni sat, their ancient faces etched with deep concern.

"We must search the city from end to end," R'hira said, echoing what Master Jadaris had said to him not an hour before. "Every room, and every drawer of every desk. We must find these Linking Books and destroy them, else no one here is safe."

"Is it possible?" another of them asked. "Have we the time or the numbers to make such a search?"

"No," R'hira admitted, "yet we must make the attempt. Unless we do . . . "

He stopped dead, staring in astonishment as a figure materialized in the space before the thrones.

"What in the Maker's name . . . "

"Ti'ana!" R'hira cried, standing and stepping down from his throne.

Anna looked up, her face pale, then slumped down onto the floor. Blood poured from a wound in her shoulder.

"Bring help!" R'hira cried, speaking to one of the guards who stood in the shadow surrounding them. "Quick now, Guildsman! Ti'ana is badly hurt!"

Yet even as he stooped to try to help her, another figure shimmered into being right beside her.

The man's face was blackened. His hair was aflame. Smoke curled up from his burning clothes. He was doubled up, almost choking for breath, but even in that state R'hira recognized him at once.

"Veovis!"

PART SEVEN: LAST DAYS

I T WAS OVER. THE EVIDENCE HAD BEEN
heard, the verdict of the Council unanimously
given. It remained now only for the Five Lords to
announce the sentence.

The great chamber was hushed as Lord R'hira got
to his feet and, stepping from his throne, stood over the
kneeling Veovis.

Veovis was chained at hand and foot. His head had
been shaved and he wore a simple prison gown of rust
red, which showed his bare arms and calves. Seated just
behind the kneeling prisoner, looking on attentively, were
Aitrus and his wife, Ti'ana, who, because of her part in
things, had been allowed to attend this final ceremony.

It was only two weeks since that moment when, to
the astonishment of the five great Lords, both Ti'ana
and Veovis had linked through into this self-same
chamber. Both Aitrus and his wife were now much
improved from their wounds. Aitrus sat there with his
head bound, Ti'ana with a bandage about her wounded
shoulder.

There was a silent tension in the chamber as R'hira
looked about him at the seated ranks of guildsmen.

"Veovis," R'hira said quietly. "You have betrayed the trust of this Council. You have deceived us and stolen from us, destroyed our property, and . . . yes, *murdered* our fellow guildsmen. Such behavior is without parallel in all our long history, and it is felt that our sentence ought to reflect that. I therefore declare that you, Veovis, son of Rakeri, Lord of D'ni, shall be taken from here to the steps of the Library and there, at the seventeenth hour, before witnesses, be beheaded for your treachery."

There was a sharp intake of breath. Beheaded! It was unheard of. But Lord R'hira seemed as hard as granite as he looked about him.

"Such is the decision of the Five Lords. Will anybody speak for the accused?"

It was a traditional request at such moments, when a prisoner had been sentenced, and though this sentence was without recent parallel, it was clear that none among the Five expected anyone to speak.

Anna stood.

"Forgive me, Lord R'hira. I know I am here as a guest of the Council and as such have no right to voice my feelings; even so, I *would* like to speak in favor of the prisoner."

R'hira turned, looking to his fellows. There was a moment of eye contact among the ancients and then R'hira turned back.

"If anyone deserves the chance to speak, it is you, Ti'ana, though why you should wish to utter a word in favor of this miscreant is quite beyond my imagining. Step forward."

At that moment Veovis screamed, "That barbaric animal is going to speak on my behalf?! Never! I won't allow it!"

"Silence," R'hira shouted with the pounding of his hand.

Veovis continued in his rage. "She's a traitor, not one of us! She has breached the sanctity of the D'ni blood! Don't you see!?"

"Guards, remove him!" R'hira shouted. "Now!"

They dragged the screaming man from the room. Calm returned to the chamber.

Anna stepped out. She bowed to each of the Five in turn, then turned about, facing the ranks of guildsmen.

"My Lords . . . Guildsmen. I do not wish to play down the severity of what your once-fellow Veovis has been found guilty of. Nor have I reason to feel anything but hatred for the man who tried to kill my husband and, but for a poorly aimed shot, would undoubtedly have killed me. Yet as an outsider, a newcomer to the great empire of D'ni, let me make an observation.

"This great cavern is an island of reason, of rational, considered behavior. You D'ni have developed codes of behavior, ways of dealing with situations, that are the result of thousands of years of experience. The most important of those codes, and the wisest of all, perhaps, is that which deals with those who transgress and step outside the codes. Until now, the D'ni have only rarely taken a life for a life. Until now, you have chosen the path of segregation, of cutting out the bad from your midst and isolating it, as a surgeon might isolate a virus. That, I would argue, is the path of sanity, whereas this . . ."

Anna paused, as if she could read the objection that was in most of their minds.

"I know what you are thinking. He escaped once. He might well escape again. And the so-called Philosopher, A'Gaeris, is still at large. Such factors must, I agree, come into your thinking. But there is one important factor that has not been considered, and that is precisely why Veovis behaved as he did."

Anna took something from her pocket and held it up. It was a notebook of some kind.

"I have here a journal—A'Gaeris's private journal—which I took from his room in the Age from which they launched their attacks on D'ni. Had I not been ill these past few weeks, I might have read it sooner—and then could have laid this before the Council as evidence in Lord Veovis's favor, for its contents are most revelatory. As it is, I offer it to you now as a plea for clemency."

Lord R'hira, who had been listening in silence until this moment, now spoke up.

"Forgive me, Ti'ana, but what might that villain A'Gaeris possibly have to say that would excuse the prisoner's behavior?"

Anna turned, facing him. "It is all here, my Lord, every last part of it, fully documented in A'Gaeris's own hand. How he planned things; how he forged papers; how he worked through Guildsman Suahrnir to ensnare Lord Veovis into his perverse schemes; even how he manipulated my husband into going to Master Jadaris with what he 'knew.'

"Whatever he has done since, that first great wrong cannot be denied. Veovis was an innocent man. Think, then, of the bitterness he must have felt in being stripped of all title and incarcerated upon that prison rock. Oh, it is no excuse for what he subsequently did, yet I offer it as explanation."

Lord R'hira took the book from Anna and read a page or two, blinking from time to time. Then he looked up.

"We must have time to study this, Ti'ana."

"Of course," she said, giving him a grateful bow. "But as you study it, my Lord, consider the balance of good and ill that exists in all men, and try to imagine in what circumstances that balance could be tilted either way—toward great good, or toward the kind of behavior Veovis displayed toward the society that spurned him."

R'hira gave a tiny nod, his eyes smiling at Anna, then he turned, his eyes quickly gauging the response of his fellow Lords. There were nods.

"Very well," he said, turning back. "The sentence of this Council is set in abeyance until this matter can be fully considered. Until then the prisoner will be placed under constant guard."

As the meeting broke up and guildsmen began to drift out of the chamber and into the nearby rooms, R'hira came over to Anna.

"I am grateful for your intercession, Ti'ana, yet one thing bothers me. You may be right. Veovis may once have been innocent. Yet that is in the past. If we do not end his life for what he subsequently did, then we have but a single course before us, and that is to incarcerate him for the rest of his natural life. Such a course we tried before . . . and failed with. What if we fail a second time?"

"Then make sure you do not, Lord R'hira. Make a new and special Age for him, then, once he is safe within that place, burn the book so that no one can help him escape. Vigilance, not vengeance should be your byword."

R'hira bowed his head, impressed by her words. "Well spoken, Ti'ana.

She gave a little bow.

"Oh, and Ti'ana . . . do not worry. Whatever we decide, Veovis will *never* be allowed his freedom."

A'GAERIS SAT AT HIS DESK, STUDYING THE notebook. The wooden door of the hut was closed, the blinds drawn against the sunlight. From outside came the busy sound of sawing and hammering.

He closed the book then nodded to himself. Standing, he yawned and stretched. He was wearing a simple rust-red gown that fitted tightly at the waist. A pair of D'ni glasses rested atop his freshly shaven head. Walking over to the door, he pulled them down over his eyes, then stepped outside.

Just below the hillock on which the hut stood, in a clearing between the trees, his slaves were hard at work. Already the basic frame of the room had been constructed. Now they were building the seats and shelves and, at the center of it all, the podium.

He walked down, stopping at the edge of the clearing to take out the notebook once again, turning to the page he had been looking at a moment earlier. For a moment he compared Suahrnir's sketches to the room that was being constructed in the clearing, then he slipped the book away once more. There was no doubting it, Suahrnir had had a good eye. No detail had evaded him. Everything he needed was here. Every measurement.

He began to laugh; a deep, hearty laughter that rolled from his corpulent frame, making the natives glance up at him fearfully before returning to their work.

"But we shall change all that," he said, as his laughter subsided. "No rules. No guidelines. Nothing but what I want."

The thought of it sent a tiny shiver up his spine.

"Nothing . . . but what *I* want."

THE PREPARATIONS WERE METICULOUS.

Four of the guild's finest Writers were assigned the task of making the new Age; each of them allocated one specific strand of the whole. Working to Lord R'hira's brief, in copy books that had no power to link, they patiently produced their words, passing on their finished creations to the Grand Master of their Guild, Ja'ir, who, in coordination with Grand Master Jadaris of the Maintainers, compared the texts and made his subtle corrections, ensuring that the resultant Age was consistent and thus stable.

In all a hundred days passed in this fashion. But then it was finally done and, after consultation with Lord R'hira, a blank Book—a Kortee'nea—was taken from the Guild's Book Room and placed on a desk in a cell at the center of the Hall of the Maintainers. There it was guarded day and night, its pages never out of sight for a single instant as, one by one, the four Writers returned to copy their work into the Book.

By this means the privacy of the Book was maintained, for none of the four had any knowledge of what the other three had written. Only Jadaris and Ja'ir and R'hira, three of the most trustworthy men in the entire empire, knew that.

Meanwhile, in a cell just down the passageway, they placed Veovis, shackled hand and foot, two members of the City Guard with him every moment of the day and night, linked to him by chains of nara, waking and sleeping.

And so the days passed, until the Prison Book was done.

AT THE SEVENTEENTH HOUR ON THE DAY OF judgment the great bronze bell rang out from the tower above the Hall of the Guild of Maintainers. Far below, in the lowest level of that great labyrinthine building, in the deep shadows of the Room of Punishment, the Great Lords and Grand Masters of D'ni looked on as Veovis, his head unbowed, the cords that had bound his hands and feet cut, stepped over to the podium and faced the open Book.

As the bell rang, Veovis looked about him, no flicker of fear in those pale, intelligent eyes, only, at this final moment, a sense of great dignity. Then, as the final stroke rang out, he placed his hand upon the glowing panel and linked.

As he vanished, a sighing breath seemed to pass through the watching guildsmen. Heads turned, looking to Lord R'hira.

"It is done," he said quietly. "Master Jadaris . . . take the Book away and burn it."

Yet even as he spoke the words there was a faint disturbance of the air before the Book, the faintest blur. For the briefest instant, R'hira thought he glimpsed a figure in a rust-red prison gown, his head shaved bare.

R'hira looked about him, surprised. Was he the only one to have seen it? And what precisely had he seen? An afterimage?

Or was this some flaw in the Book itself? After all, it was rare for a Book to be made by four separate writers, and it was possible that some minor errors had crept into the text.

He frowned, then set the matter from his mind. It was of no importance. All that mattered was that they burned the Book. Then D'ni would be safe.

Master Jadaris stepped up to the podium and, closing the Book, lifted it ceremonially in both hands, then carried it from the room.

They followed, along a passageway and through into the furnace room. Here, since time immemorial, they had burned faulty Books, destroying their failed experiments and shoddy work.

But this was different. This was a world that functioned perfectly.

And so we break our own rules, R'hira thought. And even if it were for a good cause, he still felt the breach as a kind of failure.

This is not the D'ni way. We do not destroy what is healthy.

Yet Ti'ana was right. It was either this or put Veovis to death. And there was no doubt about it now: Veovis had been an innocent man when first they found him guilty and incarcerated him.

R'hira watched as the great oven door was opened and the Book slid in. There was a transparent panel in the door. Through it he could see the gray-blue cover of the Prison Book clearly. R'hira bent slightly, looking on as the oven fired and the flames began to lick the cover of the Book.

THE MONTHS PASSED SWIFTLY. THINGS QUICKLY returned to normal. For young Gehn these were strangely happy times—strange, because he had never dared hope to thrive away from his mother's side.

In his eighth year, on the last day of his first term at the Guild College, his father and mother visited him. It was an Open Day, and most of the students' parents were to be there, but for Gehn it was a very special occasion, for he had been chosen to represent the College and read out a passage from the great history of his guild that spoke of the long tradition of the Guild of Books.

The days of illness, of bullying in the night, and tearful homesickness were long behind Gehn. He had become a strong child, surprisingly tall for his age, and confident in all he did, if never outspoken. Yet he was strangely distant with his mother, as if some part of him had never quite forgiven her for sending him away. It was thus that he greeted her on this special day, with a respectful distance that might have been expected from any other student meeting the great Ti'ana, but not, perhaps, from her only son.

He bowed formally. "Mother. I am glad you came."

Anna smiled and briefly held him, but she, too, sensed how things were between them. As she stepped back, Aitrus embraced Gehn.

"Well done, Gehn!" he said, grinning down at his son. "I hear nothing but good from your Guild Masters! I am very proud of you boy. We both are!"

Gehn glanced at his mother. He could see that she was indeed proud of him, yet strangely that mattered very little beside the praise of his father. After all, his father was D'ni—of the blood—and a Council member, too. To have *his* praise was something. Yet he did not say this openly.

"I try to do my best," he said, lowering his head with the modesty that was drilled into all students.

"Guild Master Rijahna says you have a promising future, Gehn," Anna said, her smile more guarded than his father's. "Indeed, he has talked to your father of private tuition."

This was the first Gehn had heard of this. He looked to his father wide-eyed.

"Is that true?"

Aitrus nodded. "If you want it."

Gehn beamed. "Of course I want it! Who would not? Oh, I ache to be like them, Father! Like the Masters, I mean. To know what they know. To be as they are!"

Aitrus laughed. "I understand that feeling, Gehn, but you must be patient, too."

Gehn lowered his head again. "Of course." He calmed, matching his demeanor to a more somber mood. "Thank you. Thank you both. I shall make you proud of me."

Anna smiled and reached out, ruffling his hair. "We are already proud of you, Gehn. More proud than you could ever imagine."

AS GEHN FINISHED THE ORATION, ANNA FELT the tightness in her stomach vanish, her anxiety replaced by a great uprush of pride. To think he had nearly died—and not once but several times! And now here he was, standing confidently before his peers and Masters—yes, and before a great hall full of parents, too—speaking with real feeling and pride of the great tradition into which he had been born.

She glanced at Aitrus and saw the great beam of a smile on her husband's face and knew he shared all she felt.

My son.

Oh, it was difficult sometimes. Gehn could be cold and distant, but she put that down to his age, yes, and to other things. It had not been easy for him being of mixed blood. Yet he had come through it all triumphantly.

As Guild Master Rijahna stepped up to the podium, he gave a little bow to Gehn. There was the faintest trace of a smile on his lips, a trace that vanished as he turned to face the audience.

"And now, guildsmen, ladies, if you would like to come through to the refectory . . . "

But Master Rijahna had barely formed the word when the whole building shook. He looked up, surprised, as if he had imagined it, but from the murmur in the audience, from the way a number of the guildsmen and their ladies had risen to their feet, he was not alone in experiencing that tremor.

It came again, stronger this time, and with it a low rumbling noise. Dust fell from overhead.

Outside, the great bell of D'ni was sounding.

And there were only two reasons for that bell to sound: the death of one of the Five, or a threat to D'ni itself.

Rijahna swallowed back his momentary fear and leaned upon the podium.

"Ladies, guildsmen. Please remain calm."

He turned, looking to his fellow Masters and to the young pupils, who stared back at him, silent yet clearly afraid.

"It will be all right," he said quietly, his voice offering them a reassurance he did not feel. "Be calm and follow me outside and all will be well, I promise you. All will be well . . . "

ANNA SAW IT AT ONCE AS SHE EMERGED FROM the Guild Hall, there on the far side of the great cavern. A great crack had opened in the wall of the cave, and from it spewed a dark cloud of gas.

She looked to Aitrus, as if he might explain it, but from the expression on his face he seemed as dumbfounded as anyone.

"What is it?" she asked, trying not to succumb to the panic that seemed to be spreading among the people all about her. At the sight of the dark cloud some of the women had started screaming and wailing.

"I do not know," he said, unable to tear his eyes from it, "but it might be best to link away from here, until more is known."

"But you will be needed, Aitrus . . . "

He looked to her. "I did not mean myself. You and Gehn. You should take him home, to the mansion, then go to Gemedet. At once. There are provisions there."

"And you?" she asked, fearing for him suddenly.

He smiled, then kissed her. "I shall come when I can, Ti'ana. But take Gehn straightaway. And look after him."

"All right. But take care, my love. And come when you can."

"I shall," he said, then, turning, he hastened away, heading for the Guild House.

Anna hesitated a moment, watching Aitrus go, an awful feeling filling her at the sight of him making his way through the crowd; then, determined to do as he had asked, she turned, beginning to make her way back up the steps, anxious to find Gehn.

SLOWLY THE DARK CLOUD SPREAD, LIKE A mighty veil being drawn across the far side of the cavern. Inch by inch it crept across the lake, edging toward D'ni, and where it touched the surface of the lake, the light from the lake was extinguished.

The light-giving algae were dying, by the look of it; poisoned by the noxious fumes of the cloud.

And if that cloud were to reach out its fingers to D'ni city?

Then they would also die.

The city below was in turmoil. The shrieks of terror and wailing of the desperate were dreadful to hear. There were great queues now at all of the Common Libraries, as people made their way to the safety of the common Ages.

Anna stared across the cavern for a moment longer, horrified, then hurried on, taking Gehn's hand and pulling him along behind her. There was not far to go now and she was beginning to think about what she would need to pack—journals and books and the like—when the third tremor struck.

It was by far the largest of the three tremors and threw them both from their feet, showering them with dust and debris.

Walls were crumbling now. Buildings were crashing to the ground. Just up ahead of them, the front of one of their neighbors' mansions tumbled into the alleyway, throwing up a great cloud of dust.

As the tremor faded, Anna lifted herself onto her hands and knees and turned anxiously. But Gehn was fine: He had a small cut on his brow, but it was almost nothing.

"Come on," she said, getting to her feet then taking his hand again, "before the next one hits."

But they had barely gone a dozen paces when the whole cavern seemed to resound like a struck gong.

They clung to each other, waiting for the great ceiling to come down on them or the earth to open up beneath them, but despite the mighty roar of falling masonry and cracking walls, they came through untouched.

Indoors, Tasera was waiting for them anxiously.

"Thank the Maker you are here," she said, relieved to see at least two of her family home safe. "But where is Aitrus?"

"He has gone to the Guild House," Anna said, more calmly than she felt. "He will come when he can."

Tasera gave a nod of resignation. "Kahlis went, too, as soon as the first tremor struck. No doubt they will return together."

Anna nodded, then said, "I need to get one or two things from the study. Take Gehn and link through. I will follow you just as soon as I can. Aitrus said we were to link to Gemedet."

"Gemedet? But surely Ko'ah would be safer?"

"It is what he said."

Tasera bowed her head, for once giving in to her daughter-in-law. "Then go quickly, Ti'ana. I shall see you in Gemedet."

ANNA SLIPPED THE KNAPSACK ONTO HER back, then went out into the corridor. Time was pressing now, but she could not go until she had taken one final look at things. Climbing the stairs, she emerged onto the balcony then hurried over to the rail.

The great city was stretched out below where she stood, layer after layer of ancient stone streets and houses, reaching down to the great circle of the harbor and Kerath's massive arch. Though it was day, lights burned in most of the houses, for a strange twilight was falling over D'ni as the great cloud spread, its poisonous fumes dousing the lake's soft glow.

The dark cloud now filled almost half of the cavern, its color now discernible as a filthy brown. The edges of it drifted slowly, in a dreamlike fashion, more like a sluggish liquid than a gas. Even as she watched, wispy brown tendrils of the gas extended about Kerath's Arch and slowly curled across the surface of the harbor.

And where the gas touched, the algae faded, the bright glow dying like sputtering embers.

The sight of it chilled her.

Where are you, Aitrus? she wondered, looking across to the left, where the Guild House stood, its massive, tiered roof dominating the surrounding Halls. *Are you safe, my love?*

As if voicing the fear she felt at that moment, a great noise of wailing drifted up from the lower city. Many were safe now, but there were still some—hundreds, maybe more—who had not made it to the Common Libraries and the safety of the Ages. It was they who now faced the coming of the great cloud as it slowly filled the harbor with its roiling darkness, then spilled into the narrow lanes and alleyways that led up from the waterfront.

The Maker help them . . .

Yet even as she thought it, she caught a glimpse of a guildsmen hurriedly ascending the main street that led between the gates, his cloak streaming behind him as he ran. He was carrying something odd, some kind of cylinder, yet she knew at once who it was.

"Aitrus!" she yelled, waving frantically at him.

He slowed, his head turning, and then he waved back at her, hurrying on again, disappearing briefly behind a row of houses, while far below him, like the breath of fate itself, the dark gas slowly climbed the levels, destroying any living thing it touched.

IT WAS RAINING IN GEMEDET, A FRESH, PURE rain that, after the nightmare of the cavern, seemed to wash all stain of it from them as they walked down the slope toward the encampment.

Seeing them step out from among the trees, Gehn stood then ran toward them, hugging his father fiercely. The boy's hair was slicked back, his clothes soaked, but he seemed not to mind.

Picking him up, Aitrus carried Gehn down the rest of the slope and into the shelter of the cabin. Tasera looked up as they entered, a great beam of a smile lighting her face at the sight of Aitrus. Then, seeing only Anna enter behind him, she frowned.

"Where is your father, Aitrus?"

"In D'ni," Aitrus answered somberly, slipping the cylinder from his back and balancing it in the corner.

"He stayed?"

"He agreed to. Along with the Five and all the other Grand Masters. It was their plan to go to one of the Guild worlds and there to debate things further."

"Then he is safe," she said, relieved.

"For a time," Aitrus answered, taking the mask from his cloak pocket and placing it on top of the cylinder, the end of it dangling from the great silver nozzle.

"What do you mean?"

Aitrus shrugged. "I mean only that none of us knows yet what has really happened or where the gas is coming from. As for the tremors, there were no early signs in the rock, nor is there any history of such local disturbances."

"So what are we to do? Stay here?"

"For a time, yes. Until things blow over. I have been ordered to remain here for ten days. At the end of that I am to return to D'ni, wearing the mask and cylinder. Others will return at the same time. If all is well, we shall bring the people back to D'ni."

"And if it is not?" Tasera asked, her face gaunt.

Aitrus sighed. "Then we stay here . . . for a time. Until we can *make* things well again in D'ni."

THE AIR WAS A HORRIBLE, SICKLY YELLOW-brown, choking the ancient streets and alleyways, as though a wintry fog had descended upon the great tiered city in the cave. Silent it was, and dark, though not as dark now as at first.

Here and there, at crossroads and at gates, lamps had been set on the top of poles. Huge fire-marbles the size of fists glowed red, or blue, or green behind the thick glass panes of the lamps; yet their lights burned dimly, as though through depths of dark and murky water.

Silent it was, yet in that silence the creaking of a cart could now be heard, along with the shuffle of two men, making their slow way through that subterranean place.

As they came into a pool of dark red light, one could see the airtight masks that encased their heads, linked by strong hoses to the air tanks on their backs. They wore long leather boots and thick gloves that reached to their elbows.

Their cart was loaded high, pale hands and feet jutting lifelessly from the midst of that macabre bundle of rags and bones. Leaning forward, they pushed in silence, sharing the weight without complaint. Ahead, just beyond the lamp, was their destination.

Coming to the foot of the steps, they set the handles of the cart down, then began to unload, taking each body by its wrists and ankles and carrying it up into the semi-darkness of the entrance hall.

Here, too, they had placed lamps, lighting the way into the great Book Room.

It was not their first journey, nor would it be their last. For a full week now they had gone about their task, patiently, unendingly, collecting in the harvest of their sowing.

So many bodies, there were. So much illness and death. It was hard to credit that the gas had undone so many. And then the quakes.

While one held the body propped against the podium, the other took its hand and placed it over the glowing panel of the Book, moving his own hand back as the link was made.

The body shimmered for an instant and was gone.

And so on, endlessly, it seemed. A thousand corpses, maybe more: their dead hands, filled yet with living cells, linking into the Ages; their bodies wracked with illness; rife with the contagion that had swept these mortuary streets.

Looking through their masks at one another, the two men smiled grimly.

"Another, Philosopher?"

"Oh, another, my Lord. Most certainly another."

The two men laughed; a dark and bitter laughter. And then they returned, to bring another body from the cart. To send another of their dark seeds through into the Ages. Destroying the sanctuaries one at a time: finishing the work they had begun.

IT WAS THE EVENING OF THE NINTH DAY. Tomorrow Aitrus would return to D'ni. As the day ended, they sat on a platform of rock just above the falls, just Anna and Aitrus, looking out over the little world they had made.

The sun, behind them, cast their shadows long across the lush greens of the valley. For a long time they were silent, then Anna spoke.

"What do you think you will find?"

Aitrus plucked a stem of grass and put it to his mouth. Now that it was evening, he had pushed his glasses up onto his brow, but where they had sat about his eyes, his pale flesh was marked with thin red furrows. He shrugged. "Who knows? Yet I fear the worst. I had hoped some message would have come through earlier than this. Or my father . . ."

Anna reached out, laying her hand softly against his neck. He feared for his father, more than for himself. So it was with Aitrus. It was always others before himself. And that was why, ultimately, she loved him: for that selflessness in him.

"How long will you be?"

Aitrus turned slightly, looking at her. "As long as I am needed."

"And if you do not return?"

"Then you will stay here."

She began to shake her head, but he was insistent. "No, Ti'ana. You *must* do this for me. For me, and for Gehn."

The mention of Gehn stilled her objections. Aitrus was right. Gehn was still only eight. Losing one parent would be bad enough, but to lose both could prove devastating, even though Tasera would still be here.

She gave the barest nod.

"Good," Aitrus said, "then let us go back to the encampment. I have much to prepare before I leave."

IT WAS EARLY WHEN AITRUS SET OFF. ALL farewells had been said; now, as Anna looked on, Gehn cuddled against her, Aitrus pulled on the cylinder, checked it was working properly, then slipped the airtight mask down over his head.

Seeing him thus, Anna felt her stomach tighten with anxiety.

Aitrus turned, waved to them, then turned back, placing his hand against the open Linking Book.

The air about his figure swirled as if it had been transformed into some other substance, then cleared. Aitrus was gone.

Anna shivered. Words could not say the fear she felt at that moment: a dark, instinctive fear for him.

"Be brave, my darling," she said, looking down at Gehn. "Your father will come back. I promise he will."

AITRUS COULD HEAR HIS OWN BREATHING
loud within the mask as he linked into the study. He
took out the lamp he had brought and, striking the
fire-marble, lit it and held it up, looking about him.

Nothing had been disturbed, yet all had been transformed. The gas had gone, but where it had been it had
left its residue, coating everything with a thin layer of
yellow-brown paste.

The sight of it sickened him to his stomach. Was
it all like this, everywhere in D'ni? Had nothing survived untouched?

Outside in the corridor it was all the same, as
though some host of demons had repainted everything
the same hellish shade. Where his booted feet trod he
left long smearing marks upon the floor.

Aitrus swallowed. The air he breathed was clean
and pure, yet it seemed tainted somehow by what
he saw.

He went down the stairs, into the lower level of the
house. Here some of the gas remained, pooled in the
corners of rooms. Faint wisps of it drifted slowly
through open doorways.

Aitrus watched it a moment. It seemed alive,
almost; hideously, maliciously alive.

No sooner had he had the thought, than a second
followed. This was no simple chemical mix. He should

have known that by the way it had reacted with the algae in the lake. This was biological. It *was* alive.

He went out again, heading for the front door, then stopped, deciding to douse the lantern, just in case. He did so, letting the darkness embrace him, then he stepped up to the door, finding his way blindly.

Outside it was somewhat lighter, but only comparatively so. Most of the cavern was dark—darker than Aitrus had ever imagined possible—but there *were* lights, down below him and to his left, not far off if he estimated correctly; approximately where the great Halls of the guilds had once stood.

Had stood. For even in the darkness he could see evidence of the great ruin that had fallen upon D'ni. Between him and the lights, silhouetted against them, was a landscape of fallen houses and toppled walls, as if a giant had trampled his way carelessly across the rooftops.

Aitrus sighed, then began to make his way toward those lights. There would be guildsmen there, he was certain of it. Maybe even his father, Kahlis. They would have news, yes, and schemes to set things right again.

The thought of that cheered him. He *was* D'ni, after all!

Aitrus stopped and, taking out the lantern, lit it again. Then, holding it up before him, he began to make his way through the ruin of the streets and lanes, heading for the Guild House.

THE GUILD HOUSE WAS EMPTY, ITS GREAT doors, which had once been proudly guarded, were now wide open. It had been built well and had withstood the ravages of the great quakes that had struck the city, yet all about it was a scene of devastation that had taken Aitrus's breath. There was barely a building that had not been damaged.

And everywhere the sickly yellow-brown residue of the gas.

Aitrus stood in the great Council chamber, facing the five thrones, his lantern held up before him. It was here that he had left his father. Here that he had made his promise to return on the tenth day. So where were they all? Had they been and gone? Or had they never come?

There was one sure and certain way to find out.

He walked through, into one of the tiny rooms that lay behind the great chamber. There, open on the desk, was a Linking Book. As all else, it was covered with the pastelike residue, yet the glow of the linking panel could be glimpsed. Though a thin layer of the paste covered the glowing rectangle, a hand print could be clearly seen upon it.

Someone had linked *after* the gas had settled.

Aitrus went across and, using the sleeve of his cloak, wiped the right-hand page clean. At once the glow came clear. If the Five Lords and his father were anywhere, they were there, in that Age.

He doused the lantern and stowed it, then placed his hand upon the panel. He linked.

At once Aitrus found himself in a low cave. Sunlight filtered in from an entrance just above him. He could hear birdsong and the lulling noise of the sea washing against the shoreline.

He sighed, relieved. All was well.

Releasing the clamp at the side of his mask, he eased it up, taking a deep gulp of the refreshing air, then, reaching behind him, switched off the air supply. He would need it when he returned to D'ni.

Quickly he climbed the twist of steps that had been cut into the side of the cave wall, pausing only to take out his glasses and slip them on. Then, his spirits raised, he stepped out, into the sunlight.

The buildings were just below him, at the end of a long grassy slope. They blazed white in the sunlight, their perfect domes and arches blending with the green of the surrounding wood, the deep blue of the shimmering sea that surrounded the island.

They would be inside the Great Library, of course, debating what to do. That was why they were delayed, why they had not come. Even so, Aitrus was surprised that they had not set a guard by the Linking Book.

He stopped dead, blinking, taking that in.

There *would* have been a guard. There always *was* a guard. In fact, he had never come here, before now, without there being a guard in the cave.

Something was wrong.

Aitrus drew his dagger then walked on, listening for any sound. Coming around the side of the library, he slowed. The silence was strange, unnatural. The great wooden door was open. Inside the room was shadowy dark.

The elders of D'ni sat in their seats about the chamber, thirty, maybe forty in all. In the darkness they seemed to be resting, yet their stillness was not the stillness of sleep.

Slipping his dagger back into its sheath, Aitrus took out his lamp and lit it, then stepped into the chamber.

In the glow of the lantern he could see the dreadful truth of things. They were dead, every last one of them, dead, their faces pulled back, the chins slightly raised, as if in some final exhalation.

Aitrus shuddered, then turned.

"Father . . . "

Kahlis sat in a chair close by the door, his back to the sunlight spilling in from outside. His hands rested on the arms of the chair, almost casually it seemed, yet the fingers gripped the wood tightly and the face had that same stiffness in it that all the other faces had, as if they had been caught suddenly and unawares by some invisible enemy.

Aitrus groaned and sank down to his knees, his head lowered before his father. For a long while he remained so. Then, slowly, he raised his head again.

"What in the Maker's name has happened here?"

Aitrus turned, looking up into the masked face of the newcomer. The man was standing in the doorway, the sunlight behind him. He was wearing the purple cloak of the Guild of Ink-Makers, but Aitrus could not make out his features clearly in the gloom.

"It's some kind of virus," he began, then, seeing that the other made to unmask himself, shook his head. "No! Keep that on!"

The guildsman let his hand fall away from the strap, then looked about him. "Are they all dead?" he asked, a note of hopelessness entering his voice.

"Yes," Aitrus answered bleakly. "Or so it seems."

THE GRAVE WAS NEW, THE EARTH FRESHLY turned. Nearby, as if surprised, a guard lay on his back, dead, his hands gripping each other as if they fought, his jaws tightly clenched.

Aitrus stared at the guard a moment, then, looking to his fellow guildsman, Jiladis, he picked up the spade once more and began to dig, shoveling the last of the dark earth back into the hole. They really were all dead—guildsmen and guards, servants and natives. Not one had survived the plague, if plague it was.

And himself? Was *he* now infected with it?

The last book of commentary told the tale. They had found it open on a desk in one of the other buildings, its scribe, an ancient of two hundred years or more, slumped over it. The body had come through a week ago, only two days after the evacuation of D'ni. They had burned it, naturally, but the damage had been done.

"What will you do?" Jiladis asked, his voice muted through the mask he still wore.

"I suppose I will go back," Aitrus answered. "To D'ni, anyway."

And there was the problem. If he *was* infected, he could not go back to Gemedet, for he could not risk infecting Gehn and Anna and his mother. Yet was it fair not to let them know what had happened here?

Besides which, he needed to get back, now that he knew what was happening, for he had to return to the mansion and get the Linking Book. Gemedet at least would then be safe.

If he was not already too late.

"I shall come with you," Jiladis said finally. "There's nothing here."

Aitrus nodded, then looked up at the open sky and at the sun winking fiercely down at him.

The surface. He could always make his way to the surface.

Yes. But what about any others who had survived? Could he persuade Jiladis, for instance, that his future lay on the surface?

Aitrus set the spade aside, then knelt, murmuring the D'ni words of parting over the grave. Then, standing again, he made his own, more informal farewell.

"Goodbye, my father. May you find peace in the next Age, and may Yavo, the Maker, receive your soul."

Aitrus lingered awhile, his eyes closed as he remembered the best of his father. Then he turned and slowly walked away, making his way back to the linking cave, Jiladis following slowly after.

THE DOOR TO THE FAMILY BOOK ROOM HAD been smashed open, the shelves of the room ransacked. On the podium the Book of Ko'ah lay open, its pages smeared, a clear handprint over the panel.

Aitrus stared at it in shock.

Signs of desecration were everywhere—smeared footprints in the hallways and in almost every room—but had they gone upstairs.

His heart almost in his mouth, Aitrus slipped and skidded up the stairs in his haste.

His workroom was at the far end of the corridor. Footsteps led along the corridor toward it. Aitrus stopped dead, staring at them in horror.

So they had been here, too.

In the doorway he paused, looking about him. A circle of footprints went halfway into the room then came away.

He frowned, not understanding, then rushed across the room. The Book of Gemedet was where he had left it on the desk. The open pages were undisturbed, the thin layer of pasty residue untouched.

Aitrus sighed with relief. Taking a clean cloth from a drawer, he cleaned the cover carefully, then tucked it into the knapsack beside the other things he had packed for the journey.

He had taken extra cylinders from the Hall of the Guild of Miners and food from the sealed vaults in the Hall of the Caterers—enough for an eight-day journey.

If he had eight days.

And Anna? Would she keep her word? Would she stay in Gemedet and not try to come after him? He hoped so. For if she linked here, there would be no linking back for her. Not to Gemedet, anyway, for the book would be with him, and he was going to the surface.

Aitrus went to the front door and looked out across the darkness of the cavern.

He had seen them, yesterday, on his return, or thought he did: the ghostly figures of A'Gaeris and Veovis, pushing their cart of death. And, seeing them, he had known that nowhere was safe from them: not in D'ni, anyway, nor in any of the linked Ages.

If he and Anna and the boy were to have any kind of life, it would have to be up there, on the surface. But were the tunnels still open? Or had the great quakes that had flattened so much in D'ni destroyed them also?

He would have to go and see for himself. If he lived that long. If sickness did not take him on the journey.

IT WAS THE EVENING OF THE SIXTEENTH DAY, and Anna sat at Gehn's bedside, listening to his gentle snores in the shadows of the room. A book of D'ni tales lay beside her, facedown where she had put it. Worn out by a day of playing in the woods, Gehn had fallen asleep even as she read to him. Not that she minded. Anything that took his mind off his father's prolonged absence was welcome, and it was good to see him sleep so deeply and peacefully.

Leaning across, she kissed his brow, then stood and went outside. The stars were out now, bright against the sable backdrop of the sky. Anna yawned and stretched. She had barely slept this past week. Each day she expected him back, and each day, when he did not come, she feared the very worst.

Tasera, she knew, felt it almost as keenly as she did; maybe more so, for she, after all, had both a husband and a son who were missing; yet Tasera found it much easier to cope with than she did, for she was D'ni and had that rocklike D'ni stoicism. Had it been a thousand days, Tasera would have waited still, patient to the last.

Am I so impatient, then? Anna asked herself, walking over to the rock at the head of the valley.

She smiled, knowing what Aitrus would have said. It was the difference in their life expectancy, or so he argued. She was a short fuse and burned fast, while he . . .

Come back, she pleaded silently, looking out into the star-filled night. *Wherever you are—whenever you are—come back to me, Aitrus.*

If they had to spend the rest of their years on Gemedet, she would be content, if only she could be with him.

And if that is not your fate?

It was her father's voice. It was a long time since she had heard that voice—a long, long time since she had needed the comfort of it.

He has been a good man to you, Anna.

"Yes," she said quietly, speaking to the air. "I could not have wished for a better partner."

But now you must learn to be alone.

She blinked. There was such certainty in that voice. "No," she said, after a moment. "He will come back. He promised, and he always keeps his promises."

The voice was silent.

"Ti'ana?"

Anna started, then turned. Tasera was standing not ten paces from her, just below her on the slope. She must have been walking down by the stream. Coming closer, Tasera looked at her and frowned.

"Who were you talking to?"

Anna looked aside, then answered her honestly. "I was speaking to my father."

"Ah . . . " Tasera stepped closer, so that Anna could see her eyes clearly in the half-light. "And what did he say?"

"He said I must learn to be alone."

Tasera watched her a moment, then nodded. "I fear it might be so."

"But I thought . . . "

"Kahlis is not there. I cannot feel him anymore. No matter where he was, no matter *when*, he was always there, with me. So it is when you have lived with a man a century and more. But suddenly there is a gap—an absence, if you like. He is not there anymore. Something has happened to him."

Tasera fell silent.

"I did not know. I thought . . . " Anna frowned. What *had* she thought? That only *she* felt like that? That only she and he were related to each other in that strange, nonphysical manner? No. For how could that possibly be? Even so, sometimes it felt as if they were the books of each other—to which each one linked. And when one of those books was destroyed, what then? Would there no longer be a connection? Would there only be a gap, an awful, yawning abyss?

The thought of it terrified her. To be *that* alone.

"I am sorry, Tasera," Anna said finally. "I do hope you are wrong."

"And I," Tasera said, reaching out to take her hands. "And I."

AITRUS WOKE. THE DARKNESS IN HIS HEAD was matched by the darkness in which he lay. It was damp and cold and his whole body ached, yet the air was fresher than he remembered it.

He put his hand up to his face, surprised. The mask . . .

And then he remembered. The air had given out. He had had to take off the mask or suffocate. And that was when he had linked—linked back to Gemedet.

Aitrus lay there a while, letting his eyes grow accustomed to the darkness of the cave. It had to be night outside, for not a trace of sunlight filtered down from above. He listened, straining to hear some sound, but it was hard to know whether he was imagining it or not. For eight days now he had known nothing but silence. The awful, echoing silence of the rock.

All of his life, he realized now, there had been noises all about him—the faint murmur of the great fans that brought the air into the caverns, or the dull concussion from a mining rig, busy excavating in the deep; the noises of the city itself, or of boats out on the lake; the bells that sounded out each hour of every day, and the normal noises of the household all about him. Such sounds had formed the continuum of his existence, ceaseless and unnoticed. Until now.

Now death had come to D'ni. Yes, and to every part of its once great empire. Even in the tunnels he had found the dead—Miners at their work, or Maintainers, whose job it was to patrol the great perimeter.

Yes, and he had even found the source of death: the great machine that had proved D'ni's bane. In one of the lower caverns he had come upon it, its huge canisters empty now. They had used such machines in the Guild of Surveyors, to provide air for tricky excavations, or before a regular supply could be pumped up from D'ni itself. But Veovis had used it to pump poisons back into D'ni, letting D'ni's own circulatory system distribute it to every tiny niche.

Even had they switched the great fans down, which eventually they did, it would have proved a bleak choice: to suffocate from lack of air, or die of the poisonous bacteria that that same air carried.

It was not until he saw the machine that he knew for sure; not until then that he knew Anna had been wrong to intercede.

It is not her fault, he kept telling himself; *she was not to know.* Yet it was hard to see it otherwise. All of this death, all of this vast suffering and misery, was down to a single man, Veovis. For all that A'Gaeris had been a willing partner, it was Veovis's bitterness, his anger and desire for revenge, that had been behind this final, futile act. And if he had been dead?

Then my father would yet be alive. And Lord R'hira. And Master Jadaris. And Jerahl . . .

Aitrus sat up, shaking his head, but the darkness kept coming back. *Ti'ana is to blame. My darling wife, Ti'ana.*

"No!"

Outside a bird flapped away between the trees.

It was the first natural sound he had heard in days.

Aitrus sniffed the air. It smelled sweet. He could still smell the rubber of the mask upon his face, but this air was different. It lacked the strange metallic taste of the air he had grown accustomed to.

Slowly, almost stumblingly, he climbed up, until he stood at the mouth of the cave, looking down through the trees toward the encampment. It seemed empty, deserted, but then it was late.

He sighed. *I ought to wash,* he thought. *More than that, I ought to burn these clothes, or bury them. Just in case . . .*

In truth, he ought not to have come. Indeed, he would not have come but for the fact that lack of air had addled his brain. But now that he was back he would make the best of things.

At least the Linking Book was relatively safe; though who knew how thorough Veovis would be? If he chose to search the tunnels, then he might come upon it, lying there, and then even Gemedet would not be safe.

The thought of it petrified him.

He had the urge to cough. Stifling it, he turned, looking up beyond the cave. If he remembered correctly, there was a path that led up and to the left, curving across to the head of the falls. He would find a place up there and bury the suit, then wash himself.

And then he would come back here, naked, the bearer of ill news, to face his mother and his wife.

THEY HAD FOUND AITRUS UP BY THE POOL, beside the waterfall, his body bathed in sweat, his eyes staring. Getting two servants to carry him, they had brought him back to the encampment and laid him on the bed. Then, for the next three days, Tasera and Anna took turns tending him, bathing his brow, and holding his hand while the fever raged on.

On the morning of the fourth day he finally woke. Anna had been sleeping in the tent nearby when Gehn came and shook her.

"Mother! Mother! Father is awake!"

She hurried across to the cabin to find Aitrus awake, his eyes clear and lucid. Tasera sat beside him, smiling and holding his hand. He looked weak, but he was alive, and seeing Anna, a faint smile came to his lips.

"Ti'ana . . ."

His voice was little more than a breath.

"Do not talk," she said, going over to kneel beside the bed and take his hand.

"I must," he said, the words the faintest whisper.

"No," she said. "You must rest. You must get back your strength."

But Aitrus shook his head. "I am dying, Ti'ana. I know it. But I have been given this moment and I must use it."

He paused, coughing a little, then continued, his voice wavering a little.

"They are dead. Everyone . . . dead. My father . . . I buried him. And D'ni . . . D'ni is ended. But there is a way out. Through the tunnels. I mapped it. My notebook . . . "

"Yes, yes," Anna said, impatiently. "But you must rest now, Aitrus, *please.*"

For a moment his eyes blinked closed. With an effort he opened them again, his eyes looking to Anna pleadingly. "You must go, Ti'ana. Please. Promise me you will go. You are not safe here . . . "

"Why? Why aren't we safe here?"

But Aitrus had drifted into sleep again. His head had fallen back and his breathing was shallow.

"Let him sleep," Tasera said, looking to Anna, as if concern for her boy was the only thing in the universe; yet Anna could see that Aitrus's news had shocked her. Indeed, it had shocked them both. Then, suddenly, she remembered Gehn.

She whirled about. Gehn was standing in the doorway, staring, his face aghast.

"It isn't true," he said, his voice tiny. "Tell me it isn't true!"

But she could not lie, and as he saw it in her face, so that look returned: a look of purest horror. Turning, he fled.

"Gehn!" she cried, going to the doorway. "Gehn! Come back!"

But Gehn was already at the edge of the wood. With the barest glance back, he disappeared among the trees.

Anna turned back, looking to Tasera, but Tasera was not there. Her eyes seemed distant and hollow now and her shoulders sagged, as if her son's soft words—so quiet, so insubstantial—had broken her. Even as Anna looked, a tear trickled down Tasera's cheek and fell.

Gone. All of it gone. But how was that possible? Surely some had survived?

She stared at Aitrus, wondering what else he had not told her. Why was this Age not safe? Why?

"Tell me, Aitrus," she said quietly. "*Please* tell me."

But Aitrus did not answer her.

AFTERNOON TASERA TOOK TO HER BED, COMPLAINING of a migraine. Anna, thinking it had to do with Kahlis's death, decided it was best to leave her be to grieve.

Having made certain Tasera was comfortable, she went to see if she could find where Gehn had got to. There was no sign of him. But when she returned two hours later it was to find that Tasera had worsened considerably.

Not only that, but the two servants who had helped carry Aitrus down from the pool were now displaying the exact same symptoms he had shown. They had been suffering from minor stomach pains for days, but now both of them had gone down with a full-blown fever.

As the afternoon became evening, Anna began to grow worried. Aitrus still showed no sign of waking, yet it was for Tasera she was most concerned, for she had slipped into a fretful, fevered sleep. Then, just after sundown, Anna went to check on the two servants, whom she had placed nearby in the storage tent, and found that one of them had died.

She was standing there, outside the tent, when Gehn wandered back into the camp.

"Gehn?"

Gehn did not even glance at her, but walked on past her, going inside the cabin.

Anna walked across. Gehn was sitting in a corner, in the darkness, staring at his father's reclining form. She watched him a moment, her heart going out to him. Then, taking the lantern from the side, she struck the fire-marble, closed the plate, and hung it on the hook overhead.

In its sudden glow she could see that Gehn had been crying.

"Gehn? Are you all right?"

He turned his head and looked at her, coldly, sullenly, then looked away.

"Two of the servants are ill," she said quietly.

Gehn made no gesture, no response. He simply stared at his father.

"Gehn . . . we must think of leaving here."

But Gehn was like a statue, his child's face hard and cold as it stared at his dying father.

THAT NIGHT THE REST OF THE SERVANTS RAN away. While Gehn slept, Anna sat beside Tasera, bathing her face and holding her hand. Yet in the early hours of morning, Aitrus's mother convulsed and died.

Anna sat there for a long time afterward, staring into space. Gehn was asleep in the corner. Aitrus lay nearby, his shallow breathing barely audible. In this one room was her whole world—all that mattered to her, anyway—and it was slowly falling apart about her.

Just as before, she thought, real despair touching her for the first time.

She stood up abruptly then crossed the room, picking up the bag Aitrus had brought back with him from D'ni. She had been busy until now even to remember it, but now she sat down and rummaged through it.

Here was his journal, that he kept with him at all times.

Lighting a lamp, she opened the notebook and began to leaf through it, stopping finally at a series of maps and diagrams Aitrus had made. The first were of the tunnels leading to the cavern where the machines were and, beyond it, several miles distant, the Lodge. Aitrus had added to this map, drawing thick dark lines across a number of the tunnels. It was clear that they were blocked. Indeed, looking at the map, she saw that there was no access to the surface by this route. On the next page was another map, but this one ended in dead-ends and white, unfilled space.

Anna looked up, understanding. Aitrus had spent the last week or so tramping through the tunnels, trying to find a route for their escape, spending his precious energies so that they might find a safe way to the surface.

Aitrus was dying, she knew that now for certain. Yet even at the end he had been true. Even at the end he had thought of others before himself. Of her, and Gehn.

She looked back at the journal. The next map was different—much more complex than the others. It extended over several pages.

Anna smiled, appreciating what he had done here. Elevations, rock-types, physical details—all were noted down. It was a real labyrinth, but Aitrus had done his best to make each twist and turn as clear as he could. She traced the zigzag line of it with her finger over several pages, then looked up, laughing softly.

The volcano! It came out at the old dormant volcano where her father and she had used to stop on their way to Tadjinar.

She smiled and spoke softly to the air. "You did well, my love."

"Did I?"

His voice, so unexpected, startled her. She turned to find him sitting up, watching her.

"Aitrus?"

"We have to go."

Anna blinked. *You are dying*, she thought. *You are not going anywhere.* But he was insistent.

"You must pack, Ti'ana. Now, while there is still time."

"Time for what?"

"I am coming with you," he said, then coughed. "Back to D'ni. I will help you find the way."

"But you are ill, Aitrus."

In answer he threw back the sheet and, steadying himself against the wall with one hand, slowly stood.

His eyes looked to her imploringly. "I must do this, Ti'ana. Do you understand that?"

She stared at him, her fear and love for him mixed violently at that moment, and then she nodded. "I understand."

PACKING THE LAST FEW THINGS INTO THE bag, Anna slipped it onto her back and went outside, into the sunlight. Gehn was just below her, standing beside his father, supporting him, as they looked down at Tasera's grave.

Anna sighed, then walked across. Gehn was wearing the suit she had made for him and the mask lay loose about his neck. His own knapsack was on his back.

"Are you ready?"

Both Gehn and Aitrus looked to her and nodded. Then, on impulse, Gehn ran down the slope and, bending, leaned out over the edge.

Anna looked to Aitrus and frowned, wondering what he was doing, but in a moment Gehn was back, holding out a tiny sheath of white flowers for her to take. Two other bunches were in his other hand.

She took them from him, then, knowing what he intended, cast the flowers onto Tasera's grave and stepped back, allowing Gehn and Aitrus to do the same.

"Farewell, dear Mother," Aitrus said, looking out past the mound at the beauty of the valley. "You will be with me always."

Gehn stood there a moment, then, bowing his head, scattered the flowers and said his own farewell: "Goodbye, Grandmother. May we meet again in the next Age."

Anna blinked, surprised. He seemed to have grown up so much these past few weeks. She put out her hand to him.

"Come, Gehn. We must go now."

Gehn hesitated a moment, then, with a glance at his father, reached out and took her hand. Anna gave it a little squeeze, then, turning from the grave, began to climb the slope, heading for the linking cave, Aitrus following behind.

IT WAS THE TWENTY-SECOND DAY AFTER THE FALL.

Anna stood beside Aitrus on the balcony of the mansion, Gehn in front of her, her arms about his shoulders as they looked out over the ruins of D'ni. To her surprise the air had proved clean, and after several tests in the workroom, they had decided to remove their masks. There was no trace now of the gas that had wreaked such havoc, though its residue remained, like a dried crust over everything. Moreover, someone had reactivated the great fans that brought the air into the cavern, and the algae of the lake had recovered enough to give off a faint, almost twilight glow. In that faint illumination they could see the extent of the devastation.

The sight was desolate beyond all words. What had once been the most magnificent of cities was now a mausoleum, an empty, echoing shell of its former glory.

She could feel Gehn trembling and knew that he was close to tears. All that he had ever known lay within the compass of his sight. His shattered hopes and dreams were here displayed, naked to the eye. Why, even the great rock that stood in the very midst of the lake had split, like wood before the axe.

"Come," she said gently, meeting Aitrus's eyes. "Let us go from here."

Walking down through the dead streets, their sense of desolation grew. Barely a house stood without great cracks in its walls; barely a wall or gate remained undamaged. From time to time the rubble of a house would block their way and they were forced to backtrack, but eventually they came out by the harbor's edge.

The great statues that had once lined the harbor wall were cracked or fallen. The great merchant fleet that once had anchored here now rested on the harbor's floor. They could see their long shadows thirty, forty feet below the surface.

Anna turned, looking about her. There was no sign anywhere of a boat, and they needed a boat. Without one there was no chance of getting across the lake.

"There are boathouses to the east of the harbor," Aitrus said, "down by the lake's edge. There will be barges there."

But the boathouses were burned, the barges smashed. Someone had made sure they could not get across. Aitrus sighed and sat, his remaining strength almost spent.

"I'll go and look," Anna said, gesturing to Gehn that he should sit with his father and take care of him. "There must be something."

In a moment she was back, her eyes shining. "There is!" she said. "One boat. A small thing, but big enough for us three."

Aitrus's eyes came up, suspicion in them. "Was it tied up?"

She nodded, then frowned. "What is it?"

But Aitrus merely shook his head. "Nothing. Let us go at once."

Gehn helped his father stand, then supported him as they made their way toward where the boat was moored. They were not halfway across when a fearful cry rang out from the lower city at their backs.

All three of them turned, shocked by the sudden sound.

It came again.

Aitrus looked to his wife. "Go to the boat, Ti'ana. Take Gehn and wait there for me. It might be Jiladis."

"But Aitrus . . . "

"Go to the boat. I'll join you in a while."

Anna hesitated, reluctant to let him go, yet she knew that this, too, was his duty—to help his fellow guildsmen if in need. Taking Gehn's hand she led him away, but all the while she kept glancing back at Aitrus, watching as he slowly crossed the open harbor front, then disappeared into one of the narrow alleyways.

"Come, Gehn," she said. "Let us secure the boat for when your father returns."

AITRUS LEANED AGAINST THE WALL, DOUBLED up, getting his breath. The pain in his limbs and in his stomach was growing worse and he felt close now to exhaustion. Moreover, he was lost. Or, at least, he had no idea just where the sounds had come from. He had thought it was from somewhere in this locality, but now that he was here there was nothing. The deserted streets were silent.

Across from him a sign hung over the shadowed door of a tavern. There were no words, but the picture could be glimpsed, even through the layer of gray-brown residue. It showed a white, segmented worm, burrowing blindly through the rock. The sight of it made him frown, as if at some vague, vestigial memory. The Blind Worm. Where had he heard mention of that before?

Aitrus straightened, looking up. The windows of the upper story were open, the shutters thrown back.

Even as he looked, there came a loud, distinctive groan.

So he had not been wrong. Whoever it was, they were up there, in that second-floor room.

Aitrus crossed the street then slowly pushed the door open, listening. The groan came again. A set of narrow stairs led up to his right. They were smeared, as if many feet had used them. Cautiously, looking about him all the while, he slipped inside and began to climb them, careful to make no noise.

He was almost at the top when, from the room above came a grunt and then another pained groan. Something creaked.

Aitrus stopped then turned his head, looking up into the open doorway just behind him, beyond the turn in the stairs.

A soft, scraping noise came from the room, and then a tiny gasp of pain. That sound released Aitrus. Finding new reserves of energy, he hurried up the final steps.

Standing in the doorway, he gasped, astonished by the sight that met his eyes.

It was a long, low-ceilinged room, with windows overlooking the harbor. In the center of the room a table was overturned and all three chairs. Blood smeared the floor surrounding them, trailing away across the room. And at the end of that trail of blood, attempting to pull himself up onto the window ledge, was Veovis, the broad blade of a butcher's cleaver buried deep in his upper back.

"Veovis!"

But Veovis seemed unaware of his presence. His fingers clutched at the stone ledge as his feet tried to push himself up, his face set in an expression of grim determination.

Horrified, Aitrus rushed halfway across the room, yet even as he did, Veovis collapsed and fell back, groaning.

Aitrus knelt over him.

"Veovis . . . Veovis, it is Aitrus. What happened here?"

There was a movement in Veovis's face. His eyes blinked and then he seemed to focus on Aitrus's face. And with that came recognition.

"What happened?"

Veovis laughed, then coughed. Blood was on his lips. His voice, when he spoke, came raggedly, between pained breaths.

"My colleague and I . . . we had a little . . . *disagreement.*"

The ironic smile was pained.

"A'Gaeris?"

Veovis closed his eyes then gave the faintest nod.

"And you fought?"

Veovis's eyes flickered open. "It was no fight . . . He . . . " Veovis swallowed painfully. "He stabbed me . . . when my back was turned."

Veovis grimaced, fighting for his breath. Aitrus thought he was going to die, right there and then, but slowly Veovis's breathing normalized again and his eyes focused on Aitrus once more.

"I would not do it."

"What? What wouldn't you do?"

"The Age he wanted . . . I would not write it." A tiny spasm ran through Veovis. Aitrus gripped him.

"Tell me," he said. "I need to know."

Veovis almost smiled. "And I need to tell you."

He swallowed again, then. "He wanted a special place . . . a place where we could be gods."

"Gods?"

Veovis nodded.

It was the ultimate heresy, the ultimate misuse of the great Art: to mistake Writing, the ability to link with preexistent worlds, with true creation. And at the end, Veovis, it seemed, had refused to step over that final line. He looked up at Aitrus now.

Aitrus blinked. Suddenly, the image of his workroom had come to his mind—the trail of footprints leading halfway to the Book but no farther.

"Was that you?" he asked softly. "In my workroom, I mean."

Veovis took two long breaths, then nodded.

"But why? After all you did, why let *us* live?"

"Because she spoke out for me. Because . . . she said there was good in me . . . And she was right . . . even at the end."

Veovis closed his eyes momentarily, the pain overwhelming him, then he continued, struggling now to get the words out before there were no more words.

"It was as if there was a dark cloud in my head, poisoning my thoughts. I felt . . . " Veovis groaned, "nothing. Nothing but hatred, anyway. Blind hatred. Of everything and everyone."

There was a shout, from outside. Carefully laying Veovis down, he went to the window and looked out, what he saw filling him with dismay.

"What is it?" Veovis asked from below him.

Out on the lake a single boat was heading out toward the distant islands. Standing at its stern, steering it, was the distinctive figure of A'Gaeris. And before him in the boat, laying on the bare planks, their hands and feet bound, were Anna and Gehn.

"It's A'Gaeris," he said quietly. "He has Ti'ana and my son."

"Then you must save her, Aitrus."

Aitrus gave a bleak cry. "How? A'Gaeris has the only boat, and I am too weak to swim."

"Then *link* there."

Aitrus turned and looked down at the dying man. "Where is he taking them?"

Veovis looked up at him, his eyes clear now, as if he had passed beyond all pain. "To K'veer. That's where we are based. That's where all the Books are now. We've been collecting them. Hundreds of them. Some are in the Book Room, but most are on the Age I made for him. They are in the cabin on the south island. That's where you link to. The Book of that Age is in my study."

Aitrus knelt over Veovis again. "I understand. But how does that help me? That's in K'veer. How do I get *there?*"

In answer, Veovis gestured toward his left breast. There was a deep pocket there, and something in it. Aitrus reached inside and took out a slender book.

"He did not know I had this," Veovis said, smiling now. "It links to Nidur Gemat. There is a Book there that links directly to my study on K'veer. You can use them to get to the island before he does."

Aitrus stared at the Book a moment, then looked back at Veovis.

Veovis met his eyes. "Do you *still* not trust me, Aitrus! Then listen. The Book I mentioned. It has a green cover. It is there that A'Gaeris plans to go. It is there that you might trap him. You understand?"

Aitrus hesitated a moment, then. "I will trust you, for I have no choice, and perhaps there *is* some good in you at the last."

THE CITY WAS RECEDING NOW. IN AN HOUR HE would be back in K'veer. A'Gaeris turned from the sight and looked back at his captives where they lay at the bottom of the boat.

He would have killed them there and then, at the harbor's edge, and thought nothing of it, but the woman had betrayed the fact that her husband was still abroad.

And so, he would use them as his bait. And once he had Aitrus, he would destroy all three of them, for he had not the sentimental streak that had ruined his once-companion, Veovis.

"He will not come for us, you know."

A'Gaeris looked down at the woman disdainfully. "Of course he'll come. The man's a sentimental fool. He came before, didn't he?"

"But not this time. He'll wait for you. In D'ni."

"While you and your son are my captives?" A'Gaeris laughed. "Why, he will be out of his mind with worry, don't you think?"

He saw how that silenced her. Yes, with the two of them safe in a cell on K'veer he could go back and settle things with Guildsman Aitrus once and for all.

For there was only one boat in all of D'ni now, and he had it.

"No," he said finally. "He'll wait there at the harbor until I bring the boat back. And then I'll have him. Oh yes, Ti'ana. You can be certain of it!"

THE FIRST BOOK HAD LINKED HIM TO A ROOM IN the great house on Nidur Gemat, filled with Veovis's things. There, after a brief search, he found the second Book that linked to this, more familiar room on the island of K'veer, a place he had often come in better times.

Aitrus stood there a moment, leaning heavily against the desk, a bone-deep weariness making his head spin. Then, knowing he had less than an hour to make his preparations, he looked about him.

The Book with the emerald green cover was on a table in the far corner of the room, beside a stack of other, older Books. Going across to them, Aitrus felt a sudden despair, thinking of what had been done here. So much endeavor had come to naught, here in this room. And for what reason? Envy? Revenge? Or was it simple malice?

Was A'Gaeris mad?

Aitrus groaned, thinking of the end to which Veovis had come. Then, determined to make one final, meaningful effort, he lifted the Book and carried it back over to the desk.

There he sat, opening the Book and reading through the first few pages. After a while he lifted his head, nodding to himself. Here it was, nakedly displayed: what Veovis might, in time, have become; a great Master among Masters, as great, perhaps, as the legendary Ri'Neref.

He began to cough, a hacking, debilitating cough, then put his fingers to his lips. There was blood there now. He, too, was dying.

Taking a cloth from his pocket, Aitrus wiped his mouth and then began, dipping the pen and scoring

out essential phrases and adding in others at the end of
the book. Trimming and pruning this most perfect of
Ages. *Preparing* it.

And all the while he thought of Anna and of Gehn,
and prayed silently that they would be all right.

A'GAERIS CLIMBED THE STEPS OF THE HARBOR
at K'veer, Anna and the boy just in front of him, goad-
ed on by the point of his knife.

At the top he paused and, grasping the loose ends
of the ropes by which their hands were bound,
wrapped them tightly about his left hand. Then, leading the two behind him like a pair of hounds, he went
inside the mansion.

K'veer had not been untouched by the tremors, and
parts of its impressive architecture had cracked and
fallen away into the surrounding lake, yet enough of it
remained for it to be recognizable. Anna, who had
wondered where they were going, now felt a sense of
resignation descend on her.

If Veovis was here then there was nothing Aitrus
could do.

Anna glanced at her son. Gehn's face was closed,
his eyes sullen, as if this latest twist were no more

than could be expected. Yet he was bearing up, for all his trials, and she felt a strange twinge of pride in him for that.

She was about to speak, when she caught the scent of burning. A'Gaeris, too, must have noticed it at the same moment, for he stopped suddenly and frowned.

For a moment he sniffed the air, as if he had been mistaken, then, with a bellow, he began to hurriedly climb the stairs, dragging them along after him.

As they approached the Book Room the smell of burning grew and grew until, at a turn in the stairs, they could see the flickering glow of a fire up ahead of them.

A'Gaeris roared. "My Books!"

For a moment, as he tugged at the rope, Anna almost fell, but she kept her footing. Gehn did, however. She heard his cry and saw that A'Gaeris had let go of the rope that held him. But there was no time to see if he was all right. The next instant she found herself behind A'Gaeris in the doorway to the Book Room. Beyond him the room was brilliantly lit. Smoke bellowed from a stack of burning Books. And just to one side of the flaming pile—a Book in one hand, a flaming torch in the other—stood Aitrus.

A'Gaeris slammed the great door shut behind him, then took a step toward Aitrus, yet even as he did, Aitrus raised the torch and called to him:

"Come any closer and I'll burn the rest of your Books, A'Gaeris! I know where they are. I've *seen* them. In the cabin on the south island. I linked there. I can link there now, unless . . . "

Anna felt A'Gaeris's hand reach out and grasp her roughly, and then his arm was about her neck, the dagger raised, its point beneath her neck.

"I have your wife, Aitrus. Go near those Books and I shall kill her."

"Kill her and I shall destroy your Books. I'll link through and put them to the torch. And what will you have then, *Master* Philosopher? Nothing. Not now that you've killed Veovis."

Anna could feel A'Gaeris trembling with anger. Any false move and she would be dead.

"Give me that Book," he said once more in a low growl. "Give it to me, or Ti'ana dies."

Aitrus was smiling now. He lifted the Book slightly. "This is a masterful work. I know Veovis was proud of it."

A'Gaeris stared at Aitrus. "It was called Ederat."

"No," Aitrus said, his eyes meeting Anna's. "Veovis had another name for it. He called it Be-el-ze-bub."

Anna caught her breath. She stared at him, loving him more in that instant than she had ever loved him.

I love you, she mouthed.

Aitrus answered her with his eyes.

"Well?" he asked, returning his attention to A'Gaeris. "Do we have a deal? The Book—and all those Books within—for my wife?"

But A'Gaeris simply laughed.

Aitrus lowered the torch. His eyes went to the cover of the Book, then, with a final loving look at Anna, he placed the hand that held the burning torch upon the glowing panel.

A'Gaeris howled. Thrusting Anna away from him he ran across the room.

"Aitrus!" she yelled as his figure shimmered and vanished. "Aitrus!"

But he was gone. The great Book fell with a thud to the floor beside the burning stack.

A'Gaeris threw himself at it in unseemly haste and almost wrenched the cover from the spine forcing it open.

Anna watched, her heart in her throat as, his chest heaving, A'Gaeris looked across at her and, with a smile that was half snarl, placed his hand against the descriptive panel and linked.

EVEN AS HE LINKED INTO THE CAVE, A'GAERIS stumbled, doubling up in pain. The air was burning, the reek of sulphur choking. The first breath seared his lungs. Putting out an arm, A'Gaeris staggered forward, howling, looking about him desperately for the Linking Book back to D'ni. Yet even as he did, a great crack appeared in the floor of the cavern. The heat intensified. There was a glimpse of brilliant orange-redness, one stark moment of realization, and then the rock slab on which he stood tilted forward, A'Gaeris's shrill cry of surprise cut off as he tumbled into the molten flow.

And then silence. The primal, unheard silence of the great cauldron of creation.

ANNA CRIED QUIETLY, CROUCHING OVER THE green-covered Book and studying the glowing image there.

For a moment or two there was the temptation to follow him: to end it all, just as Aitrus had. Then someone hammered on the Book Room door.

It brought her back to herself. *Gehn.*

Anna turned to face the smoldering pile of ashes that had once been D'ni Books, then dropped the green-covered Book upon the rest. Sparks scattered. A cloud of smoke wafted up toward the high ceiling of the room. A moment later, flames began to lick the burnished leather of the cover.

For a moment she simply stared, feeling the gap there now where the other book of her life had been, just as Tasera had described it. Then, getting to her feet again, she turned, even as the knocking came again, more urgently this time, and began to walk across.

THE SUN WAS EDGING ABOVE THE mountains far to the east as the figure of a woman emerged from the lip of the volcano, cradling a sleeping child. The desert floor was still in deep shadow. It lay like a dark sea about the bright, black-mouthed circle of the caldera. The woman paused, lifting her chin, slowly scanning the surrounding desert, then began to descend the rock-littered slope, her shadow stretched out long and thin behind her, black against the dawn's red.

As she came closer to the cleft, a light wind began to blow, lifting the dark strands of her hair behind her. Sand danced across the rock then settled. The woman seemed gaunt and wraithlike, and the child in her arms was but skin and bone, yet there was a light in her eyes, a vitality, that was like the fire from the deep earth.

Seeing the cleft, she slowed, looking about her once more, then went across and knelt, laying the child down gently on a narrow ledge of rock. Taking the two packs from her shoulders, she set them down. Then, using her hands and feet to find her way, she ducked down into the dark gash of the cleft.

There was a pool down there at the foot of the cleft. In the predawn darkness it was filled with stars, reflected from the sky far overhead. Like a shadow, she knelt beside it, scooping up a handful of the pure, cool water, and drank. Refreshed, she turned, still kneeling, and looked about her. It was cool down here, and there was water. With a little work it could be more.

Anna nodded, then stood, wiping her hands against her shirt. "Here," she said. "We'll begin again here."

R AND MILLER—WHO ALONG WITH HIS brother Robyn discovered and brought to life the secrets of D'ni empire in the megahit CD-ROM world MYST and the novel Myst: The Book of Atrus— rather enjoys his simple life . . . one that now includes a garage at his home in the Pacific Northwest. And when he has the time, he carefully practices his form and technique at his self-designed 14-hole, Certified Cross Country, Off-Road disc-golf course. On rare occasions he invites only the best of friends or employees over for a weekend disc-golf slaughtering.

David Wingrove is the author of the *Chung Kuo* series of novels, which include *The Middle Kingdom, The Broken Wheel, The White Mountain, The Stone Within,* and *Beneath the Tree of Heaven.* He also co-authored, with Brian Aldiss, *Trillion Year Spree: The History of Science,* a volume which won the prestigious Hugo and *Locus* Awards for best nonfiction work in the science fiction genre. He lives in North London with his wife and three daughters.

Chris Brandkamp, when he's not being slaughtered in disc-golf by Rand, manages Cyan's business affairs. He also enjoys all sorts of outdoor activities, for example chipping (grinding huge trees into pea-size pieces). And no, that's not what happened to his fingers!

Richard Watson is the keeper of the D'ni. His expertise in D'ni culture, language, and events is exceeded only by his skill at Mario Brothers.

Ryan Miller (a.k.a. Rand and Robyn's little brother) is the most competitive of the Miller brothers. When the Dallas Cowboys won the Superbowl, it allowed him to relax and transfer his competitive energy into working with his brothers, repairing his sewer pipe and gas line, having a kid, and writing his own novel.

IF YOU LOVED MYST: THE BOOK OF TI'ANA, BE SURE
TO CATCH RAND MILLER'S NEWEST NOVEL,
MYST: THE BOOK OF D'NI.
COMING SOON FROM HYPERION.

PROLOGUE

A SEABIRD CALLS. THE *UNKNOWING ONE*
STANDS AT THE RAIL. PEACE. THE CIRCLE
CLOSED, THE LAST WORD WRITTEN.

—FROM THE *KOROKH JIMAH*: VV.
13245–46

THE CAVERN WAS SILENT. A FAINT MIST drifted on the surface of the water, underlit by the dull orange glow that seemed to emanate from deep within the lake. Vast walls of granite climbed on every side while overhead, unsensed, a solid shelf of rock a mile thick shut off all view of stars and moon.

Islands littered the lake, twisted spikes of darkness jutting from the level surface of the water, and there, on the far side of the cavern, one single, massive rock, split yet still standing, like the splintered trunk of a tree, its peak hidden in the darkness.

Beyond it lay the city, wreathed in stillness, its ancient buildings clinging to the walls of the cavern.

D'ni slept, dreamless and in ruins. And yet the air was fresh. It moved, circulating between the caverns, the distant noise of the vast rotating blades little more than the suggestion of a sound, a faint, whumping pulse *beneath* the silence.

The mist parted briefly as a boat slid across the

waters, the faintest ripple marking its passage, and then it, too, was gone, vanished into the blackness.

It was night in D'ni. A night that had lasted now for almost seventy years.

In the streets of the city the mist coiled on the cold stone of ancient cobbles like something living. Yet nothing lived there now; only the mosses and fungi that grew from every niche and cranny.

Empty it was, as though it had stood thus for a thousand years. Level after level lay open to the eye, abandoned and neglected. A thousand empty lanes, ten thousand empty rooms, a desolate landscape of crumbling walls and fallen masonry everywhere one looked.

In the great curve between the city's marbled flanks lay the harbor, the shadows of sunken boats in its glowing depths, and across the harbor's mouth a great arch of stone, Kerath's Arch, as it was known, its pitted surface webbed with cracks.

Silence. A preternatural silence. And then a sound. Faint at first and distant, and yet clear. The tap, tap, tap of metal against stone.

High above, in the narrow lanes of the upper city, a shadow stopped beneath a partly fallen gate and turned to look. The sound had come from the far end of the cavern; from one of the islands scattered on the lake out there.

Mist swirled, then silence fell again.

And then new sounds: a whirring, high-pitched mechanical screech, followed by the low burr of a power drill. And then the tapping once again, the sound of it echoing out across the water.

K'veer. The noises were coming from K'veer.

Two miles across the lake and there it is, the island rising like a huge black corkscrew from the glowing lake, its once crisp outline softened by a recent rockfall.

Coming closer, the noise grows in volume, the sound of drilling constant now, as is the clang, clang, clang of massive hammers pounding the stone. The island shakes beneath the onslaught, the carved stone trembling like a sounding bell.

But no one is woken by that dreadful din. The ancient rooms are dark and empty. All, that is, but one, at the very foot of the island, down beneath the surface of the lake. There, deep in the rock, lies the oldest room of all, a chamber of marbled pillars and cold stone, sealed off by an angry father to teach his son a lesson.

Now, forty years on, that same chamber is filled with busy men in dark, protective suits. Their brows beaded with sweat, they toil beneath the arc lights, a dozen of them standing between the two big hydraulic props, working at the face of the wall with hammer and drill, while others scamper back and forth, lifting and carrying the fallen stone, stacking it in a great heap on the far side of the chamber.

A figure stands beside the left-handed prop, looking on. Atrus, son of Gehn, once-prisoner in this chamber. After a while, he glances at the open notebook in his hand, then looks up again, calling out something to those closest to him.

A face looks up and nods, then turns back. The message is passed along the line.

There is a moment's pause. A welcome silence.

Walking across, Atrus crouches between two of the men and leans forward, examining the wall, prising his fingers deep into the crack, then turns and shakes his head.

He stands back, letting them continue, watching them go to it with a vengeance, the noise deafening now, as if all of them know that one more push will see the job through.

Slowly the chamber fills with dust and grit. And then one of them withdraws and, straightening up, cuts the power to his drill. Turning, he lifts his protective visor and grins.

All about him the others stand back, looking on.

Atrus returns to the wall and , crouching, pushes his hand deep into the crack, edging this way and that, feeling high and low. Satisfied, he eases back and, taking a marker from his pocket, stands, drawing and outline on the stone. The outline of a door.

At his signal, one of the drill men steps forward and begins to cut along the mark.

Swiftly it's done. A dozen hammer blows and the stone falls away.

The stone is quickly cleared, and as the rest look on, Atrus steps forward one last time. He holds a cutting tool with a chunky barrel the thickness of his arm. Placing the circle of its teeth about the circle of the lock—a circle that overlaps the thick frame of the door—he braces himself, then gently squeezes the trigger, letting it bite slowly into the surface. Only then, when the cutter has a definite grip on the metal, does he begin to push, placing his whole weight behind it.

There is a growling whine, a sharp, burning smell, different in kind from the earlier smells of stone and dust and lubricant. And then, abruptly, it's over. There is the clatter of the lock as it falls into the corridor beyond, the descending whine of the drill as it stutters into silence.

Setting the drill down, he raises his visor, then pulls the protective helmet off and lets it fall.

Atrus straightened and, with a single meaningful glance at the watching men, turned back to face the doorway. Forty years he had waited for this. Forty long years.

Placing his booted foot against the surface, he pushed hard, feeling the metal resist at first, then give.

Slowly, silently, it swung back.

A good D'ni door, he thought, *with good stone hinges that never rust. A door built to last.*

And as the door swung back he saw for the first time in a long while the empty corridor and, at its end, the twist of steps that led up into the house, where, long ago, his father, Gehn, had taught him how to write. Where he had first learned the truth about D'ni. Yes, and other things, too.

Irras came and stood by his shoulder. "Will you not go through, Master Atrus?"

Atrus turned, meeting the young man's eyes. "One should not hurry moments like this, Irras. I have waited forty years. Another forty seconds will not harm."

Irras lowered his eyes, abashed.

"Besides," Atrus went on, "we do not know yet whether D'ni is occupied or not."

"You think it might be?" The look of shock on Irras's face was almost comical.

"If it *is*," Atrus said, "then they will know we are here. We've made enough noise to wake the dead."

"Then maybe we should arm ourselves."

"Against other D'ni?" Atrus smiled. "No, Irras. If anyone's here, they will be friends, not foes. Like us, they will have returned for a reason."

Atrus turned back, looking toward the steps, then, brushing the dust from his leather gloves and boots, he stepped through, into the dimly lit corridor.

PART ONE

Rivers of fire. Even the rocks burn.
An island rises from the sea.
Dark magic in an errant phrase.
The people bow to the Lord of Error.

—from the *Ejemah'Terak*, Book Seven,
vv. 328–31

SEABIRDS WHEELED AND CALLED IN THE AIR above the bay, a flutter of white above the blue. It was hot, and, looking at the village, Marrim drew her hair back from her face, then gathered the braided strands together, fastening them at the nape of her neck. But for her father she would have had it cut like a man's long ago. After all, she did a man's job, why should she not wear her hair like a man's? But she was loathe to upset her father. It was hard enough for him to understand all the changes that had come to Averone, let alone comprehend the urge to explore and understand that this had been woken in his youngest daughter,

From where she stood, on the promontory, the whole of her small world was open to her gaze. For all her childhood it had been enough. The six great circular lodge houses, the river, the broad fields where they had planted the crops, and, beyond them, the woods where they had hunted and played. World enough, until Atrus and Catherine appeared.

Now she could barely imagine how it had been

before they'd come. How she had ever survived without this urge in her, this need to know.

And now, almost as suddenly as it had begun, it was to end. Only that morning they had dismantled the last of the workshops and cleared the ground where it had been. So Atrus had promised the elders of the village when he had first come here, yet Marrim could not understand why it had to be. They had come so far so quickly. Why *did* it have to end? For certain, she herself could not easily return to being what she was. No. She had changed. And this world, while it still drew her emotionally, was no longer big enough for her. She wanted more. Atrus's Books had opened her mind to the infinite possibilities that existed, and she wanted to see, if not all, then at least *some* of those possibilities.

And yet tomorrow they would be gone. Atrus and Catherine, and all they stood for.

There had to be a way to prevent that. Or if not, a way of going with them. If only Atrus would ask. But even then there were the elders—her father among them—and they would never agree. As much as they liked Atrus, they did not welcome the changes he had brought to Averone. They saw the excitement in their children's eyes and to them it was a threat. Atrus had understood that. It was why he had agreed to destroy all that he had built here once it had served his needs. But he could not destroy what was in her head. Nor the seeds he had planted in the heads of others, such as Irras and Carrad. Marrim knew they shared her frustration. They, too, felt constrained now by this tiny world of theirs.

She let her thoughts grow still, watching the movements down below her, in the village. Each of the great lodge houses had four large doorways, at north, south, east, and west; the massive entrances framed by the polished jarras trunks—cut from the largest trees in the woods. As she looked, three people emerged from the south doorway of her own lodge, their figures tiny against the great boles of the ancient trees; yet she recognized them at once.

Atrus stood to the left, the distinctive lenses that he wore pulled down over his face, his long cloak hanging loose in the windless air. Beside him, in a long flowing gown of green, stood Catherine, her hair tied back. Facing them, talking to them, was her father.

She groaned. Doubtless her father was asking Atrus not to interfere. And Atrus, being the man he was, would respect her father's wishes.

Her spirits low, she began to walk back down to the village, heading toward the river, away from her own lodge and the three figures who stood there debating her future. And as she walked she remembered the first time she had seen Atrus and Catherine, that morning when they had, so it seemed, stepped from the air and into their lives. Wide-eyed, the villagers had come out from their lodges to stare at the two strangers, while the elders quickly gathered to form a welcoming party.

She remembered how difficult that first meeting had been, with neither party able to speak the other's language. And yet even then Atrus had found ways to communicate with them. His hands had drawn pictures in the air, and they had somehow understood. He wanted their help. She remembered the gesture clearly: how he had put his arms straight out toward the elders, palms open, and then slowly drawn them in, as if to embrace something to his chest.

In the days that had followed, she had barely let them out of her sight, hovering at the back of a circle of curious youngsters who had followed the two strangers everywhere they went. And slowly she had begun to pick up the odd word or two until, emboldened by familiarity, she had dared to speak to the woman.

She remembered vividly how Catherine had turned to face her, the surprise in her eyes slowly turning to a smile. She had repeated the words Marrim had uttered, then gently beckoned her across.

So it had begun, four years ago this summer.

Marrim smiled, recalling the long hours she had spent learning the D'ni tongue, and afterward—in the library on Chroma'Agana—how she had sat at her books long into the night, learning the written script.

Even now she had not mastered it fully. But now it did not matter. For tonight, after the feast, they would be gone, the Linking Book burned, that whole world of experience barred to her, *if* the elders had their way.

The thought of it filled her with dread. It would be like locking her in a room and throwing away the key.

No, she thought. *Worse than that. Much worse.*